THE WORLD'S CLASSICS

DAISY MILLER

HENRY JAMES was born in New York in 1843 of ancestry both Irish and Scottish. He received a remarkably cosmopolitan education in New York, London, Paris and Geneva, and entered law school at Harvard in 1862. After 1866, he lived mostly in Europe, at first writing critical articles, reviews, and short stories for American periodicals. He lived in London for more than twenty years, and in 1898 moved to Rye, where his later novels were written. Under the influence of an ardent sympathy for the British cause in the First World War, Henry James was in 1915 naturalised a British subject. He died in 1916.

In his early novels, which include *Roderick Hudson* (1875) and *The Portrait of a Lady* (1881), he was chiefly concerned with the impact of the older civilisation of Europe upon American life. He analysed English character with extreme subtlety in such novels as *What Maisie Knew* (1897) and *The Awkward Age* (1899). In his last three great novels, *The Wings of the Dove* (1902), *The Ambassadors* (1903), and *The Golden Bowl* (1904), he returned to the 'international' theme of the contrast of American and European character.

JEAN GOODER is a Fellow of Newnham College, Cambridge.

THE WORLD'S CLASSICS

HENRY JAMES
Daisy Miller
and Other Stories

Edited with an introduction
and notes by
JEAN GOODER

Oxford   New York
OXFORD UNIVERSITY PRESS

Oxford University Press, Walton Street, Oxford OX2 6DP

Oxford New York
Athens Auckland Bangkok Bombay
Calcutta Cape Town Dar es Salaam Delhi
Florence Hong Kong Istanbul Karachi
Kuala Lumpur Madras Madrid Melbourne
Mexico City Nairobi Paris Singapore
Taipei Tokyo Toronto

and associated companies in
Berlin Ibadan

Oxford is a trade mark of Oxford University Press

'Daisy Miller' first published 1878; published in the New York Edition 1909
'Pandora' first published 1884; published in the New York Edition 1909
'The Patagonia' first published 1888; published in the New York Edition 1909
'Four Meetings' first published 1877; published in the New York Edition 1909

Introduction, Notes on the texts, Further reading, Notes and list of Variant
readings © Jean Gooder 1985
Chronology © Leon Edel 1963
This World's Classics paperback first published 1985

British Library Cataloguing in Publication Data
Data available

Library of Congress Cataloging in Publication Data
James, Henry, 1843-1916.
Daisy Miller and other stories.
(The World's classics)
Bibliography: p.
Contents: Daisy Miller—Pandora—
The Patagonia—Four Meetings.
I. Gooder, Jean. II. Title.
PS2112.G6 1985 813'.4 84—29480
ISBN 0 19-281618-7 (pbk.)

9 10 8

Printed in Great Britain by
BPC Paperbacks Ltd
Aylesbury, Bucks

CONTENTS

ACKNOWLEDGEMENTS

I WOULD like to acknowledge a special debt to Philip Horne's original work on James's revisions to the New York Edition, in particular his chapter on 'Daisy Miller'. I am also grateful to the following for their help with some of the notes: John Dugdale, Tamara Follini, Miss Caroline Goodfellow, Professor U. Limentani, and Dr Eve Mason.

Acknowledgement is also due to Macmillan and Co. Ltd for the use of their 1922 edition of the New York text of the Henry James's tales and Preface.

INTRODUCTION

In a minute there is time
For decisions and revisions which a
minute will reverse.
The Love Song of J. Alfred Prufrock

I

'You don't observe—you know—you imagine.' The
challenge to one of James's narrators goes to the heart of
fiction. Necessarily we interpret what we encounter,
draw the lines which define and bound what we
perceive; but the reality of such lines is a matter of
convention. Boundaries once familiar may become
worn or strained, putting old certainties in jeopardy.
The distinction between observation and imagination
is treacherous: once admitted, it questions not only
what is 'true', but the tools of verification. Observation
can never be simple, for it implicates the observer. The
novelist—seizing on what James calls the opportunity
to 'Dramatise, dramatise!'—may be thought of as
observing the observers, imaginatively.

Few of the boundaries of our world are clear or
stable. Within Henry James's lifetime the very 'bound-
ary' separating Europe from America changed. Steam,
the screw propeller, and then the turbine engine were
to cut the blank wastes of the North Atlantic from the
nineteen or so days it would have taken the James
family to cross from Boston to Liverpool in 1843, to a

bare ten days—less by the 1880s—literally opening the old world to the new. The effects were immense. Though James visited Europe more than once as a child, his family was unusual. It was not until after the Civil War that passenger steamships made tourism familiar. Indirectly, at least, the four stories collected here witness the change. They come out of a new social mobility and the new internationalism that attended it. They also suggest how, even if these boundaries had altered, the journey across the Atlantic remained a passage in many senses. A space remained between the continents. The mere being at sea meant a peculiar suspension of normal contacts and constraints. In mid-ocean, the narrator of 'The Patagonia' says, 'everything becomes absolute'. The sight of land brings a 'return to reality', to the conditional, perhaps leaving disquietingly open the question of what has happened.

The new traffic from America was the outcome of many social changes. Set in the 1870s, 'Daisy Miller' was so popular that one critic was moved to ask what this tale alone might not have done 'to swell the receipts, in the '80's and '90's, of the American tourist agencies'. Families with notions of geography as incoherent as the Millers now made their way from hotel to hotel round Europe; or, more ambitiously, like the Days in 'Pandora', made a two-year trip taking in Palestine and Greece as well as the better-known tourist routes through France and Italy. Young men eager to study at the art schools and universities of Europe sailed regularly from Boston and New York. The cost of the fare and the European exchange rates brought the crossing just within the range of a single and self-supporting school-teacher like Caroline Spencer in 'Four Meetings'. For a growing number of Americans, Europe was no longer an image: it had become accessible to the tourist who travelled by 'car', Baedecker guide-book in hand, as well as to the long-term expatriate resident. Behind this foreground 'Pandora' lets us just glimpse the very different passengers who filled the steerage class of the big ships sailing westward—the thousands upon thousands of emigrants leaving the poverty, political insecurity and persecution of Europe for the New World.

The contrasted worlds of Europe and America gave James his celebrated international theme. But other, less tangible boundaries exist within his fiction—what James meant when he spoke of the 'manners, customs, usages, habits, forms' that make 'the very stuff' of the novelist's work. 'Usages' and 'habits' are hardly neutral: they are the means by which a society articulates its values, or identifies threats to them. What does not conform to custom may be looked on as an anomaly. The reaction to an anomaly may entail fear of contagion, and take the form of suppression or rejection; or it may become an energetic organising principle which absorbs the strange, adapting its categories to include what is new. When James confronts old with new, native with foreign, or sophisticated with innocent, he is not dealing with social or national characteristics so much as constructing a symbolic language capable of very fine degrees of differentiation. If enough is at stake in such an encounter, ambiguity—or uncertainty of definition—may become intolerable. James's stories dramatise the price of resolving uncertainty. An empiricist by nature, he warns us in his Preface that 'a perfect definition of terms . . . is not of this muddled world.' 'A human, a "personal" adventure', he adds,

is no *a priori*, no positive and absolute and inelastic thing, but just a matter of relation and appreciation—a name we conveniently give, after the fact, to any passage, to any situation, that has added the sharp taste of uncertainty to a quickened sense of life.

II

Philosophical scepticism from James shouldn't surprise us. His extraordinary family background taught
him to respect 'inconsistencies' and 'contradictions',
and the James children met few boundaries of the usual
kind. But their imaginative freedom had its drawbacks.
It was not reassuring to be told, for example, when they
asked their father which church they belonged to, that
they could 'plead nothing less than the whole privilege
of Christendom', that there was no communion from
which they need feel themselves excluded. Such
unhelpful extravagance of choice brought James the
sober reflection that it might be better to suffer
exclusion than to belong nowhere. The precarious
balance between pain and delight in the uncertainties of
childhood reappears in the creative writer's principle of
refusing to regard questions as things to be closed.
'Nothing', James was to write to a reviewer of 'Daisy
Miller' in March 1879, 'is my *last word* about
anything—I am interminably super-subtle and analy-
tic—and with the blessing of heaven, I shall live to
make all sorts of representations of all sorts of things.'
As a critic, James pressed the point. Writing on Taine's
history of English literature in 1872, he openly
preferred the scrupulous inquiries of another French-
man, Sainte-Beuve, to the methodological rigour of
Taine. Sainte-Beuve's very horror of dogmas and
formulas was to James his 'living testimony to the
importance of the facts'. For Taine, the truth seemed to
lie stored up, 'to be released by a few lively hammer
blows'; while for Sainte-Beuve it was rather 'a diffused
and imponderable essence, as vague as the carbon in
the air which nourishes vegetation, and, like it, to be
disengaged by patient chemistry'. Such vagueness is
not a weakness of conception in a writer: it is a means of
resisting a premature conclusion. James often enacts

the process through a narrator, whose task it becomes to disengage the truth of events by a patient chemistry of understanding—to mediate between the 'facts' and the reader. James's narrators are usually conscious of what is difficult in this task, and become increasingly uneasy about the degree of their own implication in what happens. They perceive, in the course of telling their story, a responsibility for their own words fatal to their moral security. They relinquish the vantage of the 'inveterate, almost professional observer' (as the narrator in 'The Patagonia' describes himself), surrendering their apparent neutrality. Their new uncertainty is the very occasion of the story.

In 'Four Meetings'—an unusually concentrated tale—the tension between observation and imagination is painfully acute. It is hardly a 'story': it is quite simply the narrator's recollection of the four separate occasions on which he had met the little New England school-teacher, Caroline Spencer. Yet as he begins he immediately hesitates, caught between his objective sense of her as 'a touching specimen of a type' and the more compelling memory of the last time he had seen her. His thought breaks off as he lets go the conventional expressions of regret at hearing of her death, not knowing what to replace them with. As he reviews their meetings, it comes out that a difficulty had always faced him. Quite unconsciously, Caroline Spencer had disconcerted him. Ordinary social usages seemed barely to register with her, making *his* courtesies seem insincere. He never sounds the note of candour which he might have offered her. He had asked to be introduced to her as someone who might care more for the tales of an experienced traveller than for 'flirting' at a party; and she does, indeed, respond to the photographs of Europe that he shows her rather than to his gallantries. It is at the thought of Italy that she looks as pretty as if he had been making love to her.

Her enthusiasm meets his over Byron, and he is prompted to speak thoughts which have evidently preoccupied him before—thoughts which have for him a large general bearing, but which have a vivid relevance to her. He finds her intense imaginative response to the very idea of Europe a 'condition' which is distinctively American. She has 'the great American disease', and she's 'got it "bad"'. In the speech that follows he gives free rein to a diagnosis of the 'morbid' and 'monstrous' appetite for the picturesque *at any price* which is for him the mark of the American imagination. The condition is inherited: the images which fill the sufferer's mind are antecedent to experience; and when experience comes, what it does is 'merely confirm and consecrate our confident dream'. The eloquence of this speech is the more to be noted in that it is almost entirely introduced into the story as it was revised. In his own intensity at the time the narrator barely notices Caroline Spencer's response: 'I've dreamt of everything—I'll know it all!' He had not been much struck either by her earlier admission, that her preoccupation with Europe was an obsession which 'kills any interest in things nearer home.' Yet the narrator has gone far towards confirming her own 'confident dream': he discovers how that collusive exchange foreshadows her history.

So intent is Caroline Spencer on realising her dream that she doesn't at first recognise the narrator when they meet again at the little café in Le Havre. (Nor does she later when he visits her at her home.) The barely touched coffee before her, she apologises, may have gone to her head. As she tells her story, the narrator can see everything that she finds 'so delicious and romantic' yielding to the basest of realities. Her 'book-nourished fancy' has taught her to recognise everything but the truth. He can neither intervene nor undeceive her. The dignity of her conception is proof against worldly appeal and self-interest. She has shed her tears and submitted to circumstances. The quiet stoicism with which she has simply given up everything leaves the narrator compassionate and outraged, as he watches her cousin dine off the proceeds with indecent relish. The farewell flourish the painter gives him with his preposterous hat is 'like the wave of a banner over a conquered field'.

As the narrator calls on Caroline Spencer for the last time in North Verona, the image of defeat comes back to him: he finds the 'Countess' 'encamped upon the stricken field' of the school-teacher's life. He sees that Caroline Spencer has connived in exalted good faith with the agents of her fate: her passion for the picturesque, though, has not quite cheated her of her dream. Meeting her mute appeal to his authority, he can no more bring himself to expose the imposture then than he had been able to do during her scant thirteen hours in France. For this victim the 'great American disease' had proved fatal: at whatever price, Caroline Spencer had clung to her dream and let it determine her experience. *Has* the narrator described a general condition? Or did he suggest to her receptive mind a metaphor of which she made a reality? He cannot complete his broken thought of the beginning without going back on that large premise about the nature of the American imagination—without acknowledging the responsibility its utterance has given him. His silence at the end has a delicate duplicity: it respects Caroline Spencer's self-deception; does it also take the measure of his own? He knows, at least, 'the sharp taste of uncertainty'.

III

There is a risk in making 'manners' or 'customs' the ground of human drama. Manners date, and customs change. Looking back on these stories James saw many notes that belonged to the past. Daisy and Pandora were frankly topical figures: it was *because* they were so that they were 'subjects'. But there is a half-truth here. If 'Pandora' catches a moment of American social history with open comedy, it is dispiriting to find 'Daisy Miller' described as 'a piece of superseded social history'. The story's first readers were quick to pick up what was immediate and contemporary: whether they liked or disliked what they saw, everyone took Daisy for the new type of American girl abroad. Her name became a sobriquet, passing into the language. (There was even a fashion for 'Daisy Miller' hats in the millinery shops.) A perverse consequence of its popularity was that the tale proved a godsend to the etiquette writers of Victorian England, and America: it was just the text from which to preach the risks of independence to the young female, or the threat that an unchaperoned girl constituted to proper, parentally overseen relations between the sexes. It was read, in other words, as social satire. One can see why James should have had misgivings about success on these terms. Theodora Bosanquet (much later, James's secretary) remembered that his feeling about the continued success of 'Daisy Miller' was like that of 'some *grande dame* possessing a jewel-case richly stocked with glowing rubies and flashing diamonds, but condemned by her admirers always to appear in the single string of moonstones worn at her first dance'. But James confesses with characteristic irony in the Preface that he found his theme of the 'international young ladies' by seeing what he *couldn't* take on. He couldn't take on workaday America and risk (as he puts it) a 'spill' in Wall Street. The question of what was left to write about when nineteen-twentieths of American town life were closed to him posed drastic alternatives: to give up writing, or—for the time, at least, to give up

America. Not being able to 'afford' either, James was driven to use every inch of the meagre ground left. He resorted to the subtle patience he admired in Sainte-Beuve, and trusted, Micawber-like, that something '*would*' turn up'.

What 'turned up' was not the down-town New York of W. D. Howells's realist fiction, nor the political corruption of post-Civil War America which so struck Henry Adams. Certainly not the coast-to-coast rack-eteering and commercialism that Mark Twain knew. Rather, a Janus-faced America, conscious of its distinctive New England past, and displaying some of the brasher elements of the Gilded Age. Many aspects of his native land may have remained for James 'a great neglected quarry', but he found the necessary and ingenious angle of vision to meet his problem: he discovered the world of 'up-town'. It was the world from which the 'best' society came—even if it chose, like Mrs Costello or Mrs Dangerfield, to live abroad—and to which the new wealth aspired. The Millers from Schenectady hardly knew what they were doing in Europe, but they could—conspicuously—pay their way; and Pandora Day's tour was a calculated step in her progress from Utica to Murray Hill. Mrs Dangerfield might decline her acquaintance on the transatlantic crossing, but Pandora was (rightly) confident that she would find herself on visiting terms with that lady within a couple of 'seasons'. Social mobility and the crude power of cash were producing new pressures, new dramas of assimilation or aliena-tion. When the stony-faced Mrs Walker turns her back on Daisy in Rome, she is resisting what she sees as an intolerable challenge to her world. Her action is a rejection of the new. It anticipates the greater cruelty of Winterbourne in his final meeting with Daisy. The manners and customs of this 'up-town' world could give James all the subject-matter that he needed.

Despite (or perhaps because of) its earlier popularity 'Daisy Miller' now seems rather coolly regarded. The charm of the setting and of Daisy herself have prompted critics to either a sentimental, or a compensatingly hard line. In the sentimental version Daisy may die innocent or 'wronged', but she understands her fate so little that we respond only to its pathos. To the tougher mind Daisy is at best an example of James's favourite theme: the superiority of the American girl to all the world—the superiority in question, however (according to Leavis), being of a kind to make Daisy's freedoms in the face of European conventions 'insufferable in any civilised society'. Both verdicts are more like Taine's hammer blows than Sainte-Beuve's patient chemistry. And, ironically, too ready a habit of interpretation is what the story itself dramatises. Throughout, Daisy is seen through Winterbourne's eyes, heard through his ears—on *her* side for the most part unguardedly, since (unlike Pandora Day or Grace Mavis) Daisy seems unaware that the manners of up-state New York are not of universal currency, and that she looks and behaves quite differently from her European counterparts. Neither does she realise how critically such differences may be appraised by her own countrymen. Winterbourne's appraisal of Daisy is, of course, the dramatic centre of the story. From the start it is ambivalent. Although American, Winterbourne has been long enough in Europe to have acquired an exact sense of the prevailing forms, and possibly to have lost touch with what he calls the 'young American tone'. His meeting with a strikingly pretty compatriot in decidedly unconventional circumstances is a challenge to his sophistication. In a running internal dialogue his mind plays to and fro over the distinction between what he observes—Daisy's naturalness—and what he should infer —her concealed intentions. For a man of urbanity and wit he seems remarkably afraid of being compromised.

A desire to interpret correctly is hardly conventional in itself; and a wish to relate the particular to the general may well be a sign of intelligence. Winterbourne amuses himself with possible terms of analysis. His exchange with little Randolph Miller takes him with easy assurance to his first large category—'American girls are the best girls!'—just as his quick admiration for Daisy is cast in a similarly general form—'How pretty they are!'—as though this too were something common to all American girls. The comedy of his witty assimilation of particular to general carries over to his next speculations on the risks of all that is unconventional in the behaviour of such girls. His apprehension about *their* alleged boldness leaves him blind to what is predatory in his own responses. As he resorts to conversational strategies to find out who Daisy is, he is conscious of taking freedoms beyond the codes he knows, but he is less concerned to assess his own conduct than to penetrate Daisy's. It is a matter of relief when he lights on a formula that satisfies him—that she was, after all, 'only a pretty American flirt': he can give himself up to a connoisseur's appreciation of the girl's charms. A little later, and again with conscious impropriety, he finds himself proposing an expedition with her to the Castle of Chillon. He can detect in her 'no mockery nor irony'.

Winterbourne's aunt, however, supplies a less tractable system of categories. Even by American standards, she insists, the Miller family is 'horribly common'. If Daisy is pretty, she is nevertheless 'of the last crudity'. Mrs Costello chooses to insinuate an 'intimacy' with the courier, and discriminates trenchantly between the liberty permitted her granddaughters in New York and the licence taken by Daisy. Winterbourne is 'vexed, even a little humiliated' that he should be able to rely so little in such a matter on either his instinct or his reason. He feels the force of his aunt's prediction that he is 'sure to make some great mistake' while wishing, quite distinctly, to see more of Daisy. His gallantry becomes audacity: for him the trip to Chillon has all the Victorian overtones of an 'adventure', yet he can discover no answering consciousness on Daisy's part. The taunt of commonness is at odds with the impeccable taste of her turnout for the occasion, just as Daisy's preference for taking the little public steamer up the lake is at odds with his idea of a private carriage. Daisy hardly takes the sentimental advantage of the outing that Winterbourne had looked for. She is in fact, by the end, 'quite distractingly passive'. It is Mrs Costello and the superbly whiskered Eugenio who ensure the full implications of Daisy's having gone out 'all alone' with a gentleman. Caught between his own contradictions of gallantry and impropriety, Winterbourne revises his formula: if Daisy is not a consummate coquette, she must be too simple to be a schemer at all. The puzzle is only to determine whether her 'case' is one of calculation or incoherence. The exercise becomes a refinement of classification, which seems to be the condition of Winterbourne's urbanity and self-esteem. At any rate, he keeps his promise and follows her to Rome.

In the second part of the story the speculations take on a darker cast. The uncertainties of Vevey are intensified for Winterbourne as he is greeted with the public versions of 'how far' Daisy is going in Rome. The 'child of the Swiss lakeside' has become a text-book case for study in Mrs Walker's circle, and Winterbourne can neither admit nor discount the common verdict. Yet the very openness of her rendez-vous with Giovanelli in the Pincian Gardens is so provocative as to make him hesitate to reach the obvious conclusion. The relationship looks no more like an intrigue, and is no more clandestine, than his own visit to Chillon with her had been. He becomes aware that he wants an answer to what puzzles him in the girl's conduct which should be definite before it was favourable. Daisy's resistance to Mrs Walker's well-meant interference produces a crisis of doubt: it has implicated him with 'the voice of civilisation', while making him aware that he must choose between the criteria of the world he knows and an uncertain alliance with a girl whose nature he cannot fathom. The glimpse of Daisy with Giovanelli, half-concealed by her parasol in an attitude of casual intimacy, is enough to send him back to the world he knew. 'American flirting', he tells her severely, 'has no place in *this* system.'

Winterbourne wants, with growing urgency, 'trustworthy information' about Daisy. He cannot interpret the information he has, and cannot bring himself to trust her without knowing more. As his grounds for mistrust accumulate he is less and less able to resist the common view of Daisy. He sees her literally as an 'anomaly', and comes to believe that what he had at first taken for a 'gay indifference' is, rather, a sign that she is 'powerless either to heed or to suffer'. At Mrs Walker's soirée he sees for the first time that Daisy is aware of his dilemma, that she has taken the 'force of his logic': he understands her 'single small queer glance' and her spirited preference for weak tea to sound advice. Yet half in irritation, half in sympathy, he retreats to his formula—'the name of little American flirts was incoherence.' His ambivalence is fatal. He merely resents the sense that he has been reduced to logic-chopping.

It is Daisy who meets the cold shoulders of the polite world, but Winterbourne who seems, in her word, 'lonesome'. As he takes it upon himself to advise her, his tone and language become so formal that Daisy objects he has 'no more "give" than a ramrod'. He imposes the terms of his world upon her, meeting *her* terms nowhere. When she asks, on the Palatine Hill, whether *he* thinks she is going around too much with Giovanelli, his reply is callously impersonal: 'Everyone thinks so—if you care to know.' He is too intent on his own idea to hear a challenge in her answer, or to sense the possible reproach in her suggestion that he might have wanted to 'say something' on her behalf. What he notices is his reaction to her sudden declaration that she is engaged—'it was for a moment like testing a heart-beat.' Yet all he can hear in her instant and self-contradictory retraction is perversity: she is once again denying him a certainty which is comprehensible.

Certainty comes with the chance encounter late at night in the Colosseum. It brings both 'horror' and 'relief'. What Winterbourne feels then is anger at his earlier hesitancies, shame for what now seem misplaced scruples of definition: 'The whole riddle of her contradictions had grown easy to read.' His arrest is so complete that he only belatedly takes in where he is—he has heard, rather than seen, Daisy and her companion, who have been sitting in the shadow of the massive ruin while he himself was crossing the moon-drenched arena. For the first time in the story, *he* has been the person directly in view. He tells Daisy with brutal explicitness that it is no longer a matter of importance whether he had 'believed' her. The reach of his words is given in Daisy's parting cry that she 'doesn't care' whether or not she has the 'Roman fever'. The 'exquisite little fatalist' has made her only direct appeal from that hard judgement. Mrs Walker's gesture had been a snobbish cut: Winterbourne's is a deliberate refusal of comprehension or pity, which Daisy perfectly understands. As she takes his 'point' in the sinister moonlight, Daisy 'appraised him a moment, roughness and all'. In that instant the truth between them might have been reached; but Winterbourne is locked in his conviction that 'any rupture of any law or any deviation from any custom' is intolerable. He does not even feel remorse until he learns, so much too late at the Protestant cemetery, what Giovanelli had to say. At the close he responds to Mrs Costello's question with the same stiffness for which Daisy had mocked him: 'She would have appreciated one's esteem.' The story returns to the unresolved ambiguity of its opening: still unable to commit himself, Winterbourne turns away. He can measure neither the transgressions nor the innocence he has met. He only knows, without knowing what it meant, that he would never have been 'afraid' of Daisy. He had 'studied' her to her cost, and to his own loss.

IV

'Pandora' belongs with 'Daisy Miller' and the much later 'Julia Bride'. It opens with the neatly contrived joke in which the young German diplomat, going to his first assignment in the United States, is discovered earnestly preparing himself for the experience by reading the latest Tauchnitz edition of 'Daisy Miller', and noting in that story elements which seem to correspond with his own situation. 'Pandora' transmutes to comedy the failures of understanding which had led to tragedy in 'Daisy Miller', but the nature and the ends of its comedy are open to question. Is it simply a 'study of manners'? Or did James on this occasion find the vantage point for a 'quickened vision' of his native country? Ezra Pound, at least, thought 'Pandora' one of the best of James's shorter pieces: he said it should pass as 'a sop to America's virginal charm' and a counterweight to Daisy Miller. He enjoyed James's alertness to 'the Teuton', and such details as the picture of Mr and Mrs Day, so competently tucked up on deck by their daughter, closing their eyes 'after the fashion of a pair of household dogs who expect to be scratched'. He also reflected on James's description of Pandora's success as 'purely personal'—though he took the phrase to apply to the story whereas James meant it of his heroine, and in a way which is a clue to his real subject. Pandora's 'success' is exactly what makes her different from Daisy, and the way in which it is 'entirely personal' (Pound was misquoting when he wrote 'purely') makes for a deliberate irony of perspective between the two stories.

'Pandora' was nothing like the big hit that 'Daisy Miller' had been. None of James's American stories was. It was prompted by his visit to America over the winter of 1881–2, and in particular by his first ever stay in Washington. The *Notebooks* record his desire to 'DO Henry Adams and his wife', to write something of the 'very lovely memories of last winter'. The Adamses reappear as the Bonnycastles of the tale: intelligent, witty and well-informed witnesses to the political life of the capital, who delight in defining and deconstructing its apparent boundaries. Like Henry Adams, Alfred Bonnycastle 'was not in politics, though politics were much in him'. And like Clover Adams, Mrs Bonnycastle is uncompromisingly selective about the company she will admit: neither was prepared to tolerate fools, knaves or bores. ('I have asked Henry James NOT to bring his friend Oscar Wilde when he comes,' wrote Mrs Adams in January 1882; 'I must keep out thieves and noodles or else take down my sign and go West.') 'Pandora' echoes several of the political moments of Henry Adams's anonymously published novel, *Democracy*, but the effect of these undeclared references is not simply to stress what is topical. Mrs Bonnycastle's mockery—like Beatrice's in *Much Ado About Nothing*—serves as a damaging touchstone to certain kinds of pretentiousness, in particular the attribution of misplaced significance to what cannot bear thematic weight.

We might begin with the title. Mrs Dangerfield saw Pandora's name as 'in the highest degree typical': that is, she saw it as evidence of embarrassing cultural aspiration of a deeply provincial order. We may be meant to wonder what the girl from Utica has to do with the legendary figure who brought about the ruin of man. Is there some teasing analogy between the forbidden box given the Greek Pandora, containing all the ills of the world, and the trunk symbolically opened by a Customs Officer as the Day family return from their two years abroad? At best I see only an unstated play on newer meanings to the name: the 'Pandora' dolls of the world of fashion were indeed figures for exhibition (see note to p. 97.2) and point with specific irony to the way in which the heroine's success may be thought of as 'personal'. A 'Pandora' hardly has a personality: she is merely a model upon which others hang their designs. Yet the Pandora of the story is resourceful, capable, and sure of what she wants. Mrs Dangerfield underestimates her candidate when she informs Count Otto that such a girl can't 'have' a social position—there simply weren't opera boxes to be had in up-state New York—and that it was unfair even to pose such systematically analytical questions about her status. Pandora took her culture systematically enough: she had seen to it that her family spent three hours on the Acropolis—'I guess they won't forget that!'—and for deck-reading on the homeward crossing she had Sainte-Beuve, Renan, and 'by way of dissipation' the poetry of Alfred de Musset. She proves a receptive and enthusiastic tourist in Washington, managing to turn her eagerly gathered impressions to practical advantage with exemplary promptness. The point is that, just as Daisy is seen through the eyes of her critics, so Pandora is the subject of speculation by a solemnly apprehensive German diplomat and his American informants. Like Winterbourne, Vogelstein is at first warned off a young American girl by an older woman who claims authoritative social experience. If a long stay in Europe has left Winterbourne 'morally muddled', Vogelstein's anxieties come from facing the New World. He naturally wishes to acquit himself well in a post of national consequence and dreads mistakes. Like Winterbourne, again, he seeks the assurance of definite information, particularly on the peculiar freedom of American girls who, by account, are so 'apt to advance . . . straight upon their victim'. The Count does not compromise himself as Winterbourne does, but as the *Donau* approaches New York he regrets that he has profited so little from the opportunity of enjoying Pandora Day's company. So many questions, for him, remain unanswered.

The scene at the New Jersey docks with which the first part closes is perfect: the noise, heat, ramshackle crowds, waiting hackney-coachmen, heaps of luggage, and the odour of the rotting piles, all register for the new arrivals the bristling challenge of America. Amid the Count's uncertainty as to whether he should tip an American Customs Officer, and the struggles of his English manservant haggling for a cab (it turns out that the only viable language of communication is German), we are left with Pandora's ringing tones, admonishing Vogelstein, as she busies herself with her family's affairs: 'I hope you'll judge us correctly!' The young man has hardly the means of 'judging' at all.

Two years in Washington do little to allay Vogelstein's anxieties. They are, if anything, increased by his getting to know the Bonnycastles who seem to have 'solved all their problems successfully'. As a foreigner and an aristocrat, he is dismayed by the mixture of the homespun and the monumental among the elected representatives of the world's largest nation. Hearing that a Miss Day is in Washington, he wonders doubtingly whether this could possibly be the 'heroine of the *Donau*'. He further wonders whether he will prove to have met her hope: '*Had* he judged America correctly?' He recognises Pandora at a party, engaged in private *tête-à-tête* with the President himself—extracting a promise, it appears, from the ruler of fifty million people—and makes his first notable mistake: he does not take what he sees seriously enough. The evening ends with his recourse to the Bonnycastles for a thoroughgoing analysis of the identity and career of the girl from Utica. The result is the clever and witty set-piece on the genesis and evolution of the 'self-made girl'. The Bonnycastles enjoy sporting with their social Darwinism; the Count has to make what he can of this flagrant example of the modern. He begins to suspect that his curiosity is not as perfectly disinterested as that of his hosts. As he shows Pandora round the Capitol and calls on her the following day, he persuades himself, with a certain want of logic, that he wasn't 'in real danger'. For the first time he forgets the warnings of native caution: on the picnic at Arlington he may even be said to relax. He considers Pandora's virtues as the wife of an aspiring diplomat, though suspecting that she might require 'several thorough lessons' if it came to talking to the Kaiser rather than the President. He feels secure as they wander round Mount Vernon; yet he senses that the day is a turning point—'he was under a charm that made him feel he was watching his own life and that his susceptibilities were beyond his control.'

It is on the return journey down the Potomac that Mrs Bonnycastle adds a final 'fact' to her definition of the self-made girl: that she usually has an 'impediment' in the form of an improbably long attachment, to which it is thought she will 'stick'. The end mirrors the close of the first part. As the boat docks back in Washington, Vogelstein finds himself standing just behind Pandora and, a mere spectator, witnesses the nearly soundless exchange between the girl and a gentleman who has evidently come to meet her. She has, he learns, got her promise from the President. The Count has failed to judge correctly the very features of America which most interested him. We may conclude lightheartedly enough that his rationalism was naïve and his elaborate caution unwarranted. Like Winterbourne he has not risked commitment until too late. But here no one suffers but himself: he is never faced with a painfully alien truth about himself, as Winterbourne is. He simply has no place in Pandora's scheme of things. The final note is Mrs Bonnycastle's immoderate shriek of mirth. It is a hint of the hysteria which reappears more dangerously in *The Bostonians*. The social forms and realities of the democratic capital have defeated the pedantic young man: the lines of demarcation, the codes by which people can be 'recognised' and accounted for, are so confusing and uncertain, that no 'system' could be applied. In default of the security of facts and figures, Vogelstein feels himself 'reduced to his mere personality'. Self-made as she is, Pandora slips through this formless world unscathed: the very uncertainties of definition are the condition of her personal success. As Mrs Bonnycastle says, it is a condition they had all helped to make.

V

The theme of collective responsibility darkens in 'The Patagonia'. The characters here are brought together by the ordinary chance of circumstances and share a fine, slow, mid-summer Atlantic crossing from Boston to Liverpool. At the start the narrator has learned that an old friend whom he has not seen for a long time is due to sail on the same ship, and he visits her on the eve of their departure. She tells him that her son, whom he hardly knows, may be travelling with them. In the course of the hot evening two strangers call: a mother and her daughter. They have been urged by mutual acquaintances to appeal to Mrs Nettlepoint's goodwill in befriending the daughter during the voyage. The girl, Grace Mavis, is travelling alone to meet her fiancé in England. It turns out that Mrs Nettlepoint's son and the girl have met before; the narrator remembers the fiancé, Mr Porterfield, from Paris some ten years ago. The degrees of acquaintanceship are not perfectly clear. Once on board the passengers are committed to a curious intimacy for the duration of the crossing. The social world of the ship is made up of elements partly familiar and partly unfamiliar, in an enforced community. Mrs Nettlepoint, a wretched sailor, dreads the voyage. Grateful that she can rely on her son, Jasper, to discharge her duties towards their *protégée*, she intends to keep to her cabin. The narrator warns her lightly that such a retreat will not guarantee her immunity from the dramas of personal relationships which make the interest of such crossings: she will participate, he explains, if only at secondhand, through the reports of her visitors. An experienced traveller, he knows the 'sea-change' which comes over those well 'out' in the ocean—the change by which, subtly, 'things that were nobody's business soon become everybody's business'. Or, as Mrs Peck puts it later, if you 'knew someone' you 'had some rights in them.' As an 'inveterate observer', he proposes to enjoy the opportunities for licensed speculation afforded by the vacant days before them. Mrs Nettlepoint protests that he is abusing the distinction between observing and imagining.

During the first days out the narrator does indeed enjoy that special sense of unreality and safety which prevail at sea. Yet he knows that a ship is also a place in which whispers carry. In the vast open spaces of the sea there is no agent of 'compression', 'no sounding board to make speakers responsible'. There is a common sense of everyone having taken their seats as in a theatre, and waiting for some action to begin. The narrator's image of the ship as 'a great school of gossip' takes on a more sinister point, as, gradually, the actors distinguish themselves from the spectators. The process seems to have no clear origin. As he reads peaceably on deck, even the narrator has an almost hallucinatory sense of his French novel having been the agent that 'set them in motion'. Yet there is no 'text': only the collusion of the witnesses to take the drama through its successive stages.

What happens can be seen as an emblem of how a group works—in this case, a group of people operating within civilised codes of behaviour who become irretrievably implicated in events with which they have no necessary connection. Even the Captain is powerless to arrest what everyone can see to be going on. There are constant verbal anticipations of the finale, yet when it comes it is shocking. What takes place throughout is obscure. Everyone feels under a spell which is only broken by the sight of land. As the narrator puts it, 'we make a little world here together and we can't blink its condition.' He sees this 'condition' without being able to foresee its outcome. He sees how her 'maternal immorality' implicates Mrs Nettlepoint; he measures the selfishness of Jasper Nettlepoint, and the force of the implacable Mrs Peck's cry: 'Ah she's afraid.' He even feels himself to have 'interfered' in Grace Mavis's situation, 'in some degree to her loss'. All that is 'absolute' is that, veiled and reserved, only once breaking down in her appeal to Mrs Nettlepoint, the girl has gone alone to her fate. Everyone was 'somehow responsible'. There can be no sure definition of human liability or complicity—no safe distinction between observation and imagination.

JEAN GOODER

NOTE ON THE TEXTS

THE four stories collected here were written over roughly ten years. Each originally appeared in a periodical, to be reprinted in book form with some revisions to the text and punctuation. In the case of 'Daisy Miller' especially there were further alterations to later reprintings. All four were chosen by James for inclusion in the New York Edition of *The Novels and Tales* (1907–9). They are given here in this final form, together with the relevant parts of the Preface to Volume XVIII.

The source of 'Daisy Miller' was an anecdote that James heard in Rome during the autumn of 1877. He wrote the story early in the new year on his return to London. It appeared in two parts, in the June and July numbers of the *Cornhill Magazine*, 1878, under the title 'Daisy Miller: A Study'. James did not move quickly enough to secure the American rights and the story was pirated over the summer in both Boston and New York. In November Harper's brought out an authorised edition—No. 82 of their Half-Hour Series—selling 20,000 copies within weeks. Macmillan brought out the first book edition in 1879, putting 'Daisy Miller' with 'Four Meetings' and 'An International Episode'. The story was popular and was reprinted several times: by Macmillan in 1880 and 1888; and by Harper in 1883, 1892 and 1902. It was one of the most extensively revised of all James's works for the New York Edition. (It has been estimated that 90 per cent of the sentences were altered in some way and some 15 per cent more material added.) James also wrote a very different dramatic version of the story, *Daisy Miller: A*

Comedy in Three Acts, which was published in 1883.

'Pandora' first came out in two instalments in the *New York Sun*, on 1 and 8 June 1884. It was twice reprinted in book form in 1885: with 'The Author of Beltraffio' by James R. Osgood of Boston in January; and in February as part of a three-volume collection called *Stories Revived* by Macmillan. It was revised for Volume XVIII of the New York Edition over the summer of 1908. The *Notebooks* record James's initial conception for the story and a sketch of its main theme in the entry for 29 January 1884.

'The Patagonia' first appeared in the *English Illustrated Magazine* for August and September 1888. It was reprinted in book form in 1889, as part of a two-volume collection of tales published by Macmillan in London and New York. The first volume was given over to 'A London Life'; the second put 'The Patagonia' with 'The Liar' and 'Mrs Temperley'. The story was omitted from the Continental Edition of 1891, and then lightly revised for inclusion in Volume XVIII of the New York Edition. The first sketch of its subject is in the *Notebook* entry for 5 January 1888. Mrs Kemble's anecdote of Barry St Leger and the young married woman with whom he sailed from India is further developed in the entry for 11 March 1888.

The earliest of these stories, 'Four Meetings', first came out in *Scribner's Monthly* in November 1877. It was reprinted in 1879, in the first book edition of 'Daisy Miller' (see above). It had originally appeared in three parts: at this stage the central section at Le Havre was divided to make the present four. It was included in Volume 13 of the Macmillan Collective Edition of 1883, with 'Daisy Miller', 'Longstaff's Marriage' and 'Benvolio'; and reissued in Boston by James R. Osgood in 1885 with 'The Author of Beltraffio'. Theodora Bosanquet tells us that it was revised 'with extreme care' for Volume XVI of the New York Edition. The alterations amounted to some 12,000 words, including four major insertions and extensive rewriting in the final section. The Preface does not mention the story, and there is no record of its origins.

The Scribner Archive at Princeton shows that James

sent off the Preface, together with his revised copy for 'Daisy Miller', in September 1908. He saw the Preface as his best and most important—'as winding up the series of Shorter Things and taking in all I have to say about them'. It was a shock to him to learn in December that there was too much material for the single projected volume. Rather than cut out some of the tales, Scribner's proposed dividing them over two volumes. Although James complied promptly, he was left with difficult decisions about the regrouping of his stories, and the necessity of breaking up the Preface. In the end he saw no principle of redistribution '*but* the mere mechanical one', which would see that each volume had the right number of pages. 'Julia Bride' ends Volume XVII; and 'Daisy Miller' was chosen to head the new Volume XVIII, 'even though it perches her in a queer place'. For James the 'majestic coherence' of his conception had suffered, but he held to his original intention in putting 'Pandora' and 'The Patagonia' with 'Daisy Miller'. The other stories in the volume are 'The Marriages', 'The Real Thing', 'Brooksmith', 'The Beldonald Holbein', 'The Story in It', 'Flickerbridge', and 'Mrs Medwin'.

FURTHER READING

MANY of James's novels and tales involve comparisons between European and American manners, on both sides of the Atlantic. The following list of his writings is restricted to those where such contrasts are most dramatically direct.

I. JAMES'S WRITINGS

Novels

Dates are of the first edition.

Roderick Hudson (1875)   The Portrait of a Lady (1881)
The American (1877)   The Wings of the Dove (1902)
The Europeans (1878)   The Ambassadors (1903)

Tales

Dates are of the first (usually magazine) publication. The versions as first published in book form are reprinted in *The Complete Tales of Henry James*, ed. Leon Edel (London, 1962–4). The earliest versions are now being reprinted as *The Tales of Henry James*, ed. Maqbool Aziz (Oxford, 1973–). Both 'Four Meetings' and 'Daisy Miller' appear in vol. 3 (1984).

'A Passionate Pilgrim' (1871)

'Madame de Mauves' (1874)

'An International Episode' (1878–9)

'The Pension Beaurepas' (1879)

'A Bundle of Letters' (1879)

'The Point of View' (1882)

'The Siege of London' (1883)

'Lady Barberina' (1884)

'A New England Winter' (1884)

'"Europe"' (1899)

'Miss Gunton of Poughkeepsie' (1900)

'Julia Bride' (1908)

Other writings

Transatlantic Sketches (1875)	*Portraits of Places* (1883)
French Poets and Novelists (1878)	*The American Scene* (1907)
Hawthorne (1879)	*Italian Hours* (1909)

Autobiography, ed. F. W. Dupee (London, 1956). This includes *A Small Boy and Others* (1913), *Notes of a Son and Brother* (1914), and *The Middle Years* (1917); repr. Princeton, New Jersey, 1983.

Letters, ed. Percy Lubbock, 2 vols (London, 1920).

Letters, ed. Leon Edel, 4 vols (Cambridge, Mass., and London, 1974–84).

The Notebooks of Henry James, ed. F. O. Matthiessen and Kenneth B. Murdock (New York, 1947; repr. Chicago and London, 1981).

Selected Literary Criticism, ed. Morris Shapira, introduction by F. R. Leavis (London, 1963; repr. Cambridge, 1981).

The Scenic Art, ed. Allen Wade (London, 1949).

The American Essays of Henry James, ed. Leon Edel (New York, 1956).

Literary Reviews and Essays by Henry James, ed. Albert Mordell (New York, 1957).

II. BIOGRAPHY

Matthiessen, F. O., *The James Family* (New York, 1947).

Edel, Leon, *The Life of Henry James*, 5 vols (London, 1953–72); revised edn, 2 vols (London, 1977).

III. BIBLIOGRAPHY

Edel, Leon, and Dan H. Laurence, with James Rambeau, *A Bibliography of Henry James*, 3rd edn (Oxford, 1982).

Ricks, Beatrice, *Henry James: A Bibliography of Secondary Works* (Metuchen, New Jersey, 1975).

The Humanities Index provides an annual supplement to Ricks.

IV. CRITICISM

Arvin, Newton, 'Henry James and the Almighty Dollar', *Hound & Horn*, VII, April–May, 1934.

Aziz, Maqbool, '*Four Meetings*: A Caveat for James Critics', *Essays in Criticism*, 18, 1968.

Booth, Wayne C., *The Rhetoric of Fiction* (Chicago, 1961).

Bosanquet, Theodora, 'The Revised Version', *The Little Review*, 5, Aug. 1918.

Buitenhuis, Peter, *The Grasping Imagination* (Toronto, 1970).

Deakin, Motley F., 'Daisy Miller, Tradition and the European Heroine', *Comparative Literature Studies*, VI, 1, March 1969.

Dupee, F. W., ed., *The Question of Henry James* (London, 1947).

Eliot, T. S., 'In Memory', *The Little Review*, 5, Aug. 1918; repr. in Edmund Wilson; *The Shock of Recognition* (London, 1956).

Gale, Robert L., *The Caught Image* (Chapel Hill, 1964).

Gard, Roger, ed., *Henry James: The Critical Heritage* (London, 1968).

Holloway, J., Introduction to *Daisy Miller*, Heritage Press edn (New York, 1969).

Horne, F. P., 'A Textual and Critical Study of the New York Edition of The Novels and Tales of Henry James', unpublished Ph.D. thesis, Cambridge University Library, 1984.

Hoxie, Elizabeth F., 'Mrs Grundy adopts Daisy Miller', *New England Quarterly*, 19, Dec. 1946.

Leavis, F. R., *The Great Tradition* (London, 1948).

Matthiessen, F. O., *The Major Phase* (New York, 1944).

Ohmann, Carol, '*Daisy Miller*: A Study of Changing Intentions', *American Literature*, 36, March 1964.

FURTHER READING

Poirier, Richard, *The Comic Sense of Henry James* (London, 1960).

Pound, Ezra, 'Henry James: A Shake Down', *The Little Review*, 5, Aug. 1918; repr. in *The Literary Essays of Ezra Pound*, ed. T. S. Eliot (London, 1954).

Rowe, John Carlos, *Henry Adams and Henry James: The Emergence of a Modern Consciousness* (Ithaca and London, 1976).

Samuels, Charles T., *The Ambiguity of Henry James* (Illinois, 1971).

Stafford, William T., ed., *James's Daisy Miller* (New York, 1963).

Tanner, Tony, *The Reign of Wonder: Naivety and Reality in American Literature* (Cambridge, 1965).

——, ed., *Henry James*, Modern Judgements (London, 1968).

Winters, Yvor, *In Defense of Reason* (London, 1960).

CHRONOLOGY OF HENRY JAMES

COMPILED BY LEON EDEL

1843	Born 15 April at No. 21 Washington Place, New York City.
1843–4	Taken abroad by parents to Paris and London: period of residence at Windsor.
1845–55	Childhood in Albany and New York.
1855–8	Attends schools in Geneva, London, Paris and Boulogne-sur-mer and is privately tutored.
1858	James family settles in Newport, Rhode Island.
1859	At scientific school in Geneva. Studies German in Bonn.
1860	At school in Newport. Receives back injury on eve of Civil War while serving as volunteer fireman. Studies art briefly. Friendship with John La Farge.
1862–3	Spends term in Harvard Law School.
1864	Family settles in Boston and then in Cambridge. Early anonymous story and unsigned reviews published.
1865	First signed story published in *Atlantic Monthly*.
1869–70	Travels in England, France and Italy. Death of his beloved cousin Minny Temple.
1870	Back in Cambridge, publishes first novel in *Atlantic*, *Watch and Ward*.
1872–4	Travels with sister Alice and aunt in Europe; writes impressionistic travel sketches for the *Nation*. Spends autumn in Paris and goes to Italy to write first large novel.
1874–5	On completion of *Roderick Hudson* tests New York City as residence; writes much literary journalism for

xxxvi

Nation. First three books published: *Transatlantic Sketches*, *A Passionate Pilgrim* (tales) and *Roderick Hudson*.

1875–6   Goes to live in Paris. Meets Ivan Turgenev and through him Flaubert, Zola, Daudet, Maupassant and Edmond de Goncourt. Writes *The American*.

1876–7   Moves to London and settles in 3 Bolton Street, Piccadilly. Revisits Paris, Florence, Rome.

1878   'Daisy Miller' published in London establishes fame on both sides of the Atlantic. Publishes first volume of essays (*French Poets and Novelists*) and *The Europeans*.

1879–82   *Washington Square*, *Confidence*, *The Portrait of a Lady*.

1881–3   Revisits Boston: first visit to Washington. Death of parents.

1884–6   Returns to London. Sister Alice comes to live near him. Fourteen-volume collection of novels and tales published. Writes *The Bostonians* and *The Princess Casamassima*, published in the following year.

1886   Moves to flat at 34 De Vere Gardens West.

1887   Sojourn in Italy, mainly Florence and Venice. 'The Aspern Papers', *The Reverberator*, 'A London Life'. Friendship with grand-niece of Fenimore Cooper—Constance Fenimore Woolson.

1888   *Partial Portraits* and several collections of tales.

1889–90   *The Tragic Muse*.

1890–1   Dramatises *The American*, which has a short run. Writes four comedies, rejected by producers.

1892   Alice James dies in London.

1894   Miss Woolson commits suicide in Venice. James journeys to Italy and visits her grave in Rome.

1895   He is booed at first night of his play *Guy Domville*. Deeply depressed, he abandons the theatre.

1896–7   *The Spoils of Poynton*, *What Maisie Knew*.

1898   Takes long lease of Lamb House, in Rye, Sussex. *The Turn of the Screw* published.

1899–1900 *The Awkward Age*, *The Sacred Fount*. Friendship with Conrad and Wells.

1902–4 *The Ambassadors*, *The Wings of the Dove* and *The Golden Bowl*. Friendships with H. C. Andersen and Jocelyn Persse.

1905 Revisits USA after 20-year absence, lectures on Balzac and the speech of Americans.

1906–10 *The American Scene*. Edits selective and revised New York Edition of his works in 24 volumes. Friendship with Hugh Walpole.

1910 Death of brother, William James.

1913 Sargent paints his portrait as 70th birthday gift from some 300 friends and admirers. Writes autobiographies, *A Small Boy and Others*, and *Notes of a Son and Brother*.

1914 *Notes on Novelists*. Visits wounded in hospitals.

1915 Becomes a British subject.

1916 Given Order of Merit. Dies 28 February in Chelsea, aged 72. Funeral in Chelsea Old Church. Ashes buried in Cambridge, Mass., family plot.

1976 Commemorative tablet unveiled in Poets' Corner of Westminster Abbey, 17 June.

PREFACE*

IT was in Rome during the autumn of 1877 ; a friend then living there but settled now in a South less weighted with appeals and memories happened to mention——which she might perfectly not have done—— some simple and uninformed American lady of the previous winter, whose young daughter, a child of nature and of freedom, accompanying her from hotel to hotel, had " picked up " by the wayside, with the best conscience in the world, a good-looking Roman, of vague identity, astonished at his luck, yet (so far as might be, by the pair) all innocently, all serenely exhibited and introduced : this at least till the occur- rence of some small social check, some interrupting incident, of no great gravity or dignity, and which I forget. I had never heard, save on this showing, of the amiable but not otherwise eminent ladies, who weren't in fact named, I think, and whose case had merely served to point a familiar moral ; and it must have been just their want of salience that left a margin for the small pencil - mark inveterately signifying, in such connexions, " Dramatise, dramatise ! " The result of my recognising a few months later the sense of my pencil-mark was the short chronicle of " Daisy Miller," which I indited in London the following spring and then addressed, with no conditions attached, as I remember, to the editor of a magazine that had its seat of publication at Philadelphia and had lately appeared to appreciate my contributions. That gentleman how-

* The relevant part of the Preface to Vol. XVIII of the New York Edition is reproduced here.

ever (an historian of some repute) promptly returned me my missive, and with an absence of comment that struck me at the time as rather grim—as, given the circumstances, requiring indeed some explanation : till a friend to whom I appealed for light, giving him the thing to read, declared it could only have passed with the Philadelphian critic for " an outrage on American girlhood." This was verily a light, and of bewildering intensity ; though I was presently to read into the matter a further helpful inference. To the fault of being outrageous this little composition added that of being essentially and pre-eminently a *nouvelle*; a signal example in fact of that type, foredoomed at the best, in more cases than not, to editorial disfavour. If accordingly I was afterwards to be cradled, almost blissfully, in the conception that " Daisy " at least, among my productions, might approach " success," such success for example, on her eventual appearance, as the state of being promptly pirated in Boston—a sweet tribute I hadn't yet received and was never again to know—the irony of things yet claimed its rights, I couldn't but long continue to feel, in the circumstance that quite a special reprobation had waited on the first appearance in the world of the ultimately most prosperous child of my invention. So doubly discredited, at all events, this bantling met indulgence, with no great delay, in the eyes of my admirable friend the late Leslie Stephen and was published in two numbers of *The Cornhill Magazine* (1878).

It qualified itself in that publication and afterwards as " a Study " ; for reasons which I confess I fail to recapture unless they may have taken account simply of a certain flatness in my poor little heroine's literal denomination. Flatness indeed, one must have felt, was the very sum of her story; so that perhaps after all the attached epithet was meant but as a deprecation, addressed to the reader, of any great critical hope of stirring scenes. It provided for mere concentration, and on an object scant and superficially vulgar—from which, however, a sufficiently brooding tenderness might eventually extract a shy incongruous charm. I suppress at all events here the appended qualification —in view of the simple truth, which ought from the first to have been apparent to me, that my little exhibition is made to no degree whatever in critical but, quite inordinately and extravagantly, in poetical terms. It comes back to me that I was at a certain hour long afterwards to have reflected, in this connexion, on the characteristic free play of the whirligig of time. It was in Italy again—in Venice and in the prized society of an interesting friend, now dead, with whom I happened to wait, on the Grand Canal, at the animated water-steps of one of the hotels. The considerable little terrace there was so disposed as to make a salient stage for certain demonstrations on the part of two young girls, children *they*, if ever, of nature and of free-dom, whose use of those resources, in the general public eye, and under our own as we sat in the gondola, drew from the lips of a second companion, sociably afloat with us, the remark that there before us, with no sign absent, were a couple of attesting Daisy Millers. Then it was that, in my charming hostess's prompt protest, the whirligig, as I have called it, at once betrayed itself. " How can you liken *those* creatures to a figure of which the only fault is touchingly to have transmuted so sorry a type and to have, by a poetic artifice, not only led our judgement of it astray, but made *any* judgement quite impossible ? " With which this gentle lady and admirable critic turned on the author himself. " You *know* you quite falsified, by the turn you gave it, the thing you had begun with having in mind, the thing you had had, to satiety, the chance of ' observing ' : your pretty perversion of it, or your unprincipled mystification of our sense of it, does it really too much honour—in spite of which, none the less, as anything charming or touching always to that extent justifies itself, we after a fashion forgive and understand you. But why *waste* your romance ? There are cases, too many, in which you've done it again ; in which, provoked by a spirit of observation at first no doubt sufficiently sincere, and with the measured and felt truth fairly twitching your sleeve, you have yielded to your incurable prejudice in favour of grace—to whatever it is in you that makes so inordinately for form and prettiness and pathos ; not to say sometimes for misplaced drolling. Is it that you've after all too much imagination ? Those awful young women capering at the hotel-door, *they* are the real little Daisy Millers that were ; whereas yours in the tale is such a one, more's the pity, as—for pitch of the ingenuous, for quality of the artless—couldn't possibly have been at all." My answer to all which bristled of course with more professions than I can or need report here ; the chief of them inevitably to the effect that my supposedly typical little figure was of course pure poetry, and had never been anything else ; since this is what helpful imagination, in however slight a dose, ever directly makes for. As for the original grossness of readers, I daresay I added, that was another matter—but one which at any rate had then quite ceased to signify.

A good deal of the same element has doubtless sneaked into " Pandora," which I also reprint here for congruity's sake, and even while the circumstances attending the birth of this anecdote, given to the light in a New York newspaper (1884), pretty well lose themselves for me in the mists of time. I do nevertheless connect " Pandora " with one of the scantest of memoranda, twenty words jotted down in New York during a few weeks spent there a year or two before. I had put a question to a friend about a young lady present at a certain pleasure-party, but present in rather perceptibly unsupported and unguaranteed fashion, as without other connexions, without more operative " backers," than a proposer possibly half-hearted and a slightly sceptical seconder ; and had been answered to the effect that she was an interesting representative of a new social and local variety, the " self-made," or at least self-making, girl, whose sign was that—given some measurably amusing appeal in her to more or less ironic curiosity or to a certain complacency of patronage —she was anywhere made welcome enough if she only came, like one of the dismembered charges of Little Bo-Peep, leaving her " tail " behind her. Docked of all natural appendages and having enjoyed, as was supposed, no natural advantages ; with the " line drawn," that is, at her father and her mother, her sisters and her brothers, at everything that was hers, and with the presumption crushing as against these adjuncts, she was yet held free to prove her case and sail her boat herself ; even quite quaintly or quite touchingly free, as might be—working out thus on her own lines her social salvation. This was but five-and-twenty years ago ; yet what to-day most strikes me in the connexion, and quite with surprise, is that at a period so recent there should have been novelty for me in a situation so little formed by more contemporary lights to startle or waylay. The evolution of varieties moves fast ; the Pandora Days can no longer, I fear, pass for quaint or fresh or for exclusively native to any one tract of Anglo-Saxon soil. Little Bo-Peep's charges may, as manners have developed, leave their tails behind them for the season, but quite knowing what they have done with them and where they shall find them again—as is proved for the most part by the promptest disavowal of any apparent ground for ruefulness. To " dramatise " the hint thus gathered was of course, rudimentarily, to see the self-made girl apply her very first independent measure to the renovation of her house, founding its fortunes, introducing her parents, placing her brothers, marrying her sisters (this care on her own behalf being—a high note of superiority—quite secondary), in fine floating the heavy mass on the flood she had learned to breast. Something of that sort must have proposed itself to me at that time as the latent " drama " of the case ; very little of which, however, I am obliged to recognise, was to struggle to the surface. What is more to the point is the moral I at present find myself drawing from the fact that, then turning over my American impressions, those proceeding from a brief but profusely peopled stay in New York, I should have fished up that none so very precious particle as one of the pearls of the collection. Such a circumstance comes back, for me, to that fact of my insuperably restricted experience and my various missing American clues—or rather at least to my felt lack of the most important of them all—on which the current of these remarks has already led me to dilate. There had been indubitably and multitudinously, for me, in my native city, the world " down-town "—since how otherwise should the sense of " going " down, the sense of hovering at the narrow gates and skirting the so violently overscored outer face of the monstrous labyrinth that stretches from Canal Street to the Battery, have taken on, to me, the intensity of a worrying, a tormenting impression ? Yet it was an impression any attempt at the active cultivation of which, one had been almost violently admonished, could but find one in the last degree unprepared and uneducated. It was essentially New York, and New York was, for force and accent, nothing else worth speaking of ; but without the special lights it remained impenetrable and inconceivable ; so that one but mooned about superficially, circumferentially, taking in, through the pores of whatever wistfulness, no good material at all. I had had to retire, accordingly, with my yearning presumptions all unverified—presumptions, I mean, as to the privilege of the imaginative initiation, as to the hived stuff of drama, at the service there of the literary adventurer really informed enough and bold enough ; and with my one drop of comfort the observation already made—that at least I descried, for my own early humiliation and exposure, no semblance of such a competitor slipping in at any door or perched, for raking the scene, on any coign of vantage. *That* invidious attestation of my own appointed and incurable deafness to the major key I frankly surmise I could scarce have borne. For there it was ; not only that the major key was " down-town " but that down-town was, all itself, the major key—absolutely, exclusively ; with the inevitable consequence that if the minor was " up-town," and (by a parity of reasoning) up-town the minor, so the field was meagre and the inspiration thin for any unfortunate practically banished from the true pasture. Such an unfortunate, even at the time I speak of, had still to confess to the memory of a not inconsiderably earlier season when, seated for several months at the very moderate altitude of Twenty-Fifth Street, he felt himself day by day alone in that scale of the balance ; alone, I mean, with the music-masters and French pastry-cooks, the ladies and children—immensely present and immensely numerous these, but testifying with a collective voice to the extraordinary absence (save as pieced together through a thousand gaps and indirectnesses) of a serious male interest. One had heard and seen novels and plays appraised as lacking, detrimentally, a serious female ; but the higher walks in that community might at the period I speak of have formed a picture bright and animated, no doubt, but marked with the very opposite defect.

Here it was accordingly that loomed into view more than ever the anomaly, in various ways dissimulated to a first impression, rendering one of the biggest and loudest of cities one of the very least of Capitals ; together with the immediate reminder, on the scene, that an adequate muster of Capital characteristics would have remedied half my complaint. To have lived in capitals, even in some of the smaller, was to be sure of that and to know why—and all the more was this a consequence of having happened to live in some of the greater. Neither scale of the balance, in these, had ever struck one as so monstrously heaped-up at the expense of the other ; there had been manners and customs enough, so to speak, there had been features and functions, elements, appearances, social material, enough to go round. The question was to have appeared, however, and the question was to remain, this interrogated mystery of what American town-life had left to entertain the observer withal when nineteen twentieths of it, or in other words the huge organised mystery of the consummately, the supremely applied money-passion, were inexorably closed to him. My own practical answer figures here perforce in the terms, and in them only, of such propositions as are constituted by the four or five longest tales comprised in this series. What it came to was that up-town would do for me simply what up-town could—and seemed in a manner apologetically conscious that this mightn't be described as much. The kind of appeal to interest embodied in these portrayals and in several of their like companions was the measure of the whole minor exhibition, which affected me as virtually saying : " Yes I'm either *that*—that range and order of things, or I'm nothing at all ; therefore make the most of me ! " Whether " Daisy Miller," " Pandora," " The Patagonia," " Miss Gunton," " Julia Bride " and *tutti quanti* do in fact conform to any such admonition would be an issue by itself and which mustn't overcome my shyness ; all the more that the point of interest is really but this—that I was on the basis of the loved *nouvelle* form, with the best will in the world and the best conscience, almost helplessly cornered. To ride the *nouvelle* down-town, to prance and curvet and caracole with it there—that would have been the true ecstasy. But a single " spill "—such as I so easily might have had in Wall Street or wherever—would have forbidden me, for very shame, in the eyes of the expert and the knowing, ever to mount again ; so that in short it wasn't to be risked on any terms.

There were meanwhile the alternatives of course—that I might renounce the *nouvelle*, or else might abjure that " American life " the characteristic towniness of which was lighted for me, even though so imperfectly, by New York and Boston—by those centres only. Such extremities, however, I simply couldn't afford—artistically, sentimentally, financially, or by any other sacrifice—to face ; and if the fact nevertheless remains that an adjustment, under both the heads in question, had eventually to take place, every inch of my doubtless meagre ground was yet first contested, every turn and twist of my scant material economically used. Add to this that if the other constituents of the volume, the intermediate ones, serve to specify what I was then thrown back on, I needn't perhaps even at the worst have found within my limits a thinness of interest to resent : seeing that still after years the common appeal remained sharp enough to flower again into such a composition as " Julia Bride " (which independently of its appearance here has seen the light but in *Harper's Magazine*, 1908). As I wind up with this companion-study to " Daisy Miller " the considerable assortment of my shorter tales I seem to see it symbolise my sense of my having waited with something of a subtle patience, my having still hoped as against hope that the so ebbing and obliging seasons would somehow strike for me some small flash of what I have called the major light—would suffer, I mean, to glimmer out, through however odd a crevice or however vouchsafed a contact, just enough of a wandering air from the down-town penetralia as might embolden, as might inform, as might, straining a point, even conceivably inspire (always where the *nouvelle*, and the *nouvelle* only, should be concerned) ; all to the advantage of my extension of view and my variation of theme. A whole passage of intellectual history, if the term be not too pompous, occupies in fact, to my present sense, the waiting, the so fondly speculative interval : in which I seem to see myself rather a high and dry, yet irrepressibly hopeful artistic Micawber, cocking an ostensibly confident hat and practising an almost passionate system of " bluff " ; insisting, in fine, that something (out of the just-named penetralia) *would* turn up if only the right imaginative hanging-about on the chance, if only the true intelligent attention, were piously persisted in. . . . It's as if the international young ladies, felt by me as once more, as verily once too much, my appointed thematic doom, had inspired me with the fond thought of attacking them at an angle and from a quarter by which the peril and discredit of their rash inveteracy might be a bit conjured away.

These in fact are the saving sanities of the dramatic poet's always rather mad undertaking—the rigour of his artistic need to cultivate almost at any price variety of appearance and experiment, to dissimulate likenesses, samenesses, stalenesses, by the infinite play of a form pretending to a life of its own. There are not so many quite distinct things in his field, I think, as there are sides by which the main masses may be approached ; and he is after all but a nimble

besieger or nocturnal sneaking adventurer who perpetually plans, watches, circles for penetrable places.
I offer " Fordham Castle " positively for a rare little
memento of that truth : once I had to be, for the light
wind of it in my sails, " internationally " American,
what amount of truth my subject mightn't aspire
to was urgently enough indicated—which condition
straightway placed it in the time-honoured category ;
but the range of choice as to treatment, by which I
mean as to my pressing the clear liquor of amusement
and refreshment from the golden apple of composition,
that blest freedom, with its infinite power of renewal,
was still my resource, and I felt myself invoke it not
in vain. There was always the difficulty—I have in
the course of these so numerous preliminary observations repeatedly referred to it, but the point is so
interesting that it can scarce be made too often—that
the simplest truth about a human entity, a situation,
a relation, an aspect of life, however small, on behalf of
which the claim to charmed attention is made, strains
ever, under one's hand, more intensely, *most* intensely,
to justify that claim ; strains ever, as it were, toward
the uttermost end or aim of one's meaning or of its
own numerous connexions ; struggles at each step,
and in defiance of one's raised admonitory finger,
fully and completely to express itself. Any real art
of representation is, I make out, a controlled and
guarded acceptance, in fact a perfect economic
mastery, of that conflict : the general sense of the
expansive, the explosive principle in one's material
thoroughly noted, adroitly allowed to flush and colour
and animate the disputed value, but with its other
appetites and treacheries, its characteristic space-
hunger and space-cunning, kept down. The fair flower
of this artful compromise is to my sense the secret of
" foreshortening "—the particular economic device for
which one must have a name and which has in its

single blessedness and its determined pitch, I think, a higher price than twenty other clustered loosenesses ; and just because full-fed statement, just because the picture of as many of the conditions as possible made and kept proportionate, just because the surface iridescent, even in the short piece, by what is beneath it and what throbs and gleams through, are things all conducive to the only compactness that has a charm, to the only spareness that has a force, to the only simplicity that has a grace—those, in each order, that produce the *rich* effect.

Let me say, however, that such reflexions never helped to close my eyes, at any moment, to all that had come and gone, over the rest of the field, in the fictive world of adventure more complacently so called—the American world, I particularly mean, that might have put me so completely out of countenance by having drawn its inspiration, that of thousands of celebrated works, neither from up-town nor from down-town nor from my lady's chamber, but from the vast wild garden of " unconventional " life in no matter what part of our country. I grant in fact that this demonstration of how consummately my own meagrely-conceived sources were to be dispensed with by the more initiated minds would but for a single circumstance, grasped at in recovery of self-respect, have thrown me back in absolute dejection on the poverty of my own categories. Why hadn't so quickened a vision of the great neglected native quarry *at large* more troubled my dreams, instead of leaving my imagination on the whole so resigned ? Well, with many reasons I could count over, there was one that all exhaustively covered the ground and all completely answered the question : the reflexion, namely, that the common sign of the productions " unconventionally " prompted (and this positively without exception) was nothing less than the birth-

1

mark of Dialect, general or special—dialect with the
literary rein loose on its agitated back and with its
shambling power of traction, not to say, more analytic-
ally, of *at*traction, trusted for all such a magic might
be worth. Distinctly that was the odd case : the
key to the *whole* of the treasure of romance independently garnered was the riot of the vulgar tongue. One
might state it more freely still and the truth would be
as evident : the plural number, the vulgar tongues,
each with its intensest note, but pointed the moral
more luridly. Grand generalised continental riot
or particular pedantic, particular discriminated and
" sectional " and self-conscious riot—to feel the thick
breath, to catch the ugly snarl, of all or of either, was
to be reminded afresh of the only conditions that
guard the grace, the only origins that save the honour,
or even the life, of dialect : those precedent to the
invasion, to the sophistication, of schools and unconscious of the smartness of echoes and the taint
of slang. The thousands of celebrated productions
raised their monument but to the bastard vernacular
of communities disinherited of the felt difference
between the speech of the soil and the speech of
the newspaper, and capable thereby, accordingly, of
taking slang for simplicity, the composite for the
quaint and the vulgar for the natural. These were
unutterable depths, and, as they yawned about one,
what appreciable coherent sound did they seem most
to give out ? Well, to my ear surely, at the worst,
none that determined even a tardy compunction.
The monument was there, if one would, but was one
to regret one's own failure to have contributed a
stone ? Perish, and all ignobly, the thought ! . . .

HENRY JAMES.

DAISY MILLER

I

AT the little town of Vevey, in Switzerland, there is a particularly comfortable hotel ; there are indeed many hotels, since the entertainment of tourists is the business of the place, which, as many travellers will remember, is seated upon the edge of a remarkably blue lake—a lake that it behoves every tourist to visit. The shore of the lake presents an unbroken array of establishments of this order, of every category, from the " grand hotel " of the newest fashion, with a chalk-white front, a hundred balconies, and a dozen flags flying from its roof, to the small Swiss pension of an elder day, with its name inscribed in German-looking lettering upon a pink or yellow wall and an awkward summer-house in the angle of the garden. One of the hotels at Vevey, however, is famous, even classical, being distinguished from many of its upstart neighbours by an air both of luxury and of maturity. In this region, through the month of June, American travellers are extremely numerous ; it may be said indeed that Vevey assumes at that time some of the characteristics of an American watering-place. There are sights and sounds that evoke a vision, an echo, of Newport and Saratoga. There is a flitting hither and thither of " stylish " young girls, a rustling of muslin flounces, a rattle of dance-music in the morning hours, a sound of high-pitched voices at all times. You receive an impression of these things at the excellent inn of the "Trois Couronnes," and are transported in fancy to the Ocean House or to Congress Hall. But at the "Trois Couronnes," it must be added, there are other features much at variance with these suggestions : neat German waiters who look like secretaries of legation ; Russian princesses sitting in the garden ; little Polish boys walking about, held by the hand, with their governors ; a view of the snowy crest of the Dent du Midi and the picturesque towers of the Castle of Chillon.

I hardly know whether it was the analogies or the differences that were uppermost in the mind of a young American, who, two or three years ago, sat in the garden of the "Trois Couronnes," looking about him rather idly at some of the graceful objects I have mentioned. It was a beautiful summer morning, and in whatever fashion the young American looked at things they must have seemed to him charming. He had come from Geneva the day before, by the little steamer, to see his aunt, who was staying at the hotel —Geneva having been for a long time his place of residence. But his aunt had a headache—his aunt had almost always a headache—and she was now shut up in her room smelling camphor, so that he was at liberty to wander about. He was some seven-and-twenty years of age ; when his friends spoke of him they usually said that he was at Geneva "studying." When his enemies spoke of him they said—but after all he had no enemies : he was extremely amiable and generally liked. What I should say is simply that when certain persons spoke of him they conveyed that the reason of his spending so much time at Geneva was that he was extremely devoted to a lady who lived there—a foreign lady, a person older than himself. Very few Americans—truly I think none—had ever seen this lady, about whom there were some singular stories. But Winterbourne had an old attachment for the little capital of Calvinism ; he had been put to school there as a boy and had afterwards even gone, on trial—trial of the grey old " Academy " on the steep and stony hillside—to college there ; circumstances which had led to his forming a great many youthful friendships. Many of these he had kept, and they were a source of great satisfaction to him.

After knocking at his aunt's door and learning that she was indisposed he had taken a walk about the town and then he had come in to his breakfast. He had now finished that repast, but was enjoying a small cup of coffee which had been served him on a little table in the garden by one of the waiters who looked like *attachés*. At last he finished his coffee and lit a cigarette. Presently a small boy came walking along the path—an urchin of nine or ten. The child, who was diminutive for his years, had an aged expression of countenance, a pale complexion and sharp little features. He was dressed in knickerbockers and had red stockings that displayed his poor little spindle-shanks ; he also wore a brilliant red cravat. He carried in his hand a long alpenstock, the sharp point of which he thrust into everything he approached—the flower-beds, the garden-benches, the trains of the ladies' dresses. In front of Winterbourne he paused, looking at him with a pair of bright and penetrating little eyes.

" Will you give me a lump of sugar ? " he asked in a small sharp hard voice—a voice immature and yet somehow not young.

Winterbourne glanced at the light table near him, on which his coffee-service rested, and saw that several morsels of sugar remained. " Yes, you may take one," he answered ; " but I don't think too much sugar good for little boys."

This little boy stepped forward and carefully selected three of the coveted fragments, two of which

5

he buried in the pocket of his knickerbockers, depositing the other as promptly in another place. He poked his alpenstock, lance-fashion, into Winterbourne's bench and tried to crack the lump of sugar with his teeth.

" Oh blazes ; it's har-r-d ! " he exclaimed, divesting vowel and consonants, pertinently enough, of any taint of softness.

Winterbourne had immediately gathered that he might have the honour of claiming him as a countryman. " Take care you don't hurt your teeth," he said paternally.

" I haven't got any teeth to hurt. They've all come out. I've only got seven teeth. Mother counted them last night, and one came out right afterwards. She said she'd slap me if any more came out. I can't help it. It's this old Europe. It's the climate that makes them come out. In America they didn't come out. It's these hotels."

Winterbourne was much amused. " If you eat three lumps of sugar your mother will certainly slap you," he ventured.

" She's got to give me some candy then," rejoined his young interlocutor. " I can't get any candy here —any American candy. American candy's the best candy."

" And are American little boys the best little boys ? " Winterbourne asked.

" I don't know. *I'm* an American boy," said the child.

" I see you're one of the best ! " the young man laughed.

" Are you an American man ? " pursued this vivacious infant. And then on his friend's affirmative reply, " American men are the best," he declared with assurance.

His companion thanked him for the compliment,

and the child, who had now got astride of his alpenstock, stood looking about him while he attacked
another lump of sugar. Winterbourne wondered if he
himself had been like this in his infancy, for he had
been brought to Europe at about the same age.

" Here comes my sister ! " cried his young compatriot. " She's an American girl, you bet ! "

Winterbourne looked along the path and saw a
beautiful young lady advancing. " American girls are
the best girls," he thereupon cheerfully remarked to
his visitor.

" My sister ain't the best ! " the child promptly
returned. " She's always blowing at me."

" I imagine that's your fault, not hers," said
Winterbourne. The young lady meanwhile had
drawn near. She was dressed in white muslin, with a
hundred frills and flounces and knots of pale-coloured
ribbon. Bareheaded, she balanced in her hand a
large parasol with a deep border of embroidery ; and
she was strikingly, admirably pretty. " How pretty
they are ! " thought our friend, who straightened himself in his seat as if he were ready to rise.

The young lady paused in front of his bench,
near the parapet of the garden, which overlooked the
lake. The small boy had now converted his alpenstock into a vaulting-pole, by the aid of which he was
springing about in the gravel and kicking it up not a
little. " Why Randolph," she freely began, " what
are you doing ? "

" I'm going up the Alps ! " cried Randolph. " This
is the way ! " And he gave another extravagant jump,
scattering the pebbles about Winterbourne's ears.

" That's the way they come down," said Winterbourne.

" He's an American man ! " proclaimed Randolph
in his harsh little voice.

The young lady gave no heed to this circumstance,

7

but looked straight at her brother. "Well, I guess you'd better be quiet," she simply observed.

It seemed to Winterbourne that he had been in a manner presented. He got up and stepped slowly toward the charming creature, throwing away his cigarette. "This little boy and I have made acquaintance," he said with great civility. In Geneva, as he had been perfectly aware, a young man wasn't at liberty to speak to a young unmarried lady save under certain rarely-occurring conditions ; but here at Vevey what conditions could be better than these ?—a pretty American girl coming to stand in front of you in a garden with all the confidence in life. This pretty American girl, whatever that might prove, on hearing Winterbourne's observation simply glanced at him ; she then turned her head and looked over the parapet, at the lake and the opposite mountains. He wondered whether he had gone too far, but decided that he must gallantly advance rather than retreat. While he was thinking of something else to say the young lady turned again to the little boy, whom she addressed quite as if they were alone together. "I should like to know where you got that pole."

"I bought it !" Randolph shouted.

"You don't mean to say you're going to take it to Italy !"

"Yes, I'm going to take it t' Italy !" the child rang out.

She glanced over the front of her dress and smoothed out a knot or two of ribbon. Then she gave her sweet eyes to the prospect again. "Well, I guess you'd better leave it somewhere," she dropped after a moment.

"Are you going to Italy ?" Winterbourne now decided very respectfully to inquire.

She glanced at him with lovely remoteness. "Yes, sir," she then replied. And she said nothing more.

" And are you—a—thinking of the Simplon ? " he pursued with a slight drop of assurance.

" I don't know," she said. " I suppose it's some mountain. Randolph, what mountain are we thinking of ? "

" Thinking of ? "—the boy stared.

" Why going right over."

" Going to where ? " he demanded.

" Why right down to Italy "—Winterbourne felt vague emulations.

" I don't know," said Randolph. " I don't want to go t' Italy. I want to go to America."

" Oh Italy's a beautiful place ! " the young man laughed.

" Can you get candy there ? " Randolph asked of all the echoes.

" I hope not," said his sister. " I guess you've had enough candy, and mother thinks so too."

" I haven't had any for ever so long—for a hundred weeks ! " cried the boy, still jumping about.

The young lady inspected her flounces and smoothed her ribbons again ; and Winterbourne presently risked an observation on the beauty of the view. He was ceasing to be in doubt, for he had begun to perceive that she was really not in the least embarrassed. She might be cold, she might be austere, she might even be prim ; for that was apparently—he had already so generalised—what the most " distant " American girls did : they came and planted themselves straight in front of you to show how rigidly unapproachable they were. There hadn't been the slightest flush in her fresh fairness however ; so that she was clearly neither offended nor fluttered. Only she was composed—he had seen that before too—of charming little parts that didn't match and that made no *ensemble* ; and if she looked another way when he spoke to her, and seemed not particularly to hear him, this was simply her habit, her manner, the result of her having no idea whatever of " form " (with such a tell-tale appendage as Randolph where in the world would she have got it ?) in any such connexion. As he talked a little more and pointed out some of the objects of interest in the view, with which she appeared wholly unacquainted, she gradually, none the less, gave him more of the benefit of her attention ; and then he saw that act unqualified by the faintest shadow of reserve. It wasn't however what would have been called a " bold " front that she presented, for her expression was as decently limpid as the very cleanest water. Her eyes were the very prettiest conceivable, and indeed Winterbourne hadn't for a long time seen anything prettier than his fair country-woman's various features—her complexion, her nose, her ears, her teeth. He took a great interest generally in that range of effects and was addicted to noting and, as it were, recording them ; so that in regard to this young lady's face he made several observations. It wasn't at all insipid, yet at the same time wasn't pointedly—what point, on earth, could she ever make ?—expressive ; and though it offered such a collection of small finenesses and neatnesses he mentally accused it—very forgivingly—of a want of finish. He thought nothing more likely than that its wearer would have had her own experience of the action of her charms, as she would certainly have acquired a resulting confidence ; but even should she depend on this for her main amusement her bright sweet superficial little visage gave out neither mockery nor irony. Before long it became clear that, however these things might be, she was much disposed to conversation. She remarked to Winterbourne that they were going to Rome for the winter—she and her mother and Randolph. She asked him if he was a " real American " ; she wouldn't have taken him for one ; he seemed more like a German—this flower was gathered as from a large field of comparison—especially when he spoke. Winterbourne, laughing, answered that he had met Germans who spoke like Americans, but not, so far as he remembered, any American with the resemblance she noted. Then he asked her if she mightn't be more at ease should she occupy the bench he had just quitted. She answered that she liked hanging round, but she none the less resignedly, after a little, dropped to the bench. She told him she was from New York State—" if you know where that is " ; but our friend really quickened this current by catching hold of her small slippery brother and making him stand a few minutes by his side.

"Tell me your honest name, my boy." So he artfully proceeded.

In response to which the child was indeed unvarnished truth. "Randolph C. Miller. And I'll tell you hers." With which he levelled his alpenstock at his sister.

"You had better wait till you're asked ! " said this young lady quite at her leisure.

"I should like very much to know *your* name," Winterbourne made free to reply.

"Her name's Daisy Miller ! " cried the urchin. "But that ain't her real name ; that ain't her name on her cards."

"It's a pity you haven't got one of my cards ! " Miss Miller quite as naturally remarked.

"Her real name's Annie P. Miller," the boy went on.

It seemed, all amazingly, to do her good. "Ask him *his* now "—and she indicated their friend.

But to this point Randolph seemed perfectly indifferent ; he continued to supply information with regard to his own family. "My father's name is Ezra B. Miller. My father ain't in Europe—he's in a better place than Europe." Winterbourne for a moment supposed this the manner in which the child had been taught to intimate that Mr. Miller had been removed to the sphere of celestial rewards. But Randolph immediately added : " My father's in Schenectady. He's got a big business. My father's rich, you bet."

" Well ! " ejaculated Miss Miller, lowering her parasol and looking at the embroidered border. Winterbourne presently released the child, who departed, dragging his alpenstock along the path. " He don't like Europe," said the girl as with an artless instinct for historic truth. " He wants to go back."

" To Schenectady, you mean ? "

" Yes, he wants to go right home. He hasn't got any boys here. There's one boy here, but he always goes round with a teacher. They won't let him play."

" And your brother hasn't any teacher ? " Winterbourne inquired.

It tapped, at a touch, the spring of confidence. " Mother thought of getting him one — to travel round with us. There was a lady told her of a very good teacher ; an American lady—perhaps you know her—Mrs. Sanders. I think she came from Boston. She told her of this teacher, and we thought of getting him to travel round with us. But Randolph said he didn't want a teacher travelling round with us. He said he wouldn't have lessons when he was in the cars. And we *are* in the cars about half the time. There was an English lady we met in the cars—I think her name was Miss Featherstone ; perhaps you know her. She wanted to know why I didn't give Randolph lessons —give him ' instruction,' she called it. I guess he could give me more instruction than I could give him. He's very smart."

" Yes," said Winterbourne ; " he seems very smart."

" Mother's going to get a teacher for him as soon as we get t' Italy. Can you get good teachers in Italy ? "

" Very good, I should think," Winterbourne hastened to reply.

" Or else she's going to find some school. He ought to learn some more. He's only nine. He's going to college." And in this way Miss Miller continued to converse upon the affairs of her family and upon other topics. She sat there with her extremely pretty hands, ornamented with very brilliant rings, folded in her lap, and with her pretty eyes now resting upon those of Winterbourne, now wandering over the garden, the people who passed before her and the beautiful view. She addressed her new acquaintance as if she had known him a long time. He found it very pleasant. It was many years since he had heard a young girl talk so much. It might have been said of this wandering maiden who had come and sat down beside him upon a bench that she chattered. She was very quiet, she sat in a charming tranquil attitude ; but her lips and her eyes were constantly moving. She had a soft slender agreeable voice, and her tone was distinctly sociable. She gave Winterbourne a report of her movements and intentions, and those of her mother and brother, in Europe, and enumerated in particular the various hotels at which they had stopped. " That English lady in the cars," she said—" Miss Feather-stone—asked me if we didn't all live in hotels in America. I told her I had never been in so many hotels in my life as since I came to Europe. I've never seen so many—it's nothing but hotels." But Miss Miller made this remark with no querulous accent ; she appeared to be in the best humour with everything. She declared that the hotels were very good when once you got used to their ways and that Europe was perfectly entrancing. She wasn't disappointed—not a bit. Perhaps it was because she had heard so much about it before. She had ever so many intimate friends who had been there ever so many times, and that way she had got thoroughly posted. And then she had had ever so many dresses and things from Paris. Whenever she put on a Paris dress she felt as if she were in Europe.

"It was a kind of a wishing-cap," Winterbourne smiled.

"Yes," said Miss Miller at once and without examining this analogy ; " it always made me wish I was here. But I needn't have done that for dresses. I'm sure they send all the pretty ones to America ; you see the most frightful things here. The only thing I don't like," she proceeded, " is the society. There ain't any society—or if there is I don't know where it keeps itself. Do you ? I suppose there's some society somewhere, but I haven't seen anything of it. I'm very fond of society and I've always had plenty of it. I don't mean only in Schenectady, but in New York. I used to go to New York every winter. In New York I had lots of society. Last winter I had seventeen dinners given me, and three of them were by gentlemen," added Daisy Miller. " I've more friends in New York than in Schenectady—more gentlemen friends ; and more young lady friends too," she resumed in a moment. She paused again for an instant ; she was looking at Winterbourne with all her prettiness in her frank grey eyes and in her clear rather uniform smile. " I've always had," she said, " a great deal of gentlemen's society."

Poor Winterbourne was amused and perplexed—above all he was charmed. He had never yet heard a young girl express herself in just this fashion ; never at least save in cases where to say such things was to have at the same time some rather complicated consciousness about them. And yet was he to accuse Miss

Daisy Miller of an actual or a potential *arrière-pensée*, as they said at Geneva? He felt he had lived at Geneva so long as to have got morally muddled; he had lost the right sense for the young American tone. Never indeed since he had grown old enough to appreciate things had he encountered a young compatriot of so " strong " a type as this. Certainly she was very charming, but how extraordinarily communicative and how tremendously easy! Was she simply a pretty girl from New York State—were they all like that, the pretty girls who had had a good deal of gentlemen's society? Or was she also a designing, an audacious, in short an expert young person? Yes, his instinct for such a question had ceased to serve him, and his reason could but mislead. Miss Daisy Miller looked extremely innocent. Some people had told him that after all American girls *were* exceedingly innocent, and others had told him that after all they weren't. He must on the whole take Miss Daisy Miller for a flirt —a pretty American flirt. He had never as yet had relations with representatives of that class. He had known here in Europe two or three women—persons older than Miss Daisy Miller and provided, for respectability's sake, with husbands — who were great coquettes; dangerous terrible women with whom one's light commerce might indeed take a serious turn. But this charming apparition wasn't a coquette in that sense; she was very unsophisticated; she was only a pretty American flirt. Winterbourne was almost grateful for having found the formula that applied to Miss Daisy Miller. He leaned back in his seat; he remarked to himself that she had the finest little nose he had ever seen; he wondered what were the regular conditions and limitations of one's intercourse with a pretty American flirt. It presently became apparent that he was on the way to learn.

" Have you been to that old castle? " the girl soon

asked, pointing with her parasol to the far-shining walls of the Château de Chillon.

"Yes, formerly, more than once," said Winterbourne. "You too, I suppose, have seen it?"

"No, we haven't been there. I want to go there dreadfully. Of course I mean to go there. I wouldn't go away from here without having seen that old castle."

"It's a very pretty excursion," the young man returned, "and very easy to make. You can drive, you know, or you can go by the little steamer."

"You can go in the cars," said Miss Miller.

"Yes, you can go in the cars," Winterbourne assented.

"Our courier says they take you right up to the castle," she continued. "We were going last week, but mother gave out. She suffers dreadfully from dyspepsia. She said she couldn't any more go——!" But this sketch of Mrs. Miller's plea remained unfinished. "Randolph wouldn't go either; ·he says he don't think much of old castles. But I guess we'll go this week if we can get Randolph."

"Your brother isn't interested in ancient monuments?" Winterbourne indulgently asked.

He now drew her, as he guessed she would herself have said, every time. "Why no, he says he don't care much about old castles. He's only nine. He wants to stay at the hotel. Mother's afraid to leave him alone, and the courier won't stay with him; so we haven't been to many places. But it will be too bad if we don't go up there." And Miss Miller pointed again at the Château de Chillon.

"I should think it might be arranged," Winterbourne was thus emboldened to reply. "Couldn't you get some one to stay—for the afternoon—with Randolph?"

Miss Miller looked at him a moment, and then

with all serenity, " I wish *you'd* stay with him ! " she said.

He pretended to consider it. " I'd much rather go to Chillon with you."

" With me ? " she asked without a shadow of emotion.

She didn't rise blushing, as a young person at Geneva would have done ; and yet, conscious that he had gone very far, he thought it possible she had drawn back. " And with your mother," he answered very respectfully.

But it seemed that both his audacity and his respect were lost on Miss Daisy Miller. " I guess mother wouldn't go—for *you*," she smiled. " And she ain't much *bent* on going, anyway. She don't like to ride round in the afternoon." After which she familiarly proceeded : " But did you really mean what you said just now—that you'd like to go up there ? "

" Most earnestly I meant it," Winterbourne declared.

" Then we may arrange it. If mother will stay with Randolph I guess Eugenio will."

" Eugenio ? " the young man echoed.

" Eugenio's our courier. He doesn't like to stay with Randolph—he's the most fastidious man I ever saw. But he's a splendid courier. I guess he'll stay at home with Randolph if mother does, and then we can go to the castle."

Winterbourne reflected for an instant as lucidly as possible : " we " could only mean Miss Miller and himself. This prospect seemed almost too good to believe ; he felt as if he ought to kiss the young lady's hand. Possibly he would have done so,—and quite spoiled his chance ; but at this moment another person — presumably Eugenio — appeared. A tall handsome man, with superb whiskers and wearing a velvet morning-coat and a voluminous watch-guard, approached the young lady, looking sharply at her companion. " Oh Eugenio ! " she said with the friendliest accent.

Eugenio had eyed Winterbourne from head to foot ; he now bowed gravely to Miss Miller. " I have the honour to inform Mademòiselle that luncheon's on table."

Mademoiselle slowly rose. " See here, Eugenio, I'm going to that old castle anyway."

" To the Château de Chillon, Mademoiselle ? " the courier inquired. " Mademoiselle has made arrangements ? " he added in a tone that struck Winterbourne as impertinent.

Eugenio's tone apparently threw, even to Miss Miller's own apprehension, a slightly ironical light on her position. She turned to Winterbourne with the slightest blush. " You won't back out ? "

" I shall not be happy till we go ! " he protested.

" And you're staying in this hotel ? " she went on. " And you're really American ? "

The courier still stood there with an effect of offence for the young man so far as the latter saw in it a tacit reflexion on Miss Miller's behaviour and an insinuation that she " picked up " acquaintances. " I shall have the honour of presenting to you a person who'll tell you all about me," he said, smiling, and referring to his aunt.

" Oh well, we'll go some day," she beautifully answered ; with which she gave him a smile and turned away. She put up her parasol and walked back to the inn beside Eugenio. Winterbourne stood watching her, and as she moved away, drawing her muslin furbelows over the walk, he spoke to himself of her natural elegance.

DAISY MILLER

II

He had, however, engaged to do more than proved feasible in promising to present his aunt, Mrs. Costello, to Miss Daisy Miller. As soon as that lady had got better of her headache he waited on her in her apartment and, after a show of the proper solicitude about her health, asked if she had noticed in the hotel an American family—a mamma, a daughter and an obstreperous little boy.

" An obstreperous little boy and a preposterous big courier ? " said Mrs. Costello. " Oh yes, I've noticed them. Seen them, heard them and kept out of their way." Mrs. Costello was a widow of fortune, a person of much distinction and who frequently intimated that if she hadn't been so dreadfully liable to sick-headaches she would probably have left a deeper impress on her time. She had a long pale face, a high nose and a great deal of very striking white hair, which she wore in large puffs and over the top of her head. She had two sons married in New York and another who was now in Europe. This young man was amusing himself at Homburg and, though guided by his taste, was rarely observed to visit any particular city at the moment selected by his mother for her appearance there. Her nephew, who had come to Vevey expressly to see her, was therefore more attentive than, as she said, her very own. He had imbibed at Geneva the idea that one must be irreproachable in all such forms. Mrs. Costello hadn't seen him for many years and was now greatly pleased with him, manifesting her approbation by initiating him into many of the secrets of that social sway which, as he could see she would like him to think, she exerted from her stronghold in Forty-Second Street. She admitted that she was very exclusive, but if he had been better acquainted with New York he would see that one had to be. And her picture of the minutely hierarchical constitution of the society of that city, which she presented to him in many different lights, was, to Winterbourne's imagination, almost oppressively striking.

He at once recognised from her tone that Miss Daisy Miller's place in the social scale was low. " I'm afraid you don't approve of them," he pursued in reference to his new friends.

" They're horribly common "—it was perfectly simple. " They're the sort of Americans that one does one's duty by just ignoring."

" Ah you just ignore them ? "—the young man took it in.

" I can't *not*, my dear Frederick. I wouldn't if I hadn't to, but I have to."

" The little girl's very pretty," he went on in a moment.

" Of course she's very pretty. But she's of the last crudity."

" I see what you mean of course," he allowed after another pause.

" She has that charming look they all have," his aunt resumed. " I can't think where they pick it up ; and she dresses in perfection—no, you don't know how well she dresses. I can't think where they get their taste."

" But, my dear aunt, she's not, after all, a Comanche savage."

" She is a young lady," said Mrs. Costello, " who has an intimacy with her mamma's courier ! "

" An ' intimacy ' with him ? " Ah there it was !

" There's no other name for such a relation. But the skinny little mother's just as bad ! They treat the courier as a familiar friend—as a gentleman and a scholar. I shouldn't wonder if he dines with them. Very likely they've never seen a man with such good manners, such fine clothes, so *like* a gentleman—or a scholar. He probably corresponds to the young lady's idea of a count. He sits with them in the garden of an evening. I think he smokes in their faces."

Winterbourne listened with interest to these disclosures ; they helped him to make up his mind about Miss Daisy. Evidently she was rather wild. " Well," he said, " I'm not a courier and I didn't smoke in her face, and yet she was very charming to me."

" You had better have mentioned at first," Mrs. Costello returned with dignity, " that you had made her valuable acquaintance."

" We simply met in the garden and talked a bit."

" By appointment—no ? Ah that's still to come ! Pray what did you say ? "

" I said I should take the liberty of introducing her to my admirable aunt."

" Your admirable aunt's a thousand times obliged to you."

" It was to guarantee my respectability."

" And pray who's to guarantee hers ? "

" Ah you're cruel ! " said the young man. " She's a very innocent girl."

" You don't say that as if you believed it," Mrs. Costello returned.

" She's completely uneducated," Winterbourne acknowledged, " but she's wonderfully pretty, and in short she's very nice. To prove I believe it I'm going to take her to the Château de Chillon."

Mrs. Costello made a wondrous face. " You two

are going off there together ? I should say it proved just the contrary. How long had you known her, may I ask, when this interesting project was formed ? You haven't been twenty-four hours in the house."

" I had known her half an hour ! " Winterbourne smiled.

" Then she's just what I supposed."

" And what do you suppose ? "

" Why that she's a horror."

Our youth was silent for some moments. " You really think then," he presently began, and with a desire for trustworthy information, " you really think that—— " But he paused again while his aunt waited.

" Think what, sir ? "

" That she's the sort of young lady who expects a man sooner or later to—well, we'll call it carry her off ? "

" I haven't the least idea what such young ladies expect a man to do. But I really consider you had better not meddle with little American girls who are uneducated, as you mildly put it. You've lived too long out of the country. You'll be sure to make some great mistake. You're too innocent."

" My dear aunt, not so much as that comes fo ! " he protested with a laugh and a curl of his moustache.

" You're too guilty then ! "

He continued all thoughtfully to finger the ornament in question. " You won't let the poor girl know you then ? " he asked at last.

" Is it literally true that she's going to the Château de Chillon with you ? "

" I've no doubt she fully intends it."

" Then, my dear Frederick," said Mrs. Costello, " I must decline the honour of her acquaintance. I'm an old woman, but I'm not too old—thank heaven —to be honestly shocked ! "

" But don't they all do these things—the little American girls at home ? " Winterbourne inquired.

Mrs. Costello stared a moment. " I should like to see my granddaughters do them ! " she then grimly returned.

This seemed to throw some light on the matter, for Winterbourne remembered to have heard his pretty cousins in New York, the daughters of this lady's two daughters, called " tremendous flirts." If therefore Miss Daisy Miller exceeded the liberal license allowed to these young women it was probable she did go even by the American allowance rather far. Winterbourne was impatient to see her again, and it vexed, it even a little humiliated him, that he shouldn't by instinct appreciate her justly.

Though so impatient to see her again he hardly knew what ground he should give for his aunt's refusal to become acquainted with her ; but he discovered promptly enough that with Miss Daisy Miller there was no great need of walking on tiptoe. He found her that evening in the garden, wandering about in the warm starlight after the manner of an indolent sylph and swinging to and fro the largest fan he had ever beheld. It was ten o'clock. He had dined with his aunt, had been sitting with her since dinner, and had just taken leave of her till the morrow. His young friend frankly rejoiced to renew their intercourse ; she pronounced it the stupidest evening she had ever passed.

" Have you been all alone ? " he asked with no intention of an epigram and no effect of her perceiving one.

" I've been walking round with mother. But mother gets tired walking round," Miss Miller explained.

" Has she gone to bed ? "

" No, she doesn't like to go to bed. She doesn't

sleep scarcely any—not three hours. She says she doesn't know how she lives. She's dreadfully nervous. I guess she sleeps more than she thinks. She's gone somewhere after Randolph ; she wants to try to get him to go to bed. He doesn't like to go to bed."

The soft impartiality of her *constatations,* as Winterbourne would have termed them, was a thing by itself —exquisite little fatalist as they seemed to make her. "Let us hope she'll persuade him," he encouragingly said.

"Well; she'll talk to him all she can—but he doesn't like her to talk to him " : with which Miss Daisy opened and closed her fan. "She's going to try to get Eugenio to talk to him. But Randolph ain't afraid of Eugenio. Eugenio's a splendid courier, but he can't make much impression on Randolph ! I don't believe he'll go to bed before eleven." Her detachment from any invidious judgement of this was, to her companion's sense, inimitable ; and it appeared that Randolph's vigil was in fact triumphantly prolonged, for Winterbourne attended her in her stroll for some time without meeting her mother. "I've been looking round for that lady you want to introduce me to," she resumed—" I guess she's your aunt." Then on his admitting the fact and expressing some curiosity as to how she had learned it, she said she had heard all about Mrs. Costello from the chambermaid. She was very quiet and very *comme il faut* ; she wore white puffs ; she spoke to no one and she never dined at the common table. Every two days she had a headache. "I think that's a lovely description, headache and all ! " said Miss Daisy, chattering along in her thin gay voice. "I want to know her ever so much. I know just what *your* aunt would be ; I know I'd like her. She'd be very exclusive. I like a lady to be exclusive ; I'm dying to be exclusive myself. Well, I guess we *are* exclusive, mother and I. We don't speak to any one—or they don't speak to us. I suppose it's about the same thing. Anyway, I shall be ever so glad to meet your aunt."

Winterbourne was embarrassed — he could but trump up some evasion. "She'd be most happy, but I'm afraid those tiresome headaches are always to be reckoned with."

The girl looked at him through the fine dusk. "Well, I suppose she doesn't have a headache every day."

He had to make the best of it. "She tells me she wonderfully does." He didn't know what else to say. Miss Miller stopped and stood looking at him. Her prettiness was still visible in the darkness; she kept flapping to and fro her enormous fan. "She doesn't want to know me!" she then lightly broke out. "Why don't you say so? You needn't be afraid. *I'm* not afraid!" And she quite crowed for the fun of it.

Winterbourne distinguished however a wee false note in this : he was touched, shocked, mortified by it. "My dear young lady, she knows no one. She goes through life immured. It's her wretched health."

The young girl walked on a few steps in the glee of the thing. "You needn't be afraid," she repeated. "Why should she want to know me?" Then she paused again ; she was close to the parapet of the garden, and in front of her was the starlit lake. There was a vague sheen on its surface, and in the distance were dimly-seen mountain forms. Daisy Miller looked out at these great lights and shades and again proclaimed a gay indifference—"Gracious! she *is* exclusive!" Winterbourne wondered if she were seriously wounded and for a moment almost wished her sense of injury might be such as to make it becoming in him to reassure and comfort her. He had a pleasant sense that she would be all accessible to a

respectful tenderness at that moment. He felt quite
ready to sacrifice his aunt — conversationally ; to
acknowledge she was a proud rude woman and to make
the point that they needn't mind her. But before he
had time to commit himself to this questionable
mixture of gallantry and impiety, the young lady,
resuming her walk, gave an exclamation in quite
another tone. " Well, here's mother ! I guess she
hasn't got Randolph to go to bed." The figure of a
lady appeared, at a distance, very indistinct in the
darkness ; it advanced with a slow and wavering step
and then suddenly seemed to pause.

" Are you sure it's your mother ? Can you make
her out in this thick dusk ? " Winterbourne asked.

" Well," the girl laughed, " I guess I know my
own mother ! And when she has got on my shawl too.
She's always wearing my things."

The lady in question, ceasing now to approach,
hovered vaguely about the spot at which she had
checked her steps.

" I'm afraid your mother doesn't see you," said
Winterbourne. " Or perhaps," he added—thinking,
with Miss Miller, the joke permissible — " perhaps
she feels guilty about your shawl."

" Oh it's a fearful old thing ! " his companion
placidly answered. " I told her she could wear it if
she didn't mind looking like a fright. She won't come
here because she sees you."

" Ah then," said Winterbourne, " I had better leave
you."

" Oh no—come on ! " the girl insisted.

" I'm afraid your mother doesn't approve of my
walking with you."

She gave him, he thought, the oddest glance. " It
isn't for me ; it's for you—that is it's for *her*. Well,
I don't know who it's for ! But mother doesn't like
any of my gentlemen friends. She's right down timid.

26

She always makes a fuss if I introduce a gentleman.
But I *do* introduce them—almost always. If I didn't
introduce my gentlemen friends to mother," Miss
Miller added, in her small flat monotone, " I shouldn't
think I was natural."

" Well, to introduce me," Winterbourne remarked,
" you must know my name." And he proceeded to
pronounce it.

" Oh my—I can't say all that ! " cried his companion, much amused. But by this time they had
come up to Mrs. Miller, who, as they drew near,
walked to the parapet of the garden and leaned on it,
looking intently at the lake and presenting her back to
them. " Mother ! " said the girl in a tone of decision
—upon which the elder lady turned round. " Mr.
Frederick Forsyth Winterbourne," said the latter's
young friend, repeating his lesson of a moment
before and introducing him very frankly and prettily.
" Common " she might be, as Mrs. Costello had pronounced her ; yet what provision was made by that
epithet for her queer little native grace ?

Her mother was a small spare light person, with a
wandering eye, a scarce perceptible nose, and, as to
make up for it, an unmistakable forehead, decorated
—but too far back, as Winterbourne mentally described it—with thin much-frizzled hair. Like her
daughter Mrs. Miller was dressed with extreme
elegance ; she had enormous diamonds in her ears.
So far as the young man could observe, she gave him
no greeting—she certainly wasn't looking at him.
Daisy was near her, pulling her shawl straight.
" What are you doing, poking round here ? " this
young lady inquired—yet by no means with the
harshness of accent her choice of words might have
implied.

" Well, I don't know "—and the new-comer
turned to the lake again.

" I shouldn't think you'd want that shawl ! "
Daisy familiarly proceeded.

" Well—I do ! " her mother answered with a sound
that partook for Winterbourne of an odd strain
between mirth and woe.

" Did you get Randolph to go to bed ? " Daisy
asked.

" No, I couldn't induce him "—and Mrs. Miller
seemed to confess to the same mild fatalism as her
daughter. " He wants to talk to the waiter. He *likes*
to talk to that waiter."

" I was just telling Mr. Winterbourne," the girl
went on ; and to the young man's ear her tone might
have indicated that she had been uttering his name all
her life.

" Oh yes ! " he concurred—" I've the pleasure of
knowing your son."

Randolph's mamma was silent ; she kept her
attention on the lake. But at last a sigh broke from
her. " Well, I don't see how he lives ! "

" Anyhow, it isn't so bad as it was at Dover,"
Daisy at least opined.

" And what occurred at Dover ? " Winterbourne
desired to know.

" He wouldn't go to bed at all. I guess he sat up
all night—in the public parlour. He wasn't in bed at
twelve o'clock : it seemed as if he couldn't budge."

" It was half-past twelve when *I* gave up," Mrs.
Miller recorded with passionless accuracy.

It was of great interest to Winterbourne. " Does he
sleep much during the day ? "

" I guess he doesn't sleep *very* much," Daisy
rejoined.

" I wish he just *would* ! " said her mother. " It
seems as if he *must* make it up somehow."

" Well, I guess it's we that make it up. I think
he's real tiresome," Daisy pursued.

After which, for some moments, there was silence. "Well, Daisy Miller," the elder lady then unexpectedly broke out, "I shouldn't think you'd want to talk against your own brother!"

"Well, he *is* tiresome, mother," said the girl, but with no sharpness of insistence.

"Well, he's only nine," Mrs. Miller lucidly urged.

"Well, he wouldn't go up to that castle, anyway," her daughter replied as for accommodation. "I'm going up there with Mr. Winterbourne."

To this announcement, very placidly made, Daisy's parent offered no response. Winterbourne took for granted on this that she opposed such a course; but he said to himself at the same time that she was a simple easily-managed person and that a few deferential protestations would modify her attitude. "Yes," he therefore interposed, "your daughter has kindly allowed me the honour of being her guide."

Mrs. Miller's wandering eyes attached themselves with an appealing air to her other companion, who, however, strolled a few steps further, gently humming to herself. "I presume you'll go in the cars," she then quite colourlessly remarked.

"Yes, or in the boat," said Winterbourne.

"Well, of course I don't know," Mrs. Miller returned. "I've never been up to that castle."

"It is a pity you shouldn't go," he observed, beginning to feel reassured as to her opposition. And yet he was quite prepared to find that as a matter of course she meant to accompany her daughter.

It was on this view accordingly that light was projected for him. "We've been thinking ever so much about going, but it seems as if we couldn't. Of course Daisy—she wants to go round everywhere. But there's a lady here—I don't know her name—she says she shouldn't think we'd want to go to see castles *here*; she should think we'd want to wait till we got t'

Italy. It seems as if there would be so many there,"
continued Mrs. Miller with an air of increasing confidence. " Of course we only want to see the principal
ones. We visited several in England," she presently
added.

" Ah yes, in England there are beautiful castles,"
said Winterbourne. " But Chillon here is very well
worth seeing."

" Well, if Daisy feels up to it——" said Mrs. Miller
in a tone that seemed to break under the burden of
such conceptions. " It seems as if there's nothing she
won't undertake."

" Oh I'm pretty sure she'll enjoy it ! " Winterbourne declared. And he desired more and more to
make it a certainty that he was to have the privilege of
a *tête-à-tête* with the young lady who was still strolling
along in front of them and softly vocalising. " You're
not disposed, madam," he inquired, " to make the so
interesting excursion yourself ? "

So addressed Daisy's mother looked at him an
instant with a certain scared obliquity and then walked
forward in silence. Then, " I guess she had better
go alone," she said simply.

It gave him occasion to note that this was a very
different type of maternity from that of the vigilant
matrons who massed themselves in the forefront of
social intercourse in the dark old city at the other end
of the lake. But his meditations were interrupted
by hearing his name very distinctly pronounced by
Mrs. Miller's unprotected daughter. " Mr. Winterbourne ! " she piped from a considerable distance.

" Mademoiselle ! " said the young man.

" Don't you want to take me out in a boat ? "

" At present ? " he asked.

" Why of course ! " she gaily returned.

" Well, Annie Miller ! " exclaimed her mother.

" I beg you, madam, to let her go," he hereupon

eagerly pleaded ; so instantly had he been struck with the romantic side of this chance to guide through the summer starlight a skiff freighted with a fresh and beautiful young girl.

" I shouldn't think she'd want to," said her mother. " I should think she'd rather go indoors."

" I'm sure Mr. Winterbourne wants to *take* me," Daisy declared. " He's so awfully devoted ! "

" I'll row you over to Chillon under the stars."

" I don't believe it ! " Daisy laughed.

" Well ! " the elder lady again gasped, as in rebuke of this freedom.

" You haven't spoken to me for half an hour," her daughter went on.

" I've been having some very pleasant conversation with your mother," Winterbourne replied.

" Oh pshaw ! I want you to take me out in a boat ! " Daisy went on as if nothing else had been said. They had all stopped and she had turned round and was looking at her friend. Her face wore a charming smile, her pretty eyes gleamed in the darkness, she swung her great fan about. No, he felt, it was impossible to be prettier than that.

" There are half a dozen boats moored at that landing-place," and he pointed to a range of steps that descended from the garden to the lake. " If you'll do me the honour to accept my arm we'll go and select one of them."

She stood there smiling ; she threw back her head ; she laughed as for the drollery of this. " I like a gentleman to be formal ! "

" I assure you it's a formal offer."

" I was bound I'd make you say something," Daisy agreeably mocked.

" You see it's not very difficult," said Winterbourne. " But I'm afraid you're chaffing me."

" I think not, sir," Mrs. Miller shyly pleaded.

"Do then let me give you a row," he persisted to Daisy.

"It's quite lovely, the way you say that!" she cried in reward.

"It will be still more lovely to do it."

"Yes, it would be lovely!" But she made no movement to accompany him; she only remained an elegant image of free light irony.

"I guess you'd better find out what time it is," her mother impartially contributed.

"It's eleven o'clock, Madam," said a voice with a foreign accent out of the neighbouring darkness; and Winterbourne, turning, recognised the florid personage he had already seen in attendance. He had apparently just approached.

"Oh Eugenio," said Daisy, "I'm going out with Mr. Winterbourne in a boat!"

Eugenio bowed. "At this hour of the night, Mademoiselle?"

"I'm going with Mr. Winterbourne," she repeated with her shining smile. "I'm going this very minute."

"Do tell her she can't, Eugenio," Mrs. Miller said to the courier.

"I think you had better not go out in a boat, Mademoiselle," the man declared.

Winterbourne wished to goodness this pretty girl were not on such familiar terms with her courier; but he said nothing, and she meanwhile added to his ground. "I suppose you don't think it's proper! My!" she wailed; "Eugenio doesn't think anything's proper."

"I'm nevertheless quite at your service," Winterbourne hastened to remark.

"Does Mademoiselle propose to go alone?" Eugenio asked of Mrs. Miller.

"Oh no, with this gentleman!" cried Daisy's mamma for reassurance.

" I *meant* alone with the gentleman." The courier looked for a moment at Winterbourne—the latter seemed to make out in his face a vague presumptuous intelligence as at the expense of their companions—and then solemnly and with a bow, " As Mademoiselle pleases ! " he said.

But Daisy broke off at this. " Oh I hoped you'd make a fuss ! I don't care to go now."

" Ah but I myself shall make a fuss if you don't go," Winterbourne declared with spirit.

" That's all I want—a little fuss ! " With which she began to laugh again.

" Mr Randolph has retired for the night ! " the courier hereupon importantly announced.

" Oh Daisy, now we can go then ! " cried Mrs. Miller.

Her daughter turned away from their friend, all lighted with her odd perversity. " Good-night—I hope you're disappointed or disgusted or something ! "

He looked at her gravely, taking her by the hand she offered. " I'm puzzled, if you want to know ! " he answered.

" Well, I hope it won't keep you awake ! " she said very smartly ; and, under the escort of the privileged Eugenio, the two ladies passed toward the house.

Winterbourne's eyes followed them ; he was indeed quite mystified. He lingered beside the lake a quarter of an hour, baffled by the question of the girl's sudden familiarities and caprices. But the only very definite conclusion he came to was that he should enjoy deucedly " going off " with her somewhere.

Two days later he went off with her to the Castle of Chillon. He waited for her in the large hall of the hotel, where the couriers, the servants, the foreign tourists were lounging about and staring. It wasn't the place he would have chosen for a tryst, but she had placidly appointed it. She came tripping downstairs, buttoning her long gloves, squeezing her folded parasol against her pretty figure, dressed exactly in the way that consorted best, to his fancy, with their adventure. He was a man of imagination and, as our ancestors used to say, of sensibility ; as he took in her charming air and caught from the great staircase her impatient confiding step the note of some small sweet strain of romance, not intense but clear and sweet, seemed to sound for their start. He could have believed he was *really* going " off " with her. He led her out through all the idle people assembled—they all looked at her straight and hard : she had begun to chatter as soon as she joined him. His preference had been that they should be conveyed to Chillon in a carriage, but she expressed a lively wish to go in the little steamer— there would be such a lovely breeze upon the water and they should see such lots of people. The sail wasn't long, but Winterbourne's companion found time for many characteristic remarks and other demonstrations, not a few of which were, from the extremity of their candour, slightly disconcerting. To the young man himself their small excursion showed so far delightfully irregular and incongruously intimate that, even allowing for her habitual sense of freedom, he had some expectation of seeing her appear to find in it the same savour. But it must be confessed that he was in this particular rather disappointed. Miss Miller was highly animated, she was in the brightest spirits ; but she was clearly not at all in a nervous flutter—as she should have been to match *his* tension ; she avoided neither his eyes nor those of any one else ; she neither coloured from an awkward consciousness when she looked at him nor when she saw that people were looking at herself. People continued to look at her a great deal, and Winterbourne could at least take pleasure in his pretty companion's distinguished air. He had been privately afraid she would talk loud, laugh overmuch, and even perhaps desire to move extravagantly about the boat. But he quite forgot his fears ; he sat smiling with his eyes on her face while, without stirring from her place, she delivered herself of a great number of original reflexions. It was the most charming innocent prattle he had ever heard, for, by his own experience hitherto, when young persons were so ingenuous they were less articulate and when they were so confident were more sophisticated. If he had assented to the idea that she was " common," at any rate, *was* she proving so, after all, or was he simply getting used to her commonness ? Her discourse was for the most part of what immediately and superficially surrounded them, but there were moments when it threw out a longer look or took a sudden straight plunge.

"What on *earth* are you so solemn about ? " she suddenly demanded, fixing her agreeable eyes on her friend's.

"*Am* I solemn ? " he asked. " I had an idea I was grinning from ear to ear."

"You look as if you were taking me to a prayer-meeting or a funeral. If that's a grin your ears are very near together."

"Should you like me to dance a hornpipe on the deck ? "

"Pray do, and I'll carry round your hat. It will pay the expenses of our journey."

"I never was better pleased in my life," Winterbourne returned.

She looked at him a moment, then let it renew her amusement. " I like to make you say those things. You're a queer mixture ! "

In the castle, after they had landed, nothing could exceed the light independence of her humour. She tripped about the vaulted chambers, rustled her skirts in the corkscrew staircases, flirted back with a pretty little cry and a shudder from the edge of the oubliettes and turned a singularly well-shaped ear to everything Winterbourne told her about the place. But he saw she cared little for medieval history and that the grim ghosts of Chillon loomed but faintly before her. They had the good fortune to have been able to wander without other society than that of their guide ; and Winterbourne arranged with this companion that they shouldn't be hurried—that they should linger and pause wherever they chose. He interpreted the bargain generously—Winterbourne on his side had been generous—and ended by leaving them quite to themselves. Miss Miller's observations were marked by no logical consistency ; for anything she wanted to say she was sure to find a pretext. She found a great many, in the tortuous passages and rugged embrasures of the place, for asking her young man sudden questions about himself, his family, his previous history, his tastes, his habits, his designs, and for supplying information on corresponding points in her own situation. Of her own tastes, habits and designs the charming creature was prepared to give the most definite and indeed the most favourable account.

" Well, I hope you know enough ! " she exclaimed after Winterbourne had sketched for her something of the story of the unhappy Bonnivard. " I never saw a man that knew so much ! " The history of Bonnivard had evidently, as they say, gone into one ear and out of the other. But this easy erudition struck her none the less as wonderful, and she was soon quite sure she wished Winterbourne would travel with them and " go round " with them : they too in that case might learn something about something. " Don't you want to come and teach Randolph ? " she asked ; " I guess he'd improve with a gentleman teacher." Winterbourne was certain that nothing could possibly please him so much, but that he had unfortunately other

occupations. " Other occupations ? I don't believe
a speck of it ! " she protested. " What do you mean
now ? You're not in business." The young man
allowed that he was not in business, but he had en-
gagements which even within a day or two would
necessitate his return to Geneva. " Oh bother ! " she
panted, " I don't believe it ! " and she began to talk
about something else. But a few moments later, when
he was pointing out to her the interesting design of an
antique fireplace, she broke out irrelevantly : " You
don't mean to say you're going back to Geneva ? "

" It is a melancholy fact that I shall have to report
myself there to-morrow."

She met it with a vivacity that could only flatter him.
" Well, Mr. Winterbourne, I think you're horrid ! "

" Oh don't say such dreadful things ! " he quite
sincerely pleaded—" just at the last."

" The last ? " the girl cried ; " I call it the very
first ! I've half a mind to leave you here and go
straight back to the hotel alone." And for the next
ten minutes she did nothing but call him horrid.
Poor Winterbourne was fairly bewildered ; no young
lady had as yet done him the honour to be so agitated
by the mention of his personal plans. His companion,
after this, ceased to pay any attention to the curiosities
of Chillon or the beauties of the lake ; she opened fire
on the special charmer in Geneva whom she appeared
to have instantly taken it for granted that he was
hurrying back to see. How did Miss Daisy Miller
know of that agent of his fate in Geneva ? Winterbourne, who denied the existence of such a person, was
quite unable to discover ; and he was divided between
amazement at the rapidity of her induction and
amusement at the directness of her criticism. She
struck him afresh, in all this, as an extraordinary
mixture of innocence and crudity. " Does she never
allow you more than three days at a time ? " Miss

Miller wished ironically to know. " Doesn't she give you a vacation in summer ? there's no one so hard-worked but they can get leave to go off somewhere at this season. I suppose if you stay another day she'll come right after you in the boat. Do wait over till Friday and I'll go down to the landing to see her arrive ! " He began at last even to feel he had been wrong to be disappointed in the temper in which his lady had embarked. If he had missed the personal accent, the personal accent was now making its appearance. It sounded very distinctly, toward the end, in her telling him she'd stop " teasing " him if he'd promise her solemnly to come down to Rome that winter.

" That's not a difficult promise to make," he hastened to acknowledge. " My aunt has taken an apartment in Rome from January and has already asked me to come and see her."

" I don't want you to come for your aunt," said Daisy ; " I want you just to come for me." And this was the only allusion he was ever to hear her make again to his invidious kinswoman. He promised her that at any rate he would certainly come, and after this she forbore from teasing. Winterbourne took a carriage and they drove back to Vevey in the dusk ; the girl at his side, her animation a little spent, was now quite distractingly passive.

In the evening he mentioned to Mrs. Costello that he had spent the afternoon at Chillon with Miss Daisy Miller.

" The Americans—of the courier ? " asked this lady.

" Ah happily the courier stayed at home."

" She went with you all alone ? "

" All alone."

Mrs. Costello sniffed a little at her smelling-bottle. " And that," she exclaimed, " is the little abomination you wanted me to know ! "

III

WINTERBOURNE, who had returned to Geneva the day after his excursion to Chillon, went to Rome toward the end of January. His aunt had been established there a considerable time and he had received from her a couple of characteristic letters. " Those people you were so devoted to last summer at Vevey have turned up here, courier and all," she wrote. " They seem to have made several acquaintances, but the courier continues to be the most *intime*. The young lady, however, is also very intimate with various third-rate Italians, with whom she rackets about in a way that makes much talk. Bring me that pretty novel of Cherbuliez's—' Paule Méré '—and don't come later than the 23rd."

Our friend would in the natural course of events, on arriving in Rome, have presently ascertained Mrs. Miller's address at the American banker's and gone to pay his compliments to Miss Daisy. " After what happened at Vevey I certainly think I may call upon them," he said to Mrs. Costello.

" If after what happens—at Vevey and everywhere —you desire to keep up the acquaintance, you're very welcome. Of course you're not squeamish—a man may know every one. Men are welcome to the privilege ! "

" Pray what is it then that ' happens '—here for instance ? " Winterbourne asked.

39

" Well, the girl tears about alone with her un-mistakably lòw foreigners. As to what happens further you must apply elsewhere for information. She has picked up half a dozen of the regular Roman fortune-hunters of the inferior sort and she takes them about to such houses as she may put *her* nose into. When she comes to a party—such a party as she can come to—she brings with her a gentleman with a good deal of manner and a wonderful moustache."

" And where's the mother ? "

" I haven't the least idea. They're very dreadful people."

Winterbourne thought them over in these new lights. " They're very ignorant—very innocent only, and utterly uncivilised. Depend on it they're not ' bad.' "

"They're hopelessly vulgar," said Mrs. Costello. " Whether or no being hopelessly vulgar is being ' bad ' is a question for the metaphysicians. They're bad enough to blush for, at any rate ; and for this short life that's quite enough."

The news that his little friend the child of nature of the Swiss lakeside was now surrounded by half a dozen wonderful moustaches checked Winterbourne's impulse to go straightway to see her. He had perhaps not definitely flattered himself that he had made an ineffaceable impression upon her heart, but he was annoyed at hearing of a state of affairs so little in harmony with an image that had lately flitted in and out of his own meditations ; the image of a very pretty girl looking out of an old Roman window and asking herself urgently when Mr. Winterbourne would arrive. If, however, he determined to wait a little before reminding this young lady of his claim to her faithful remembrance, he called with more promptitude on two or three other friends. One of these friends was an American lady who had spent several winters at

Geneva, where she had placed her children at school.
She was a very accomplished woman and she lived in
Via Gregoriana. Winterbourne found her in a little
crimson drawing-room on a third floor ; the room was
filled with southern sunshine. He hadn't been there
ten minutes when the servant, appearing in the doorway, announced complacently " Madame Mila ! "
This announcement was presently followed by the
entrance of little Randolph Miller, who stopped in the
middle of the room and stood staring at Winterbourne. An instant later his pretty sister crossed the
threshold ; and then, after a considerable interval, the
parent of the pair slowly advanced.

" I guess I know you ! " Randolph broke ground
without delay.

" I'm sure you know a great many things "—and
his old friend clutched him all interestedly by the
arm. " How's your education coming on ? "

Daisy was engaged in some pretty babble with her
hostess, but when she heard Winterbourne's voice she
quickly turned her head with a " Well, I declare ! "
which he met smiling. " I told you I should come,
you know."

" Well, I didn't believe it," she answered.

" I'm much obliged to you for that," laughed the
young man.

" You might have come to see me then," Daisy
went on as if they had parted the week before.

" I arrived only yesterday."

" I don't believe any such thing ! " the girl declared
afresh.

Winterbourne turned with a protesting smile to her
mother, but this lady evaded his glance and, seating
herself, fixed her eyes on her son. " We've got a
bigger place than this," Randolph hereupon broke out.
" It's all gold on the walls."

Mrs. Miller, more of a fatalist apparently than ever,

turned uneasily in her chair. " I told you if I was to bring you you'd say something ! " she stated as for the benefit of such of the company as might hear it.

" I told *you* ! " Randolph retorted. " I tell *you*, sir ! " he added jocosely, giving Winterbourne a thump on the knee. " It *is* bigger too ! "

As Daisy's conversation with her hostess still occupied her Winterbourne judged it becoming to address a few words to her mother—such as " I hope you've been well since we parted at Vevey."

Mrs. Miller now certainly looked at him—at his chin. " Not very well, sir," she answered.

" She's got the dyspepsia," said Randolph. " I've got it too. Father's got it bad. But I've got it worst ! "

This proclamation, instead of embarrassing Mrs. Miller, seemed to soothe her by reconstituting the environment to which she was most accustomed. " I suffer from the liver," she amiably whined to Winterbourne. " I think it's this climate ; it's less bracing than Schenectady, especially in the winter season. I don't know whether you know we reside at Schenectady. I was saying to Daisy that I certainly hadn't found any one like Dr. Davis and I didn't believe I *would*. Oh up in Schenectady, he stands first ; they think everything of Dr. Davis. He has so much to do, and yet there was nothing he wouldn't do for *me*. He said he never saw anything like my dyspepsia, but he was bound to get at it. I'm sure there was nothing he wouldn't try, and I didn't care what he did to me if he only brought me relief. He was just going to try something new, and I just longed for it, when we came right off. Mr. Miller felt as if he wanted Daisy to see Europe for herself. But I couldn't help writing the other day that I supposed it was all right for Daisy, but that I didn't know as I *could* get on much longer without Dr. Davis. At Schenectady he stands at the very top ; and there's a great deal of sickness there too. It affects my sleep."

Winterbourne had a good deal of pathological gossip with Dr. Davis's patient, during which Daisy chattered unremittingly to her own companion. The young man asked Mrs. Miller how she was pleased with Rome. " Well, I must say I'm disappointed," she confessed. " We had heard so much about it—I suppose we had heard too much. But we couldn't help that. We had been led to expect something different."

Winterbourne, however, abounded in reassurance. " Ah wait a little, and you'll grow very fond of it."

" I hate it worse and worse every day ! " cried Randolph.

" You're like the infant Hannibal," his friend laughed.

" No I ain't—like any infant ! " Randolph declared at a venture.

" Well, that's so—and you never *were* ! " his mother concurred. " But we've seen places," she resumed, " that I'd put a long way ahead of Rome." And in reply to Winterbourne's interrogation, " There's Zürich—up there in the mountains," she instanced ; " I think Zürich's real lovely, and we hadn't heard half so much about it."

" The best place we've seen's the *City of Richmond* ! " said Randolph.

" He means the ship," Mrs. Miller explained. " We crossed in that ship. Randolph had a good time on the *City of Richmond*."

" It's the best place *I've* struck," the child repeated. " Only it was turned the wrong way."

" Well, we've got to turn the right way sometime," said Mrs. Miller with strained but weak optimism. Winterbourne expressed the hope that her daughter at least appreciated the so various interest of Rome, and she declared with some spirit that Daisy was quite carried away. " It's on account of the society—the society's splendid. She goes round everywhere ; she has made a great number of acquaintances. Of course she goes round more than I do. I must say they've all been very sweet—they've taken her right in. And then she knows a great many gentlemen. Oh she thinks there's nothing like Rome. Of course it's a great deal pleasanter for a young lady if she knows plenty of gentlemen."

By this time Daisy had turned her attention again to Winterbourne, but in quite the same free form. " I've been telling Mrs. Walker how mean you were ! "

" And what's the evidence you've offered ? " he asked, a trifle disconcerted, for all his superior gallantry, by her inadequate measure of the zeal of an admirer who on his way down to Rome had stopped neither at Bologna nor at Florence, simply because of a certain sweet appeal to his fond fancy, not to say to his finest curiosity. He remembered how a cynical compatriot had once told him that American women —the pretty ones, and this gave a largeness to the axiom—were at once the most exacting in the world and the least endowed with a sense of indebtedness.

" Why, you were awfully mean up at Vevey," Daisy said. " You wouldn't do most anything. You wouldn't stay there when I asked you."

" Dearest young lady," cried Winterbourne, with generous passion, " have I come all the way to Rome only to be riddled by your silver shafts ? "

" Just hear him say that ! "—and she gave an affectionate twist to a bow on her hostess's dress. " Did you ever hear anything so quaint ? "

" So ' quaint,' my dear ? " echoed Mrs. Walker more critically—quite in the tone of a partisan of Winterbourne.

" Well, I don't know "—and the girl continued to

finger her ribbons. "Mrs. Walker, I want to tell you something."

"Say, mother-r," broke in Randolph with his rough ends to his words, "I tell you you've got to go. Eugenio'll raise something!"

"I'm not afraid of Eugenio," said Daisy with a toss of her head. "Look here, Mrs. Walker," she went on, "you know I'm coming to your party."

"I'm delighted to hear it."

"I've got a lovely dress."

"I'm very sure of that."

"But I want to ask a favour—permission to bring a friend."

"I shall be happy to see any of your friends," said Mrs. Walker, who turned with a smile to Mrs. Miller.

"Oh they're not my friends," cried that lady, squirming in shy repudiation. "It seems as if they didn't take to *me*—I never spoke to one of them!"

"It's an intimate friend of mine, Mr. Giovanelli," Daisy pursued without a tremor in her young clearness or a shadow on her shining bloom.

Mrs. Walker had a pause and gave a rapid glance at Winterbourne. "I shall be glad to see Mr. Giovanelli," she then returned.

"He's just the finest kind of Italian," Daisy pursued with the prettiest serenity. "He's a great friend of mine and the handsomest man in the world —except Mr. Winterbourne! He knows plenty of Italians, but he wants to know some Americans. It seems as if he was crazy about Americans. He's tremendously bright. He's perfectly lovely!"

It was settled that this paragon should be brought to Mrs. Walker's party, and then Mrs. Miller prepared to take her leave. "I guess we'll go right back to the hotel," she remarked with a confessed failure of the larger imagination.

" You may go back to the hotel, mother," Daisy replied, " but I'm just going to walk round."

" She's going to go it with Mr. Giovanelli," Randolph unscrupulously commented.

" I'm going to go it on the Pincio," Daisy peaceably smiled, while the way that she " condoned " these things almost melted Winterbourne's heart.

" Alone, my dear—at this hour ? " Mrs. Walker asked. The afternoon was drawing to a close—it was the hour for the throng of carriages and of contemplative pedestrians. " I don't consider it's safe, Daisy," her hostess firmly asserted.

" Neither do I then," Mrs. Miller thus borrowed confidence to add. " You'll catch the fever as sure as you live. Remember what Dr. Davis told you ! "

" Give her some of that medicine before she starts in," Randolph suggested.

The company had risen to its feet ; Daisy, still showing her pretty teeth, bent over and kissed her hostess. " Mrs. Walker, you're too perfect," she simply said. " I'm not going alone ; I'm going to meet a friend."

" Your- friend won't keep you from catching the fever even if it *is* his own second nature," Mrs. Miller observed.

" Is it Mr. Giovanelli that's the dangerous attraction ? " Mrs. Walker asked without mercy.

Winterbourne was watching the challenged girl ; at this question his attention quickened. She stood there smiling and smoothing her bonnet-ribbons ; she glanced at Winterbourne. Then, while she glanced and smiled, she brought out all affirmatively and without a shade of hesitation : " Mr. Giovanelli—the beautiful Giovanelli."

" My dear young friend "—and, taking her hand, Mrs. Walker turned to pleading—" don't prowl off to the Pincio at this hour to meet a beautiful Italian."

"Well, he speaks first-rate English," Mrs. Miller incoherently mentioned.

"Gracious me," Daisy piped up, "I don't want to do anything that's going to affect my health—or my character either! There's an easy way to settle it." Her eyes continued to play over Winterbourne. "The Pincio's only a hundred yards off, and if Mr. Winterbourne were as polite as he pretends he'd offer to walk right in with me!"

Winterbourne's politeness hastened to proclaim itself, and the girl gave him gracious leave to accompany her. They passed downstairs before her mother, and at the door he saw Mrs. Miller's carriage drawn up, with the ornamental courier whose acquaintance he had made at Vevey seated within. "Good-bye, Eugenio," cried Daisy; "I'm going to take a walk!" The distance from Via Gregoriana to the beautiful garden at the other end of the Pincian Hill is in fact rapidly traversed. As the day was splendid, however, and the concourse of vehicles, walkers and loungers numerous, the young Americans found their progress much delayed. This fact was highly agreeable to Winterbourne, in spite of his consciousness of his singular situation. The slow-moving, idly-gazing Roman crowd bestowed much attention on the extremely pretty young woman of English race who passed through it, with some difficulty, on his arm; and he wondered what on earth had been in Daisy's mind when she proposed to exhibit herself unattended to its appreciation. His own mission, to her sense, was apparently to consign her to the hands of Mr. Giovanelli; but, at once annoyed and gratified, he resolved that he would do no such thing.

"Why haven't you been to see me?" she meanwhile asked. "You can't get out of that."

"I've had the honour of telling you that I've only just stepped out of the train."

" You must have stayed in the train a good while after it stopped ! " she derisively cried. " I suppose you were asleep. You've had time to go to see Mrs. Walker."

" I knew Mrs. Walker—— " Winterbourne began to explain.

" I know where you knew her. You knew her at Geneva. She told me so. Well, you knew me at Vevey. That's just as good. So you ought to have come." She asked him no other question than this ; she began to prattle about her own affairs. " We've got splendid rooms at the hotel ; Eugenio says they're the best rooms in Rome. We're going to stay all winter—if we don't die of the fever ; and I guess we'll stay then ! It's a great deal nicer than I thought ; I thought it would be fearfully quiet—in fact I was sure it would be deadly pokey. I foresaw we should be going round all the time with one of those dreadful old men who explain about the pictures and things. But we only had about a week of that, and now I'm enjoying myself. I know ever so many people, and they're all so charming. The society's extremely select. There are all kinds—English and Germans and Italians. I think I like the English best. I like their style of conversation. But there are some lovely Americans. I never saw anything so hospitable. There's something or other every day. There's not much dancing—but I must say I never thought dancing was everything. I was always fond of conversation. I guess I'll have plenty at Mrs. Walker's— her rooms are so small." When they had passed the gate of the Pincian Gardens Miss Miller began to wonder where Mr. Giovanelli might be. " We had better go straight to that place in front, where you look at the view."

Winterbourne at this took a stand. " I certainly shan't help you to find him."

48

" Then I shall find him without you," Daisy said with spirit.

" You certainly won't leave me ! " he protested.

She burst into her familiar little laugh. " Are you afraid you'll get lost—or run over ? But there's Giovanelli leaning against that tree. He's staring at the women in the carriages : did you ever see anything so cool ? "

Winterbourne descried hereupon at some distance a little figure that stood with folded arms and nursing its cane. It had a handsome face, a hat artfully poised, a glass in one eye and a nosegay in its buttonhole. Daisy's friend looked at it a moment and then said : " Do you mean to speak to that thing ? "

" Do I mean to speak to him ? Why, you don't suppose I mean to communicate by signs ! "

" Pray understand then," the young man returned, " that I intend to remain with you."

Daisy stopped and looked at him without a sign of troubled consciousness, with nothing in her face but her charming eyes, her charming teeth and her happy dimples. " Well, she's a cool one ! " he thought.

" I don't like the way you say that," she declared. " It's too imperious."

" I beg your pardon if I say it wrong. The main point's to give you an idea of my meaning."

The girl looked at him more gravely, but with eyes that were prettier than ever. " I've never allowed a gentleman to dictate to me or to interfere with anything I do."

" I think that's just where your mistake has come in," he retorted. " You should sometimes listen to a gentleman—the right one."

At this she began to laugh again. " I do nothing but listen to gentlemen ! Tell me if Mr. Giovanelli is the right one."

The gentleman with the nosegay in his bosom had

now made out our two friends and was approaching Miss Miller with obsequious rapidity. He bowed to Winterbourne as well as to the latter's compatriot ; he seemed to shine, in his coxcombical way, with the desire to please and the fact of his own intelligent joy, though Winterbourne thought him not a bad-looking fellow. But he nevertheless said to Daisy : " No, he's not the right one."

She had clearly a natural turn for free introductions ; she mentioned with the easiest grace the name of each of her companions to the other. She strolled forward with one of them on either hand ; Mr. Giovanelli, who spoke English very cleverly—Winterbourne afterwards learned that he had practised the idiom upon a great many American heiresses— addressed her a great deal of very polite nonsense. He had the best possible manners, and the young American, who said nothing, reflected on that depth of Italian subtlety, so strangely opposed to Anglo-Saxon simplicity, which enables people to show a smoother surface in proportion as they're more acutely displeased. Giovanelli of course had counted upon something more intimate—he had not bargained for a party of three ; but he kept his temper in a manner that suggested far-stretching intentions. Winterbourne flattered himself he had taken his measure. " He's anything but a gentleman," said the young American ; " he isn't even a very plausible imitation of one. He's a music-master or a penny-a-liner or a third-rate artist. He's awfully on his good behaviour, but damn his fine eyes ! " Mr. Giovanelli had indeed great advantages ; but it was deeply disgusting to Daisy's other friend that something in her shouldn't have instinctively discriminated against such a type. Giovanelli chattered and jested and made himself agreeable according to his honest Roman lights. It was true that if he was an imitation the imitation was studied. " Nevertheless," Winterbourne said to himself, " a nice girl ought to know ! " And then he came back to the dreadful question of whether this *was* in fact a nice girl. Would a nice girl—even allowing for her being a little American flirt—make a rendezvous with a presumably low-lived foreigner ? The rendezvous in this case indeed had been in broad daylight and in the most crowded corner of Rome ; but wasn't it possible to regard the choice of these very circumstances as a proof more of vulgarity than of anything else ? Singular though it may seem, Winterbourne was vexed that the girl, in joining her *amoroso*, shouldn't appear more impatient of his own company, and he was vexed precisely because of his inclination. It was impossible to regard her as a wholly unspotted flower—she lacked a certain indispensable fineness ; and it would therefore much simplify the situation to be able to treat her as the subject of one of the visitations known to romancers as " lawless passions." That she should seem to wish to get rid of him would have helped him to think more lightly of her, just as to be able to think more lightly of her would have made her less perplexing. Daisy at any rate continued on this occasion to present herself as an inscrutable combination of audacity and innocence.

She had been walking some quarter of an hour, attended by her two cavaliers and responding in a tone of very childish gaiety, as it after all struck one of them, to the pretty speeches of the other, when a carriage that had detached itself from the revolving train drew up beside the path. At the same moment Winterbourne noticed that his friend Mrs. Walker— the lady whose house he had lately left—was seated in the vehicle and was beckoning to him. Leaving Miss Miller's side, he hastened to obey her summons—and all to find her flushed, excited, scandalised. " It's really too dreadful "—she earnestly appealed to him.

" That crazy girl mustn't do this sort of thing. She mustn't walk here with you two men. Fifty people have remarked her."

Winterbourne—suddenly and rather oddly rubbed the wrong way by this—raised his grave eyebrows. " I think it's a pity to make too much fuss about it."

" It's a pity to let the girl ruin herself ! "

" She's very innocent," he reasoned in his own troubled interest.

" She's very reckless," cried Mrs. Walker, " and goodness knows how far—left to itself—it may go. Did you ever," she proceeded to inquire, " see anything so blatantly imbecile as the mother ?   After you had all left me just now I couldn't sit still for thinking of it. It seemed too pitiful not even to attempt to save them. I ordered the carriage and put on my bonnet and came here as quickly as possible. Thank heaven I've found you ! "

" What do you propose to do with us ? " Winterbourne uncomfortably smiled.

" To ask her to get in, to drive her about here for half an hour—so that the world may see she's not running absolutely wild—and then take her safely home."

" I don't think it's a very happy thought," he said after reflexion, " but you're at liberty to try."

Mrs. Walker accordingly tried. The young man went in pursuit of their young lady who had simply nodded and smiled, from her distance, at her recent patroness in the carriage and then had gone her way with her own companion. On learning, in the event, that Mrs. Walker had followed her, she retraced her steps, however, with a perfect good grace and with Mr. Giovanelli at her side. She professed herself " enchanted " to have a chance to present this gentleman to her good friend, and immediately achieved the introduction ; declaring with it, and as if it were of as little importance, that she had never in her life seen anything so lovely as that lady's carriage-rug.

" I'm glad you admire it," said her poor pursuer, smiling sweetly. " Will you get in and let me put it over you ! "

" Oh no, thank you ! "—Daisy knew her mind. " I'll admire it ever so much more as I see you driving round with it."

" Do get in and drive round *with* me," Mrs. Walker pleaded.

" That would be charming, but it's so fascinating just as I am ! "—with which the girl radiantly took in the gentlemen on either side of her.

" It may be fascinating, dear child, but it's not the custom here," urged the lady of the victoria, leaning forward in this vehicle with her hands devoutly clasped.

" Well, it ought to be then ! " Daisy imperturbably laughed. " If I didn't walk I'd expire."

" You should walk with your mother, dear," cried Mrs. Walker with a loss of patience.

" With my mother dear ? " the girl amusedly echoed. Winterbourne saw she scented interference. " My mother never walked ten steps in her life. And then, you know," she blandly added, " I'm more than five years old."

" You're old enough to be more reasonable. You're old enough, dear Miss Miller, to be talked about."

Daisy wondered to extravagance. " Talked about ? What do you mean ? "

" Come into my carriage and I'll tell you."

Daisy turned shining eyes again from one of the gentlemen beside her to the other. Mr. Giovanelli was bowing to and fro, rubbing down his gloves and laughing irresponsibly ; Winterbourne thought the

scene the most unpleasant possible. " I don't think I
want to know what you mean," the girl presently said.
" I don't think I should like it."

Winterbourne only wished Mrs. Walker would tuck
up her carriage-rug and drive away ; but this lady, as
she afterwards told him, didn't feel she could " rest
there." " Should you prefer being thought a very
reckless girl ? " she accordingly asked.

" Gracious me ! " exclaimed Daisy. She looked
again at Mr. Giovanelli, then she turned to her other
companion. There was a small pink flush in her
cheek ; she was tremendously pretty. " Does Mr.
Winterbourne think," she put to him with a wonderful
bright intensity of appeal, " that—to save my reputation—I ought to get into the carriage ? "

It really embarrassed him ; for an instant he cast
about—so strange was it to hear her speak that
way of her " reputation." But he himself in fact had
to speak in accordance with gallantry. The finest
gallantry here was surely just to tell her the truth ;
and the truth, for our young man, as the few indications I have been able to give have made him known
to the reader, was that his charming friend should
listen to the voice of civilised society. He took in
again her exquisite prettiness and then said the
more distinctly : " I think you should get into the
carriage."

Daisy gave the rein to her amusement. " I never
heard anything so stiff ! If this is improper, Mrs.
Walker," she pursued, " then I'm *all* improper, and
you had better give me right up. Good-bye ; I hope
you'll have a lovely ride ! "—and with Mr. Giovanelli, who made a triumphantly obsequious salute,
she turned away.

Mrs. Walker sat looking after her, and there were
tears in Mrs. Walker's eyes. " Get in here, sir," she
said to Winterbourne, indicating the place beside her.

The young man answered that he felt bound to accompany Miss Miller; whereupon the lady of the victoria declared that if he refused her this favour she would never speak to him again. She was evidently wound up. He accordingly hastened to overtake Daisy and her more faithful ally, and, offering her his hand, told her that Mrs. Walker had made a stringent claim on his presence. He had expected her to answer with something rather free, something still more significant of the perversity from which the voice of society, through the lips of their distressed friend, had so earnestly endeavoured to dissuade her. But she only let her hand slip, as she scarce looked at him, through his slightly awkward grasp; while Mr. Giovanelli, to make it worse, bade him farewell with too emphatic a flourish of the hat.

Winterbourne was not in the best possible humour as he took his seat beside the author of his sacrifice. "That was not clever of you," he said candidly, as the vehicle mingled again with the throng of carriages.

"In such a case," his companion answered, "I don't want to be clever—I only want to be *true*!"

"Well, your truth has only offended the strange little creature—it has only put her off."

"It has happened very well"—Mrs. Walker accepted her work. "If she's so perfectly determined to compromise herself the sooner one knows it the better—one can act accordingly."

"I suspect she meant no great harm, you know," Winterbourne maturely opined.

"So I thought a month ago. But she has been going too far."

"What has she been doing?"

"Everything that's not done here. Flirting with any man she can pick up; sitting in corners with mysterious Italians; dancing all the evening with the same partners; receiving visits at eleven o'clock at night. Her mother melts away when the visitors come."

" But her brother," laughed Winterbourne, " sits up till two in the morning."

" He must be edified by what he sees. I'm told that at their hotel every one's talking about her and that a smile goes round among the servants when a gentleman comes and asks for Miss Miller."

" Ah we needn't mind the servants ! " Winterbourne compassionately signified. " The poor girl's only fault," he presently added, " is her complete lack of education."

" She's naturally indelicate," Mrs. Walker, on her side, reasoned. " Take that example this morning. How long had you known her at Vevey ? "

" A couple of days."

" Imagine then the taste of her making it a personal matter that you should have left the place ! "

He agreed that taste wasn't the strong point of the Millers—after which he was silent for some moments ; but only at last to add : " I suspect, Mrs. Walker, that you and I have lived too long at Geneva ! " And he further noted that he should be glad to learn with what particular design she had made him enter her carriage.

" I wanted to enjoin on you the importance of your ceasing your relations with Miss Miller ; that of your not appearing to flirt with her ; that of your giving her no further opportunity to expose herself ; that of your in short letting her alone."

" I'm afraid I can't do anything quite so enlightened as *that*," he returned. " I like her awfully, you know."

" All the more reason you shouldn't help her to make a scandal."

" Well, there shall be nothing scandalous in my attentions to her," he was willing to promise.

" There certainly will be in the way she takes them. But I've said what I had on my conscience," Mrs. Walker pursued. " If you wish to rejoin the young lady I'll put you down. Here, by the way, you have a chance."

The carriage was engaged in that part of the Pincian drive which overhangs the wall of Rome and over-looks the beautiful Villa Borghese. It is bordered by a large parapet, near which are several seats. One of these, at a distance, was occupied by a gentleman and a lady, toward whom Mrs. Walker gave a toss of her head. At the same moment these persons rose and walked to the parapet. Winterbourne had asked the coachman to stop ; he now descended from the car-riage. His companion looked at him a moment in silence and then, while he raised his hat, drove ma-jestically away. He stood where he had alighted ; he had turned his eyes toward Daisy and her cavalier. They evidently saw no one ; they were too deeply occupied with each other. When they reached the low garden-wall they remained a little looking off at the great flat-topped pine-clusters of Villa Borghese ; then the girl's attendant admirer seated himself familiarly on the broad ledge of the wall. The western sun in the opposite sky sent out a brilliant shaft through a couple of cloud-bars ; whereupon the gallant Giovanelli took her parasol out of her hands and opened it. She came a little nearer and he held the parasol over her ; then, still holding it, he let it so rest on her shoulder that both of their heads were hidden from Winterbourne. This young man stayed but a moment longer ; then he began to walk. But he walked—not toward the couple united beneath the parasol, rather toward the residence of his aunt Mrs. Costello.

IV

HE flattered himself on the following day that there
was no smiling among the servants when he at least
asked for Mrs. Miller at her hotel. This lady and her
daughter, however, were not at home; and on the next
day after, repeating his visit, Winterbourne again was
met by a denial. Mrs. Walker's party took place on
the evening of the third day, and in spite of the final
reserves that had marked his last interview with that
social critic our young man was among the guests.
Mrs. Walker was one of those pilgrims from the
younger world who, while in contact with the elder,
make a point, in their own phrase, of studying European society; and she had on this occasion collected
several specimens of diversely-born humanity to
serve, as might be, for text-books. When Winterbourne arrived the little person he desired most to find
wasn't there; but in a few moments he saw Mrs.
Miller come in alone, very shyly and ruefully. This
lady's hair, above the dead waste of her temples, was
more frizzled than ever. As she approached their
hostess Winterbourne also drew near.

" You see I've come all alone," said Daisy's unsupported parent. "I'm so frightened I don't know what
to do; it's the first time I've ever been to a party alone
—especially in this country. I wanted to bring Randolph or Eugenio or some one, but Daisy just pushed
me off by myself. I ain't used to going round alone."

"And doesn't your daughter intend to favour us with her society?" Mrs. Walker impressively inquired.

"Well, Daisy's all dressed," Mrs. Miller testified with that accent of the dispassionate, if not of the philosophic, historian with which she always recorded the current incidents of her daughter's career. "She got dressed on purpose before dinner. But she has a friend of hers there; that gentleman—the handsomest of the Italians—that she wanted to bring. They've got going at the piano—it seems as if they couldn't leave off. Mr. Giovanelli does sing splendidly. But I guess they'll come before very long," Mrs. Miller hopefully concluded.

"I'm sorry she should come—in that particular way," Mrs. Walker permitted herself to observe.

"Well, I told her there was no use in her getting dressed before dinner if she was going to wait three hours," returned Daisy's mamma. "I didn't see the use of her putting on such a dress as that to sit round with Mr. Giovanelli."

"This is most horrible!" said Mrs. Walker, turning away and addressing herself to Winterbourne. "*Elle s'affiche, la malheureuse*. It's her revenge for my having ventured to remonstrate with her. When she comes I shan't speak to her."

Daisy came after eleven o'clock, but she wasn't, on such an occasion, a young lady to wait to be spoken to. She rustled forward in radiant loveliness, smiling and chattering, carrying a large bouquet and attended by Mr. Giovanelli. Every one stopped talking and turned and looked at her while she floated up to Mrs. Walker. "I'm afraid you thought I never was coming, so I sent mother off to tell you. I wanted to make Mr. Giovanelli practise some things before he came; you know he sings beautifully, and I want you to ask him to sing. This is Mr. Giovanelli; you know I in-

59

troduced him to you ; he's got the most lovely voice and he knows the most charming set of songs. I made him go over them this evening on purpose ; we had the greatest time at the hotel." Of all this Daisy delivered herself with the sweetest brightest loudest confidence, looking now at her hostess and now at all the room, while she gave a series of little pats, round her very white shoulders, to the edges of her dress. " Is there any one I know ? " she as undiscourageably asked.

" I think every one knows you ! " said Mrs. Walker as with a grand intention ; and she gave a very cursory greeting to Mr. Giovanelli. This gentleman bore himself gallantly ; he smiled and bowed and showed his white teeth, he curled his moustaches and rolled his eyes and performed all the proper functions of a handsome Italian at an evening party. He sang, very prettily, half a dozen songs, though Mrs. Walker afterwards declared that she had been quite unable to find out who asked him. It was apparently not Daisy who had set him in motion—this young lady being seated a distance from the piano and though she had publicly, as it were, professed herself his musical patroness or guarantor, giving herself to gay and audible discourse while he warbled.

" It's a pity these rooms are so small ; we can't dance," she remarked to Winterbourne as if she had seen him five minutes before.

" I'm not sorry we can't dance," he candidly returned. " I'm incapable of a step."

" Of course you're incapable of a step," the girl assented. " I should think your legs *would* be stiff cooped in there so much of the time in that victoria."

" Well, they were very restless there three days ago," he amicably laughed ; " all they really wanted was to dance attendance on you."

" Oh my other friend—my friend in need—stuck to me ; he seems more at one with his limbs than you are—I'll say that for him. But did you ever hear anything so cool," Daisy demanded, " as Mrs. Walker's wanting me to get into her carriage and drop poor Mr. Giovanelli, and under the pretext that it was proper ? People have different ideas ! It would have been most unkind ; he had been talking about that walk for ten days."

" He shouldn't have talked about it at all," Winterbourne decided to make answer on this : " he would never have proposed to a young lady of this country to walk about the streets of Rome with him."

" About the streets ? " she cried with her pretty stare. " Where then would he have proposed to her to walk ? The Pincio ain't the streets either, I guess ; and I besides, thank goodness, am not a young lady of this country. The young ladies of this country have a dreadfully pokey time of it, by what I can discover ; I don't see why I should change my habits for *such* stupids."

" I'm afraid your habits are those of a ruthless flirt," said Winterbourne with studied severity.

" Of course they are ! "—and she hoped, evidently, by the manner of it, to take his breath away. " I'm a fearful frightful flirt ! Did you ever hear of a nice girl that wasn't ? But I suppose you'll tell me now I'm not a nice girl."

He remained grave indeed under the shock of her cynical profession. " You're a very nice girl, but I wish you'd flirt with me, and me only."

" Ah thank you, thank you very much : you're the last man I should think of flirting with. As I've had the pleasure of informing you, you're too stiff."

" You say that too often," he resentfully remarked.

Daisy gave a delighted laugh. " If I could have the sweet hope of making you angry I'd say it again."

" Don't do that—when I'm angry I'm stiffer than ever. But if you won't flirt with me do cease at least to flirt with your friend at the piano. They don't," he declared as in full sympathy with " them," " understand that sort of thing here."

" I thought they understood nothing else ! " Daisy cried with startling world-knowledge.

" Not in young unmarried women."

" It seems to me much more proper in young unmarried than in old married ones," she retorted.

" Well," said Winterbourne, " when you deal with natives you must go by the custom of the country. American flirting is a purely American silliness ; it has—in its ineptitude of innocence—no place in *this* system. So when you show yourself in public with Mr. Giovanelli and without your mother——"

" Gracious, poor mother ! "—and she made it beautifully unspeakable.

Winterbourne had a touched sense for this, but it didn't alter his attitude. " Though *you* may be flirting, Mr. Giovanelli isn't—he means something else."

" He isn't preaching at any rate," she returned. " And if you want very much to know, we're neither of us flirting—not a little speck. We're too good friends for that. We're real intimate friends."

He was to continue to find her thus at moments inimitable. " Ah," he then judged, " if you're in love with each other it's another affair altogether ! "

She had allowed him up to this point to speak so frankly that he had no thought of shocking her by the force of his logic ; yet she now none the less immediately rose, blushing visibly and leaving him mentally to exclaim that the name of little American flirts was incoherence. " Mr. Giovanelli at least," she answered, sparing but a single small queer glance for it, a queerer small glance, he felt, than he had ever yet had from her — " Mr. Giovanelli never says to me such very disagreeable things."

It had an effect on him—he stood staring. The subject of their contention had finished singing ; he left the piano, and his recognition of what—a little awkwardly—didn't take place in celebration of this might nevertheless have been an acclaimed operatic tenor's series of repeated ducks before the curtain. So he bowed himself over to Daisy. " Won't you come to the other room and have some tea ? " he asked— offering Mrs. Walker's slightly thin refreshment as he might have done all the kingdoms of the earth.

Daisy at last turned on Winterbourne a more natural and calculable light. He was but the more muddled by it, however, since so inconsequent a smile made nothing clear—it seemed at the most to prove in her a sweetness and softness that reverted instinctively to the pardon of offences. " It has never occurred to Mr. Winterbourne to offer me any tea," she said with her finest little intention of torment and triumph.

" I've offered you excellent advice," the young man permitted himself to growl.

" I prefer weak tea ! " cried Daisy, and she went off with the brilliant Giovanelli. She sat with him in the adjoining room, in the embrasure of the window, for the rest of the evening. There was an interesting performance at the piano, but neither of these con- versers gave heed to it. When Daisy came to take leave of Mrs. Walker this lady conscientiously re- paired the weakness of which she had been guilty at the moment of the girl's arrival—she turned her back straight on Miss Miller and left her to depart with what grace she might. Winterbourne happened to be near the door ; he saw it all. Daisy turned very pale and looked at her mother, but Mrs. Miller was humbly unconscious of any rupture of any law or of any deviation from any custom. She appeared indeed to have felt an incongruous impulse to draw attention

to her own striking conformity. " Good-night, Mrs.
Walker," she said ; " we've had a beautiful evening.
You see if I let Daisy come to parties without me I
don't want her to go away without me." Daisy
turned away, looking with a small white prettiness,
a blighted grace, at the circle near the door : Winterbourne saw that for the first moment she was too
much shocked and puzzled even for indignation. He
on his side was greatly touched.

" That was very cruel," he promptly remarked to
Mrs. Walker.

But this lady's face was also as a stone. " She
never enters my drawing-room again."

Since Winterbourne then, hereupon, was not to
meet her in Mrs. Walker's drawing-room he went as
often as possible to Mrs. Miller's hotel. The ladies
were rarely at home, but when he found them the
devoted Giovanelli was always present. Very often
the glossy little Roman, serene in success, but not
unduly presumptuous, occupied with Daisy alone
the florid salon enjoyed by Eugenio's care, Mrs.
Miller being apparently ever of the opinion that discretion is the better part of solicitude. Winterbourne
noted, at first with surprise, that Daisy on these occasions was neither embarrassed nor annoyed by his
own entrance ; but he presently began to feel that she
had no more surprises for him and that he really
liked, after all, not making out what she was " up to."
She showed no displeasure for the interruption of her
tête-à-tête with Giovanelli ; she could chatter as freshly
and freely with two gentlemen as with one, and this
easy flow had ever the same anomaly for her earlier
friend that it was so free without availing itself of
its freedom. Winterbourne reflected that if she was
seriously interested in the Italian it was odd she
shouldn't take more trouble to preserve the sanctity
of their interviews, and he liked her the better for

64

her innocent-looking indifference and her inexhaustible gaiety. He could hardly have said why, but she struck him as a young person not formed for a troublesome jealousy. Smile at such a betrayal though the reader may, it was a fact with regard to the women who had hitherto interested him that, given certain contingencies, Winterbourne could see himself afraid —literally afraid—of these ladies. It pleased him to believe that even were twenty other things different and Daisy should love him and he should know it and like it, he would still never be afraid of Daisy. It must be added that this conviction was not altogether flattering to her : it represented that she was nothing every way if not light.

But she was evidently very much interested in Giovanelli. She looked at him whenever he spoke ; she was perpetually telling him to do this and to do that ; she was constantly chaffing and abusing him. She appeared completely to have forgotten that her other friend had said anything to displease her at Mrs. Walker's entertainment. One Sunday afternoon, having gone to Saint Peter's with his aunt, Winterbourne became aware that the young woman held in horror by that lady was strolling about the great church under escort of her coxcomb of the Corso. It amused him, after a debate, to point out the exemplary pair—even at the cost, as it proved, of Mrs. Costello's saying when she had taken them in through her eye-glass : " That's what makes you so pensive in these days, eh ? "

" I hadn't the least idea I was pensive," he pleaded.

" You're very much preoccupied ; you're always thinking of something."

" And what is it," he asked, " that you accuse me of thinking of ? "

" Of that young lady's, Miss Baker's, Miss Chand-

ler's — what's her name ? — Miss Miller's intrigue
with that little barber's block."

" Do you call it an intrigue," he asked—" an affair
that goes on with such peculiar publicity ? "

" That's their folly," said Mrs. Costello, " it's not
their merit."

" No," he insisted with a hint perhaps of the preoccupation to which his aunt had alluded—" I don't
believe there's anything to be called an intrigue."

" Well "—and Mrs. Costello dropped her glass—
" I've heard a dozen people speak of it : they say she's
quite carried away by him."

" They're certainly as thick as thieves," our embarrassed young man allowed.

Mrs. Costello came back to them, however, after a
little ; and Winterbourne recognised in this a further
illustration — than that supplied by his own condition—of the spell projected by the case. " He's
certainly very handsome. One easily sees how it is.
She thinks him the most elegant man in the world,
the finest gentleman possible. She has never seen
anything like him—he's better even than the courier.
It was the courier probably who introduced him,
and if he succeeds in marrying the young lady the
courier will come in for a magnificent commission."

" I don't believe she thinks of marrying him,"
Winterbourne reasoned, " and I don't believe he
hopes to marry her."

" You may be very sure she thinks of nothing at all.
She romps on from day to day, from hour to hour, as
they did in the Golden Age. I can imagine nothing
more vulgar," said Mrs. Costello, whose figure of
speech scarcely went on all fours. " And at the same
time," she added, " depend upon it she may tell you
any moment that she is ' engaged.' "

" I think that's more than Giovanelli really expects," said Winterbourne.

" And who is Giovanelli ? "

" The shiny—but, to do him justice, not greasy—little Roman. I've asked questions about him and learned something. He's apparently a perfectly respectable little man. I believe he's in a small way a *cavaliere avvocato*. But he doesn't move in what are called the first circles. I think it really not absolutely impossible the courier introduced him. He's evidently immensely charmed with Miss Miller. If she thinks him the finest gentleman in the world, he, on his side, has never found himself in personal contact with such splendour, such opulence, such personal daintiness, as this young lady's. And then she must seem to him wonderfully pretty and interesting. Yes, he can't really hope to pull it off. That must appear to him too impossible a piece of luck. He has nothing but his handsome face to offer, and there's a substantial, a possibly explosive Mr. Miller in that mysterious land of dollars and six-shooters. Giovanelli's but too conscious that he hasn't a title to offer. If he were only a count or a *marchese* ! What on earth can he make of the way they've taken him up ? "

" He accounts for it by his handsome face and thinks Miss Miller a young lady *qui se passe ses fantaisies !* "

" It's very true," Winterbourne pursued, " that Daisy and her mamma haven't yet risen to that stage of—what shall I call it ?—of culture, at which the idea of catching a count or a *marchese* begins. I believe them intellectually incapable of that conception."

" Ah but the *cavaliere avvocato* doesn't believe them ! " cried Mrs. Costello.

Of the observation excited by Daisy's " intrigue " Winterbourne gathered that day at Saint Peter's sufficient evidence. A dozen of the American colonists in Rome came to talk with his relative, who sat on a small portable stool at the base of one of the great pilasters. The vesper-service was going forward in splendid chants and organ-tones in the adjacent choir, and meanwhile, between Mrs. Costello and her friends, much was said about poor little Miss Miller's going really "too far." Winterbourne was not pleased with what he heard ; but when, coming out upon the great steps of the church, he saw Daisy, who had emerged before him, get into an open cab with her accomplice and roll away through the cynical streets of Rome, the measure of her course struck him as simply there to take. He felt very sorry for her—not exactly that he believed she had completely lost her wits, but because it was painful to see so much that was pretty and undefended and natural sink so low in human estimation. He made an attempt after this to give a hint to Mrs. Miller. He met one day in the Corso a friend—a tourist like himself—who had just come out of the Doria Palace, where he had been walking through the beautiful gallery. His friend " went on " for some moments about the great portrait of Innocent X., by Velasquez, suspended in one of the cabinets of the palace, and then said : " And in the same cabinet, by the way, I enjoyed sight of an image of a different kind ; that little American who's so much more a work of nature than of art and whom you pointed out to me last week." In answer to Winterbourne's inquiries his friend narrated that the little American—prettier now than ever—was seated with a companion in the secluded nook in which the papal presence is enshrined.

" All alone ? " the young man heard himself disingenuously ask.

" Alone with a little Italian who sports in his button-hole a stack of flowers. The girl's a charming beauty, but I thought I understood from you the other day that she's a young lady *du meilleur monde*."

" So she is ! " said Winterbourne ; and having

assured himself that his informant had seen the
interesting pair but ten minutes before, he jumped
into a cab and went to call on Mrs. Miller. She
was at home, but she apologised for receiving him
in Daisy's absence.

" She's gone out somewhere with Mr. Giovanelli.
She's always going round with Mr. Giovanelli."

" I've noticed they're intimate indeed," Winterbourne concurred.

" Oh it seems as if they couldn't live without each
other ! " said Mrs. Miller. " Well, he's a real gentleman anyhow. I guess I have the joke on Daisy—
that she *must* be engaged ! "

" And how does your daughter *take* the joke ? "

" Oh she just says she ain't. But she might as *well*
be ! " this philosophic parent resumed. " She goes on
as if she was. But I've made Mr. Giovanelli promise
to tell me if Daisy don't. I'd want to write to Mr.
Miller about it—wouldn't you ? "

Winterbourne replied that he certainly should ;
and the state of mind of Daisy's mamma struck
him as so unprecedented in the annals of parental
vigilance that he recoiled before the attempt to
educate at a single interview either her conscience or
her wit.

After this Daisy was never at home and he ceased to
meet her at the houses of their common acquaintance,
because, as he perceived, these shrewd people had
quite made up their minds as to the length she must
have gone. They ceased to invite her, intimating that
they wished to make, and make strongly, for the
benefit of observant Europeans, the point that though
Miss Daisy Miller was a pretty American girl all right,
her behaviour wasn't pretty at all — was in fact
regarded by her compatriots as quite monstrous.
Winterbourne wondered how she felt about all the
cold shoulders that were turned upon her, and

sometimes found himself suspecting with impatience
that she simply didn't feel and didn't know. He
set her down as hopelessly childish and shallow, as
such mere giddiness and ignorance incarnate as was
powerless either to heed or to suffer. Then at other
moments he couldn't doubt that she carried about in
her elegant and irresponsible little organism a defiant,
passionate, perfectly observant consciousness of the
impression she produced. He asked himself whether
the defiance would come from the consciousness of
innocence or from her being essentially a young person
of the reckless class. Then it had to be admitted, he
felt, that holding fast to a belief in her " innocence "
was more and more but a matter of gallantry too fine-
spun for use. As I have already had occasion to relate,
he was reduced without pleasure to this chopping of
logic and vexed at his poor fallibility, his want of in-
stinctive certitude as to how far her extravagance
was generic and national and how far it was crudely
personal. Whatever it was he had helplessly missed
her, and now it was too late. She was " carried away "
by Mr. Giovanelli.

A few days after his brief interview with her
mother he came across her at that supreme seat of
flowering desolation known as the Palace of the
Cæsars. The early Roman spring had filled the air
with bloom and perfume, and the rugged surface of
the Palatine was muffled with tender verdure. Daisy
moved at her ease over the great mounds of ruin that
are embanked with mossy marble and paved with
monumental inscriptions. It seemed to him he had
never known Rome so lovely as just then. He looked
off at the enchanting harmony of line and colour that
remotely encircles the city—he inhaled the softly
humid odours and felt the freshness of the year and
the antiquity of the place reaffirm themselves in deep
interfusion. It struck him also that Daisy had never

showed to the eye for so utterly charming ; but this had been his conviction on every occasion of their meeting. Giovanelli was of course at her side, and Giovanelli too glowed as never before with something of the glory of his race.

" Well," she broke out upon the friend it would have been such mockery to designate as the latter's rival, " I should think you'd be quite lonesome ! "

" Lonesome ? " Winterbourne resignedly echoed.

" You're always going round by yourself. Can't you get any one to walk with you ? "

" I'm not so fortunate," he answered, " as your gallant companion."

Giovanelli had from the first treated him with distinguished politeness ; he listened with a deferential air to his remarks ; he laughed punctiliously at his pleasantries ; he attached such importance as he could find terms for to Miss Miller's cold compatriot. He carried himself in no degree like a jealous wooer ; he had obviously a great deal of tact ; he had no objection to any one's expecting a little humility of him. It even struck Winterbourne that he almost yearned at times for some private communication in the interest of his character for common sense ; a chance to remark to him as another intelligent man that, bless him, *he* knew how extraordinary was their young lady and didn't flatter himself with confident—at least *too* confident and too delusive—hopes of matrimony and dollars. On this occasion he strolled away from his charming charge to pluck a sprig of almond-blossom which he carefully arranged in his button-hole.

" I know why you say that," Daisy meanwhile observed. " Because you think I go round too much with *him* ! " And she nodded at her discreet attendant.

" Every one thinks so—if you care to know," was all Winterbourne found to reply.

" Of course I care to know ! "—she made this point with much expression. " But I don't believe a word of it. They're only pretending to be shocked. They don't really care a straw what I do. Besides, I don't go round so much."

" I think you'll find they do care. They'll show it —disagreeably," he took on himself to state.

Daisy weighed the importance of that idea. " How —disagreeably ? "

" Haven't you noticed anything ? " he compassionately asked.

" I've noticed *you*. But I noticed you've no more ' give ' than a ramrod the first time ever I saw you."

" You'll find at least that I've more ' give ' than several others," he patiently smiled.

" How shall I find it ? "

" By going to see the others."

" What will they do to me ? "

" They'll show you the cold shoulder. Do you know what that means ? "

Daisy was looking at him intently ; she began to colour. " Do you mean as Mrs. Walker did the other night ? "

" Exactly as Mrs. Walker did the other night."

She looked away at Giovanelli, still titivating with his almond-blossom. Then with her attention again on the important subject : " I shouldn't think you'd let people be so unkind ! "

" How can I help it ? "

" I should think you'd want to say something."

" I do want to say something "—and Winterbourne paused a moment. " I want to say that your mother tells me she believes you engaged."

" Well, I guess she does," said Daisy very simply.

The young man began to laugh. " And does Randolph believe it ? "

" I guess Randolph doesn't believe anything."

This testimony to Randolph's scepticism excited Winterbourne to further mirth, and he noticed that Giovanelli was coming back to them. Daisy, observing it as well, addressed herself again to her countryman. " Since you've mentioned it," she said, " I *am* engaged." He looked at her hard—he had stopped laughing. " You don't believe it ! " she added.

He asked himself, and it was for a moment like testing a heart-beat ; after which, " Yes, I believe it ! " he said.

" Oh no, you don't," she answered. " But *if* you possibly do," she still more perversely pursued— " well, I ain't ! "

Miss Miller and her constant guide were on their way to the gate of the enclosure, so that Winterbourne, who had but lately entered, presently took leave of them. A week later on he went to dine at a beautiful villa on the Cælian Hill, and, on arriving, dismissed his hired vehicle. The evening was perfect and he promised himself the satisfaction of walking home beneath the Arch of Constantine and past the vaguely-lighted monuments of the Forum. Above was a moon half-developed, whose radiance was not brilliant but veiled in a thin cloud-curtain that seemed to diffuse and equalise it. When on his return from the villa at eleven o'clock he approached the dusky circle of the Colosseum the sense of the romantic in him easily suggested that the interior, in such an atmosphere, would well repay a glance. He turned aside and walked to one of the empty arches, near which, as he observed, an open carriage—one of the little Roman street cabs—was stationed. Then he passed in among the cavernous shadows of the great structure and emerged upon the clear and silent arena. The place had never seemed to him more impressive. One half of the gigantic circus was in deep shade while the other slept in the luminous dusk. As he stood there he began to murmur Byron's famous lines out of " Manfred " ; but before he had finished his quotation he remembered that if nocturnal meditation thereabouts was the fruit of a rich literary culture it was none the less deprecated by medical science. The air of other ages surrounded one ; but the air of other ages, coldly analysed, was no better than a villainous miasma. Winterbourne sought, however, toward the middle of the arena, a further reach of vision, intending the next moment a hasty retreat. The great cross in the centre was almost obscured ; only as he drew near did he make it out distinctly. He thus also distinguished two persons stationed on the low steps that formed its base. One of these was a woman seated ; her companion hovered before her.

Presently the sound of the woman's voice came to him distinctly in the warm night-air. " Well, he looks at us as one of the old lions or tigers may have looked at the Christian martyrs ! " These words were winged with their accent, so that they fluttered and settled about him in the darkness like vague white doves. It was Miss Daisy Miller who had released them for flight.

" Let us hope he's not very hungry "—the bland Giovanelli fell in with her humour. " He'll have to take *me* first ; you'll serve for dessert."

Winterbourne felt himself pulled up with final horror now—and, it must be added, with final relief. It was as if a sudden clearance had taken place in the ambiguity of the poor girl's appearances and the whole riddle of her contradictions had grown easy to read. She was a young lady about the *shades* of whose perversity a foolish puzzled gentleman need no longer trouble his head or his heart. That once questionable quantity *had* no shades—it was a mere black little blot. He stood there looking at her, looking at her companion too, and not reflecting that

74

though he saw them vaguely he himself must have been more brightly presented. He felt angry at all his shiftings of view—he felt ashamed of all his tender little scruples and all his witless little mercies. He was about to advance again, and then again checked himself ; not from the fear of doing her injustice, but from a sense of the danger of showing undue exhilaration for this disburdenment of cautious criticism. He turned away toward the entrance of the place ; but as he did so he heard Daisy speak again.

"Why it was Mr. Winterbourne ! He saw me and he cuts me dead ! "

What a clever little reprobate she was, he was amply able to reflect at this, and how smartly she feigned, how promptly she sought to play off on him, a surprised and injured innocence ! But nothing would induce him to cut her either " dead " or to within any measurable distance even of the famous " inch " of her life. He came forward again and went toward the great cross. Daisy had got up and Giovanelli lifted his hat. Winterbourne had now begun to think simply of the madness, on the ground of exposure and infection, of a frail young creature's lounging away such hours in a nest of malaria. What if she *were* the most plausible of little reprobates ? That was no reason for her dying of the *perniciosa*. " How long have you been ' fooling round ' here ? " he asked with conscious roughness.

Daisy, lovely in the sinister silver radiance, appraised him a moment, roughness and all. " Well, I guess all the evening." She answered with spirit and, he could see even then, with exaggeration. " I never saw anything so quaint."

" I'm afraid," he returned, " you'll not think a bad attack of Roman fever very quaint. This is the way people catch it. I wonder," he added to Giovanelli,

" that you, a native Roman, should countenance such extraordinary rashness."

" Ah," said this seasoned subject, " for myself I have no fear."

" Neither have I—for you ! " Winterbourne retorted in French. " I'm speaking for this young lady."

Giovanelli raised his well-shaped eyebrows and showed his shining teeth, but took his critic's rebuke with docility. " I assured Mademoiselle it was a grave indiscretion, but when was Mademoiselle ever prudent ? "

" I never was sick, and I don't mean to be ! " Mademoiselle declared. " I don't look like much, but I'm healthy ! I was bound to see the Colosseum by moonlight—I wouldn't have wanted to go home without *that* ; and we've had the most beautiful time, haven't we, Mr. Giovanelli ? If there has been any danger Eugenio can give me some pills. Eugenio has got some splendid pills."

" *I* should advise you then," said Winterbourne, " to drive home as fast as possible and take one ! "

Giovanelli smiled as for the striking happy thought. " What you say is very wise. I'll go and make sure the carriage is at hand." And he went forward rapidly.

Daisy followed with Winterbourne. He tried to deny himself the small fine anguish of looking at her, but his eyes themselves refused to spare him, and she seemed moreover not in the least embarrassed. He spoke no word ; Daisy chattered over the beauty of the place : " Well, I *have* seen the Colosseum by moonlight—that's one thing I can rave about ! " Then noticing her companion's silence she asked him why he was so stiff—it had always been her great word. He made no answer, but he felt his laugh an immense negation of stiffness. They passed under one of the dark archways ; Giovanelli was in front with the carriage. Here Daisy stopped a moment, looking at her compatriot. " *Did* you believe I was engaged the other day ? "

" It doesn't matter now what I believed the other day ! " he replied with infinite point.

It was a wonder how she didn't wince for it. " Well, what do you believe now ? "

" I believe it makes very little difference whether you're engaged or not ! "

He felt her lighted eyes fairly penetrate the thick gloom of the vaulted passage—as if to seek some access to him she hadn't yet compassed. But Giovanelli, with a graceful inconsequence, was at present all for retreat. " Quick, quick ; if we get in by midnight we're quite safe ! "

Daisy took her seat in the carriage and the fortunate Italian placed himself beside her. " Don't forget Eugenio's pills ! " said Winterbourne as he lifted his hat.

" I don't care," she unexpectedly cried out for this, " whether I have Roman fever or not ! " On which the cab-driver cracked his whip and they rolled across the desultory patches of antique pavement.

Winterbourne—to do him justice, as it were—mentioned to no one that he had encountered Miss Miller at midnight in the Colosseum with a gentleman ; in spite of which deep discretion, however, the fact of the scandalous adventure was known a couple of days later, with a dozen vivid details, to every member of the little American circle, and was commented accordingly. Winterbourne judged thus that the people about the hotel had been thoroughly empowered to testify, and that after Daisy's return there would have been an exchange of jokes between the porter and the cab-driver. But the young man became aware at the same moment of how thoroughly it had ceased to ruffle him that the little American

flirt should be " talked about " by low-minded menials.
These sources of current criticism a day or two
later abounded still further : the little American flirt
was alarmingly ill and the doctors now in possession
of the scene. Winterbourne, when the rumour came
to him, immediately went to the hotel for more
news. He found that two or three charitable
friends had preceded him and that they were being
entertained in Mrs. Miller's salon by the all-efficient
Randolph.

" It's going round at night that way, you bet—
that's what has made her so sick. She's always going
round at night. I shouldn't think she'd want to—
it's so plaguey dark over here. You can't see anything over here without the moon's right up. In
America they don't go round by the moon ! " Mrs.
Miller meanwhile wholly surrendered to her genius
for unapparent uses ; her salon knew her less than
ever, and she was presumably now at least giving her
daughter the advantage of her society. It was clear
that Daisy was dangerously ill.

Winterbourne constantly attended for news from
the sick-room, which reached him, however, but with
worrying indirectness, though he once had speech,
for a moment, of the poor girl's physician and once
saw Mrs. Miller, who, sharply alarmed, struck him
as thereby more happily inspired than he could have
conceived and indeed as the most noiseless and light-
handed of nurses. She invoked a good deal the re-
mote shade of Dr. Davis, but Winterbourne paid her
the compliment of taking her after all for less monstrous a goose. To this indulgence indeed something
she further said perhaps even more insidiously disposed him. " Daisy spoke of you the other day quite
pleasantly. Half the time she doesn't know what
she's saying, but that time I think she did. She gave
me a message—she told me to tell you. She wanted

you to know she never was engaged to that handsome Italian who was always round. I'm sure I'm very glad ; Mr. Giovanelli hasn't been near us since she was taken ill. I thought he was so much of a gentleman, but I don't call that very polite ! A lady told me he was afraid I hadn't approved of his being round with her so much evenings. Of course it ain't as if their evenings were as pleasant as ours—since *we* don't seem to feel that way about the poison. I guess I *don't* see the point now ; but I suppose he knows I'm a lady and I'd scorn to raise a fuss. Anyway, she wants you to realise she ain't engaged. I don't know why she makes so much of it, but she said to me three times ' Mind you tell Mr. Winterbourne.' And then she told me to ask if you remembered the time you went up to that castle in Switzerland. But I said I wouldn't give any such messages as *that*. Only if she ain't engaged I guess I'm glad to realise it too."

But, as Winterbourne had originally judged, the truth on this question had small actual relevance. A week after this the poor girl died ; it had been indeed a terrible case of the *perniciosa*. A grave was found for her in the little Protestant cemetery, by an angle of the wall of imperial Rome, beneath the cypresses and the thick spring-flowers. Winterbourne stood there beside it with a number of other mourners ; a number larger than the scandal excited by the young lady's career might have made probable. Near him stood Giovanelli, who came nearer still before Winterbourne turned away. Giovanelli, in decorous mourning, showed but a whiter face ; his button-hole lacked its nosegay and he had visibly something urgent— and even to distress—to say, which he scarce knew how to " place." He decided at last to confide it with a pale convulsion to Winterbourne. " She was the most beautiful young lady I ever saw, and the most

amiable." To which he added in a moment : " Also
—naturally !—the most innocent."

Winterbourne sounded him with hard dry eyes,
but presently repeated his words, " The most innocent ? "

" The most innocent ! "

It came somehow so much too late that our friend
could only glare at its having come at all. " Why the
devil," he asked, " did you take her to that fatal
place ? "

Giovanelli raised his neat shoulders and eyebrows
to within suspicion of a shrug. " For myself I had no
fear ; and *she*—she did what she liked."

Winterbourne's eyes attached themselves to the
ground. " She did what she liked ! "

It determined on the part of poor Giovanelli a
further pious, a further candid, confidence. " If she
had lived I should have got nothing. She never would
have married me."

It had been spoken as if to attest, in all sincerity,
his disinterestedness, but Winterbourne scarce knew
what welcome to give it. He said, however, with a
grace inferior to his friend's : " I daresay not."

The latter was even by this not discouraged. " For
a moment I hoped so. . But no. I'm convinced."

Winterbourne took it in ; he stood staring at the
raw protuberance among the April daisies. When he
turned round again his fellow-mourner had stepped
back.

He almost immediately left Rome, but the following summer he again met his aunt Mrs. Costello at
Vevey. Mrs. Costello extracted from the charming
old hotel there a value that the Miller family hadn't
mastered the secret of. In the interval Winterbourne
had often thought of the most interesting member
of that trio—of her mystifying manners and her
queer adventure. One day he spoke of her to his

aunt—said it was on his conscience he had done her injustice.

" I'm sure I don't know "—that lady showed caution. " How did your injustice affect her ? "

" She sent me a message before her death which I didn't understand at the time. But I've understood it since. She would have appreciated one's esteem."

" She took an odd way to gain it ! But do you mean by what you say," Mrs. Costello asked, " that she would have reciprocated one's affection ? "

As he made no answer to this she after a little looked round at him—he hadn't been directly within sight ; but the effect of that wasn't to make her repeat her question. He spoke, however, after a while. " You were right in that remark that you made last summer. I was booked to make a mistake. I've lived too long in foreign parts." And this time she herself said nothing.

Nevertheless he soon went back to live at Geneva, whence there continue to come the most contradictory accounts of his motives of sojourn : a report that he's " studying " hard — an intimation that he's much interested in a very clever foreign lady.

PANDORA

I

It has long been the custom of the North German
Lloyd steamers, which convey passengers from
Bremen to New York, to anchor for several hours in
the pleasant port of Southampton, where their human
cargo receives many additions. An intelligent young
German, Count Otto Vogelstein, hardly knew a few
years ago whether to condemn this custom or approve
it. He leaned over the bulwarks of the *Donau* as the
American passengers crossed the plank—the travellers
who embark at Southampton are mainly of that
nationality — and curiously, indifferently, vaguely,
through the smoke of his cigar, saw them absorbed in
the huge capacity of the ship, where he had the agreeable consciousness that his own nest was comfortably
made. To watch from such a point of vantage the
struggles of those less fortunate than ourselves—of
the uninformed, the unprovided, the belated, the bewildered—is an occupation not devoid of sweetness,
and there was nothing to mitigate the complacency
with which our young friend gave himself up to it ;
nothing, that is, save a natural benevolence which had
not yet been extinguished by the consciousness of
official greatness. For Count Vogelstein was official,
as I think you would have seen from the straightness
of his back, the lustre of his light elegant spectacles, and
something discreet and diplomatic in the curve of his
moustache, which looked as if it might well contribute

to the principal function, as cynics say, of the lips—
the active concealment of thought. He had been appointed to the secretaryship of the German legation at
Washington and in these first days of the autumn was
about to take possession of his post. He was a model
character for such a purpose—serious civil ceremoni-
ous curious stiff, stuffed with knowledge and convinced that, as lately rearranged, the German Empire
places in the most striking light the highest of all the
possibilities of the greatest of all the peoples. He was
quite aware, however, of the claims to economic and
other consideration of the United States, and that this
quarter of the globe offered a vast field for study.

The process of inquiry had already begun for him,
in spite of his having as yet spoken to none of his
fellow-passengers; the case being that Vogelstein
inquired not only with his tongue, but with his eyes—
that is with his spectacles—with his ears, with his
nose, with his palate, with all his senses and organs.
He was a highly upright young man, whose only fault
was that his sense of comedy, or of the humour of
things, had never been specifically disengaged from
his several other senses. He vaguely felt that something should be done about this, and in a general
manner proposed to do it, for he was on his way to
explore a society abounding in comic aspects. This
consciousness of a missing measure gave him a certain
mistrust of what might be said of him ; and if circum-
spection is the essence of diplomacy our young aspirant promised well. His mind contained several
millions of facts, packed too closely together for the
light breeze of the imagination to draw through the
mass. He was impatient to report himself to his
superior in Washington, and the loss of time in an
English port could only incommode him, inasmuch as
the study of English institutions was no part of his
mission. On the other hand the day was charming ;

the blue sea, in Southampton Water, pricked all over
with light, had no movement but that of its infinite
shimmer. Moreover he was by no means sure that he
should be happy in the United States, where doubtless
he should find himself soon enough disembarked. He
knew that this was not an important question and that
happiness was an unscientific term, such as a man of
his education should be ashamed to use even in the
silence of his thoughts. Lost none the less in the in-
considerate crowd and feeling himself neither in his
own country nor in that to which he was in a manner
accredited, he was reduced to his mere personality ;
so that during the hour, to save his importance, he
cultivated such ground as lay in sight for a judgement
of this delay to which the German steamer was sub-
jected in English waters. Mightn't it be proved, facts,
figures and documents—or at least watch— in hand,
considerably greater than the occasion demanded ?

Count Vogelstein was still young enough in diplomacy to think it necessary to have opinions. He had
a good many indeed which had been formed without
difficulty ; they had been received ready-made from
a line of ancestors who knew what they liked. This
was of course—and under pressure, being candid, he
would have admitted it —an unscientific way of
furnishing one's mind. Our young man was a stiff
conservative, a Junker of Junkers ; he thought
modern democracy a temporary phase and expected
to find many arguments against it in the great Republic. In regard to these things it was a pleasure to
him to feel that, with his complete training, he had
been taught thoroughly to appreciate the nature of
evidence. The ship was heavily laden with German
emigrants, whose mission in the United States differed
considerably from Count Otto's. They hung over the
bulwarks, densely grouped ; they leaned forward on
their elbows for hours, their shoulders kept on a level

with their ears; the men in furred caps, smoking long-bowled pipes, the women with babies hidden in remarkably ugly shawls. Some were yellow Germans and some were black, and all looked greasy and matted with the sea-damp. They were destined to swell still further the huge current of the Western democracy; and Count Vogelstein doubtless said to himself that they wouldn't improve its quality. Their numbers, however, were striking, and I know not what he thought of the nature of this particular evidence.

The passengers who came on board at Southampton were not of the greasy class; they were for the most part American families who had been spending the summer, or a longer period, in Europe. They had a great deal of luggage, innumerable bags and rugs and hampers and sea-chairs, and were composed largely of ladies of various ages, a little pale with anticipation, wrapped also in striped shawls, though in prettier ones than the nursing mothers of the steerage, and crowned with very high hats and feathers. They darted to and fro across the gangway, looking for each other and for their scattered parcels; they separated and reunited, they exclaimed and declared, they eyed with dismay the occupants of the forward quarter, who seemed numerous enough to sink the vessel, and their voices sounded faint and far as they rose to Vogelstein's ear over the latter's great tarred sides. He noticed that in the new contingent there were many young girls, and he remembered what a lady in Dresden had once said to him — that America was the country of the Mädchen. He wondered whether he should like that, and reflected that it would be an aspect to study, like everything else. He had known in Dresden an American family in which there were three daughters who used to skate with the officers, and some of the ladies now coming on board struck him as of that same habit, except that in the Dresden days feathers weren't worn quite so high.

At last the ship began to creak and slowly budge, and the delay at Southampton came to an end. The gangway was removed and the vessel indulged in the awkward evolutions that were to detach her from the land. Count Vogelstein had finished his cigar, and he spent a long time in walking up and down the upper deck. The charming English coast passed before him, and he felt this to be the last of the old world. The American coast also might be pretty — he hardly knew what one would expect of an American coast ; but he was sure it would be different. Differences, however, were notoriously half the charm of travel, and perhaps even most when they couldn't be expressed in figures, numbers, diagrams or the other merely useful symbols. As yet indeed there were very few among the objects presented to sight on the steamer. Most of his fellow-passengers appeared of one and the same persuasion, and that persuasion the least to be mistaken. They were Jews and commercial to a man. And by this time they had lighted their cigars and put on all manner of seafaring caps, some of them with big ear-lappets which somehow had the effect of bringing out their peculiar facial type. At last the new voyagers began to emerge from below and to look about them, vaguely, with that suspicious expression of face always to be noted in the newly embarked and which, as directed to the receding land, resembles that of a person who begins to perceive himself the victim of a trick. Earth and ocean, in such glances, are made the subject of a sweeping objection, and many travellers, in the general plight, have an air at once duped and superior, which seems to say that they could easily go ashore if they would.

It still wanted two hours of dinner, and by the time Vogelstein's long legs had measured three or four miles on the deck he was ready to settle himself in his sea-chair and draw from his pocket a Tauchnitz novel by an American author whose pages, he had been assured, would help to prepare him for some of the oddities. On the back of his chair his name was painted in rather large letters, this being a precaution taken at the recommendation of a friend who had told him that on the American steamers the passengers—especially the ladies—thought nothing of pilfering one's little comforts. His friend had even hinted at the correct reproduction of his coronet. This marked man of the world had added that the Americans are greatly impressed by a coronet. I know not whether it was scepticism or modesty, but Count Vogelstein had omitted every pictured plea for his rank ; there were others of which he might have made use. The precious piece of furniture which on the Atlantic voyage is trusted never to flinch among universal concussions was emblazoned simply with his title and name. It happened, however, that the blazonry was huge ; the back of the chair was covered with enormous German characters. This time there can be no doubt : it was modesty that caused the secretary of legation, in placing himself, to turn this portion of his seat outward, away from the eyes of his companions —to present it to the balustrade of the deck. The ship was passing the Needles—the beautiful uttermost point of the Isle of Wight. Certain tall white cones of rock rose out of the purple sea ; they flushed in the afternoon light and their vague rosiness gave them a human expression in face of the cold expanse toward which the prow was turned ; they seemed to say farewell, to be the last note of a peopled world. Vogelstein saw them very comfortably from his place and after a while turned his eyes to the other quarter, where the elements of air and water managed to make between them so comparatively poor an opposition.

Even his American novelist was more amusing than
that, and he prepared to return to this author. In the
great curve which it described, however, his glance was
arrested by the figure of a young lady who had just
ascended to the deck and who paused at the mouth of
the companionway.

This was not in itself an extraordinary phenomenon;
but what attracted Vogelstein's attention was the
fact that the young person appeared to have fixed her
eyes on him. She was slim, brightly dressed, rather
pretty ; Vogelstein remembered in a moment that he
had noticed her among the people on the wharf at
Southampton. She was soon aware he had observed
her ; whereupon she began to move along the deck
with a step that seemed to indicate a purpose of
approaching him. Vogelstein had time to wonder
whether she could be one of the girls he had known at
Dresden ; but he presently reflected that they would
now be much older than that. It was true they were
apt to advance, like this one, straight upon their
victim. Yet the present specimen was no longer
looking at him, and though she passed near him it
was now tolerably clear she had come above but to
take a general survey. She was a quick handsome
competent girl, and she simply wanted to see what
one could think of the ship, of the weather, of the
appearance of England, from such a position as that ;
possibly even of one's fellow-passengers. She satisfied
herself promptly on these points, and then she looked
about, while she walked, as if in keen search of a
missing object ; so that Vogelstein finally arrived at a
conviction of her real motive. She passed near him
again and this time almost stopped, her eyes bent upon
him attentively. He thought her conduct remarkable
even after he had gathered that it was not at his face,
with its yellow moustache, she was looking, but at the
chair on which he was seated. Then those words of

his friend came back to him—the speech about the
tendency of the people, especially of the ladies, on the
American steamers to take to themselves one's little
belongings. Especially the ladies, he might well say ;
for here was one who apparently wished to pull from
under him the very chair he was sitting on. He was
afraid she would ask him for it, so he pretended
to read, systematically avoiding her eye. He was
conscious she hovered near him, and was moreover
curious to see what she would do. It seemed to him
strange that such a nice-looking girl—for her appearance was really charming—should endeavour by
arts so flagrant to work upon the quiet dignity of a
secretary of legation. At last it stood out that she was
trying to look round a corner, as it were—trying to see
what was written on the back of his chair. "She wants
to find out my name ; she wants to see who I am ! "
This reflexion passed through his mind and caused
him to raise his eyes. They rested on her own—which
for an appreciable moment she didn't withdraw. The
latter were brilliant and expressive, and surmounted
a delicate aquiline nose, which, though pretty, was
perhaps just a trifle too hawk-like. It was the oddest
coincidence in the world ; the story Vogelstein had
taken up treated of a flighty forward little American
girl who plants herself in front of a young man in the
garden of an hotel. Wasn't the conduct of this young
lady a testimony to the truthfulness of the tale, and
wasn't Vogelstein himself in the position of the young
man in the garden ? That young man—though with
more, in such connexions in general, to go upon—ended
by addressing himself to his aggressor, as she might
be called, and after a very short hesitation Vogelstein
followed his example. " If she wants to know who I
am she's welcome," he said to himself ; and he got out
of the chair, seized it by the back and, turning it
round, exhibited the superscription to the girl. She

coloured slightly, but smiled and read his name, while Vogelstein raised his hat.

" I'm much obliged to you. That's all right," she remarked as if the discovery had made her very happy.

It affected him indeed as all right that he should be Count Otto Vogelstein ; this appeared even rather a flippant mode of disposing of the fact. By way of rejoinder he asked her if she desired of him the surrender of his seat.

" I'm much obliged to you ; of course not. I thought you had one of our chairs, and I didn't like to ask you. It looks exactly like one of ours ; not so much now as when you sit in it. Please sit down again. I don't want to trouble you. We've lost one of ours, and I've been looking for it everywhere. They look so much alike ; you can't tell till you see the back. Of course I see there will be no mistake about yours," the young lady went on with a smile of which the serenity matched her other abundance. " But we've got such a small name—you can scarcely see it," she added with the same friendly intention. " Our name's just Day—you mightn't think it *was* a name, might you ? if we didn't make the most of it. If you see that on anything, I'd be so obliged if you'd tell me. It isn't for myself, it's for my mother ; she's so dependent on her chair, and that one I'm looking for pulls out so beautifully. Now that you sit down again and hide the lower part it does look just like ours. Well, it must be somewhere. You must excuse me ; I wouldn't disturb you."

This was a long and even confidential speech for a young woman, presumably unmarried, to make to a perfect stranger ; but Miss Day acquitted herself of it with perfect simplicity and self-possession. She held up her head and stepped away, and Vogelstein could see that the foot she pressed upon the clean smooth deck was slender and shapely. He watched her dis-

appear through the trap by which she had ascended,
and he felt more than ever like the young man in his
American tale. The girl in the present case was older
and not so pretty, as he could easily judge, for the
image of her smiling eyes and speaking lips still hovered
before him. He went back to his book with the feeling
that it would give him some information about her.
This was rather illogical, but it indicated a certain
amount of curiosity on the part of Count Vogelstein.
The girl in the book had a mother, it appeared, and so
had this young lady ; the former had also a brother,
and he now remembered that he had noticed a young
man on the wharf—a young man in a high hat and a
white overcoat—who seemed united to Miss Day by
this natural tie. And there was some one else too, as
he gradually recollected, an older man, also in a high
hat, but in a black overcoat—in black altogether—
who completed the group and who was presumably the
head of the family. These reflexions would indicate
that Count Vogelstein read his volume of Tauchnitz
rather interruptedly. Moreover they represented but
the loosest economy of consciousness ; for wasn't he
to be afloat in an oblong box for ten days with such
people, and could it be doubted he should see at least
enough of them ?

It may as well be written without delay that he saw
a great deal of them. I have sketched in some detail
the conditions in which he made the acquaintance of
Miss Day, because the event had a certain importance
for this fair square Teuton ; but I must pass briefly
over the incidents that immediately followed it. He
wondered what it was open to him, after such an introduction, to do in relation to her, and he determined
he would push through his American tale and discover
what the hero did. But he satisfied himself in a very
short time that Miss Day had nothing in common
with the heroine of that work save certain signs of

habitat and climate—and save, further, the fact that
the male sex wasn't terrible to her. The local stamp
sharply, as he gathered, impressed upon her he estimated indeed rather in a borrowed than in a natural
light, for if she was native to a small town in the
interior of the American continent one of their fellow-
passengers, a lady from New York with whom he had
a good deal of conversation, pronounced her " atro-
ciously " provincial. How the lady arrived at this
certitude didn't appear, for Vogelstein observed that
she held no communication with the girl. It was true
she gave it the support of her laying down that certain
Americans could tell immediately who other Americans were, leaving him to judge whether or no she
herself belonged to the critical or only to the criticised
half of the nation. Mrs. Dangerfield was a handsome
confidential insinuating woman, with whom Vogelstein felt his talk take a very wide range indeed. She
convinced him rather effectually that even in a great
democracy there are human differences, and that
American life was full of social distinctions, of delicate
shades, which foreigners often lack the intelligence to
perceive. Did he suppose every one knew every one
else in the biggest country in the world, and that one
wasn't as free to choose one's company there as in
the most monarchical and most exclusive societies ?
She laughed such delusions to scorn as Vogelstein
tucked her beautiful furred coverlet—they reclined
together a great deal in their elongated chairs—well
over her feet. How free an American lady was to
choose her company she abundantly proved by not
knowing any one on the steamer but Count Otto.

He could see for himself that Mr. and Mrs. Day
had not at all her grand air. They were fat plain
serious people who sat side by side on the deck for
hours and looked straight before them. Mrs. Day had
a white face, large cheeks and small eyes : her forehead

was surrounded with a multitude of little tight black curls ; her lips moved as if she had always a lozenge in her mouth. She wore entwined about her head an article which Mrs. Dangerfield spoke of as a " nuby," a knitted pink scarf concealing her hair, encircling her neck and having among its convolutions a hole for her perfectly expressionless face. Her hands were folded on her stomach, and in her still, swathed figure her little bead-like eyes, which occasionally changed their direction, alone represented life. Her husband had a stiff grey beard on his chin and a bare spacious upper lip, to which constant shaving had imparted a hard glaze. His eyebrows were thick and his nostrils wide, and when he was uncovered, in the saloon, it was visible that his grizzled hair was dense and perpendicular. He might have looked rather grim and truculent hadn't it been for the mild familiar accommodating gaze with which his large light-coloured pupils — the leisurely eyes of a silent man — appeared to consider surrounding objects. He was evidently more friendly than fierce, but he was more diffident than friendly. He liked to have you in sight, but wouldn't have pretended to understand you much or to classify you, and would have been sorry it should put you under an obligation. He and his wife spoke sometimes, but seldom talked, and there was something vague and patient in them, as if they had become victims of a wrought spell. The spell however was of no sinister cast ; it was the fascination of prosperity, the confidence of security, which sometimes makes people arrogant, but which had had such a different effect on this simple satisfied pair, in whom further development of every kind appeared to have been happily arrested.

Mrs. Dangerfield made it known to Count Otto that every morning after breakfast, the hour at which he wrote his journal in his cabin, the old couple were

guided upstairs and installed in their customary
corner by Pandora. This she had learned to be the
name of their elder daughter, and she was immensely
amused by her discovery. " Pandora "—that was in
the highest degree typical; it placed them in the social
scale if other evidence had been wanting ; you could
tell that a girl was from the interior, the mysterious
interior about which Vogelstein's imagination was
now quite excited, when she had such a name as that.
This young lady managed the whole family, even a
little the small beflounced sister, who, with bold
pretty innocent eyes, a torrent of fair silky hair, a
crimson fez, such as is worn by male Turks, very
much askew on top of it, and a way of galloping and
straddling about the ship in any company she could
pick up—she had long thin legs, very short skirts and
stockings of every tint—was going home, in elegant
French clothes, to resume an interrupted education.
Pandora overlooked and directed her relatives ; Vogelstein could see this for himself, could see she was very
active and decided, that she had in a high degree the
sentiment of responsibility, settling on the spot most
of the questions that could come up for a family from
the interior.

The voyage was remarkably fine, and day after day
it was possible to sit there under the salt sky and feel
one's self rounding the great curves of the globe. The
long deck made a white spot in the sharp black circle
of the ocean and in the intense sea-light, while the
shadow of the smoke-streamers trembled on the
familiar floor, the shoes of fellow-passengers, distinctive now, and in some cases irritating, passed and
repassed, accompanied, in the air so tremendously
" open," that rendered all voices weak and most
remarks rather flat, by fragments of opinion on the
run of the ship. Vogelstein by this time had finished
his little American story and now definitely judged

that Pandora Day was not at all like the heroine. She
was of quite another type ; much more serious and
strenuous, and not at all keen, as he had supposed,
about making the acquaintance of gentlemen. Her
speaking to him that first afternoon had been, he was
bound to believe, an incident without importance for
herself ; in spite of her having followed it up the next
day by the remark, thrown at him as she passed, with
a smile that was almost fraternal : " It's all right, sir !
I've found that old chair." After this she hadn't
spoken to him again and had scarcely looked at him.
She read a great deal, and almost always French
books, in fresh yellow paper ; not the lighter forms of
that literature, but a volume of Sainte-Beuve, of Renan
or at the most, in the way of dissipation, of Alfred de
Musset. She took frequent exercise and almost always
walked alone, apparently not having made many
friends on the ship and being without the resource of
her parents, who, as has been related, never budged
out of the cosy corner in which she planted them for
the day.

Her brother was always in the smoking - room,
where Vogelstein observed him, in very tight clothes,
his neck encircled with a collar like a palisade. He
had a sharp little face, which was not disagreeable ;
he smoked enormous cigars and began his drinking
early in the day : but his appearance gave no sign of
these excesses. As regards euchre and poker and the
other distractions of the place he was guilty of none.
He evidently understood such games in perfection,
for he used to watch the players, and even at moments
impartially advise them ; but Vogelstein never saw
the cards in his hand. He was referred to as regards
disputed points, and his opinion carried the day. He
took little part in the conversation, usually much
relaxed, that prevailed in the smoking-room, but from
time to time he made, in his soft flat youthful voice,

a remark which every one paused to listen to and which was greeted with roars of laughter. Vogelstein, well as he knew English, could rarely catch the joke ; but he could see at least that these must be choice specimens of that American humour admired and practised by a whole continent and yet to be rendered accessible to a trained diplomatist, clearly, but by some special and incalculable revelation. The young man, in his way, was very remarkable, for, as Vogelstein heard some one say once after the laughter had subsided, he was only nineteen. If his sister didn't resemble the dreadful little girl in the tale already mentioned, there was for Vogelstein at least an analogy between young Mr. Day and a certain small brother —a candy-loving Madison, Hamilton or Jefferson— who was, in the Tauchnitz volume, attributed to that unfortunate maid. This was what the little Madison would have grown up to at nineteen, and the improvement was greater than might have been expected.

The days were long, but the voyage was short, and it had almost come to an end before Count Otto yielded to an attraction peculiar in its nature and finally irresistible, and, in spite of Mrs. Dangerfield's emphatic warning, sought occasion for a little continuous talk with Miss Pandora. To mention that this impulse took effect without mentioning sundry other of his current impressions with which it had nothing to do is perhaps to violate proportion and give a false idea ; but to pass it by would be still more unjust. The Germans, as we know, are a transcendental people, and there was at last an irresistible appeal for Vogel stein in this quick bright silent girl who could smile and turn vocal in an instant, who imparted a rare originality to the filial character, and whose profile was delicate as she bent it over a volume which she cut as she read, or presented it in musing attitudes, at the side of the ship, to the horizon they had left behind.

But he felt it to be a pity, as regards a possible acquaintance with her, that her parents should be heavy little burghers, that her brother should not correspond to his conception of a young man of the upper class, and that her sister should be a Daisy Miller *en herbe*. Repeatedly admonished by Mrs. Dangerfield, the young diplomatist was doubly careful as to the relations he might form at the beginning of his sojourn in the United States. That lady reminded him, and he had himself made the observation in other capitals, that the first year, and even the second, is the time for prudence. One was ignorant of proportions and values ; one was exposed to mistakes and thankful for attention, and one might give one's self away to people who would afterwards be as a millstone round one's neck : Mrs. Dangerfield struck and sustained that note, which resounded in the young man's imagination. She assured him that if he didn't " look out " he would be committing himself to some American girl with an impossible family. In America, when one committed one's self, there was nothing to do but march to the altar, and what should he say for instance to finding himself a near relation of Mr. and Mrs. P. W. Day ?—since such were the initials inscribed on the back of the two chairs of that couple. Count Otto felt the peril, for he could immediately think of a dozen men he knew who had married American girls. There appeared now to be a constant danger of marrying the American girl ; it was something one had to reckon with, like the railway, the telegraph, the discovery of dynamite, the Chassepôt rifle, the Socialistic spirit : it was one of the complications of modern life.

It would doubtless be too much to say that he feared being carried away by a passion for a young woman who was not strikingly beautiful and with whom he had talked, in all, but ten minutes. But, as

we recognise, he went so far as to wish that the human
belongings of a person whose high spirit appeared
to have no taint either of fastness, as they said in
England, or of subversive opinion, and whose mouth
had charming lines, should not be a little more distinguished.   There was an effect of drollery in her behaviour to these subjects of her zeal, whom she seemed
to regard as a care, but not as an interest ; it was
as if they had been entrusted to her honour and she
had engaged to convey them safe to a certain point ;
she was detached and inadvertent, and then suddenly
remembered, repented and came back to tuck them
into their blankets, to alter the position of her mother's
umbrella, to tell them something about the run of
the ship.   These little offices were usually performed
deftly, rapidly, with the minimum of words, and when
their daughter drew near them Mr. and Mrs. Day
closed their eyes after the fashion of a pair of household dogs who expect to be scratched.

One morning she brought up the Captain of the
ship to present to them ; she appeared to have a
private and independent acquaintance with this officer,
and the introduction to her parents had the air of a
sudden happy thought. It wasn't so much an introduction as an exhibition, as if she were saying to him :
" This is what they look like ; see how comfortable I
make them.   Aren't they rather queer and rather
dear little people ?   But they leave me perfectly free.
Oh I can assure you of that.   Besides, you must see
it for yourself."   Mr. and Mrs. Day looked up at the
high functionary who thus unbent to them with very
little change of countenance ; then looked at each
other in the same way.   He saluted, he inclined
himself a moment ; but Pandora shook her head, she
seemed to be answering for them ; she made little
gestures as if in explanation to the good Captain of
some of their peculiarities, as for instance that he

needn't expect them to speak. They closed their eyes at last ; she appeared to have a kind of mesmeric influence on them, and Miss Day walked away with the important friend, who treated her with evident consideration, bowing very low, for all his importance, when the two presently after separated. Vogelstein could see she was capable of making an impression ; and the moral of our little matter is that in spite of Mrs. Dangerfield, in spite of the resolutions of his prudence, in spite of the limits of such acquaintance as he had momentarily made with her, in spite of Mr. and Mrs. Day and the young man in the smoking-room, she had fixed his attention.

It was in the course of the evening after the scene with the Captain that he joined her, awkwardly, abruptly, irresistibly, on the deck, where she was pacing to and fro alone, the hour being auspiciously mild and the stars remarkably fine. There were scattered talkers and smokers and couples, unrecognisable, that moved quickly through the gloom. The vessel dipped with long regular pulsations ; vague and spectral under the low stars, its swaying pinnacles spotted here and there with lights, it seemed to rush through the darkness faster than by day. Count Otto had come up to walk, and as the girl brushed past him he distinguished Pandora's face—with Mrs. Dangerfield he always spoke of her as Pandora—under the veil worn to protect it from the sea-damp. He stopped, turned, hurried after her, threw away his cigar— then asked her if she would do him the honour to accept his arm. She declined his arm but accepted his company, and he allowed her to enjoy it for an hour. They had a great deal of talk, and he was to remember afterwards some of the things she had said. There was now a certainty of the ship's getting into dock the next morning but one, and this prospect afforded an obvious topic. Some of Miss Day's ex-

pressions struck him as singular, but of course, as
he was aware, his knowledge of English was not nice
enough to give him a perfect measure.

"I'm not in a hurry to arrive ; I'm very happy
here," she said. "I'm afraid I shall have such a
time putting my people through."

"Putting them through ? "

"Through the Custom-House. We've made so
many purchases. Well, I've written to a friend to
come down, and perhaps he can help us. He's very
well acquainted with the head. Once I'm chalked I
don't care. I feel like a kind of blackboard by this
time anyway. We found them awful in Germany."

Count Otto wondered if the friend she had written
to were her lover and if they had plighted their troth,
especially when she alluded to him again as " that
gentleman who's coming down." He asked her about
her travels, her impressions, whether she had been
long in Europe and what she liked best, and she put it
to him that they had gone abroad, she and her family,
for a little fresh experience. Though he found her
very intelligent he suspected she gave this as a reason
because he was a German and she had heard the
Germans were rich in culture. He wondered what
form of culture Mr. and Mrs. Day had brought back
from Italy, Greece and Palestine—they had travelled
for two years and been everywhere—especially when
their daughter said : " I wanted father and mother to
see the best things. I kept them three hours on the
Acropolis. I guess they won't forget that ! " Perhaps
it was of Phidias and Pericles they were thinking,
Vogelstein reflected, as they sat ruminating in their
rugs. Pandora remarked also that she wanted to
show her little sister everything while she was comparatively unformed (" comparatively ! " he mutely
gasped) ; remarkable sights made so much more
impression when the mind was fresh : she had read

something of that sort somewhere in Goethe. She had wanted to come herself when she was her sister's age ; but her father was in business then and they couldn't leave Utica. The young man thought of the little sister frisking over the Parthenon and the Mount of Olives and sharing for two years, the years of the school-room, this extraordinary pilgrimage of her parents ; he wondered whether Goethe's dictum had been justified in this case. He asked Pandora if Utica were the seat of her family, if it were an important or typical place, if it would be an interesting city for him, as a stranger, to see. His companion replied frankly that this was a big question, but added that all the same she would ask him to " come and visit us at our home " if it weren't that they should probably soon leave it.

" Ah, you're going to live elsewhere ? " Vogelstein asked, as if that fact too would be typical.

" Well, I'm working for New York. I flatter myself I've loosened them while we've been away," the girl went on. " They won't find in Utica the same charm ; that was my idea. I want a big place, and of course Utica—— ! " She broke off as before a complex statement.

" I suppose Utica is inferior—— ? " Vogelstein seemed to see his way to suggest.

" Well no, I guess I can't have you call Utica inferior. It isn't supreme—that's what's the matter with it, and I hate anything middling," said Pandora Day. She gave a light dry laugh, tossing back her head a little as she made this declaration. And looking at her askance in the dusk, as she trod the deck that vaguely swayed, he recognised something in her air and port that matched such a pronouncement.

" What's her social position ? " he inquired of Mrs. Dangerfield the next day. " I can't make it out at all—it's so contradictory. She strikes me as having much cultivation and much spirit. Her appearance, too, is very neat. Yet her parents are complete little burghers. That's easily seen."

" Oh, social position," and Mrs. Dangerfield nodded two or three times portentously. " What big expressions you use ! Do you think everybody in the world has a social position ? That's reserved for an infinitely small majority of mankind. You can't have a social position at Utica any more than you can have an opera-box. Pandora hasn't got one ; where, if you please, should she have got it ? Poor girl, it isn't fair of you to make her the subject of such questions as that."

" Well," said Vogelstein, " if she's of the lower class it seems to me very—very——" And he paused a moment, as he often paused in speaking English, looking for his word.

" Very what, dear Count ? "

" Very significant, very representative."

" Oh dear, she isn't of the lower class," Mrs. Dangerfield returned with an irritated sense of wasted wisdom. She liked to explain her country, but that somehow always required two persons.

" What is she then ? "

" Well, I'm bound to admit that since I was at home last she's a novelty. A girl like that with such people—it *is* a new type."

" I like novelties "—and Count Otto smiled with an air of considerable resolution. He couldn't however be satisfied with a demonstration that only begged the question ; and when they disembarked in New York he felt, even amid the confusion of the wharf and the heaps of disembowelled baggage, a certain acuteness of regret at the idea that Pandora and her family were about to vanish into the unknown. He had a consolation however : it was apparent that for some reason or other—illness or absence from town—the gentleman to whom she had written had not, as she said, come down. Vogelstein was glad —he couldn't have told you why—that this sympathetic person had failed her ; even though without him Pandora had to engage single-handed with the United States Custom-House. Our young man's first impression of the Western world was received on the landing-place of the German steamers at Jersey City —a huge wooden shed covering a wooden wharf which resounded under the feet, an expanse palisaded with rough-hewn piles that leaned this way and that, and bestrewn with masses of heterogeneous luggage. At one end, toward the town, was a row of tall painted palings, behind which he could distinguish a press of hackney-coachmen, who brandished their whips and awaited their victims, while their voices rose, incessant, with a sharp strange sound, a challenge at once fierce and familiar. The whole place, behind the fence, appeared to bristle and resound. Out there was America, Count Otto said to himself, and he looked toward it with a sense that he should have to muster resolution. On the wharf people were rushing about amid their trunks, pulling their things together, trying to unite their scattered parcels. They were heated and angry, or else quite bewildered and discouraged. The few that had succeeded in collecting their battered boxes had an air of flushed indifference to the efforts of their neighbours, not even looking at people with whom they had been fondly intimate on the steamer. A detachment of the officers of the Customs was in attendance, and energetic passengers were engaged in attempts to drag them toward their luggage or to drag heavy pieces toward them. These functionaries were good-natured and taciturn, except when occasionally they remarked to a passenger whose open trunk stared up at them, eloquent, imploring, that they were afraid the voyage had been

" rather glassy." They had a friendly leisurely speculative way of discharging their duty, and if they perceived a victim's name written on the portmanteau
they addressed him by it in a tone of old acquaintance.
Vogelstein found however that if they were familiar
they weren't indiscreet. He had heard that in
America all public functionaries were the same, that
there wasn't a different *tenue*, as they said in France,
for different positions, and he wondered whether at
Washington the President and ministers, whom he
expected to see—to *have* to see—a good deal of, would
be like that.

He was diverted from these speculations by the
sight of Mr. and Mrs. Day seated side by side upon
a trunk and encompassed apparently by the accumu-
lations of their tour. Their faces expressed more consciousness of surrounding objects than he had hitherto
recognised, and there was an air of placid expansion
in the mysterious couple which suggested that this
consciousness was agreeable. Mr. and Mrs. Day were,
as they would have said, real glad to get back. At a
little distance, on the edge of the dock, our observer
remarked their son, who had found a place where,
between the sides of two big ships, he could see the
ferry-boats pass ; the large pyramidal low-laden ferry-
boats of American waters. He stood there, patient
and considering, with his small neat foot on a coil of
rope, his back to everything that had been disembarked, his neck elongated in its polished cylinder,
while the fragrance of his big cigar mingled with the
odour of the rotting piles, and his little sister, beside
him, hugged a huge post and tried to see how far she
could crane over the water without falling in. Vogelstein's servant was off in search of an examiner ;
Count Otto himself had got his things together and
was waiting to be released, fully expecting that for a
person of his importance the ceremony would be brief.

Before it began he said a word to young Mr. Day, raising his hat at the same time to the little girl, whom he had not yet greeted and who dodged his salute by swinging herself boldly outward to the dangerous side of the pier. She was indeed still unformed, but was evidently as light as a feather.

"I see you're kept waiting like me. It's very tiresome," Count Otto said.

The young American answered without looking behind him. "As soon as we're started we'll go all right. My sister has written to a gentleman to come down."

"I've looked for Miss Day to bid her good-bye," Vogelstein went on ; "but I don't see her."

"I guess she has gone to meet that gentleman ; he's a great friend of hers."

"I guess he's her lover ! " the little girl broke out. "She was always writing to him in Europe."

Her brother puffed his cigar in silence a moment. "That was only for this. I'll tell on you, sis," he presently added.

But the younger Miss Day gave no heed to his menace ; she addressed herself only, though with all freedom, to Vogelstein. "This is New York ; I like it better than Utica."

He had no time to reply, for his servant had arrived with one of the dispensers of fortune ; but as he turned away he wondered, in the light of the child's preference, about the towns of the interior. He was naturally exempt from the common doom. The officer who took him in hand, and who had a large straw hat and a diamond breastpin, was quite a man of the world, and in reply to the Count's formal declarations only said, "Well, I guess it's all right ; I guess I'll just pass you," distributing chalk-marks as if they had been so many love-pats. The servant had done some superfluous unlocking and unbuckling, and

while he closed the pieces the officer stood there wiping
his forehead and conversing with Vogelstein. " First
visit to our country, sir ?—quite alone—no ladies ?
Of course the ladies are what we're most after." It
was in this manner he expressed himself, while the
young diplomatist wondered what he was waiting for
and whether he ought to slip something into his palm.
But this representative of order left our friend only a
moment in suspense ; he presently turned away with
the remark, quite paternally uttered, that he hoped
the Count would make quite a stay ; upon which the
young man saw how wrong he should have been to
offer a tip. It was simply the American manner,
which had a finish of its own after all. Vogelstein's
servant had secured a porter with a truck, and he was
about to leave the place when he saw Pandora Day
dart out of the crowd and address herself with much
eagerness to the functionary who had just liberated
him. She had an open letter in her hand which she
gave him to read and over which he cast his eyes,
thoughtfully stroking his beard. Then she led him
away to where her parents sat on their luggage. Count
Otto sent off his servant with the porter and followed
Pandora, to whom he really wished to address a word
of farewell. The last thing they had said to each other
on the ship was that they should meet again on shore.
It seemed improbable however that the meeting
would occur anywhere but just here on the dock ;
inasmuch as Pandora was decidedly not in society,
where Vogelstein would be of course, and as, if Utica
—he had her sharp little sister's word for it—was
worse than what was about him there, he'd be hanged
if he'd go to Utica. He overtook Pandora quickly ;
she was in the act of introducing the representative
of order to her parents, quite in the same manner in
which she had introduced the Captain of the ship.
Mr. and Mrs. Day got up and shook hands with him

and they evidently all prepared to have a little talk. " I should like to introduce you to my brother and sister," he heard the girl say, and he saw her look about for these appendages. He caught her eye as she did so, and advanced with his hand outstretched, reflecting the while that evidently the Americans, whom he had always heard described as silent and practical, rejoiced to extravagance in the social graces. They dawdled and chattered like so many Neapolitans.

" Good-bye, Count Vogelstein," said Pandora, who was a little flushed with her various exertions but didn't look the worse for it. " I hope you'll have a splendid time and appreciate our country."

" I hope you'll get through all right," Vogelstein answered, smiling and feeling himself already more idiomatic.

" That gentleman's sick that I wrote to," she rejoined ; " isn't it too bad ? But he sent me down a letter to a friend of his—one of the examiners—and I guess we won't have any trouble. Mr. Lansing, let me make you acquainted with Count Vogelstein," she went on, presenting to her fellow-passenger the wearer of the straw hat and the breastpin, who shook hands with the young German as if he had never seen him before. Vogelstein's heart rose for an instant to his throat ; he thanked his stars he hadn't offered a tip to the friend of a gentleman who had often been mentioned to him and who had also been described by a member of Pandora's family as Pandora's lover.

" It's a case of ladies this time," Mr. Lansing remarked to him with a smile which seemed to confess surreptitiously, and as if neither party could be eager, to recognition.

" Well, Mr. Bellamy says you'll do anything for *him*," Pandora said, smiling very sweetly at Mr. Lansing. " We haven't got much ; we've been gone only two years."

Mr. Lansing scratched his head a little behind, with a movement that sent his straw hat forward in the direction of his nose. " I don't know as I'd do anything for him that I wouldn't do for you," he responded with an equal geniality. " I guess you'd better open that one "—and he gave a little affectionate kick to one of the trunks.

" Oh mother, isn't he lovely ? It's only your sea-things," Pandora cried, stooping over the coffer with the key in her hand.

" I don't know as I like showing them," Mrs. Day modestly murmured.

Vogelstein made his German salutation to the company in general, and to Pandora he offered an audible good-bye, which she returned in a bright friendly voice, but without looking round as she fumbled at the lock of her trunk.

" We'll try another, if you like," said Mr. Lansing good-humouredly.

" Oh no, it has got to be this one ! Good-bye, Count Vogelstein. I hope you'll judge us correctly ! "

The young man went his way and passed the barrier of the dock. Here he was met by his English valet with a face of consternation which led him to ask if a cab weren't forthcoming.

" They call 'em 'acks 'ere, sir," said the man, " and they're beyond everything. He wants thirty shillings to take you to the inn."

Vogelstein hesitated a moment. " Couldn't you find a German ? "

" By the way he talks he *is* a German ! " said the man ; and in a moment Count Otto began his career in America by discussing the tariff of hackney-coaches in the language of the fatherland.

HE went wherever he was asked, on principle, partly
to study American society and partly because in
Washington pastimes seemed to him not so numerous
that one could afford to neglect occasions. At the end
of two winters he had naturally had a good many of
various kinds—his study of American society had
yielded considerable fruit. When, however, in April,
during the second year of his residence, he presented
himself at a large party given by Mrs. Bonnycastle
and of which it was believed that it would be the last
serious affair of the season, his being there (and still
more his looking very fresh and talkative) was not the
consequence of a rule of conduct. He went to Mrs.
Bonnycastle's simply because he liked the lady, whose
receptions were the pleasantest in Washington, and
because if he didn't go there he didn't know what he
should do ; that absence of alternatives having become
familiar to him by the waters of the Potomac. There
were a great many things he did because if he didn't
do them he didn't know what he should do. It must
be added that in this case even if there had been an
alternative he would still have decided to go to Mrs.
Bonnycastle's. If her house wasn't the pleasantest
there it was at least difficult to say which was
pleasanter ; and the complaint sometimes made of it
that it was too limited, that it left out, on the whole,
more people than it took in, applied with much less

force when it was thrown open for a general party.
Toward the end of the social year, in those soft scented
days of the Washington spring when the air began to
show a southern glow and the Squares and Circles (to
which the wide empty avenues converged according
to a plan so ingenious, yet so bewildering) to flush with
pink blossom and to make one wish to sit on benches
—under this magic of expansion and condonation
Mrs. Bonnycastle, who during the winter had been
a good deal on the defensive, relaxed her vigilance a
little, became whimsically wilful, vernally reckless, as
it were, and ceased to calculate the consequences of
an hospitality which a reference to the back files or
even to the morning's issue of the newspapers might
easily prove a mistake. But Washington life, to
Count Otto's apprehension, was paved with mistakes ;
he felt himself in a society founded on fundamental
fallacies and triumphant blunders. Little addicted as
he was to the sportive view of existence, he had said
to himself at an early stage of his sojourn that the only
way to enjoy the great Republic would be to burn
one's standards and warm one's self at the blaze.
Such were the reflexions of a theoretic Teuton who
now walked for the most part amid the ashes of his
prejudices.

Mrs. Bonnycastle had endeavoured more than once
to explain to him the principles on which she received
certain people and ignored certain others ; but it was
with difficulty that he entered into her discriminations.
American promiscuity, goodness knew, had been
strange to him, but it was nothing to the queerness of
American criticism. This lady would discourse to
him *à perte de vue* on differences where he only saw
resemblances, and both the merits and the defects of
a good many members of Washington society, as this
society was interpreted to him by Mrs. Bonnycastle,
he was often at a loss to understand. Fortunately she

had a fund of good humour which, as I have intimated, was apt to come uppermost with the April blossoms and which made the people she didn't invite to her house almost as amusing to her as those she did. Her husband was not in politics, though politics were much in him ; but the couple had taken upon themselves the responsibilities of an active patriotism ; they thought it right to live in America, differing therein from many of their acquaintances who only, with some grimness, thought it inevitable. They had that burdensome heritage of foreign reminiscence with which so many Americans were saddled ; but they carried it more easily than most of their country-people, and one knew they had lived in Europe only by their present exultation, never in the least by their regrets. Their regrets, that is, were only for their ever having lived there, as Mrs. Bonnycastle once told the wife of a foreign minister. They solved all their problems successfully, including those of knowing none of the people they didn't wish to, and of finding plenty of occupation in a society supposed to be meagrely provided with resources for that body which Vogelstein was to hear invoked, again and again, with the mixture of desire and of deprecation that might have attended the mention of a secret vice, under the name of a leisure-class. When as the warm weather approached they opened both the wings of their house-door, it was because they thought it would entertain them and not because they were conscious of a pressure. Alfred Bonnycastle all winter indeed chafed a little at the definiteness of some of his wife's reserves ; it struck him that for Washington their society was really a little too good. Vogelstein still remembered the puzzled feeling—it had cleared up somewhat now—with which, more than a year before, he had heard Mr. Bonnycastle exclaim one evening, after a dinner in his own house, when every guest but the German secretary (who often sat late with the pair) had departed : " Hang it, there's only a month left ; let us be vulgar and have some fun—let us invite the President."

This was Mrs. Bonnycastle's carnival, and on the occasion to which I began my chapter by referring the President had not only been invited but had signified his intention of being present. I hasten to add that this was not the same august ruler to whom Alfred Bonnycastle's irreverent allusion had been made. The White House had received a new tenant —the old one was then just leaving it—and Count Otto had had the advantage, during the first eighteen months of his stay in America, of seeing an electoral campaign, a presidential inauguration and a distribution of spoils. He had been bewildered during those first weeks by finding that at the national capital in the houses he supposed to be the best, the head of the State was not a coveted guest ; for this could be the only explanation of Mr. Bonnycastle's whimsical suggestion of their inviting him, as it were, in carnival. His successor went out a good deal for a President.

The legislative session was over, but this made little difference in the aspect of Mrs. Bonnycastle's rooms, which even at the height of the congressional season could scarce be said to overflow with the representatives of the people. They were garnished with an occasional Senator, whose movements and utterances often appeared to be regarded with a mixture of alarm and indulgence, as if they would be disappointing if they weren't rather odd and yet might be dangerous if not carefully watched. Our young man had come to entertain a kindness for these conscript fathers of invisible families, who had something of the toga in the voluminous folds of their conversation, but were otherwise rather bare and bald, with stony wrinkles in their faces, like busts and statues of ancient lawgivers. There seemed to him something chill and exposed in their being at once so exalted and so naked ; there were frequent lonesome glances in their eyes, as if in the social world their legislative consciousness longed for the warmth of a few comfortable laws ready-made. Members of the House were very rare, and when Washington was new to the inquiring secretary he used sometimes to mistake them, in the halls and on the staircases where he met them, for the functionaries engaged, under stress, to usher in guests and wait at supper. It was only a little later that he perceived these latter public characters almost always to be impressive and of that rich racial hue which of itself served as a livery. At present, however, such confounding figures were much less to be met than during the months of winter, and indeed they were never frequent at Mrs. Bonnycastle's. At present the social vistas of Washington, like the vast fresh flatness of the lettered and numbered streets, which at this season seemed to Vogelstein more spacious and vague than ever, suggested but a paucity of political phenomena. Count Otto that evening knew every one or almost every one. There were often inquiring strangers, expecting great things, from New York and Boston, and to them, in the friendly Washington way, the young German was promptly introduced. It was a society in which familiarity reigned and in which people were liable to meet three times a day, so that their ultimate essence really became a matter of importance.

"I've got three new girls," Mrs. Bonnycastle said. "You must talk to them all."

"All at once ? " Vogelstein asked, reversing in fancy a position not at all unknown to him. He had so repeatedly heard himself addressed in even more than triple simultaneity.

"Oh no ; you must have something different for

each ; you can't get off that way. Haven't you discovered that the American girl expects something
especially adapted to herself ? It's very well for
Europe to have a few phrases that will do for any
girl. The American girl isn't *any* girl ; she's a remarkable specimen in a remarkable species. But you must
keep the best this evening for Miss Day."

" For Miss Day ! "—and Vogelstein had a stare of
intelligence. " Do you mean for Pandora ? "

Mrs. Bonnycastle broke on her side into free amusement. " One would think you had been looking for
her over the globe ! So you know her already—and
you call her by her pet name ? "

" Oh no, I don't know her ; that is I haven't seen
her or thought of her from that day to this. We came
to America in the same ship."

" Isn't she an American then ? "

" Oh yes ; she lives at Utica—in the interior."

" In the interior of Utica ? You can't mean my
young woman then, who lives in New York, where
she's a great beauty and a great belle and has been
immensely admired this winter."

"After all," said Count Otto, considering and a little
disappointed, " the name's not so uncommon ; it's
perhaps another. But has she rather strange eyes, a
little yellow, but very pretty, and a nose a little
arched ? "

" I can't tell you all that ; I haven't seen her.
She's staying with Mrs. Steuben. She only came a
day or two ago, and Mrs. Steuben's to bring her.
When she wrote to me to ask leave she told me what I
tell you. They haven't come yet."

Vogelstein felt a quick hope that the subject of this
correspondence might indeed be the young lady he
had parted from on the dock at New York, but the
indications seemed to point another way, and he had
no wish to cherish an illusion. It didn't seem to him

probable that the energetic girl who had introduced him to Mr. Lansing would have the entrée of the best house in Washington ; besides, Mrs. Bonnycastle's guest was described as a beauty and belonging to the brilliant city.

" What's the social position of Mrs. Steuben ? " it occurred to him to ask while he meditated. He had an earnest artless literal way of putting such a question as that ; you could see from it that he was very thorough.

Mrs. Bonnycastle met it, however, but with mocking laughter. " I'm sure I don't know ! What's your own ? "—and she left him to turn to her other guests, to several of whom she repeated his question. Could they tell her what was the social position of Mrs. Steuben ? There was Count Vogelstein who wanted to know. He instantly became aware of course that he oughtn't so to have expressed himself. Wasn't the lady's place in the scale sufficiently indicated by Mrs. Bonnycastle's acquaintance with her ? Still there were fine degrees, and he felt a little unduly snubbed. It was perfectly true, as he told his hostess, that with the quick wave of new impressions that had rolled over him after his arrival in America the image of Pandora was almost completely effaced ; he had seen innumerable things that were quite as remarkable in their way as the heroine of the *Donau*, but at the touch of the idea that he might see her and hear her again at any moment she became as vivid in his mind as if they had parted the day before : he remembered the exact shade of the eyes he had described to Mrs. Bonnycastle as yellow, the tone of her voice when at the last she expressed the hope he might judge America correctly. *Had* he judged America correctly ? If he were to meet her again she doubtless would try to ascertain. It would be going much too far to say that the idea of such an ordeal was terrible

to Count Otto ; but it may at least be said that the
thought of meeting Pandora Day made him nervous.
The fact is certainly singular, but I shall not take on
myself to explain it ; there are some things that even
the most philosophic historian isn't bound to account
for.

He wandered into another room, and there, at
the end of five minutes, he was introduced by Mrs.
Bonnycastle to one of the young ladies of whom she
had spoken. This was a very intelligent girl who
came from Boston and showed much acquaintance
with Spielhagen's novels. " Do you like them ? "
Vogelstein asked rather vaguely, not taking much
interest in the matter, as he read works of fiction only
in case of a sea-voyage. The young lady from Boston
looked pensive and concentrated ; then she answered
that she liked *some* of them *very* much, but that there
were others she didn't like—and she enumerated the
works that came under each of these heads. Spielhagen is a voluminous writer, and such a catalogue
took some time ; at the end of it moreover Vogelstein's question was not answered, for he couldn't
have told us whether she liked Spielhagen or not.

On the next topic, however, there was no doubt
about her feelings. They talked about Washington
as people talk only in the place itself, revolving about
the subject in widening and narrowing circles, perch-
ing successively on its many branches, considering it
from every point of view. Our young man had been
long enough in America to discover that after half a
century of social neglect Washington had become the
fashion and enjoyed the great advantage of being
a new resource in conversation. This was especially
the case in the months of spring, when the inhabitants
of the commercial cities came so far southward to
escape, after the long winter, that final affront. They
were all agreed that Washington was fascinating, and

none of them were better prepared to talk it over than
the Bostonians. Vogelstein originally had been rather
out of step with them ; he hadn't seized their point of
view, hadn't known with what they compared this
object of their infatuation. But now he knew everything ; he had settled down to the pace ; there wasn't
a possible phase of the discussion that could find him
at a loss. There was a kind of Hegelian element in
it ; in the light of these considerations the American
capital took on the semblance of a monstrous mystical infinite *Werden*. But they fatigued Vogelstein a
little, and it was his preference, as a general thing, not
to engage the same evening with more than one new-
comer, one visitor in the freshness of initiation. This
was why Mrs. Bonnycastle's expression of a wish to
introduce him to three young ladies had startled him
a little ; he saw a certain process, in which he flattered
himself that he had become proficient, but which was
after all tolerably exhausting, repeated for each of the
damsels. After separating from his judicious Bostonian he rather evaded Mrs. Bonnycastle, contenting
himself with the conversation of old friends, pitched
for the most part in a lower and easier key.

At last he heard it mentioned that the President
had arrived, had been some half-hour in the house,
and he went in search of the illustrious guest, whose
whereabouts at Washington parties was never indicated by a cluster of courtiers. He made it a point,
whenever he found himself in company with the
President, to pay him his respects, and he had not
been discouraged by the fact that there was no
association of ideas in the eye of the great man as he
put out his hand presidentially and said, " Happy to
meet you, sir." Count Otto felt himself taken for a
mere loyal subject, possibly for an office-seeker ; and
he used to reflect at such moments that the monarchical form had its merits : it provided a line of

heredity for the faculty of quick recognition. He had now some difficulty in finding the chief magistrate, and ended by learning that he was in the tea-room, a small apartment devoted to light refection near the entrance of the house. Here our young man presently perceived him seated on a sofa and in conversation with a lady. There were a number of people about the table, eating, drinking, talking; and the couple on the sofa, which was not near it but against the wall, in a shallow recess, looked a little withdrawn, as if they had sought seclusion and were disposed to profit by the diverted attention of the others. The President leaned back; his gloved hands, resting on either knee, made large white spots. He looked eminent, but he looked relaxed, and the lady beside him ministered freely and without scruple, it was clear, to this effect of his comfortably unbending. Vogelstein caught her voice as he approached. He heard her say "Well now, remember; I consider it a promise." She was beautifully dressed, in rose-colour; her hands were clasped in her lap and her eyes attached to the presidential profile.

"Well, madam, in that case it's about the fiftieth promise I've given to-day."

It was just as he heard these words, uttered by her companion in reply, that Count Otto checked himself, turned away and pretended to be looking for a cup of tea. It wasn't usual to disturb the President, even simply to shake hands, when he was sitting on a sofa with a lady, and the young secretary felt it in this case less possible than ever to break the rule, for the lady on the sofa was none other than Pandora Day. He had recognised her without her appearing to see him, and even with half an eye, as they said, had taken in that she was now a person to be reckoned with. She had an air of elation, of success; she shone, to intensity, in her rose-coloured

dress ; she was extracting promises from the ruler of
fifty millions of people. What an odd place to meet
her, her old shipmate thought, and how little one
could tell, after all, in America, who people were !
He didn't want to speak to her yet ; he wanted to
wait a little and learn more ; but meanwhile there
was something attractive in the fact that she was just
behind him, a few yards off, that if he should turn he
might see her again. It was she Mrs. Bonnycastle
had meant, it was she who was so much admired in
New York. Her face was the same, yet he had made
out in a moment that she was vaguely prettier ; he
had recognised the arch of her nose, which suggested
a fine ambition. He took some tea, which he hadn't
desired, in order not to go away. He remembered her
entourage on the steamer ; her father and mother, the
silent senseless burghers, so little " of the world," her
infant sister, so much of it, her humorous brother with
his tall hat and his influence in the smoking-room.
He remembered Mrs. Dangerfield's warnings—yet her
perplexities too—and the letter from Mr. Bellamy,
and the introduction to Mr. Lansing, and the way
Pandora had stooped down on the dirty dock, laughing and talking, mistress of the situation, to open her
trunk for the Customs. He was pretty sure she had
paid no duties that day ; this would naturally have
been the purpose of Mr. Bellamy's letter. Was she
still in correspondence with that gentleman, and had
he got over the sickness interfering with their reunion ?
These images and these questions coursed through
Count Otto's mind, and he saw it must be quite in
Pandora's line to be mistress of the situation, for there
was evidently nothing on the present occasion that
could call itself her master. He drank his tea and as
he put down his cup heard the President, behind him,
say : " Well, I guess my wife will wonder why I don't
come home."

"Why didn't you bring her with you?" Pandora benevolently asked.

"Well, she doesn't go out much. Then she has got her sister staying with her—Mrs. Runkle, from Natchez. She's a good deal of an invalid, and my wife doesn't like to leave her."

"She must be a very kind woman"—and there was a high mature competence in the way the girl sounded the note of approval.

"Well, I guess she isn't spoiled—yet."

"I should like very much to come and see her," said Pandora.

"Do come round. Couldn't you come some night?" the great man responded.

"Well, I'll come some time. And I shall remind you of your promise."

"All right. There's nothing like keeping it up. Well," said the President, "I must bid good-bye to these bright folks."

Vogelstein heard him rise from the sofa with his companion; after which he gave the pair time to pass out of the room before him. They did it with a certain impressive deliberation, people making way for the ruler of fifty millions and looking with a certain curiosity at the striking pink person at his side. When a little later he followed them across the hall, into one of the other rooms, he saw the host and hostess accompany the President to the door and two foreign ministers and a judge of the Supreme Court address themselves to Pandora Day. He resisted the impulse to join this circle: if he should speak to her at all he would somehow wish it to be in more privacy. She continued nevertheless to occupy him, and when Mrs. Bonnycastle came back from the hall he immediately approached her with an appeal. "I wish you'd tell me something more about that girl—that one opposite and in pink."

" The lovely Day—that's what they call her, I believe ? I wanted you to talk with her."

" I find she *is* the one I've met. But she seems to be so different here. I can't make it out," said Count Otto.

There was something in his expression that again moved Mrs. Bonnycastle to mjrth. " How we do puzzle you Europeans ! You look quite bewildered."

" I'm sorry I look so—I try to hide it. But of course we're very simple. Let me ask then a simple earnest childlike question. Are her parents also in society ? "

" Parents in society ? D'où tombez-vous ? Did you ever hear of the parents of a triumphant girl in rose-colour, with a nose all her own, in society ? "

" Is she then all alone ? " he went on with a strain of melancholy in his voice.

Mrs. Bonnycastle launched at him all her laughter. " You're too pathetic. Don't you know what she is ? I supposed of course you knew."

" It's exactly what I'm asking you."

" Why she's the new type. It has only come up lately. They have had articles about it in the papers. That's the reason I told Mrs. Steuben to bring her."

" The new type ? *What* new type, Mrs. Bonny-castle ? " he returned pleadingly—so conscious was he that all types in America were new.

Her laughter checked her reply a moment, and by the time she had recovered herself the young lady from Boston, with whom Vogelstein had been talking, stood there to take leave. This, for an American type, was an old one, he was sure ; and the process of parting between the guest and her hostess had an ancient elaboration. Count Otto waited a little ; then he turned away and walked up to Pandora Day, whose group of interlocutors had now been re-enforced by a gentleman who had held an important place in the

cabinet of the late occupant of the presidential chair.
He had asked Mrs. Bonnycastle if she were " all
alone " ; but there was nothing in her present situation to show her for solitary.   She wasn't sufficiently
alone for our friend's taste ; but he was impatient and
he hoped she'd give him a few words to himself.   She
recognised him without a moment's hesitation and
with the sweetest smile, a smile matching to a shade
the tone in which she said : " I was watching you.
I wondered if you weren't going to speak to me."

" Miss Day was watching him ! " one of the foreign
ministers exclaimed ; " and we flattered ourselves that
her attention was all with us.":

" I mean before," said the girl, " while I was
talking with the President."

At which the gentlemen began to laugh, one of
them remarking that this was the way the absent were
sacrificed, even the great ; while another put on record
that he hoped Vogelstein was duly flattered.

" Oh I was watching the President too," said
Pandora.   " I've got to watch *him*.   He has promised
me something."

" It must be the mission to England," the judge
of the Supreme Court suggested.   " A good position
for a lady ; they've got a lady at the head over
there."

" I wish they would send you to *my* country," one
of the foreign ministers suggested.   " I'd immediately
get recalled."

" Why perhaps in your country I wouldn't speak
to you ! It's only because you're here," the ex-
heroine of the *Donau* returned with a gay familiarity
which evidently ranked with her but as one of the arts
of defence.   " You'll see what mission it is when it
comes out.   But I'll speak to Count Vogelstein anywhere," she went on.   " He's an older friend than any
right here.   I've known him in difficult days."

"Oh yes, on the great ocean," the young man smiled. "On the watery waste, in the tempest!"

"Oh I don't mean that so much; we had a beautiful voyage and there wasn't any tempest. I mean when I was living in Utica. That's a watery waste if you like, and a tempest there would have been a pleasant variety."

"Your parents seemed to me so peaceful!" her associate in the other memories sighed with a vague wish to say something sympathetic.

"Oh you haven't seen them ashore! At Utica they were very lively. But that's no longer our natural home. Don't you remember I told you I was working for New York? Well, I worked—I had to work hard. But we've moved."

Count Otto clung to his interest. "And I hope they're happy."

"My father and mother? Oh they will be, in time. I must give them time. They're very young yet, they've years before them. And you've been always in Washington?" Pandora continued. "I suppose you've found out everything about everything."

"Oh no—there are some things I *can't* find out."

"Come and see me and perhaps I can help you. I'm very different from what I was in that phase. I've advanced a great deal since then."

"Oh how was Miss Day in that phase?" asked a cabinet minister of the last administration.

"She was delightful of course," Count Otto said.

"He's very flattering; I didn't open my mouth!" Pandora cried. "Here comes Mrs. Steuben to take me to some other place. I believe it's a literary party near the Capitol. Everything seems so separate in Washington. Mrs. Steuben's going to read a poem. I wish she'd read it here; wouldn't it do as well?"

This lady, arriving, signified to her young friend the necessity of their moving on. But Miss Day's

companions had various things to say to her before
giving her up. She had a vivid answer for each, and
it was brought home to Vogelstein while he listened
that this would be indeed, in her development, as she
said, another phase. Daughter of small burghers as
she might be she was really brilliant. He turned away
a little and while Mrs. Steuben waited put her a
question. He had made her half an hour before the
subject of that inquiry to which Mrs. Bonnycastle
returned so ambiguous an answer ; but this wasn't
because he failed of all direct acquaintance with the
amiable woman or of any general idea of the esteem
in which she was held. He had met her in various
places and had been at her house. She was the widow
of a commodore, was a handsome mild soft swaying
person, whom every one liked, with glossy bands of
black hair and a little ringlet depending behind each
ear. Some one had said that she looked like the *vieux
jeu* idea of the queen in *Hamlet*. She had written
verses which were admired in the South, wore a full-
length portrait of the commodore on her bosom and
spoke with the accent of Savannah. She had about
her a positive strong odour of Washington. It had
certainly been very superfluous in our young man to
question Mrs. Bonnycastle about her social position.

" Do kindly tell me," he said, lowering his voice,
" what's the type to which that young lady belongs ?
Mrs. Bonnycastle tells me it's a new one."

Mrs. Steuben for a moment fixed her liquid eyes
on the secretary of legation. She always seemed to
be translating the prose of your speech into the finer
rhythms with which her own mind was familiar. " Do
you think anything's really new ? " she then began to
flute. " I'm very fond of the old ; you know that's
a weakness of we Southerners." The poor lady, it
will be observed, had another weakness as well.
" What we often take to be the new is simply the old

127

under some novel form. Were there not remarkable natures in the past ? If you doubt it you should visit the South, where the past still lingers."

Vogelstein had been struck before this with Mrs. Steuben's pronunciation of the word by which her native latitudes were designated ; transcribing it from her lips you would have written it (as the nearest approach) the Sooth. But at present he scarce heeded this peculiarity ; he was wondering rather how a woman could be at once so copious and so uninforming. What did he care about the past or even about the Sooth ? He was afraid of starting her again. He looked at her, discouraged and helpless, as bewildered almost as Mrs. Bonnycastle had found him half an hour before ; looked also at the commodore, who, on her bosom, seemed to breathe again with his widow's respirations. " Call it an old type then if you like," he said in a moment. " All I want to know is what type it *is* ! It seems impossible," he gasped, " to find out."

" You can find out in the newspapers. They've had articles about it. They write about everything now. But it isn't true about Miss Day. It's one of the first families. Her great-grandfather was in the Revolution." Pandora by this time had given her attention again to Mrs. Steuben. She seemed to signify that she was ready to move on. " Wasn't your great-grandfather in the Revolution ? " the elder lady asked. " I'm telling Count Vogelstein about him."

" Why are you asking about my ancestors ? " the girl demanded of the young German with untempered brightness. " Is that the thing you said just now that you can't find out ? Well, if Mrs. Steuben will only be quiet you never will."

Mrs. Steuben shook her head rather dreamily. " Well, it's no trouble for we of the Sooth to be quiet. There's a kind of languor in our blood. Besides, we have to be to-day. But I've got to show some energy to-night. I've got to get you to the end of Pennsylvania Avenue."

Pandora gave her hand to Count Otto and asked him if he thought they should meet again. He answered that in Washington people were always meeting again and that at any rate he shouldn't fail to wait upon her. Hereupon, just as the two ladies were detaching themselves, Mrs. Steuben remarked that if the Count and Miss Day wished to meet again the picnic would be a good chance—the picnic she was getting up for the following Thursday. It was to consist of about twenty bright people, and they'd go down the Potomac to Mount Vernon. The Count answered that if Mrs. Steuben thought him bright enough he should be delighted to join the party ; and he was told the hour for which the tryst was taken.

He remained at Mrs. Bonnycastle's after every one had gone, and then he informed this lady of his reason for waiting. Would she have mercy on him and let him know, in a single word, before he went to rest—for without it rest would be impossible—what was this famous type to which Pandora Day belonged ?

" Gracious, you don't mean to say you've not found out that type yet ! " Mrs. Bonnycastle exclaimed with a return of her hilarity. " What have you been doing all the evening ? You Germans may be thorough, but you certainly are not quick ! "

It was Alfred Bonnycastle who at last took pity on him. " My dear Vogelstein, she's the latest freshest fruit of our great American evolution. She's the self-made girl ! "

Count Otto gazed a moment. " The fruit of the great American Revolution ? Yes, Mrs. Steuben told me her great-grandfather——" but the rest of his sentence was lost in a renewed explosion of Mrs. Bonnycastle's sense of the ridiculous. He bravely pushed his advantage, such as it was, however, and, desiring his host's definition to be defined, inquired what the self-made girl might be.

" Sit down and we'll tell you all about it," Mrs. Bonnycastle said. " I like talking this way, after a party's over. You can smoke if you like, and Alfred will open another window. Well, to begin with, the self-made girl's a new feature. That, however, you know. In the second place she isn't self-made at all. We all help to make her—we take such an interest in her."

" That's only after she's made ! " Alfred Bonny-castle broke in. " But it's Vogelstein that takes an interest. What on earth has started you up so on the subject of Miss Day ? "

The visitor explained as well as he could that it was merely the accident of his having crossed the ocean in the steamer with her ; but he felt the inadequacy of this account of the matter, felt it more than his hosts, who could know neither how little actual contact he had had with her on the ship, how much he had been affected by Mrs. Dangerfield's warnings, nor how much observation at the same time he had lavished on her. He sat there half an hour, and the warm dead stillness of the Washington night—nowhere are the nights so silent—came in at the open window, mingled with a soft sweet earthy smell, the smell of growing things and in particular, as he thought, of Mrs. Steuben's Sooth. Before he went away he had heard all about the self-made girl, and there was something in the picture that strongly impressed him. She was possible doubtless only in America ; American life had smoothed the way for her. She was not fast, nor emancipated, nor crude, nor loud, and there wasn't in her, of necessity at least, a grain of the stuff of which the adventuress is made. She was simply very success-ful, and her success was entirely personal. She hadn't

been born with the silver spoon of social opportunity ;
she had grasped it by honest exertion.   You knew her
by many different signs, but chiefly, infallibly, by the
appearance of her parents.   It was her parents who
told her story ; you always saw how little her parents
could have made her.   Her attitude with regard to
them might vary in different ways.   As the great fact
on her own side was that she had lifted herself from a
lower social plane, done it all herself, and done it by
the simple lever of her personality, it was naturally to
be expected that she would leave the authors of her
mere material being in the shade.   Sometimes she had
them in her wake, lost in the bubbles and the foam
that showed where she had passed ; sometimes, as
Alfred Bonnycastle said, she let them slide altogether ;
sometimes she kept them in close confinement, resort-
ing to them under cover of night and with every precaution ; sometimes she exhibited them to the public
in discreet glimpses, in prearranged attitudes.   But
the general characteristic of the self-made girl was
that, though it was frequently understood that she was
privately devoted to her kindred, she never attempted
to impose them on society, and it was striking that,
though in some of her manifestations a bore, she was
at her worst less of a bore than they.   They were almost
always solemn and portentous, and they were for the
most part of a deathly respectability.   She wasn't
necessarily snobbish, unless it was snobbish to want
the best.   She didn't cringe, she didn't make herself
smaller than she was ; she took on the contrary a
stand of her own and attracted things to herself.
Naturally she was possible only in America—only in a
country where whole ranges of competition and comparison were absent.   The natural history of this interesting creature was at last completely laid bare to the
earnest stranger, who, as he sat there in the animated
stillness, with the fragrant breath of the Western world

in his nostrils, was convinced of what he had already
suspected, that conversation in the great Republic was
more yearningly, not to say gropingly, psychological
than elsewhere. Another thing, as he learned, that
you knew the self-made girl by was her culture, which
was perhaps a little too restless and obvious. She had
usually got into society more or less by reading, and
her conversation was apt to be garnished with literary
allusions, even with familiar quotations. Vogelstein
hadn't had time to observe this element as a developed
form in Pandora Day ; but Alfred Bonnycastle hinted
that he wouldn't trust her to keep it under in a *tête-
à-tête*. It was needless to say that these young persons
had always been to Europe ; that was usually the
first place they got to. By such arts they sometimes
entered society on the other side before they did so at
home ; it was to be added at the same time that this
resource was less and less valuable, for Europe, in the
American world, had less and less prestige and people
in the Western hemisphere now kept a watch on that
roundabout road. All of which quite applied to
Pandora Day—the journey to Europe, the culture (as
exemplified in the books she read on the ship), the
relegation, the effacement, of the family. The only
thing that was exceptional was the rapidity of her
march ; for the jump she had taken since he left her in
the hands of Mr. Lansing struck Vogelstein, even after
he had made all allowance for the abnormal homo-
geneity of the American mass, as really considerable.
It took all her cleverness to account for such things.
When she " moved " from Utica—mobilised her com-
missariat—the battle appeared virtually to have been
gained.

Count Otto called the next day, and Mrs. Steuben's
blackamoor informed him, in the communicative
manner of his race, that the ladies had gone out to pay
some visits and look at the Capitol. Pandora appar-

ently had not hitherto examined this monument, and
our young man wished he had known, the evening
before, of her omission, so that he might have offered
to be her initiator. There is too obvious a connexion
for us to fail of catching it between his regret and the
fact that in leaving Mrs. Steuben's door he reminded
himself that he wanted a good walk, and that he thereupon took his way along Pennsylvania Avenue. His
walk had become fairly good by the time he reached
the great white edifice that unfolds its repeated colon-
nades and uplifts its isolated dome at the end of a
long vista of saloons and tobacco-shops. He slowly
climbed the great steps, hesitating a little, even
wondering why he had come. The superficial reason
was obvious enough, but there was a real one behind it
that struck him as rather wanting in the solidity which
should characterise the motives of an emissary of
Prince Bismarck. The superficial reason was a belief
that Mrs. Steuben would pay her visit first—it was
probably only a question of leaving cards—and bring
her young friend to the Capitol at the hour when the
yellow afternoon light would give a tone to the blank-
ness of its marble walls. The Capitol was a splendid
building, but it was rather wanting in tone. Vogelstein's curiosity about Pandora Day had been much
more quickened than checked by the revelations made
to him in Mrs. Bonnycastle's drawing-room. It was a
relief to have the creature classified ; but he had a
desire, of which he had not been conscious before, to
see really to the end how well, in other words how completely and artistically, a girl could make herself. His
calculations had been just, and he had wandered about
the rotunda for only ten minutes, looking again at
the paintings, commemorative of the national annals,
which occupy its lower spaces, and at the simulated
sculptures, so touchingly characteristic of early
American taste, which adorn its upper reaches, when

the charming women he had been counting on presented themselves in charge of a licensed guide. He went to meet them and didn't conceal from them that he had marked them for his very own. The encounter was happy on both sides, and he accompanied them through the queer and endless interior, through labyrinths of bleak bare development, into legislative and judicial halls. He thought it a hideous place ; he had seen it all before and asked himself what senseless game he was playing. In the lower House were certain bedaubed walls, in the basest style of imitation, which made him feel faintly sick, not to speak of a lobby adorned with artless prints and photographs of eminent defunct Congressmen that was all too serious for a joke and too comic for a Valhalla. But Pandora was greatly interested ; she thought the Capitol very fine ; it was easy to criticise the details, but as a whole it was the most impressive building she had ever seen. She proved a charming fellow tourist ; she had constantly something to say, but never said it too much ; it was impossible to drag in the wake of a *cicerone* less of a lengthening or an irritating chain. Vogelstein could see too that she wished to improve her mind ; she looked at the historical pictures, at the uncanny statues of local worthies, presented by the different States—they were of different sizes, as if they had been " numbered," in a shop—she asked questions of the guide and in the chamber of the Senate requested him to show her the chairs of the gentlemen from New York. She sat down in one of them, though Mrs. Steuben told her *that* Senator (she mistook the chair, dropping into another State) was a horrid old thing.

Throughout the hour he spent with her Vogelstein seemed to see how it was she had made herself. They walked about afterwards on the splendid terrace that surrounds the Capitol, the great marble floor on which it stands, and made vague remarks—Pandora's were the most definite—about the yellow sheen of the Potomac, the hazy hills of Virginia, the far-gleaming pediment of Arlington, the raw confused-looking country. Washington was beneath them, bristling and geometrical ; the long lines of its avenues seemed to stretch into national futures. Pandora asked Count Otto if he had ever been to Athens and, on his admitting so much, sought to know whether the eminence on which they stood didn't give him an idea of the Acropolis in its prime. Vogelstein deferred the satisfaction of this appeal to their next meeting ; he was glad—in spite of the appeal—to make pretexts for seeing her again. He did so on the morrow ; Mrs. Steuben's picnic was still three days distant. He called on Pandora a second time, also met her each evening in the Washington world. It took very little of this to remind him that he was forgetting both Mrs. Dangerfield's warnings and the admonitions—long familiar to him—of his own conscience. Was he in peril of love ? Was he to be sacrificed on the altar of the American girl, an altar at which those other poor fellows had poured out some of the bluest blood in Germany and he had himself taken oath he would never seriously worship ? He decided that he wasn't in real danger, that he had rather clinched his pre-cautions. It was true that a young person who had succeeded so well for herself might be a great help to her husband ; but this diplomatic aspirant preferred on the whole that his success should be his own : it wouldn't please him to have the air of being pushed by his wife. Such a wife as that would wish to push him, and he could hardly admit to himself that this was what fate had in reserve for him—to be propelled in his career by a young lady who would perhaps attempt to talk to the Kaiser as he had heard her the other night talk to the President. Would she consent to discontinue relations with her family, or would she wish still to borrow plastic relief from that domestic background ? That her family was so impossible was to a certain extent an advantage ; for if they had been a little better the question of a rupture would be less easy. He turned over these questions in spite of his security, or perhaps indeed because of it. The security made them speculative and disinterested.

They haunted him during the excursion to Mount Vernon, which took place according to traditions long established. Mrs. Steuben's confederates assembled on the steamer and were set afloat on the big brown stream which had already seemed to our special traveller to have too much bosom and too little bank. Here and there, however, he became conscious of a shore where there was something to look at, even though conscious at the same time that he had of old lost great opportunities of an idyllic cast in not having managed to be more " thrown with " a certain young lady on the deck of the North German Lloyd. The two turned round together to hang over Alexandria, which for Pandora, as she declared, was a picture of Old Virginia. She told Vogelstein that she was always hearing about it during the Civil War, ages before. Little girl as she had been at the time she remembered all the names that were on people's lips during those years of reiteration. This historic spot had a touch of the romance of rich decay, a reference to older things, to a dramatic past. The past of Alexandria appeared in the vista of three or four short streets sloping up a hill and lined with poor brick warehouses erected for merchandise that had ceased to come or go. It looked hot and blank and sleepy, down to the shabby waterside where tattered darkies dangled their bare feet from the edge of rotting wharves. Pandora was even more interested in Mount Vernon—when at last its wooded bluff began

to command the river—than she had been in the
Capitol, and after they had disembarked and ascended
to the celebrated mansion she insisted on going into
every room it contained. She " claimed for it," as she
said—some of her turns were so characteristic both
of her nationality and her own style—the finest situation in the world, and was distinct as to the shame of
their not giving it to the President for his country-seat.
Most of her companions had seen the house often, and
were now coupling themselves in the grounds according to their sympathies, so that it was easy for Vogelstein to offer the benefit of his own experience to
the most inquisitive member of the party. They were
not to lunch for another hour, and in the interval
the young man roamed with his first and fairest
acquaintance. The breath of the Potomac, on the
boat, had been a little harsh, but on the softly-curving
lawn, beneath the clustered trees, with the river rele-
gated to a mere shining presence far below and in the
distance, the day gave out nothing but its mildness,
the whole scene became noble and genial.

Count Otto could joke a little on great occasions,
and the present one was worthy of his humour. He
maintained to his companion that the shallow painted
mansion resembled a false house, a "wing" or structure
of daubed canvas, on the stage ; but she answered him
so well with certain economical palaces she had seen
in Germany, where, as she said, there was nothing but
china stoves and stuffed birds, that he was obliged to
allow the home of Washington to be after all really
gemüthlich. What he found so in fact was the soft
texture of the day, his personal situation, the sweetness
of his suspense. For suspense had decidedly become
his portion ; he was under a charm that made him feel
he was watching his own life and that his susceptibilities were beyond his control. It hung over him that
things might take a turn, from one hour to the other,

which would make them very different from what they
had been yet; and his heart certainly beat a little faster
as he wondered what that turn might be. Why did he
come to picnics on fragrant April days with American
girls who might lead him too far? Wouldn't such
girls be glad to marry a Pomeranian count? And
would they, after all, talk that way to the Kaiser? If
he were to marry one of them he should have to give
her several thorough lessons.

In their little tour of the house our young friend and
his companion had had a great many fellow visitors,
who had also arrived by the steamer and who had
hitherto not left them an ideal privacy. But the others
gradually dispersed; they circled about a kind of
showman who was the authorised guide, a big slow
genial vulgar heavily-bearded man, with a whimsical
edifying patronising tone, a tone that had immense
success when he stopped here and there to make his
points—to pass his eyes over his listening flock, then
fix them quite above it with a meditative look and
bring out some ancient pleasantry as if it were a
sudden inspiration. He made a cheerful thing, an
echo of the platform before the booth of a country
fair, even of a visit to the tomb of the *pater patriæ*.
It is enshrined in a kind of grotto in the grounds,
and Vogelstein remarked to Pandora that he was a
good man for the place, but was too familiar. "Oh
he'd have been familiar with Washington," said the
girl with the bright dryness with which she often
uttered amusing things. Vogelstein looked at her a
moment, and it came over him, as he smiled, that she
herself probably wouldn't have been abashed even by
the hero with whom history has taken fewest liberties.
"You look as if you could hardly believe that,"
Pandora went on. "You Germans are always in
such awe of great people." And it occurred to her
critic that perhaps after all Washington would have

liked her manner, which was wonderfully fresh and
natural. The man with the beard was an ideal
minister to American shrines; he played on the
curiosity of his little band with the touch of a master,
drawing them at the right moment away to see the
classic ice-house where the old lady had been found
weeping in the belief it was Washington's grave. While
this monument was under inspection our interesting
couple had the house to themselves, and they spent
some time on a pretty terrace where certain windows
of the second floor opened—a little roofless verandah
which overhung, in a manner, obliquely, all the
magnificence of the view; the immense sweep of the
river, the artistic plantations, the last-century garden
with its big box hedges and remains of old espaliers.
They lingered here for nearly half an hour, and it
was in this retirement that Vogelstein enjoyed the
only approach to intimate conversation appointed for
him, as was to appear, with a young woman in whom
he had been unable to persuade himself that he
was not absorbed. It's not necessary, and it's not
possible, that I should reproduce this colloquy; but
I may mention that it began—as they leaned against
the parapet of the terrace and heard the cheerful voice
of the showman wafted up to them from a distance—
with his saying to her rather abruptly that he couldn't
make out why they hadn't had more talk together
when they crossed the Atlantic.

"Well, I can if you can't," said Pandora. "I'd
have talked quick enough if you had spoken to me.
I spoke to you first."

"Yes, I remember that"—and it affected him
awkwardly.

"You listened too much to Mrs. Dangerfield."

He feigned a vagueness. "To Mrs. Dangerfield?"

"That woman you were always sitting with; she
told you not to speak to me. I've seen her in New

York ; she speaks to me now herself. She recommended you to have nothing to do with me."

" Oh how can you say such dreadful things ? " Count Otto cried with a very becoming blush.

" You know you can't deny it. You weren't attracted by my family. They're charming people when you know them. I don't have a better time anywhere than I have at home," the girl went on loyally. " But what does it matter ? My family are very happy. They're getting quite used to New York. Mrs. Dangerfield's a vulgar wretch—next winter she'll call on me."

" You are unlike any Mädchen I've ever seen—I don't understand you," said poor Vogelstein with the colour still in his face.

" Well, you never *will* understand me—probably ; but what difference does it make ? "

He attempted to tell her what difference, but I've no space to follow him here. It's known that when the German mind attempts to explain things it doesn't always reduce them to simplicity, and Pandora was first mystified, then amused, by some of the Count's revelations. At last I think she was a little frightened, for she remarked irrelevantly, with some decision, that luncheon would be ready and that they ought to join Mrs. Steuben. Her companion walked slowly, on purpose, as they left the house together, for he knew the pang of a vague sense that he was losing her.

" And shall you be in Washington many days yet ? " he appealed as they went.

" It will all depend. I'm expecting important news. What I shall do will be influenced by that."

The way she talked about expecting news—and important !—made him feel somehow that she had a career, that she was active and independent, so that he could scarcely hope to stop her as she passed. It was certainly true that he had never seen any girl like

her. It would have occurred to him that the news she
was expecting might have reference to the favour she
had begged of the President, if he hadn't already
made up his mind—in the calm of meditation after
that talk with the Bonnycastles—that this favour
must be a pleasantry. What she had said to him had a
discouraging, a somewhat chilling effect ; nevertheless
it was not without a certain ardour that he inquired
of her whether, so long as she stayed in Washington,
he mightn't pay her certain respectful attentions.

" As many as you like—and as respectful ones ;
but you won't keep them up for ever ! "

" You try to torment me," said Count Otto.

She waited to explain. " I mean that I may have
some of my family."

" I shall be delighted to see them again."

Again she just hung fire. " There are some you've
never seen."

In the afternoon, returning to Washington on the
steamer, Vogelstein received a warning. It came from
Mrs. Bonnycastle and constituted, oddly enough, the
second juncture at which an officious female friend
had, while sociably afloat with him, advised him on
the subject of Pandora Day.

" There's one thing we forgot to tell you the other
night about the self-made girl," said the lady of infinite
mirth. " It's never safe to fix your affections on her,
because she has almost always an impediment somewhere in the background."

He looked at her askance, but smiled and said : " I
should understand your information—for which I'm
so much obliged—a little better if I knew what you
mean by an impediment."

" Oh I mean she's always engaged to some young
man who belongs to her earlier phase."

" Her earlier phase ? "

" The time before she had made herself—when she

lived unconscious of her powers. A young man from Utica, say. They usually have to wait ; he's probably in a store. It's a long engagement."

Count Otto somehow preferred to understand as little as possible. " Do you mean a betrothal—to take effect ? "

" I don't mean anything German and moonstruck. I mean that piece of peculiarly American enterprise a premature engagement—to take effect, but too complacently, at the end of time."

Vogelstein very properly reflected that it was no use his having entered the diplomatic career if he weren't able to bear himself as if this interesting generalisation had no particular message for him. He did Mrs. Bonnycastle moreover the justice to believe that she wouldn't have approached the question with such levity if she had supposed she should make him wince. The whole thing was, like everything else, but for her to laugh at, and the betrayal moreover of a good intention. " I see, I see—the self-made girl has of course always had a past. Yes, and the young man in the store—from Utica—is part of her past."

" You express it perfectly," said Mrs. Bonnycastle. " I couldn't say it better myself."

" But with her present, with her future, when they change like this young lady's, I suppose everything else changes. How do you say it in America ? She lets him slide."

" We don't say it at all ! " Mrs. Bonnycastle cried. " She does nothing of the sort ; for what do you take her ? She sticks to him; that at least is what we *expect* her to do," she added with less assurance. " As I tell you, the type's new and the case under consideration. We haven't yet had time for complete study."

" Oh of course I hope she sticks to him," Vogelstein declared simply and with his German accent more audible, as it always was when he was slightly agitated.

For the rest of the trip he was rather restless. He wandered about the boat, talking little with the returning picnickers. Toward the last, as they drew near Washington and the white dome of the Capitol hung aloft before them, looking as simple as a suspended snowball, he found himself, on the deck, in proximity to Mrs. Steuben. He reproached himself with having rather neglected her during an entertainment for which he was indebted to her bounty, and he sought to repair his omission by a proper deference. But the only act of homage that occurred to him was to ask her as by chance whether Miss Day were, to her knowledge, engaged.

Mrs. Steuben turned her Southern eyes upon him with a look of almost romantic compassion. "To my knowledge? Why of course I'd know! I should think you'd know too. Didn't you know she was engaged? Why she has been engaged since she was sixteen."

Count Otto gazed at the dome of the Capitol. "To a gentleman from Utica?"

"Yes, a native of her place. She's expecting him soon."

"I'm so very glad to hear it," said Vogelstein, who decidedly, for his career, had promise. "And is she going to marry him?"

"Why what do people fall in love with each other *for*? I presume they'll marry when she gets round to it. Ah if she had only been from the Sooth——!"

At this he broke quickly in : "But why have they never brought it off, as you say, in so many years?"

"Well, at first she was too young, and then she thought her family ought to see Europe—of course they could see it better *with* her—and they spent some time there. And then Mr. Bellamy had some business difficulties that made him feel as if he didn't want to marry just then. But he has given up business and I presume feels more free. Of course it's rather long, but all the while they've been engaged. It's a true, true love," said Mrs. Steuben, whose sound of the adjective was that of a feeble flute.

" Is his name Mr. Bellamy ? " the Count asked with his haunting reminiscence. " D. F. Bellamy, so ? And has he been in a store ? "

" I don't know what kind of business it was : it was some kind of business in Utica. I think he had a branch in New York. He's one of the leading gentlemen of Utica and very highly educated. He's a good deal older than Miss Day. He's a very fine man—I presume a college man. He stands very high in Utica. I don't know why you look as if you doubted it."

Vogelstein assured Mrs. Steuben that he doubted nothing, and indeed what she told him was probably the more credible for seeming to him eminently strange. Bellamy had been the name of the gentleman who, a year and a half before, was to have met Pandora on the arrival of the German steamer ; it was in Bellamy's name that she had addressed herself with such effusion to Bellamy's friend, the man in the straw hat who was about to fumble in her mother's old clothes. This was a fact that seemed to Count Otto to finish the picture of her contradictions ; it wanted at present no touch to be complete. Yet even as it hung there before him it continued to fascinate him, and he stared at it, detached from surrounding things and feeling a little as if he had been pitched out of an overturned vehicle, till the boat bumped against one of the outstanding piles of the wharf at which Mrs. Steuben's party was to disembark. There was some delay in getting the steamer adjusted to the dock, during which the passengers watched the process over its side and extracted what entertainment they might from the appearance of the various persons collected to receive it. There were darkies and loafers and hackmen, and also vague individuals, the loosest and blankest he had ever seen anywhere, with tufts on their chins, toothpicks in their mouths, hands in their pockets, rumination in their jaws and diamond pins in their shirt-fronts, who looked as if they had sauntered over from Pennsylvania Avenue to while away half an hour, forsaking for that interval their various slanting postures in the porticoes of the hotels and the door-ways of the saloons.

"Oh I'm so glad! How sweet of you to come down!" It was a voice close to Count Otto's shoulder that spoke these words, and he had no need to turn to see from whom it proceeded. It had been in his ears the greater part of the day, though, as he now perceived, without the fullest richness of expression of which it was capable. Still less was he obliged to turn to discover to whom it was addressed, for the few simple words I have quoted had been flung across the narrowing interval of water, and a gentleman who had stepped to the edge of the dock without our young man's observing him tossed back an immediate reply.

"I got here by the three o'clock train. They told me in K Street where you were, and I thought I'd come down and meet you."

"Charming attention!" said Pandora Day with the laugh that seemed always to invite the whole of any company to partake in it; though for some moments after this she and her interlocutor appeared to continue the conversation only with their eyes. Meanwhile Vogelstein's also were not idle. He looked at her visitor from head to foot, and he was aware that she was quite unconscious of his own proximity. The gentleman before him was tall, good-looking, well-dressed; evidently he would stand well not only at Utica, but, judging from the way he had planted

145

himself on the dock, in any position that circumstances might compel him to take up. He was about forty years old ; he had a black moustache and he seemed to look at the world over some counter-like expanse on which he invited it all warily and pleasantly to put down first its idea of the terms of a transaction. He waved a gloved hand at Pandora as if, when she exclaimed " Gracious, ain't they long ! " to urge her to be patient. She was patient several seconds and then asked him if he had any news. He looked at her briefly, in silence, smiling, after which he drew from his pocket a large letter with an official-looking seal and shook it jocosely above his head. This was discreetly, covertly done. No one but our young man appeared aware of how much was taking place—and poor Count Otto mainly felt it in the air. The boat was touching the wharf and the space between the pair inconsiderable.

" Department of State ? " Pandora very prettily and soundlessly mouthed across at him.

" That's what they call it."

" Well, what country ? "

" What's your opinion of the Dutch ? " the gentleman asked for answer.

" Oh gracious ! " cried Pandora.

" Well, are you going to wait for the return trip ? " said the gentleman.

Our silent sufferer turned away, and presently Mrs. Steuben and her companion disembarked together. When this lady entered a carriage with Miss Day the gentleman who had spoken to the girl followed them ; the others scattered, and Vogelstein, declining with thanks a " lift " from Mrs. Bonnycastle, walked home alone and in some intensity of meditation. Two days later he saw in a newspaper an announcement that the President had offered the post of Minister to Holland to Mr. D. F. Bellamy of Utica ; and in the

course of a month he heard from Mrs. Steuben that
Pandora, a thousand other duties performed, had
finally " got round " to the altar of her own nuptials.
He communicated this news to Mrs. Bonnycastle,
who had not heard it but who, shrieking at the queer
face he showed her, met it with the remark that there
was now ground for a new induction as to the self-
made girl.

THE PATAGONIA

I

THE houses were dark in the August night and the perspective of Beacon Street, with its double chain of lamps, was a foreshortened desert. The club on the hill alone, from its semi-cylindrical front, projected a glow upon the dusky vagueness of the Common, and as I passed it I heard in the hot stillness the click of a pair of billiard-balls. As " every one " was out of town perhaps the servants, in the extravagance of their leisure, were profaning the tables. The heat was insufferable and I thought with joy of the morrow, of the deck of the steamer, the freshening breeze, the sense of getting out to sea. I was even glad of what I had learned in the afternoon at the office of the company—that at the eleventh hour an old ship with a lower standard of speed had been put on in place of the vessel in which I had taken my passage. America was roasting, England might very well be stuffy, and a slow passage (which at that season of the year would probably also be a fine one) was a guarantee of ten or twelve days of fresh air.

I strolled down the hill without meeting a creature, though I could see through the palings of the Common that that recreative expanse was peopled with dim forms. I remembered Mrs. Nettlepoint's house— she lived in those days (they are not so distant, but there have been changes) on the water-side, a little way beyond the spot at which the Public Garden

terminates ; and I reflected that like myself she would
be spending the night in Boston if it were true that,
as had been mentioned to me a few days before at
Mount Desert, she was to embark on the morrow for
Liverpool. I presently saw this appearance confirmed
by a light above her door and in two or three of her
windows, and I determined to ask for her, having
nothing to do till bedtime. I had come out simply
to pass an hour, leaving my hotel to the blaze of its
gas and the perspiration of its porters ; but it occurred
to me that my old friend might very well not know of
the substitution of the *Patagonia* for the *Scandinavia*,
so that I should be doing her a service to prepare her
mind. Besides, I could offer to help her, to look after
her in the morning : lone women are grateful for
support in taking ship for far countries.

It came to me indeed as I stood on her door-step
that as she had a son she might not after all be so
lone ; yet I remembered at the same time that Jasper
Nettlepoint was not quite a young man to lean upon,
having—as I at least supposed—a life of his own
and tastes and habits which had long since diverted
him from the maternal side. If he did happen just
now to be at home my solicitude would of course
seem officious ; for in his many wanderings—I believed he had roamed all over the globe—he would
certainly have learned how to manage. None the
less, in fine, I was very glad to show Mrs. Nettlepoint
I thought of her. With my long absence I had lost
sight of her ; but I had liked her of old, she had been
a good friend to my sisters, and I had in regard to her
that sense which is pleasant to those who in general
have gone astray or got detached, the sense that she
at least knew all about me. I could trust her at any
time to tell people I was respectable. Perhaps I was
conscious of how little I deserved this indulgence
when it came over me that I hadn't been near her

for ages. The measure of that neglect was given by
my vagueness of mind about Jasper. However, I
really belonged nowadays to a different generation ;
I was more the mother's contemporary than the
son's.

Mrs. Nettlepoint was at home : I found her in her
back drawing-room, where the wide windows opened
to the water. The room was dusky—it was too hot
for lamps—and she sat slowly moving her fan and
looking out on the little arm of the sea which is so
pretty at night, reflecting the lights of Cambridgeport
and Charlestown. I supposed she was musing on the
loved ones she was to leave behind, her married
daughters, her grandchildren ; but she struck a note
more specifically Bostonian as she said to me, pointing
with her fan to the Back Bay : " I shall see nothing
more charming than that over there, you know ! "
She made me very welcome, but her son had told her
about the *Patagonia*, for which she was sorry, as this
would mean a longer voyage. She was a poor creature
in any boat and mainly confined to her cabin even
in weather extravagantly termed fine—as if any
weather could be fine at sea.

" Ah then your son's going with you ? " I asked.

" Here he comes, he'll tell you for himself much
better than I can pretend to." Jasper Nettlepoint
at that moment joined us, dressed in white flannel
and carrying a large fan. " Well, my dear, have you
decided ? " his mother continued with no scant irony.
" He hasn't yet made up his mind, and we sail at ten
o'clock ! "

" What does it matter when my things are put
up ? " the young man said. " There's no crowd at
this moment ; there will be cabins to spare. I'm
waiting for a telegram—that will settle it. I just
walked up to the club to see if it was come—
they'll send it there because they suppose this house

unoccupied. Not yet, but I shall go back in twenty
minutes."

" Mercy, how you rush about in this temperature ! "
the poor lady exclaimed while I reflected that it was
perhaps *his* billiard-balls I had heard ten minutes
before. I was sure he was fond of billiards.

" Rush ? not in the least. I take it uncommon
easy."

" Ah I'm bound to say you do ! " Mrs. Nettlepoint
returned with inconsequence. I guessed at a certain
tension between the pair and a want of consideration
on the young man's part, arising perhaps from selfishness. His mother was nervous, in suspense, wanting
to be at rest as to whether she should have his company on the voyage or be obliged to struggle alone.
But as he stood there smiling and slowly moving his
fan he struck me somehow as a person on whom this
fact wouldn't sit too heavily. He was of the type of
those whom other people worry about, not of those
who worry about other people. Tall and strong, he
had a handsome face, with a round head and close-
curling hair ; the whites of his eyes and the enamel
of his teeth, under his brown moustache, gleamed
vaguely in the lights of the Back Bay. I made out
that he was sunburnt, as if he lived much in the open
air, and that he looked intelligent but also slightly
brutal, though not in a morose way. His brutality,
if he had any, was bright and finished. I had to tell
him who I was, but even then I saw how little he
placed me and that my explanations gave me in his
mind no great identity or at any rate no great importance. I foresaw that he would in intercourse make
me feel sometimes very young and sometimes very
old, caring himself but little which. He mentioned, as
if to show our companion that he might safely be left to
his own devices, that he had once started from London
to Bombay at three quarters of an hour's notice.

" Yes, and it must have been pleasant for the people you were with ! "

" Oh the people I was with—— ! " he returned ; and his tone appeared to signify that such people would always have to come off as they could. He asked if there were no cold drinks in the house, no lemonade, no iced syrups ; in such weather something of that sort ought always to be kept going. When his mother remarked that surely at the club they *were* kept going he went on : " Oh yes, I had various things there ; but you know I've walked down the hill since. One should have something at either end. May I ring and see ? " He rang while Mrs. Nettlepoint observed that with the people they had in the house, an establishment reduced naturally at such a moment to its simplest expression—they were burning up candle-ends and there were no luxuries—she wouldn't answer for the service. The matter ended in her leaving the room in quest of cordials with the female domestic who had arrived in response to the bell and in whom Jasper's appeal aroused no visible intelligence.

She remained away some time and I talked with her son, who was sociable but desultory and kept moving over the place, always with his fan, as if he were properly impatient. Sometimes he seated himself an instant on the window-sill, and then I made him out in fact thoroughly good-looking—a fine brown clean young athlete. He failed to tell me on what special contingency his decision depended ; he only alluded familiarly to an expected telegram, and I saw he was probably fond at no time of the trouble of explanations. His mother's absence was a sign that when it might be a question of gratifying him she had grown used to spare no pains, and I fancied her rummaging in some close storeroom, among old pre-serve-pots, while the dull maid-servant held the candle awry. I don't know whether this same vision was in his own eyes ; at all events it didn't prevent his saying suddenly, as he looked at his watch, that I must excuse him—he should have to go back to the club. He would return in half an hour—or in less. He walked away and I sat there alone, conscious, on the dark dismantled simplified scene, in the deep silence that rests on American towns during the hot season— there was now and then a far cry or a plash in the water, and at intervals the tinkle of the bells of the horse-cars on the long bridge, slow in the suffocating night—of the strange influence, half-sweet, half-sad, that abides in houses uninhabited or about to become so, in places muffled and bereaved, where the un- heeded sofas and patient belittered tables seem (like the disconcerted dogs, to whom everything is alike sinister) to recognise the eve of a journey.

After a while I heard the sound of voices, of steps, the rustle of dresses, and I looked round, supposing these things to denote the return of Mrs. Nettlepoint and her handmaiden with the refection prepared for her son. What I saw however was two other female forms, visitors apparently just admitted, and now ushered into the room. They were not announced— the servant turned her back on them and rambled off to our hostess. They advanced in a wavering tentative unintroduced way—partly, I could see, because the place was dark and partly because their visit was in its nature experimental, a flight of imagina- tion or a stretch of confidence. One of the ladies was stout and the other slim, and I made sure in a moment that one was talkative and the other re- served. It was further to be discerned that one was elderly and the other young, as well as that the fact of their unlikeness didn't prevent their being mother and daughter. Mrs. Nettlepoint reappeared in a very few minutes, but the interval had sufficed to establish a communication—really copious for the occasion—

between the strangers and the unknown gentleman whom they found in possession, hat and stick in hand. This was not my doing—for what had I to go upon?—and still less was it the doing of the younger and the more indifferent, or less courageous, lady. She spoke but once—when her companion informed me that she was going out to Europe the next day to be married. Then she protested " Oh mother ! " in a tone that struck me in the darkness as doubly odd, exciting my curiosity to see her face.

It had taken the elder woman but a moment to come to that, and to various other things, after I had explained that I myself was waiting for Mrs. Nettlepoint, who would doubtless soon come back.

" Well, she won't know me—I guess she hasn't ever heard much about me," the good lady said ; " but I've come from Mrs. Allen and I guess that will make it all right. I presume you know Mrs. Allen ? "

I was unacquainted with this influential personage, but I assented vaguely to the proposition. Mrs. Allen's emissary was good-humoured and familiar, but rather appealing than insistent (she remarked that if her friend *had* found time to come in the afternoon—she had so much to do, being just up for the day, that she couldn't be sure—it would be all right) ; and somehow even before she mentioned Merrimac Avenue (they had come all the way from there) my imagination had associated her with that indefinite social limbo known to the properly-constituted Boston mind as the South End—a nebulous region which condenses here and there into a pretty face, in which the daughters are an " improvement " on the mothers and are sometimes acquainted with gentlemen more gloriously domiciled, gentlemen whose wives and sisters are in turn not acquainted with them.

When at last Mrs. Nettlepoint came in, accompanied by candles and by a tray laden with glasses of

coloured fluid which emitted a cool tinkling, I was in
a position to officiate as master of the ceremonies, to
introduce Mrs. Mavis and Miss Grace Mavis, to
represent that Mrs. Allen had recommended them—
nay, had urged them—just to come that way, in-
formally and without fear ; Mrs. Allen who had been
prevented only by the pressure of occupations so characteristic of her (especially when up from Mattapoisett
for a few hours' desperate shopping) from herself call-
ing in the course of the day to explain who they were
and what was the favour they had to ask of her bene-
volent friend.   Good-natured women understand each
other even when so divided as to sit residentially above
and below the salt, as who should say ; by which token
our hostess had quickly mastered the main facts : Mrs.
Allen's visit that morning in Merrimac Avenue to
talk of Mrs. Amber's great idea, the classes at the
public schools in vacation (she was interested with an
equal charity to that of Mrs. Mavis—even in such
weather !—in those of the South End) for games and
exercises and music, to keep the poor unoccupied
children out of the streets ; then the revelation that it
had suddenly been settled almost from one hour to the
other that Grace should sail for Liverpool, Mr. Porterfield at last being ready.   He was taking a little holiday ; his mother was with him, they had come over
from Paris to see some of the celebrated old buildings
in England, and he had telegraphed to say that if
Grace would start right off they would just finish it up
and be married.   It often happened that when things
had dragged on that way for years they were all
huddled up at the end.   Of course in such a case she,
Mrs. Mavis, had had to fly round.   Her daughter's
passage was taken, but it seemed too dreadful she
should make her journey all alone, the first time she
had ever been at sea, without any companion or
escort.   *She* couldn't go—Mr. Mavis was too sick :

she hadn't even been able to get him off to the seaside.

"Well, Mrs. Nettlepoint's going in that ship," Mrs. Allen had said; and she had represented that nothing was simpler than to give her the girl in charge. When Mrs. Mavis had replied that this was all very well but that she didn't know the lady, Mrs. Allen had declared that that didn't make a speck of difference, for Mrs. Nettlepoint was kind enough for anything. It was easy enough to *know* her, if that was all the trouble! All Mrs. Mavis would have to do would be to go right up to her next morning, when she took her daughter to the ship (she would see her there on the deck with her party) and tell her fair and square what she wanted. Mrs. Nettlepoint had daughters herself and would easily understand. Very likely she'd even look after Grace a little on the other side, in such a queer situation, going out alone to the gentleman she was engaged to: she'd just help her, like a good Samaritan, to turn round before she was married. Mr. Porterfield seemed to think they wouldn't wait long, once she was there: they would have it right over at the American consul's. Mrs. Allen had said it would perhaps be better still to go and see Mrs. Nettlepoint beforehand, that day, to tell her what they wanted: then they wouldn't seem to spring it on her just as she was leaving. She herself (Mrs. Allen) would call and say a word for them if she could save ten minutes before catching her train. If she hadn't come it was because she hadn't saved her ten minutes; but she had made them feel that they must come all the same. Mrs. Mavis liked that better, because on the ship in the morning there would be such a confusion. She didn't think her daughter would be any trouble—conscientiously she didn't. It was just to have some one to speak to her and not sally forth like a servant-girl going to a situation.

" I see, I'm to act as a sort of bridesmaid and to give her away," Mrs. Nettlepoint obligingly said. Kind enough in fact for anything, she showed on this occasion that it was easy enough to know her. There is notoriously nothing less desirable than an imposed aggravation of effort at sea, but she accepted without betrayed dismay the burden of the young lady's dependence and allowed her, as Mrs. Mavis said, to hook herself on. She evidently had the habit of patience, and her reception of her visitors' story reminded me afresh—I was reminded of it whenever I returned to my native land—that my dear compatriots are the people in the world who most freely take mutual accommodation for granted. They have always had to help themselves, and have rather magnanimously failed to learn just where helping others is distinguishable from that. In no country are there fewer forms and more reciprocities.

It was doubtless not singular that the ladies from Merrimac Avenue shouldn't feel they were importunate : what was striking was that Mrs. Nettlepoint didn't appear to suspect it. However, she would in any case have thought it inhuman to show this—though I could see that under the surface she was amused at everything the more expressive of the pilgrims from the South End took for granted. I scarce know whether the attitude of the younger visitor added or not to the merit of her good nature. Mr. Porterfield's intended took no part in the demonstration, scarcely spoke, sat looking at the Back Bay and the lights on the long bridge. She declined the lemonade and the other mixtures which, at Mrs. Nettlepoint's request, I offered her, while her mother partook freely of everything and I reflected—for I as freely drained a glass or two in which the ice tinkled —that Mr. Jasper had better hurry back if he wished to enjoy these luxuries.

Was the effect of the young woman's reserve meanwhile ungracious, or was it only natural that in her
particular situation she shouldn't have a flow of compliment at her command ? I noticed that Mrs. Nettlepoint looked at her often, and certainly though she
was undemonstrative Miss Mavis was interesting.
The candle-light enabled me to see that though not in
the very first flower of her youth she was still fresh and
handsome. Her eyes and hair were dark, her face was
pale, and she held up her head as if, with its thick
braids and everything else involved in it, it were an
appurtenance she wasn't ashamed of. If her mother
was excellent and common she was not common—
not at least flagrantly so—and perhaps also not excellent. At all events she wouldn't be, in appearance
at least, a dreary appendage ; which in the case of a
person " hooking on " was always something gained.
Was it because something of a romantic or pathetic
interest usually attaches to a good creature who has
been the victim of a " long engagement " that this
young lady made an impression on me from the first
—favoured as I had been so quickly with this glimpse
of her history ? I could charge her certainly with no
positive appeal ; she only held her tongue and smiled,
and. her smile corrected whatever suggestion might
have forced itself upon me that the spirit within her
was dead—the spirit of that promise of which she
found herself doomed to carry out the letter.

What corrected it less, I must add, was an odd
recollection which gathered vividness as I listened to
it—a mental association evoked by the name of Mr.
Porterfield. Surely I had a personal impression, over-
smeared and confused, of the gentleman who was
waiting at Liverpool, or who presently would be, for
Mrs. Nettlepoint's protégée. I had met him, known
him, some time, somewhere, somehow, on the other
side. Wasn't he studying something, very hard,

somewhere—probably in Paris—ten years before, and
didn't he make extraordinarily neat drawings, linear
and architectural ? Didn't he go to a table d'hôte, at
two francs twenty-five, in the Rue Bonaparte, which
I then frequented, and didn't he wear spectacles and
a Scotch plaid arranged in a manner which seemed to
say " I've trustworthy information that that's the
way they do it in the Highlands " ? Wasn't he
exemplary to positive irritation, and very poor, poor
to positive oppression, so that I supposed he had no
overcoat and his tartan would be what he slept under
at night ? Wasn't he working very hard still, and
wouldn't he be, in the natural course, not yet satisfied
that he had found his feet or knew enough to launch
out ? He would be a man of long preparations—
Miss Mavis's white face seemed to speak to one of that.
It struck me that if I had been in love with her I
shouldn't have needed to lay such a train for the
closer approach. Architecture was his line and he
was a pupil of the École des Beaux Arts. This
reminiscence grew so much more vivid with me that
at the end of ten minutes I had an odd sense of
knowing—by implication—a good deal about the
young lady.

Even after it was settled that Mrs. Nettlepoint
would do everything possible for her the other visitor
sat sipping our iced liquid and telling how " low "
Mr. Mavis had been. At this period the girl's silence
struck me as still more conscious, partly perhaps
because she deprecated her mother's free flow—she
was enough of an " improvement " to measure that—
and partly because she was too distressed by the idea
of leaving her infirm, her perhaps dying father. It
wasn't indistinguishable that they were poor and that
she would take out a very small purse for her trousseau.
For Mr. Porterfield to make up the sum his own case
would have had moreover greatly to change. If he

had enriched himself by the successful practice of his
profession I had encountered no edifice he had reared
—his reputation hadn't come to my ears.

Mrs. Nettlepoint notified her new friends that she
was a very inactive person at sea: she was prepared
to suffer to the full with Miss Mavis, but not prepared
to pace the deck with her, to struggle with her, to
accompany her to meals. To this the girl replied
that she would trouble her little, she was sure: she
was convinced she should prove a wretched sailor and
spend the voyage on her back. Her mother scoffed
at this picture, prophesying perfect weather and a
lovely time, and I interposed to the effect that if I
might be trusted, as a tame bachelor fairly sea-
seasoned, I should be delighted to give the new
member of our party an arm or any other countenance whenever she should require it. Both the ladies
thanked me for this—taking my professions with no
sort of abatement—and the elder one declared that
we were evidently going to be such a sociable group
that it was too bad to have to stay at home. She
asked Mrs. Nettlepoint if there were any one else in
our party, and when our hostess mentioned her son—
there was a chance of his embarking but (wasn't it
absurd?) he hadn't decided yet—she returned with
extraordinary candour: "Oh dear, I do hope he'll
go: that would be so lovely for Grace."

Somehow the words made me think of poor Mr.
Porterfield's tartan, especially as Jasper Nettlepoint
strolled in again at that moment. His mother at
once challenged him: it was ten o'clock; had he by
chance made up his great mind? Apparently he
failed to hear her, being in the first place surprised at
the strange ladies and then struck with the fact that
one of them wasn't strange. The young man, after a
slight hesitation, greeted Miss Mavis with a handshake
and a "Oh good-evening, how do you do?" He

didn't utter her name—which I could see he must have forgotten ; but she immediately pronounced his, availing herself of the American girl's discretion to " present " him to her mother.

" Well, you might have told me you knew him all this time ! " that lady jovially cried. Then she had an equal confidence for Mrs. Nettlepoint. "It would have saved me a worry—an acquaintance already begun."

" Ah my son's acquaintances——! " our hostess murmured.

" Yes, and my daughter's too ! " Mrs. Mavis gaily echoed. " Mrs. Allen didn't tell us *you* were going," she continued to the young man.

" She'd have been clever if she had been able to ! " Mrs. Nettlepoint sighed.

" Dear mother, I have my telegram," Jasper remarked, looking at Grace Mavis.

" I know you very little," the girl said, returning his observation.

" I've danced with you at some ball—for some sufferers by something or other."

" I think it was an inundation or a big fire," she a little languidly smiled. " But it was a long time ago —and I haven't seen you since."

" I've been in far countries—to my loss. I should have said it was a big fire."

" It was at the Horticultural Hall. I didn't remember your name," said Grace Mavis.

" That's very unkind of you, when I recall vividly that you had a pink dress."

" Oh I remember that dress—your strawberry tarletan : you looked lovely in it ! " Mrs. Mavis broke out. " You must get another just like it—on the other side."

" Yes, your daughter looked charming in it," said Jasper Nettlepoint. Then he added to the girl : " Yet you mentioned my name to your mother."

" It came back to me—seeing you here. I had no idea this was your home."

" Well, I confess it isn't, much. Oh there are some drinks ! "—he approached the tray and its glasses.

" Indeed there are and quite delicious " — Mrs. Mavis largely wiped her mouth.

" Won't you have another then ?—a pink one, like your daughter's gown."

" With pleasure, sir. Oh do see them over," Mrs. Mavis continued, accepting from the young man's hand a third tumbler.

" My mother and that gentleman ? Surely they can take care of themselves," he freely pleaded.

" Then my daughter—she has a claim as an old friend."

But his mother had by this time interposed. " Jasper, what does your telegram say ? "

He paid her no heed : he stood there with his glass in his hand, looking from Mrs. Mavis to Miss Grace.

" Ah leave her to me, madam ; I'm quite competent," I said to Mrs. Mavis.

Then the young man gave me his attention. The next minute he asked of the girl : " Do you mean you're going to Europe ? "

" Yes, to-morrow. In the same ship as your mother."

" That's what we've come here for, to see all about it," said Mrs. Mavis.

" My son, take pity on me and tell me what light your telegram throws," Mrs. Nettlepoint went on.

" I will, dearest, when I've quenched my thirst." And he slowly drained his glass.

" Well, I declare you're worse than Gracie," Mrs. Mavis commented. " She was first one thing and then the other—but only about up to three o'clock yesterday."

" Excuse me—won't you take something ? " Jasper
inquired of Gracie ; who however still declined, as if
to make up for her mother's copious *consommation*.   I
found myself quite aware that the two ladies would
do well to take leave, the question of Mrs. Nettlepoint's good will being so satisfactorily settled and the
meeting of the morrow at the ship so near at hand ;
and I went so far as to judge that their protracted
stay, with their hostess visibly in a fidget, gave the
last proof of their want of breeding.   Miss Grace after
all then was not such an improvement on her mother,
for she easily might have taken the initiative of
departure, in spite of Mrs. Mavis's evident " game "
of making her own absorption of refreshment last as
long as possible.   I watched the girl with increasing
interest ; I couldn't help asking myself a question or
two about her and even perceiving already (in a dim
and general way) that rather marked embarrassment,
or at least anxiety attended her.   Wasn't it compli-
cating that she should have needed, by remaining
long enough, to assuage a certain suspense, to learn
whether or no Jasper were going to sail ?   Hadn't
something particular passed between them on the
occasion or at the period to which we had caught
their allusion, and didn't she really not know her
mother was bringing her to *his* mother's, though she
apparently had thought it well not to betray knowledge ?   Such things were symptomatic — though
indeed one scarce knew of what—on the part of a
young lady betrothed to that curious cross-barred
phantom of a Mr. Porterfield.   But I am bound to
add that she gave me no further warrant for wonder
than was conveyed in her all tacitly and covertly
encouraging her mother to linger.   Somehow I had a
sense that *she* was conscious of the indecency of this.
I got up myself to go, but Mrs. Nettlepoint detained
me after seeing that my movement wouldn't be taken

as a hint, and I felt she wished me not to leave my fellow visitors on her hands. Jasper complained of the closeness of the room, said that it was not a night to sit in a room—one ought to be out in the air, under the sky. He denounced the windows that overlooked the water for not opening upon a balcony or a terrace, until his mother, whom he hadn't yet satisfied about his telegram, reminded him that there was a beautiful balcony in front, with room for a dozen people. She assured him we would go and sit there if it would please him.

" It will be nice and cool to-morrow, when we steam into the great ocean," said Miss Mavis, express-ing with more vivacity than she had yet thrown into any of her utterances my own thought of half an hour before. Mrs. Nettlepoint replied that it would prob-ably be freezing cold, and her son murmured that he would go and try the drawing-room balcony and report upon it. Just as he was turning away he said, smiling, to Miss Mavis : " Won't you come with me and see if it's pleasant ? "

" Oh well, we had better not stay all night ! " her mother exclaimed, but still without moving. The girl moved, after a moment's hesitation ; she rose and accompanied Jasper to the other room. I saw how her slim tallness showed to advantage as she walked, and that she looked well as she passed, with her head thrown back, into the darkness of the other part of the house. There was something rather marked, rather surprising—I scarcely knew why, for the act in itself was simple enough—in her acceptance of such a plea, and perhaps it was our sense of this that held the rest of us somewhat stiffly silent as she remained away. I was waiting for Mrs. Mavis to go, so that I myself might go ; and Mrs. Nettlepoint was waiting for her to go so that I mightn't. This doubtless made the young lady's absence appear to us

longer than it really was—it was probably very brief.
Her mother moreover, I think, had now a vague lapse
from ease. Jasper Nettlepoint presently returned to
the back drawing-room to serve his companion with
our lucent syrup, and he took occasion to remark that
it was lovely on the balcony : one really got some air,
the breeze being from that quarter. I remembered,
as he went away with his tinkling tumbler, that from
my hand, a few minutes before, Miss Mavis had not
been willing to accept this innocent offering. A little
later Mrs. Nettlepoint said : " Well, if it's so pleasant
there we had better go ourselves." So we passed to
the front and in the other room met the two young
people coming in from the balcony. I was to wonder,
in the light of later things, exactly how long they had
occupied together a couple of the set of cane chairs
garnishing the place in summer. If it had been but
five minutes that only made subsequent events more
curious. " We must go, mother," Miss Mavis immediately said ; and a moment after, with a little
renewal of chatter as to our general meeting on the
ship, the visitors had taken leave. Jasper went down
with them to the door and as soon as they had got off
Mrs. Nettlepoint quite richly exhaled her impression.
" Ah but'll she be a bore—she'll be a bore of bores ! "

" Not through talking too much, surely."

" An affectation of silence is as bad. I hate that
particular *pose* ; it's coming up very much now ; an
imitation of the English, like everything else. A girl
who tries to be statuesque at sea—that will act on
one's nerves ! "

" I don't know what she tries to be, but she succeeds
in being very handsome."

" So much the better for you. I'll leave her to you,
for I shall be shut up. I like her being placed under
my ' care ' ! " my friend cried.

" She'll be under Jasper's," I remarked.

" Ah he won't go," she wailed—" I want it too much ! "

" But I didn't see it that way. I have an idea he'll go."

" Why didn't he tell me so then—when he came in ? "

" He was diverted by that young woman—a beautiful unexpected girl sitting there."

" Diverted from his mother and her fond hope ?— his mother trembling for his decision ? "

" Well "—I pieced it together—" she's an old friend, older than we know. It was a meeting after a long separation."

" Yes, such a lot of them as he does know ! " Mrs. Nettlepoint sighed.

" Such a lot of them ? "

" He has so many female friends—in the most varied circles."

" Well, we can close round her then," I returned ; " for I on my side know, or used to know, her young man."

" Her intended ? "—she had a light of relief for this.

" The very one she's going out to. He can't, by the way," it occurred to me, " be very young now."

" How odd it sounds—her muddling after him ! " said Mrs. Nettlepoint.

I was going to reply that it wasn't odd if you knew Mr. Porterfield, but I reflected that that perhaps only made it odder. I told my companion briefly who he was—that I had met him in the old Paris days, when I believed for a fleeting hour that I could learn to paint, when I lived with the *jeunesse des écoles* ; and her comment on this was simply : " Well, he had better have come out for her ! "

" Perhaps so. She looked to me as she sat there as if she might change her mind at the last moment."

" About her marriage ? "

" About sailing. But she won't change now."

Jasper came back, and his mother instantly challenged him. " Well, *are* you going ? "

" Yes, I shall go "—he was finally at peace about it. " I've got my telegram."

" Oh your telegram ! "—I ventured a little to jeer. " That charming girl's your telegram."

He gave me a look, but in the dusk I couldn't make out very well what it conveyed. Then he bent over his mother, kissing her. " My news isn't particularly satisfactory. I'm going for *you*."

" Oh you humbug ! " she replied. But she was of course delighted.

II

PEOPLE usually spend the first hours of a voyage in
squeezing themselves into their cabins, taking their
little precautions, either so excessive or so inadequate,
wondering how they can pass so many days in such
a hole and asking idiotic questions of the stewards,
who appear in comparison rare men of the world.
My own initiations were rapid, as became an old
sailor, and so, it seemed, were Miss Mavis's, for when
I mounted to the deck at the end of half an hour I
found her there alone, in the stern of the ship, her
eyes on the dwindling continent. It dwindled very
fast for so big a place. I accosted her, having had no
conversation with her amid the crowd of leave-takers
and the muddle of farewells before we put off ; we
talked a little about the boat, our fellow-passengers
and our prospects, and then I said : " I think you
mentioned last night a name I know—that of Mr.
Porterfield."

" Oh no I didn't ! " she answered very straight
while she smiled at me through her closely - drawn
veil.

" Then it was your mother."

" Very likely it was my mother." And she continued to smile as if I ought to have known the
difference.

" I venture to allude to him because I've an idea
I used to know him," I went on.

171

" Oh I see." And beyond this remark she appeared to take no interest ; she left it to me to make any connexion.

" That is if it's the same one." It struck me as feeble to say nothing more ; so I added " My Mr. Porterfield was called David."

" Well, so is ours." " Ours " affected me as clever.

" I suppose I shall see him again if he's to meet you at Liverpool," I continued.

" Well, it will be bad if he doesn't."

It was too soon for me to have the idea that it would be bad if he did : that only came later. So I remarked that, not having seen him for so many years, it was very possible I shouldn't know him.

" Well, I've not seen him for a considerable time, but I expect I shall know him all the same."

" Oh with you it's different," I returned with harmlessly bright significance. " Hasn't he been back since those days ? "

" I don't know," she sturdily professed, " what days you mean."

" When I knew him in Paris—ages ago. He was a pupil of the École des Beaux Arts. He was studying architecture."

" Well, he's studying it still," said Grace Mavis.

" Hasn't he learned it yet ? "

" I don't know what he has learned. I shall see." Then she added for the benefit of my perhaps undue levity : " Architecture's very difficult and he's tremendously thorough."

" Oh yes, I remember that. He was an admirable worker. But he must have become quite a foreigner if it's so many years since he has been at home."

She seemed to regard this proposition at first as complicated ; but she did what she could for me. " Oh he's not changeable. If he were changeable—— "
Then, however, she paused. I daresay she had been

172

going to observe that if he were changeable he would long ago have given her up. After an instant she went on : " He wouldn't have stuck so to his profession. You can't make much by it."

I sought to attenuate her rather odd maidenly grimness. " It depends on what you call much."

" It doesn't make you rich."

" Oh of course you've got to practise it—and to practise it long."

" Yes—so Mr. Porterfield says."

Something in the way she uttered these words made me laugh—they were so calm an implication that the gentleman in question didn't live up to his principles. But I checked myself, asking her if she expected to remain in Europe long—to what one might call settle.

" Well, it will be a good while if it takes me as long to come back as it has taken me to go out."

" And I think your mother said last night that it was your first visit."

Miss Mavis, in her deliberate way, met my eyes. " Didn't mother talk ! "

" It was all very interesting."

She continued to look at me. " You don't think that," she then simply stated.

" What have I to gain then by saying it ? "

" Oh men have always something to gain."

" You make me in that case feel a terrible failure ! I hope at any rate that it gives you pleasure," I went on, " the idea of seeing foreign lands."

" Mercy—I should think so ! "

This was almost genial, and it cheered me proportionately. " It's a pity our ship's not one of the fast ones, if you're impatient."

She was silent a little ; after which she brought out : " Oh I guess it'll be fast enough ! "

That evening I went in to see Mrs. Nettlepoint and

sat on her sea-trunk, which was pulled out from under the berth to accommodate me. It was nine o'clock but not quite dark, as our northward course had already taken us into the latitude of the longer days. She had made her nest admirably and now rested from her labours ; she lay upon her sofa in a dressing-gown and a cap that became her. It was her regular practice to spend the voyage in her cabin, which smelt positively good—such was the refinement of her art ; and she had a secret peculiar to herself for keeping her port open without shipping seas. She hated what she called the mess of the ship and the idea, if she should go above, of meeting stewards with plates of supererogatory food. She professed to be content with her situation—we promised to lend each other books and I assured her familiarly that I should be in and out of her room a dozen times a day—pitying me for having to mingle in society. She judged this a limited privilege, for on the deck before we left the wharf she had taken a view of our fellow-passengers.

" Oh I'm an inveterate, almost a professional observer," I replied, " and with that vice I'm as well occupied as an old woman in the sun with her knitting. It makes me, in any situation, just inordinately and submissively *see* things. I shall see them even here and shall come down very often and tell you about them. You're not interested to-day, but you will be to-morrow, for a ship's a great school of gossip. You won't believe the number of researches and problems you'll be engaged in by the middle of the voyage."

" I ? Never in the world !—lying here with my nose in a book and not caring a straw."

" You'll participate at second hand. You'll see through my eyes, hang upon my lips, take sides, feel passions, all sorts of sympathies and indignations. I've an idea," I further developed, " that your young lady's the person on board who will interest me most."

" ' Mine ' indeed ! She hasn't been near me since we left the dock."

" There you are—you do feel she owes you something. Well," I added, " she's very curious."

" You've such cold-blooded terms ! " Mrs. Nettlepoint wailed. " Elle ne sait pas se conduire ; she ought to have come to ask about me."

" Yes, since you're under her care," I laughed. " As for her not knowing how to behave—well, that's exactly what we shall see."

" You will, but not I ! I wash my hands of her."

" Don't say that—don't say that."

Mrs. Nettlepoint looked at me a moment. " Why do you speak so solemnly ? "

In return I considered her. " I'll tell you before we land. And have you seen much of your son ? "

" Oh yes, he has come in several times. He seems very much pleased. He has got a cabin to himself."

" That's great luck," I said, " but I've an idea he's always in luck. I was sure I should have to offer him the second berth in my room."

" And you wouldn't have enjoyed that, because you don't like him," she took upon herself to say.

" What put that into your head ? "

" It isn't in my head—it's in my heart, my cœur de mère. We guess those things. You think he's selfish. I could see it last night."

" Dear lady," I contrived promptly enough to reply, " I've no general ideas about him at all. He's just one of the phenomena I am going to observe. He seems to me a very fine young man. However," I added, " since you've mentioned last night I'll admit that I thought he rather tantalised you. He played with your suspense."

" Why he came at the last just to please me," said Mrs. Nettlepoint.

I was silent a little. " Are you sure it was for
your sake ? "

" Ah, perhaps it was for yours ! "

I bore up, however, against this thrust, characteristic of perfidious woman when you présume to
side with her against a fond tormentor. " When he
went out on the balcony with that girl," I found
assurance to suggest, " perhaps she asked him to come
for *hers*."

" Perhaps she did. But why should he do everything she asks him—such as she is ? "

" I don't know yet, but perhaps I shall know later.
Not that he'll tell me—for he'll never tell me anything : he's not," I consistently opined, " one of those
who tell."

" If she didn't ask him, what you say is a great
wrong to her," said Mrs. Nettlepoint.

" Yes, if she didn't. But you say that to protect
Jasper—not to protect her," I smiled.

" You *are* cold-blooded—it's uncanny ! " my friend
exclaimed.

" Ah this is nothing yet ! Wait a while—you'll
see. At sea in general I'm awful—I exceed the
limits. If I've outraged her in thought I'll jump
overboard. There are ways of asking—a man doesn't
need to tell a woman that—without the crude words."

" I don't know what you imagine between them,"
said Mrs. Nettlepoint.

" Well, nothing," I allowed, " but what was visible
on the surface. It transpired, as the newspapers say,
that they were old friends."

" He met her at some promiscuous party—I asked
him about it afterwards. She's not a person "—my
hostess was confident—" whom he could ever think
of seriously."

" That's exactly what I believe."

" You don't observe—you know—you imagine,"

Mrs. Nettlepoint continued to argue. " How do you reconcile her laying a trap for Jasper with her going out to Liverpool on an errand of love ? "

Oh I wasn't to be caught that way ! " I don't for an instant suppose she laid a trap ; I believe she acted on the impulse of the moment. She's going out to Liverpool on an errand of marriage ; that's not necessarily the same thing as an errand of love, especially for one who happens to have had a personal impression of the gentleman she's engaged to."

" Well, there are certain decencies which in such a situation the most abandoned of her sex would still observe. You apparently judge her capable—on no evidence—of violating them."

" Ah you don't understand the shades of things," I returned. " Decencies and violations, dear lady—there's no need for such heavy artillery ! I can perfectly imagine that without the least immodesty she should have said to Jasper on the balcony, in fact if not in words : ' I'm in dreadful spirits, but if you come I shall feel better, and that will be pleasant for you too.' "

" And why is she in dreadful spirits ? "

" She isn't ! " I replied, laughing.

My poor friend wondered. " What then is she doing ? "

" She's walking with your son."

Mrs. Nettlepoint for a moment said nothing ; then she treated me to another inconsequence. " Ah she's horrid ! "

" No, she's charming ! " I protested.

" You mean she's ' curious ' ? "

" Well, for me it's the same thing ! "

This led my friend of course to declare once more that I was cold-blooded. On the afternoon of the morrow we had another talk, and she told me that in the morning Miss Mavis had paid her a long visit.

She knew nothing, poor creature, about anything, but
her intentions were good and she was evidently in her
own eyes conscientious and decorous. And Mrs.
Nettlepoint concluded these remarks with the sigh :
" Unfortunate person ! "

" You think she's a good deal to be pitied then ? "

" Well, her story sounds dreary—she told me a
good deal of it. She fell to talking little by little
and went from one thing to another. She's in that
situation when a girl *must* open herself—to some
woman."

" Hasn't she got Jasper ? " I asked.

" He isn't a woman. You strike me as jealous of
him," my companion added.

" I daresay *he* thinks so—or will before the end.
Ah no—ah no ! " And I asked Mrs. Nettlepoint if
our young lady struck her as, very grossly, a flirt.
She gave me no answer, but went on to remark that
she found it odd and interesting to see the way a girl
like Grace Mavis resembled the girls of the kind she
herself knew better, the girls of " society," at the same
time that she differed from them ; and the way the
differences and resemblances were so mixed up that on
certain questions you couldn't tell where you'd find
her. You'd think she'd feel as you did because you
had found her feeling so, and then suddenly, in regard
to some other matter—which was yet quite the same
—she'd be utterly wanting. Mrs. Nettlepoint proceeded to observe—to such idle speculations does the
vacancy of sea-hours give encouragement—that she
wondered whether it were better to be an ordinary girl
very well brought up or an extraordinary girl not
brought up at all.

" Oh I go in for the extraordinary girl under all
circumstances."

" It's true that if you're *very* well brought up you're
not, you can't be, ordinary," said Mrs. Nettlepoint,

smelling her strong salts. " You're a lady, at any rate."

" And Miss Mavis is fifty miles out—is that what you mean ? "

" Well—you've seen her mother."

" Yes, but I think your contention would be that among such people the mother doesn't count."

" Precisely, and that's bad."

" I see what you mean. But isn't it rather hard ? If your mother doesn't know anything it's better you should be independent of her, and yet if you are that constitutes a bad note." I added that Mrs. Mavis had appeared to count sufficiently two nights before. She had said and done everything she wanted, while the girl sat silent and respectful. Grace's attitude, so far as her parent was concerned, had been eminently decent.

" Yes, but she ' squirmed ' for her," said Mrs. Nettlepoint.

" Ah if you know it I may confess she has told me as much."

My friend stared. " Told *you* ? There's one of the things they do ! "

" Well, it was only a word. Won't you let me know whether you do think her a flirt ? "

" Try her yourself—that's better than asking another woman ; especially as you pretend to study folk."

" Oh your judgement wouldn't probably at all determine mine. It's as bearing on *you* I ask it." Which, however, demanded explanation, so that I was duly frank ; confessing myself curious as to how far maternal immorality would go.

It made her at first but repeat my words. " Maternal immorality ? "

" You desire your son to have every possible distraction on his voyage, and if you can make up your

179

mind in the sense I refer to that will make it all right. He'll have no responsibility."

"Heavens, how you analyse!" she cried. "I haven't in the least your passion for making up my mind."

"Then if you chance it," I returned, "you'll be more immoral still."

"Your reasoning's strange," said Mrs. Nettlepoint; "when it was you who tried to put into my head yesterday that she had asked him to come."

"Yes, but in good faith."

"What do you mean, in such a case, by that?"

"Why, as girls of that sort do. Their allowance and measure in such matters," I expounded, "is much larger than that of young persons who have been, as you say, *very* well brought up; and yet I'm not sure that on the whole I don't think them thereby the more innocent. Miss Mavis is engaged, and she's to be married next week, but it's an old old story, and there's no more romance in it than if she were going to be photographed. So her usual life proceeds, and her usual life consists—and that of *ces demoiselles* in general—in having plenty of gentlemen's society. Having it I mean without having any harm from it."

Mrs. Nettlepoint had given me due attention. "Well, if there's no harm from it what are you talking about and why am I immoral?"

I hesitated, laughing. "I retract—you're sane and clear. I'm sure she thinks there won't be any harm," I added. "That's the great point."

"The great point?"

"To be settled, I mean."

"Mercy, we're not trying them!" cried my friend. "How can *we* settle it?"

"I mean of course in our minds. There will be nothing more interesting these next ten days for our minds to exercise themselves upon."

" Then they'll get terribly tired of it," said Mrs. Nettlepoint.

" No, no—because the interest will increase and the plot will thicken. It simply can't *not*," I insisted. She looked at me as if she thought me more than Mephistophelean, and I went back to something she had lately mentioned. " So she told you everything in her life was dreary ? "

" Not everything, but most things. And she didn't tell me so much as I guessed it. She'll tell me more the next time. She'll behave properly now about coming in to see me ; I told her she ought to."

" I'm glad of that," I said. " Keep her with you as much as possible."

" I don't follow you closely," Mrs. Nettlepoint replied, " but so far as I do I don't think your remarks in the best taste."

" Well, I'm too excited, I lose my head in these sports," I had to recognise—" cold-blooded as you think me. Doesn't she like Mr. Porterfield ? "

" Yes, that's the worst of it."

I kept making her stare. " The worst of it ? "

" He's so good—there's no fault to be found with him. Otherwise she'd have thrown it all up. It has dragged on since she was eighteen : she became engaged to him before he went abroad to study. It was one of those very young and perfectly needless blunders that parents in America might make so much less possible than they do. The thing is to insist on one's daughter waiting, on the engagement's being long ; and then, after you've got that started, to take it on every occasion as little seriously as possible—to make it die out. You can easily tire it to death," Mrs. Nettlepoint competently stated. "However," she concluded, " Mr. Porterfield has taken this one seriously for some years. He has done his part to keep it alive. She says he adores her."

" His part ? Surely his part would have been to marry her by this time."

" He has really no money." My friend was even more confidently able to report it than I had been.

" He ought to have got some, in seven years," I audibly reflected.

" So I think she thinks. There are some sorts of helplessness that are contemptible. However, a small difference has taken place. That's why he won't wait any longer. His mother has come out, she has something—a little—and she's able to assist him. She'll live with them and bear some of the expenses, and after her death the son will have what there is."

" How old is she ? " I cynically asked.

" I haven't the least idea. But it doesn't, on his part, sound very heroic—or very inspiring for our friend here. He hasn't been to America since he first went out."

" That's an odd way of adoring her," I observed.

" I made that objection mentally, but I didn't express it to her. She met it indeed a little by telling me that he had had other chances to marry."

" That surprises me," I remarked. " But did she say," I asked, " that *she* had had ? "

" No, and that's one of the things I thought nice in her ; for she must have had. She didn't try to make out that he had spoiled her life. She has three other sisters and there's very little money at home. She has tried to make money ; she has written little things and painted little things—and dreadful little things they must have been ; too bad to think of. Her father has had a long illness and has lost his place—he was in receipt of a salary in connexion with some waterworks —and one of her sisters has lately become a widow, with children and without means. And so as in fact she never has married any one else, whatever opportunities she may have encountered, she appears to have just made up her mind to go out to Mr. Porterfield as the least of her evils. But it isn't very amusing."

"Well," I judged after all, "that only makes her doing it the more honourable. She'll go through with it, whatever it costs, rather than disappoint him after he has waited so long. It's true," I continued, "that when a woman acts from a sense of honour—— !"

"Well, when she does?" said Mrs. Nettlepoint, for I hung back perceptibly.

"It's often so extravagant and unnatural a proceeding as to entail heavy costs on some one."

"You're very impertinent. We all have to pay for each other all the while; and for each other's virtues as well as vices."

"That's precisely why I shall be sorry for Mr. Porterfield when she steps off the ship with her little bill. I mean with her teeth clenched."

"Her teeth are not in the least clenched. She's quite at her ease now"—Mrs. Nettlepoint could answer for that.

"Well, we must try and keep her so," I said. "You must take care that Jasper neglects nothing."

I scarce know what reflexions this innocent pleasantry of mine provoked on the good lady's part; the upshot of them at all events was to make her say: "Well, I never asked her to come; I'm very glad of that. It's all their own doing."

"'Their' own—you mean Jasper's and hers?"

"No indeed. I mean her mother's and Mrs. Allen's; the girl's too of course. They put themselves on us by main force."

"Oh yes, I can testify to that. Therefore I'm glad too. We should have missed it, I think."

"How seriously you take it!" Mrs. Nettlepoint amusedly cried.

"Ah wait a few days!"—and I got up to leave her.

183

THE *Patagonia* was slow, but spacious and comfortable, and there was a motherly decency in her long nursing rock and her rustling old-fashioned gait, the multitudinous swish, in her wake, as of a thousand proper petticoats. It was as if she wished not to present herself in port with the splashed eagerness of a young creature. We weren't numerous enough quite to elbow each other and yet weren't too few to support—with that familiarity and relief which figures and objects acquire on the great bare field of the ocean and under the great bright glass of the sky. I had never liked the sea so much before, indeed I had never liked it at all ; but now I had a revelation of how in a midsummer mood it could please. It was darkly and magnificently blue and imperturbably quiet—save for the great regular swell of its heart-beats, the pulse of its life ; and there grew to be something so agreeable in the sense of floating there in infinite isolation and leisure that it was a positive godsend the *Patagonia* was no racer. One had never thought of the sea as the great place of safety, but now it came over one that there's no place so safe from the land. When it doesn't confer trouble it takes trouble away—takes away letters and telegrams and newspapers and visits and duties and efforts, all the complications, all the superfluities and superstitions that we have stuffed into our terrene life. The simple absence of the post, when the particular conditions enable you to enjoy the great fact by which it's produced, becomes in itself a positive bliss, and the clean boards of the deck turn to the stage of a play that amuses, the personal drama of the voyage, the movement and interaction, in the strong sea-light, of figures that end by representing something—something moreover of which the interest is never, even in its keenness, too great to suffer you to slumber. I at any rate dozed to excess, stretched on my rug with a French novel, and when I opened my eyes I generally saw Jasper Nettlepoint pass with the young woman confided to his mother's care on his arm. Somehow at these moments, between sleeping and waking, I inconsequently felt that my French novel had set them in motion. Perhaps this was because I had fallen into the trick, at the start, of regarding Grace Mavis almost as a married woman, which, as every one knows, is the necessary status of the heroine of such a work. Every revolution of our engine at any rate would contribute to the effect of making her one.

In the saloon, at meals, my neighbour on the right was a certain little Mrs. Peck, a very short and very round person whose head was enveloped in a " cloud " (a cloud of dirty white wool) and who promptly let me know that she was going to Europe for the education of her children. I had already perceived—an hour after we left the dock—that some energetic measure was required in their interest, but as we were not in Europe yet the redemption of the four little Pecks was stayed. Enjoying untrammelled leisure they swarmed about the ship as if they had been pirates boarding her, and their mother was as powerless to check their licence as if she had been gagged and stowed away in the hold. They were especially to be trusted to dive between the legs of the stewards when these attendants arrived with bowls of soup for the languid ladies. Their mother was too busy counting over to her fellow-passengers all the years Miss Mavis had been engaged. In the blank of our common detachment things that were nobody's business very soon became everybody's, and this was just one of those facts that are propagated with mysterious and ridiculous speed. The whisper that carries them is very small, in the great scale of things, of air and space and progress, but it's also very safe, for there's no compression, no sounding-board, to make speakers responsible. And then repetition at sea is somehow not repetition ; monotony is in the air, the mind is flat and everything recurs—the bells, the meals, the stewards' faces, the romp of children, the walk, the clothes, the very shoes and buttons of passengers taking their exercise. These things finally grow at once so circumstantial and so arid that, in comparison, lights on the personal history of one's companions become a substitute for the friendly flicker of the lost fireside.

Jasper Nettlepoint sat on my left hand when he was not upstairs seeing that Miss Mavis had her repast comfortably on deck. His mother's place would have been next mine had she shown herself, and then that of the young lady under her care. These companions, in other words, would have been between us, Jasper marking the limit of the party in that quarter. Miss Mavis was present at luncheon the first day, but dinner passed without her coming in, and when it was half over Jasper remarked that he would go up and look after her.

" Isn't that young lady coming—the one who was here to lunch ? " Mrs. Peck asked of me as he left the saloon.

" Apparently not. My friend tells me she doesn't like the saloon."

" You don't mean to say she's sick, do you ? "

186

"Oh no, not in this weather. But she likes to be above."

" And is that gentleman gone up to her ? "

" Yes, she's under his mother's care."

" And is his mother up there, too ? " asked Mrs. Peck, whose processes were homely and direct.

" No, she remains in her cabin. People have different tastes. Perhaps that's one reason why Miss Mavis doesn't come to table," I added—" her chaperon not being able to accompany her."

" Her chaperon ? " my fellow passenger echoed.

" Mrs. Nettlepoint—the lady under whose protection she happens to be."

" Protection ? " Mrs. Peck stared at me a moment, moving some valued morsel in her mouth ; then she exclaimed familiarly " Pshaw ! " I was struck with this and was on the point of asking her what she meant by it when she continued : " Ain't we going to see Mrs. Nettlepoint ? "

" I'm afraid not. She vows she won't stir from her sofa."

" Pshaw ! " said Mrs. Peck again. " That's quite a disappointment."

" Do you know her then ? "

" No, but I know all about her." Then my companion added : " You don't mean to say she's any real relation ? "

" Do you mean to me ? "

" No, to Grace Mavis."

" None at all. They're very new friends, as I happen to know. Then you're acquainted with our young lady ? " I hadn't noticed the passage of any recognition between them at luncheon.

" Is she your young lady too ? " asked Mrs. Peck with high significance.

" Ah when people are in the same boat—literally —they belong a little to each other."

187

" That's so," said Mrs. Peck. " I don't know Miss Mavis, but I know all about her— I live opposite to her on Merrimac Avenue. I don't know whether you know that part."

" Oh yes—it's very beautiful."

The consequence of this remark was another " Pshaw ! " But Mrs. Peck went on : " When you've lived opposite to people like that for a long time you feel as if you had some rights in them—tit for tat ! But she didn't take it up to-day ; she didn't speak to me. She knows who I am as well as she knows her own mother."

" You had better speak to her first—she's constitutionally shy," I remarked.

" Shy ? She's constitutionally tough ! Why she's thirty years old," cried my neighbour. " I suppose you know where she's going."

" Oh yes—we all take an interest in that."

" That young man, I suppose, particularly." And then as I feigned a vagueness : " The handsome one who sits *there*. Didn't you tell me he's Mrs. Nettlepoint's son ? "

" Oh yes—he acts as her deputy. No doubt he does all he can to carry out her function."

Mrs. Peck briefly brooded. I had spoken jocosely, but she took it with a serious face. " Well, she might let him eat his dinner in peace ! " she presently put forth.

" Oh he'll come back ! " I said, glancing at his place. The repast continued and when it was finished I screwed my chair round to leave the table. Mrs. Peck performed the same movement and we quitted the saloon together. Outside of it was the usual vestibule, with several seats, from which you could descend to the lower cabins or mount to the promenade-deck. Mrs. Peck appeared to hesitate as to her course and then solved the problem by going neither way.

She dropped on one of the benches and looked up at me.

"I thought you said he'd come back."

"Young Nettlepoint? Yes, I see he didn't. Miss Mavis then has given him half her dinner."

"It's very kind of her! She has been engaged half her life."

"Yes, but that will soon be over."

"So I suppose—as quick as ever we land. Every one knows it on Merrimac Avenue," Mrs. Peck pursued. "Every one there takes a great interest in it."

"Ah of course—a girl like that has many friends."

But my informant discriminated. "I mean even people who don't know her."

"I see," I went on : "she's so handsome that she attracts attention—people enter into her affairs."

Mrs. Peck spoke as from the commanding centre of these. "She *used* to be pretty, but I can't say I think she's anything remarkable to-day. Anyhow, if she attracts attention she ought to be all the more careful what she does. You had better tell her that."

"Oh it's none of my business!" I easily made out, leaving the terrible little woman and going above. This profession, I grant, was not perfectly attuned to my real idea, or rather my real idea was not quite in harmony with my profession. The very first thing I did on reaching the deck was to notice that Miss Mavis was pacing it on Jasper Nettlepoint's arm and that whatever beauty she might have lost, according to Mrs. Peck's insinuation, she still kept enough to make one's eyes follow her. She had put on a crimson hood, which was very becoming to her and which she wore for the rest of the voyage. She walked very well, with long steps, and I remember that at this moment the sea had a gentle evening swell which made the great ship dip slowly, rhythmically, giving a movement that was graceful to graceful pedestrians and a more awkward one to the awkward. It was the loveliest hour of a fine day, the clear early evening, with the glow of the sunset in the air and a purple colour on the deep. It was always present to me that so the waters ploughed by the Homeric heroes must have looked. I became conscious on this particular occasion moreover that Grace Mavis would for the rest of the voyage be the most visible thing in one's range, the figure that would count most in the composition of groups. She couldn't help it, poor girl ; nature had made her conspicuous—important, as the painters say. She paid for it by the corresponding exposure, the danger that people would, as I had said to Mrs. Peck, enter into her affairs.

Jasper Nettlepoint went down at certain times to see his mother, and I watched for one of these occasions—on the third day out—and took advantage of it to go and sit by Miss Mavis. She wore a light blue veil drawn tightly over her face, so that if the smile with which she greeted me rather lacked intensity I could account for it partly by that.

" Well, we're getting on—we're getting on," I said cheerfully, looking at the friendly twinkling sea.

" Are we going very fast ? "

" Not fast, but steadily. *Ohne Hast, ohne Rast*— do you know German ? "

" Well, I've studied it—some."

" It will be useful to you over there when you travel."

" Well yes, if we do. But I don't suppose we shall much. Mr. Nettlepoint says we ought," my young woman added in a moment.

" Ah of course *he* thinks so. He has been all over the world."

" Yes, he has described some of the places. They must be wonderful. I didn't know I should like it so much."

190

" But it isn't ' Europe ' yet ! " I laughed.

Well, she didn't care if it wasn't. " I mean going on this way. I could go on for ever—for ever and ever."

" Ah you know it's not always like this," I hastened to mention.

" Well, it's better than Boston."

" It isn't so good as Paris," I still more portentously noted.

" Oh I know all about Paris. There's no freshness in that. I feel as if I had been there all the time."

" You mean you've heard so much of it ? "

" Oh yes, nothing else for ten years."

I had come to talk with Miss Mavis because she was attractive, but I had been rather conscious of the absence of a good topic, not feeling at liberty to revert to Mr. Porterfield. She hadn't encouraged me, when I spoke to her as we were leaving Boston, to go on with the history of my acquaintance with this gentleman ; and yet now, unexpectedly, she appeared to imply—it was doubtless one of the disparities mentioned by Mrs. Nettlepoint—that he might be glanced at without indelicacy.

" I see—you mean by letters," I remarked.

" We won't live in a good part. I know enough to know that," she went on.

" Well, it isn't as if there were any very bad ones," I answered reassuringly.

" Why Mr. Nettlepoint says it's regular mean."

" And to what does he apply that expression ? "

She eyed me a moment as if I were elegant at her expense, but she answered my question. " Up there in the Batignolles. I seem to make out it's worse than Merrimac Avenue."

" Worse—in what way ? "

" Why, even less where the nice people live."

" He oughtn't to say that," I returned. And I

ventured to back it up. " Don't you call Mr. Porterfield a nice person ? "

" Oh it doesn't make any difference." She watched
me again a moment through her veil, the texture of
which gave her look a suffused prettiness. " Do you
know him very little ? " she asked.

" Mr. Porterfield ? "

" No, Mr. Nettlepoint."

" Ah very little. He's very considerably my junior,
you see."

She had a fresh pause, as if almost again for my
elegance ; but she went on : " He's younger than me
too." I don't know what effect of the comic there
could have been in it, but the turn was unexpected
and it made me laugh. Neither do I know whether
Miss Mavis took offence at my sensibility on this
head, though I remember thinking at the moment
with compunction that it had brought a flush to her
cheek. At all events she got up, gathering her shawl
and her books into her arm. " I'm going down—
I'm tired."

" Tired of me, I'm afraid."

" No, not yet."

" I'm like you," I confessed. " I should like it to
go on and on."

She had begun to walk along the deck to the
companionway and I went with her. " Well, I guess
I wouldn't, after all ! "

I had taken her shawl from her to carry it, but at
the top of the steps that led down to the cabins I had
to give it back. " Your mother would be glad if she
could know," I observed as we parted.

But she was proof against my graces. " If she
could know what ? "

" How well you're getting on." I refused to be
discouraged. " And that good Mrs. Allen."

" Oh mother, mother ! She made me come, she

pushed me off." And almost as if not to say more she went quickly below.

I paid Mrs. Nettlepoint a morning visit after luncheon and another in the evening, before she " turned in." That same day, in the evening, she said to me suddenly : " Do you know what I've done ? I've asked Jasper."

" Asked him what ? "

" Why, if *she* asked him, you understand."

I wondered. " *Do* I understand ? "

" If you don't it's because you ' regular ' won't, as she says. If that girl really asked him—on the balcony—to sail with us."

" My dear lady, do you suppose that if she did he'd tell you ? "

She had to recognise my acuteness. " That's just what he says. But he says she didn't."

" And do you consider the statement valuable ? " I asked, laughing out. " You had better ask your young friend herself."

Mrs. Nettlepoint stared. " I couldn't do that."

On which I was the more amused that I had to explain I was only amused. " What does it signify now ? "

" I thought you thought everything signified. You were so full," she cried, " of signification ! "

" Yes, but we're further out now, and somehow in mid-ocean everything becomes absolute."

" What else *can* he do with decency ? " Mrs. Nettlepoint went on. " If, as my son, he were never to speak to her it would be very rude and you'd think that stranger still. Then *you* would do what he does, and where would be the difference ? "

" How do you know what he does ? I haven't mentioned him for twenty-four hours."

" Why, she told me herself. She came in this afternoon."

" What an odd thing to tell you ! " I commented.

" Not as she says it. She says he's full of attention, perfectly devoted—looks after her all the time. She seems to want me to know it, so that I may approve him for it."

" That's charming ; it shows her good conscience."

" Yes, or her great cleverness."

Something in the tone in which Mrs. Nettlepoint said this caused me to return in real surprise : " Why what do you suppose she has in her mind ? "

" To get hold of him, to make him go so far he can't retreat. To marry him perhaps."

" To marry him ? And what will she do with Mr. Porterfield ? "

" She'll ask me just to make it all right to him— or perhaps you."

" Yes, as an old friend ! "—and for a moment I felt it awkwardly possible. But I put to her seriously : " *Do* you see Jasper caught like that ? "

" Well, he's only a boy—he's younger at least than she."

" Precisely ; she regards him as a child. She remarked to me herself to-day, that is, that he's so much younger."

Mrs. Nettlepoint took this in. " Does she talk of it with you ? That shows she has a plan, that she has thought it over ! "

I've sufficiently expressed—for the interest of my anecdote—that I found an oddity in one of our young companions, but I was far from judging her capable of laying a trap for the other. Moreover my reading of Jasper wasn't in the least that he was catchable—could be made to do a thing if he didn't want to do it. Of course it wasn't impossible that he might be inclined, that he might take it—or already have taken it—into his head to go further with his mother's charge ; but to believe this I should require still more proof than his always being with her. He wanted at most to " take up with her " for the voyage. " If you've questioned him perhaps you've tried to make him feel responsible," I said to my fellow critic.

" A little, but it's very difficult. Interference makes him perverse. One has to go gently. Besides, it's too absurd—think of her age. If she can't take care of herself ! " cried Mrs. Nettlepoint.

" Yes, let us keep thinking of her age, though it's not so prodigious. And if things get very bad you've one resource left," I added.

She wondered. " To lock her up in her cabin ? "

" No—to come out of yours."

" Ah never, never ! If it takes that to save her she must be lost. Besides, what good would it do ? If I were to go above she could come below."

" Yes, but you could keep Jasper with you."

" *Could* I ? " Mrs. Nettlepoint demanded in the manner of a woman who knew her son.

In the saloon the next day, after dinner, over the red cloth of the tables, beneath the swinging lamps and the racks of tumblers, decanters and wine-glasses, we sat down to whist, Mrs. Peck, to oblige, taking a hand in the game. She played very badly and talked too much, and when the rubber was over assuaged her discomfiture (though not mine—we had been partners) with a Welsh rabbit and a tumbler of something hot. We had done with the cards, but while she waited for this refreshment she sat with her elbows on the table shuffling a pack.

" She hasn't spoken to me yet—she won't do it," she remarked in a moment.

" Is it possible there's any one on the ship who hasn't spoken to you ? "

" Not that girl — she knows too well ! " Mrs. Peck looked round our little circle with a smile of intelligence—she had familiar communicative eyes. Several of our company had assembled, according to the wont, the last thing in the evening, of those who are cheerful at sea, for the consumption of grilled sardines and devilled bones.

" What then does she know ? "

" Oh she knows *I* know."

" Well, we know what Mrs. Peck knows," one of the ladies of the group observed to me with an air of privilege.

" Well, you wouldn't know if I hadn't told you— from the way she acts," said our friend with a laugh of small charm.

" She's going out to a gentleman who lives over there—he's waiting there to marry her," the other lady went on, in the tone of authentic information. I remember that her name was Mrs. Gotch and that her mouth looked always as if she were whistling.

" Oh he knows—I've told him," said Mrs. Peck.

" Well, I presume every one knows," Mrs. Gotch contributed.

" Dear madam, is it every one's business ? " I asked.

" Why, don't you think it's a peculiar way to act ? " —and Mrs. Gotch was evidently surprised at my little protest.

" Why it's right there—straight in front of you, like a play at the theatre—as if you had paid to see it," said Mrs. Peck. " If you don't call it public——! "

" Aren't you mixing things up ? What do you call public ? "

" Why the way they go on. They're up there now."

" They cuddle up there half the night," said Mrs. Gotch. " I don't know when they come down. Any hour they like. When all the lights are out they're up there still."

" Oh you can't tire them out. They don't want relief—like the ship's watch ! " laughed one of the gentlemen.

" Well, if they enjoy each other's society what's the harm ? " another asked. " They'd do just the same on land."

" They wouldn't do it on the public streets, I presume," said Mrs. Peck. " And they wouldn't do it if Mr. Porterfield was round ! "

" Isn't that just where your confusion comes in ? " I made answer. " It's public enough that Miss Mavis and Mr. Nettlepoint are always together, but it isn't in the least public that she's going to be married."

" Why how can you say—when the very sailors know it ! The Captain knows it and all the officers know it. They see them there, especially at night, when they're sailing the ship."

" I thought there was some rule——! " submitted Mrs. Gotch.

" Well, there is—that you've got to behave yourself," Mrs. Peck explained. " So the Captain told me —he said they have some rule. He said they have to have, when people are too undignified."

" Is that the term he used ? " I inquired.

" Well, he may have said when they attract too much attention."

I ventured to discriminate. " It's we who attract the attention—by talking about what doesn't concern us and about what we really don't know."

" She said the Captain said he'd tell on her as soon as ever we arrive," Mrs. Gotch none the less serenely pursued.

" *She* said—— ? " I repeated, bewildered.

" Well, he did say so, that he'd think it his duty to inform Mr. Porterfield when he comes on to meet her—if they keep it up in the same way," said Mrs. Peck.

" Oh they'll keep it up, don't you fear ! " one of the gentlemen exclaimed.

" Dear madam, the Captain's having his joke on you," was, however, my own congruous reply.

" No, he ain't—he's right down scandalised. He says he regards us all as a real family and wants the family not to be downright coarse." I felt Mrs. Peck irritated by my controversial tone : she challenged me with considerable spirit. " How can you say I don't know it when all the street knows it and has known it for years—for years and years ? " She spoke as if the girl had been engaged at least for twenty. " What's she going out for if not to marry him ? "

" Perhaps she's going to see how he looks," suggested one of the gentlemen.

" He'd look queer—if he knew."

" Well, I guess he'll know," said Mrs. Gotch.

" She'd tell him herself—she wouldn't be afraid," the gentleman went on.

" Well she might as well kill him. He'll jump overboard," Mrs. Peck could foretell.

" Jump overboard ? " cried Mrs. Gotch as if she hoped then that Mr. Porterfield would be told.

" He has just been waiting for this—for long, long years," said Mrs. Peck.

" Do you happen to know him ? " I asked.

She replied at her convenience. " No, but I know a lady who does. Are you going up ? "

I had risen from my place—I had not ordered supper. " I'm going to take a turn before going to bed."

" Well then you'll see ! "

Outside the saloon I hesitated, for Mrs. Peck's admonition made me feel for a moment that if I went up I should have entered in a manner into her little conspiracy. But the night was so warm and splendid that I had been intending to smoke a cigar in the air

before going below, and I didn't see why I should
deprive myself of this pleasure in order to seem not to
mind Mrs. Peck. I mounted accordingly and saw a
few figures sitting or moving about in the darkness.
The ocean looked black and small, as it is apt to do at
night, and the long mass of the ship, with its vague
dim wings, seemed to take up a great part of it. There
were more stars than one saw on land and the heavens
struck one more than ever as larger than the earth.
Grace Mavis and her companion were not, so far as I
perceived at first, among the few passengers who
lingered late, and I was glad, because I hated to hear
her talked about in the manner of the gossips I had
left at supper. I wished there had been some way to
prevent it, but I could think of none but to recom-
mend her privately to reconsider her rule of discretion.
That would be a very delicate business, and perhaps
it would be better to begin with Jasper, though that
would be delicate too. At any rate one might let him
know, in a friendly spirit, to how much remark he
exposed the young lady—leaving this revelation to
work its way upon him. Unfortunately I couldn't
altogether believe that the pair were unconscious of the
observation and the opinion of the passengers. They
weren't boy and girl; they had a certain social perspective in their eye. I was meanwhile at any rate in
no possession of the details of that behaviour which
had made them—according to the version of my
good friends in the saloon—a scandal to the ship; for
though I had taken due note of them, as will already
have been gathered, I had taken really no such
ferocious, or at least such competent, note as Mrs. Peck.
Nevertheless the probability was that they knew what
was thought of them—what naturally would be—
and simply didn't care. That made our heroine out
rather perverse and even rather shameless; and yet
somehow if these were her leanings I didn't dislike her

for them. I don't know what strange secret excuses I found for her. I presently indeed encountered, on the spot, a need for any I might have at call, since, just as I was on the point of going below again, after several restless turns and—within the limit where smoking was allowed—as many puffs at a cigar as I cared for, I became aware of a couple of figures settled together behind one of the lifeboats that rested on the deck. They were so placed as to be visible only to a person going close to the rail and peering a little sidewise. I don't think I peered, but as I stood a moment beside the rail my eye was attracted by a dusky object that protruded beyond the boat and that I saw at a second glance to be the tail of a lady's dress. I bent forward an instant, but even then I saw very little more ; that scarcely mattered however, as I easily concluded that the persons tucked away in so snug a corner were Jasper Nettlepoint and Mr. Porterfield's intended. Tucked away was the odious right expression, and I deplored the fact so betrayed for the pitiful bad taste in it. I immediately turned away, and the next moment found myself face to face with our vessel's skipper. I had already had some conversation with him—he had been so good as to invite me, as he had invited Mrs. Nettlepoint and her son and the young lady travelling with them, and also Mrs. Peck, to sit at his table—and had observed with pleasure that his seamanship had the grace, not universal on the Atlantic liners, of a fine-weather manner.

" They don't waste much time—your friends in there," he said, nodding in the direction in which he had seen me looking.

" Ah well, they haven't much to lose."

" That's what I mean. I'm told *she* hasn't."

I wanted to say something exculpatory, but scarcely knew what note to strike. I could only look vaguely about me at the starry darkness and the sea that seemed to sleep. " Well, with these splendid nights and this perfect air people are beguiled into late hours."

" Yes, we want a bit of a blow," the Captain said.

I demurred. " How much of one ? "

" Enough to clear the decks ! "

He was after all rather dry and he went about his business. He had made me uneasy, and instead of going below I took a few turns more. The other walkers dropped off pair by pair—they were all men— till at last I was alone. Then after a little I quitted the field. Jasper and his companion were still behind their lifeboat. Personally I greatly preferred our actual conditions, but as I went down I found myself vaguely wishing, in the interest of I scarcely knew what, unless it had been a mere superstitious delicacy, that we might have half a gale.

Miss Mavis turned out, in sea-phrase, early ; for the next morning I saw her come up only a short time after I had finished my breakfast, a ceremony over which I contrived not to dawdle. She was alone and Jasper Nettlepoint, by a rare accident, was not on deck to help her. I went to meet her—she was en- cumbered as usual with her shawl, her sun-umbrella and a book—and laid my hands on her chair, placing it near the stern of the ship, where she liked best to be. But I proposed to her to walk a little before she sat down, and she took my arm after I had put her accessories into the chair. The deck was clear at that hour and the morning light gay ; one had an extrava- gant sense of good omens and propitious airs. I forget what we spoke of first, but it was because I felt these things pleasantly, and not to torment my companion nor to test her, that I couldn't help exclaiming cheer- fully after a moment, as I have mentioned having done the first day : " Well, we're getting on, we're getting on ! "

" Oh yes, I count every hour."

" The last days always go quicker," I said, " and the last hours—— ! "

" Well, the last hours ? " she asked ; for I had instinctively checked myself.

" Oh one's so glad then that it's almost the same as if one had arrived. Yet we ought to be grateful when the elements have been so kind to us," I added. " I hope you'll have enjoyed the voyage."

She hesitated ever so little. " Yes, much more than I expected."

" Did you think it would be very bad ? "

" Horrible, horrible ! "

The tone of these words was strange, but I hadn't much time to reflect upon it, for turning round at that moment I saw Jasper Nettlepoint come toward us. He was still distant by the expanse of the white deck, and I couldn't help taking him in from head to foot as he drew nearer. I don't know what rendered me on this occasion particularly sensitive to the impression, but it struck me that I saw him as I had never seen him before, saw him, thanks to the intense sea-light, inside and out, in his personal, his moral totality. It was a quick, a vivid revelation ; if it only lasted a moment it had a simplifying certifying effect. He was intrinsically a pleasing apparition, with his handsome young face and that marked absence of any drop in his personal arrangements which, more than any one I've ever seen, he managed to exhibit on shipboard. He had none of the appearance of wearing out old clothes that usually prevails there, but dressed quite straight, as I heard some one say. This gave him an assured, almost a triumphant air, as of a young man who would come best out of any awkwardness. I expected to feel my companion's hand loosen itself on my arm, as an indication that now she must go to him, and I was almost surprised she didn't drop me. We stopped as we met and Jasper bade us a friendly good-morning. Of course the remark that we had another lovely day was already indicated, and it led him to exclaim, in the manner of one to whom criticism came easily, " Yes, but with this sort of thing consider what one of the others would do ! "

" One of the other ships ? "

" We should be there now, or at any rate to-morrow."

" Well then I'm glad it isn't one of the others "—and I smiled at the young lady on my arm. My words offered her a chance to say something appreciative, and gave him one even more ; but neither Jasper nor Grace Mavis took advantage of the occasion. What they did do, I noticed, was to look at each other rather fixedly an instant ; after which she turned her eyes silently to the sea. She made no movement and uttered no sound, contriving to give me the sense that she had all at once become perfectly passive, that she somehow declined responsibility. We remained standing there with Jasper in front of us, and if the contact of her arm didn't suggest I should give her up, neither did it intimate that we had better pass on. I had no idea of giving her up, albeit one of the things I seemed to read just then into Jasper's countenance was a fine implication that she was his property. His eyes met mine for a moment, and it was exactly as if he had said to me " I know what you think, but I don't care a rap." What I really thought was that he was selfish beyond the limits : that was the substance of my little revelation. Youth is almost always selfish, just as it is almost always conceited, and, after all, when it's combined with health and good parts, good looks and good spirits, it has a right to be, and I easily forgive it if it be really youth. Still it's a question of degree, and what stuck out of Jasper Nettlepoint—if, of course, one had the intelligence for it—was that his egotism had a hardness, his love of his own way an avidity. These elements were jaunty and prosperous, they were accustomed to prevail. He was fond, very fond, of women ; they were necessary to him—that was in his type ; but he wasn't in the least in love with Grace Mavis. Among the reflexions I quickly made this was the one that was most to the point. There was a degree of awkwardness, after a minute, in the way we were planted there, though the apprehension of it was doubtless not in the least with himself. To dissimulate my own share in it, at any rate, I asked him how his mother might be.

His answer was unexpected. "You had better go down and see."

"Not till Miss Mavis is tired of me."

She said nothing to this and I made her walk again. For some minutes she failed to speak ; then, rather abruptly, she began : "I've seen you talking to that lady who sits at our table—the one who has so many children."

"Mrs. Peck ? Oh yes, one has inevitably talked with Mrs. Peck."

"Do you know her very well ? "

"Only as one knows people at sea. An acquaintance makes itself. It doesn't mean very much."

"She doesn't speak to me—she might if she wanted."

"That's just what she says of you—that you might speak to her."

"Oh if she's waiting for that——!" said my companion with a laugh. Then she added : "She lives in our street, nearly opposite."

"Precisely. That's the reason why she thinks you coy or haughty. She has seen you so often and seems to know so much about you."

"What does she know about me ? "

"Ah you must ask her—I can't tell you ! "

" I don't care what she knows," said my young lady. After a moment she went on : " She must have seen I ain't very sociable." And then, " What are you laughing at ? " she asked.

" Well "—my amusement was difficult to explain —" you're not very sociable, and yet somehow you are. Mrs. Peck is, at any rate, and thought that ought to make it easy for you to enter into conversation with her."

" Oh I don't care for her conversation—I know what it amounts to." I made no reply—I scarcely knew what reply to make—and the girl went on : " I know what she thinks and I know what she says." Still I was silent, but the next moment I saw my discretion had been wasted, for Miss Mavis put to me straight : " Does she make out that she knows Mr. Porterfield ? "

" No, she only claims she knows a lady who knows him."

" Yes, that's it—Mrs. Jeremie. Mrs. Jeremie's an idiot ! " I wasn't in a position to controvert this, and presently my young lady said she would sit down. I left her in her chair—I saw that she preferred it—and wandered to a distance. A few minutes later I met Jasper again, and he stopped of his own accord to say : " We shall be in about six in the evening of our eleventh day—they promise it."

" If nothing happens, of course."

" Well, what's going to happen ? "

" That's just what I'm wondering ! " And I turned away and went below with the foolish but innocent satisfaction of thinking I had mystified him.

IV

" I DON'T know what to do, and you must help me,"
Mrs. Nettlepoint said to me, that evening, as soon as
I looked in.

" I'll do what I can—but what's the matter ? "

" She has been crying here and going on—she has
quite upset me."

" Crying ? She doesn't look like that."

" Exactly, and that's what startled me. She came
in to see me this afternoon, as she has done before,
and we talked of the weather and the run of the ship
and the manners of the stewardess and other such
trifles, and then suddenly, in the midst of it, as she
sat there, on no visible pretext, she burst into tears.
I asked her what ailed her and tried to comfort her,
but she didn't explain ; she said it was nothing, the
effect of the sea, of the monotony, of the excitement,
of leaving home. I asked her if it had anything to do
with her prospects, with her marriage ; whether she
finds as this draws near that her heart isn't in it.
I told her she mustn't be nervous, that I could enter
into that—in short I said what I could. All she
replied was that she *is* nervous, very nervous, but
that it was already over ; and then she jumped up and
kissed me and went away. Does she look as if she
has been crying ? " Mrs. Nettlepoint wound up.

" How can I tell, when she never quits that horrid
veil ? It's as if she were ashamed to show her face."

" She's keeping it for Liverpool. But I don't like such incidents," said Mrs. Nettlepoint. " I think I ought to go above."

" And is that where you want me to help you ? "

" Oh with your arm and that sort of thing, yes. But I may have to look to you for something more. I feel as if something were going to happen."

" That's exactly what I said to Jasper this morning."

" And what did he say ? "

" He only looked innocent—as if he thought I meant a fog or a storm."

" Heaven forbid—it isn't that ! I shall never be good-natured again," Mrs. Nettlepoint went on ; " never have a girl put on me that way. You always pay for it—there are always tiresome complications. What I'm afraid of is after we get there. She'll throw up her engagement ; there will be dreadful scenes ; I shall be mixed up with them and have to look after her and keep her with me. I shall have to stay there with her till she can be sent back, or even take her up to London. Do you see all that ? "

I listened respectfully ; after which I observed : " You're afraid of your son."

She also had a pause. " It depends on how you mean it."

" There are things you might say to him—and with your manner ; because you have one, you know, when you choose."

" Very likely, but what's my manner to his ? Besides, I *have* said everything to him. That is I've said the great thing—that he's making her immensely talked about."

" And of course in answer to that he has asked you how you know, and you've told him you have it from me."

" I've had to tell him ; and he says it's none of your business."

207

" I wish he'd say that," I remarked, " to my face."

" He'll do so perfectly if you give him a chance. That's where you can help me. Quarrel with him—he's rather good at a quarrel ; and that will divert him and draw him off."

" Then I'm ready," I returned, " to discuss the matter with him for the rest of the voyage."

" Very well ; I count on you. But he'll ask you, as he asks me, what the deuce you want him to do."

" To go to bed ! "—and I'm afraid I laughed.

" Oh it isn't a joke."

I didn't want to be irritating, but I made my point. " That's exactly what I told you at first."

" Yes, but don't exult ; I hate people who exult. Jasper asks of me," she went on, " why he should mind her being talked about if she doesn't mind it herself."

" I'll tell him why," I replied ; and Mrs. Nettlepoint said she should be exceedingly obliged to me and repeated that she would indeed take the field.

I looked for Jasper above that same evening, but circumstances didn't favour my quest. I found him —that is I gathered he was again ensconced behind the lifeboat with Miss Mavis ; but there was a needless violence in breaking into their communion, and I put off our interview till the next day. Then I took the first opportunity, at breakfast, to make sure of it. He was in the saloon when I went in and was preparing to leave the table ; but I stopped him and asked if he would give me a quarter of an hour on deck a little later—there was something particular I wanted to say to him. He said " Oh yes, if you like "—with just a visible surprise, but I thought with plenty of assurance. When I had finished my breakfast I found him smoking on the forward-deck and I immediately began : " I'm going to say something you won't at all like ; to ask you a question you'll probably denounce for impertinent."

" I certainly shall if I find it so," said Jasper Nettle-point.

" Well, of course my warning has meant that I don't care if you do. I'm a good deal older than you and I'm a friend—of many years—of your mother. There's nothing I like less than to be meddlesome, but I think these things give me a certain right— a sort of privilege. Besides which my inquiry will speak for itself."

" Why so many damned preliminaries ? " my young man asked through his smoke.

We looked into each other's eyes a moment. What indeed was his mother's manner—her best manner —compared with his ? " Are you prepared to be responsible ? "

" To you ? "

" Dear no — to the young lady herself. I'm speaking of course of Miss Mavis."

" Ah yes, my mother tells me you have her greatly on your mind."

" So has your mother herself—now."

" She's so good as to say so—to oblige you."

" She'd oblige me a great deal more by reassuring me. I know perfectly of your knowing I've told her that Miss Mavis is greatly talked about."

" Yes, but what on earth does it matter ? "

" It matters as a sign."

" A sign of what ? "

" That she's in a false position."

Jasper puffed his cigar with his eyes on the horizon, and I had, a little unexpectedly, the sense of producing a certain effect on him. " I don't know whether it's *your* business, what you're attempting to discuss ; but it really strikes me it's none of mine. What have

I to do with the tattle with which a pack of old women console themselves for not being sea-sick ? "

" Do you call it tattle that Miss Mavis is in love with you ? "

" Drivelling."

" Then," I retorted, " you're very ungrateful. The tattle of a pack of old women has this importance, that she suspects, or she knows, it exists, and that decent girls are for the most part very sensitive to that sort of thing. To be prepared not to heed it in this case she must have a reason, and the reason must be the one I've taken the liberty to call your attention to."

" In love with me in six days, just like that ? "— and he still looked away through narrowed eyelids.

" There's no accounting for tastes, and six days at sea are equivalent to sixty on land. I don't want to make you too proud. Of course if you recognise your responsibility it's all right and I've nothing to say."

" I don't see what you mean," he presently returned.

" Surely you ought to have thought of that by this time. She's engaged to be married, and the gentleman she's engaged to is to meet her at Liverpool. The whole ship knows it—though *I* didn't tell them !— and the whole ship's watching her. It's impertinent if you like, just as I am myself, but we make a little world here together and we can't blink its conditions. What I ask you is whether you're prepared to allow her to give up the gentleman I've just mentioned for your sake."

Jasper spoke in a moment as if he didn't understand. " For my sake ? "

" To marry her if she breaks with him."

He turned his eyes from the horizon to my own, and I found a strange expression in them. " Has Miss Mavis commissioned you to go into that ? "

" Not in the least."

"Well then, I don't quite see——!"

"It isn't as from another I make it. Let it come from yourself—*to* yourself."

"Lord, you must think I lead myself a life!" he cried as in compassion for my simplicity. "That's a question the young lady may put to me any moment it pleases her."

"Let me then express the hope that she will. But what will you answer?"

"My dear sir, it seems to me that in spite of all the titles you've enumerated you've no reason to expect I'll tell you." He turned away, and I dedicated in perfect sincerity a deep sore sigh to the thought of our young woman. At this, under the impression of it, he faced me again and, looking at me from head to foot, demanded: "What is it you want me to do?"

"I put it to your mother that you ought to go to bed."

"You had better do that yourself!" he replied.

This time he walked off, and I reflected rather dolefully that the only clear result of my undertaking would probably have been to make it vivid to him that she was in love with him. Mrs. Nettlepoint came up as she had announced, but the day was half over: it was nearly three o'clock. She was accompanied by her son, who established her on deck, arranged her chair and her shawls, saw she was protected from sun and wind, and for an hour was very properly attentive. While this went on Grace Mavis was not visible, nor did she reappear during the whole afternoon. I hadn't observed that she had as yet been absent from the deck for so long a period. Jasper left his mother, but came back at intervals to see how she got on, and when she asked where Miss Mavis might be answered that he hadn't the least idea. I sat with my friend at her particular request: she told me she knew that if I didn't Mrs. Peck and Mrs. Gotch would make their approach, so that I must act as a watch-dog. She was flurried and fatigued with her migration, and I think that Grace Mavis's choosing this occasion for retirement suggested to her a little that she had been made a fool of. She remarked that the girl's not being there showed her for the barbarian she only could be, and that she herself was really very good so to have put herself out ; her charge was a mere bore : that was the end of it. I could see that my companion's advent quickened the speculative activity of the other ladies ; they watched her from the opposite side of the deck, keeping their eyes fixed on her very much as the man at the wheel kept his on the course of the ship. Mrs. Peck plainly had designs, and it was from this danger that Mrs. Nettlepoint averted her face.

" It's just as we said," she remarked to me as we sat there. " It's like the buckets in the well. When I come up everything else goes down."

" No, not at all everything else—since Jasper remains here."

" Remains ? I don't see him."

" He comes and goes—it's the same thing."

" He goes more than he comes. But *n'en parlons plus* ; I haven't gained anything. I don't admire the sea at all—what is it but a magnified water-tank ? I shan't come up again."

" I've an idea she'll stay in her cabin now," I said. " She tells me she has one to herself." Mrs. Nettlepoint replied that she might do as she liked, and I repeated to her the little conversation I had had with Jasper.

She listened with interest, but " Marry her ? Mercy ! " she exclaimed. " I like the fine freedom with which you give my son away."

" You wouldn't accept that ? "

" Why in the world should I ? "

" Then I don't understand your position."

" Good heavens, I *have* none ! It isn't a position to be tired of the whole thing."

" You wouldn't accept it even in the case I put to him—that of her believing she had been encouraged to throw over poor Porterfield ? "

" Not even—not even. Who can know what she believes ? "

It brought me back to where we had started from. " Then you do exactly what I said you would—you show me a fine example of maternal immorality."

" Maternal fiddlesticks ! It was she who began it."

" Then why did you come up to-day ? " I asked.

" To keep you quiet."

Mrs. Nettlepoint's dinner was served on deck, but I went into the saloon. Jasper was there, but not Grace Mavis, as I had half-expected. I sought to learn from him what had become of her, if she were ill—he must have thought I had an odious pertinacity—and he replied that he knew nothing whatever about her. Mrs. Peck talked to me—or tried to—of Mrs. Nettlepoint, expatiating on the great interest it had been to see her ; only it was a pity she didn't seem more sociable. To this I made answer that she was to be excused on the score of health.

" You don't mean to say she's sick on this pond ? "

" No, she's unwell in another way."

" I guess I know the way ! " Mrs. Peck laughed. And then she added : " I suppose she came up to look after her pet."

" Her pet ? " I set my face.

" Why Miss Mavis. We've talked enough about that."

" Quite enough. I don't know what that has had to do with it. Miss Mavis, so far as I've noticed, hasn't been above to-day."

" Oh it goes on all the same."

" It goes on ? "

213

" Well, it's too late."

" Too late ? "

" Well, you'll see. There'll be a row."

This wasn't comforting, but I didn't repeat it on deck. Mrs. Nettlepoint returned early to her cabin, professing herself infinitely spent. I didn't know what " went on," but Grace Mavis continued not to show. I looked in late, for a good-night to my friend, and learned from her that the girl hadn't been to her. She had sent the stewardess to her room for news, to see if she were ill and needed assistance, and the stewardess had come back with mere mention of her not being there. I went above after this ; the night was not quite so fair and the deck almost empty. In a moment Jasper Nettlepoint and our young lady moved past me together. " I hope you're better ! " I called after her ; and she tossed me over her shoulder— " Oh yes, I had a headache ; but the air now does me good ! "

I went down again—I was the only person there but they, and I wanted not to seem to dog their steps —and, returning to Mrs. Nettlepoint's room, found (her door was open to the little passage) that she was still sitting up.

" She's all right ! " I said. " She's on the deck with Jasper."

The good lady looked up at me from her book. " I didn't know you called that all right."

" Well, it's better than something else."

" Than what else ? "

" Something I was a little afraid of." Mrs. Nettlepoint continued to look at me ; she asked again what that might be. " I'll tell you when we're ashore," I said.

The next day I waited on her at the usual hour of my morning visit, and found her not a little distraught. " The scenes have begun," she said ; " you know I told you I shouldn't get through without them ! You made me nervous last night—I haven't the least idea what you meant ; but you made me horribly nervous. She came in to see me an hour ago, and I had the courage to say to her : ' I don't know why I shouldn't tell you frankly that I've been scolding my son about you.' Of course she asked what I meant by that, and I let her know. ' It seems to me he drags you about the ship too much for a girl in your position. He has the air of not remembering that you belong to some one else. There's a want of taste and even a want of respect in it.' That brought on an outbreak : she became very violent."

" Do you mean indignant ? "

" Yes, indignant, and above all flustered and excited—at my presuming to suppose her relations with my son not the very simplest in the world. I might scold him as much as I liked—that was between ourselves ; but she didn't see why I should mention such matters to herself. Did I think she allowed him to treat her with disrespect ? That idea wasn't much of a compliment to either of them ! He had treated her better and been kinder to her than most other people —there were very few on the ship who hadn't been insulting. She should be glad enough when she got off it, to her own people, to some one whom nobody would have a right to speak of. What was there in her position that wasn't perfectly natural ? what was the idea of making a fuss about her position ? Did I mean that she took it too easily—that she didn't think as much as she ought about Mr. Porterfield ? Didn't I believe she was attached to him—didn't I believe she was just counting the hours till she saw him ? That would be the happiest moment of her life. It showed how little I knew her if I thought anything else."

" All that must have been rather fine—I should

have liked to hear it," I said after quite hanging on
my friend's lips. "And what did you reply?"

"Oh I grovelled; I assured her that I accused her
—as regards my son—of nothing worse than an excess
of good nature. She helped him to pass his time—he
ought to be immensely obliged. Also that it would be
a very happy moment for me too when I should hand
her over to Mr. Porterfield."

"And will you come up to-day?"

"No indeed—I think she'll do beautifully now."

I heaved this time a sigh of relief. "All's well that
ends well!"

Jasper spent that day a great deal of time with his
mother. She had told me how much she had lacked
hitherto proper opportunity to talk over with him their
movements after disembarking. Everything changes
a little the last two or three days of a voyage; the
spell is broken and new combinations take place.
Grace Mavis was neither on deck nor at dinner, and I
drew Mrs. Peck's attention to the extreme propriety
with which she now conducted herself. She had spent
the day in meditation and judged it best to continue to
meditate.

"Ah she's afraid," said my implacable neighbour.

"Afraid of what?"

"Well, that we'll tell tales when we get there."

"Whom do you mean by 'we'?"

"Well, there are plenty—on a ship like this."

"Then I think," I returned, "we won't."

"Maybe we won't have the chance," said the
dreadful little woman.

"Oh at that moment"—I spoke from a full experience—"universal geniality reigns."

Mrs. Peck however knew little of any such law.
"I guess she's afraid all the same."

"So much the better!"

"Yes—so much the better!"

216

All the next day too the girl remained invisible, and Mrs. Nettlepoint told me she hadn't looked in. She herself had accordingly inquired by the stewardess if she might be received in Miss Mavis's own quarters, and the young lady had replied that they were littered up with things and unfit for visitors : she was packing a trunk over. Jasper made up for his devotion to his mother the day before by now spending a great deal of his time in the smoking-room. I wanted to say to him " This is much better," but I thought it wiser to hold my tongue. Indeed I had begun to feel the emotion of prospective arrival—the sense of the return to Europe always kept its intensity—and had thereby the less attention for other matters. It will doubtless appear to the critical reader that my expenditure of interest had been out of proportion to the vulgar appearances of which my story gives an account, but to this I can only reply that the event was to justify me. We sighted land, the dim yet rich coast of Ireland, about sunset, and I leaned on the bulwark and took it in. " It doesn't look like much, does it ? " I heard a voice say, beside me ; whereupon, turning, I found Grace Mavis at hand. Almost for the first time she had her veil up, and I thought her very pale.

" It will be more to-morrow," I said.

" Oh yes, a great deal more."

" The first sight of land, at sea, changes everything," I went on. " It always affects me as waking up from a dream. It's a return to reality."

For a moment she made me no response ; then she said " It doesn't look very real yet."

" No, and meanwhile, this lovely evening, one can put it that the dream's still present."

She looked up at the sky, which had a brightness, though the light of the sun had left it and that of the stars hadn't begun. " It *is* a lovely evening."

" Oh yes, with this we shall do."

She stood some moments more, while the growing dusk effaced the line of the land more rapidly than our progress made it distinct. She said nothing more, she only looked in front of her; but her very quietness prompted me to something suggestive of sympathy and service. It was difficult indeed to strike the right note—some things seemed too wide of the mark and others too importunate. At last, unexpectedly, she appeared to give me my chance. Irrelevantly, abruptly she broke out : " Didn't you tell me you knew Mr. Porterfield ? "

" Dear me, yes—I used to see him. I've often wanted to speak to you of him."

She turned her face on me and in the deepened evening I imagined her more pale. " What good would that do ? "

" Why it would be a pleasure," I replied rather foolishly.

" Do you mean for you ? "

" Well, yes—call it that," I smiled.

" Did you know him so well ? "

My smile became a laugh and I lost a little my confidence. " You're not easy to make speeches to."

" I hate speeches ! " The words came from her lips with a force that surprised me ; they were loud and hard. But before I had time to wonder she went on a little differently. " Shall you know him when you see him ? "

" Perfectly, I think." Her manner was so strange that I had to notice it in some way, and I judged the best way was jocularly ; so I added : " Shan't you ? "

" Oh perhaps you'll point him out ! " And she walked quickly away. As I looked after her there came to me a perverse, rather a provoking consciousness of having during the previous days, and especially in speaking to Jasper Nettlepoint, interfered with her situation in some degree to her loss. There was an odd

pang for me in seeing her move about alone ; I felt
somehow responsible for it and asked myself why I
couldn't have kept my hands off. I had seen Jasper
in the smoking-room more than once that day, as I
passed it, and half an hour before this had observed,
through the open door, that he was there. He had
been with her so much that without him she now
struck one as bereaved and forsaken. This was really
better, no doubt, but superficially it moved—and I
admit with the last inconsequence—one's pity. Mrs.
Peck would doubtless have assured me that their
separation was gammon : they didn't show together
on deck and in the saloon, but they made it up elsewhere. The secret places on shipboard are not numerous ; Mrs. Peck's " elsewhere " would have been
vague, and I know not what licence her imagination
took. It was distinct that Jasper had fallen off, but of
course what had passed between them on this score
wasn't so and could never be. Later on, through his
mother, I had *his* version of that, but I may remark
that I gave it no credit. Poor Mrs. Nettlepoint, on the
other hand, was of course to give it all. I was almost
capable, after the girl had left me, of going to my
young man and saying : " After all, do return to her a
little, just till we get in ! It won't make any difference after we land." And I don't think it was the fear
he would tell me I was an idiot that prevented me. At
any rate the next time I passed the door of the smoking-room I saw he had left it. I paid my usual visit to
Mrs. Nettlepoint that night, but I troubled her no
further about Miss Mavis. She had made up her mind
that everything was smooth and settled now, and it
seemed to me I had worried her, and that she had
worried herself, in sufficiency. I left her to enjoy the
deepening foretaste of arrival, which had taken possession of her mind. Before turning in I went above and
found more passengers on deck than I had ever seen

so late. Jasper moved about among them alone, but I forbore to join him. The coast of Ireland had disappeared, but the night and the sea were perfect. On the way to my cabin, when I came down, I met the stewardess in one of the passages, and the idea entered my head to say to her : " Do you happen to know where Miss Mavis is ? "

" Why she's in her room, sir, at this hour."

" Do you suppose I could speak to her ? " It had come into my mind to ask her why she had wanted to know of me if I should recognise Mr. Porterfield.

" No sir," said the stewardess ; " she has gone to bed."

" That's all right." And I followed the young lady's excellent example.

The next morning, while I dressed, the steward of my side of the ship came to me as usual to see what I wanted. But the first thing he said to me was : " Rather a bad job, sir—a passenger missing." And while I took I scarce know what instant chill from it, " A lady, sir," he went on—" whom I think you knew. Poor Miss Mavis, sir."

" *Missing ?* " I cried—staring at him and horror-stricken.

" She's not on the ship. They can't find her."

" Then where to God is she ? "

I recall his queer face. " Well sir, I suppose you know that as well as I."

" Do you mean she has jumped overboard ? "

" Some time in the night, sir—on the quiet. But it's beyond every one, the way she escaped notice. They usually sees 'em, sir. It must have been about half-past two. Lord, but she was sharp, sir. She didn't so much as make a splash. They say she 'ad come against her will, sir."

I had dropped upon my sofa—I felt faint. The man went on, liking to talk as persons of his class do

when they have something horrible to tell. She
usually rang for the stewardess early, but this morning
of course there had been no ring. The stewardess had
gone in all the same about eight o'clock and found the
cabin empty. That was about an hour previous.
Her things were there in confusion—the things she
usually wore when she went above. The stewardess
thought she had been a bit odd the night before, but
had waited a little and then gone back. Miss Mavis
hadn't turned up—and she didn't turn up. The
stewardess began to look for her—she hadn't been
seen on deck or in the saloon. Besides, she wasn't
dressed—not to show herself ; all her clothes were in
her room. There was another lady, an old lady, Mrs.
Nettlepoint—I would know her—that she was sometimes with, but the stewardess had been with *her*
and knew Miss Mavis hadn't come near her that
morning. She had spoken to *him* and they had taken
a quiet look—they had hunted everywhere. A ship's
a big place, but you did come to the end of it, and
if a person wasn't there why there it was. In short
an hour had passed and the young lady was not
accounted for : from which I might judge if she ever
would be. The watch couldn't account for her, but no
doubt the fishes in the sea could—poor miserable
pitiful lady ! The stewardess and he had of course
thought it their duty to speak at once to the Doctor,
and the Doctor had spoken immediately to the Captain.
The Captain didn't like it—they never did, but he'd
try to keep it quiet—they always did.

By the time I succeeded in pulling myself together
and getting on, after a fashion, the rest of my clothes
I had learned that Mrs. Nettlepoint wouldn't yet have
been told, unless the stewardess had broken it to her
within the previous few minutes. Her son knew, the
young gentleman on the other side of the ship—he
had the other steward ; my man had seen him come

out of his cabin and rush above, just before he came
in to me. He *had* gone above, my man was sure ; he
hadn't gone to the old lady's cabin. I catch again the
sense of my dreadfully seeing something at that
moment, catch the wild flash, under the steward's
words, of Jasper Nettlepoint leaping, with a mad compunction in his young agility, over the side of the ship.
I hasten to add, however, that no such incident was
destined to contribute its horror to poor Grace Mavis's
unwitnessed and unlighted tragic act. What followed
was miserable enough, but I can only glance at it.
When I got to Mrs. Nettlepoint's door she was there
with a shawl about her ; the stewardess had just told
her and she was dashing out to come to me. I made
her go back—I said I would go for Jasper. I went for
him but I missed him, partly no doubt because it was
really at first the Captain I was after. I found this
personage and found him highly scandalised, but he
gave me no hope that we were in error, and his displeasure, expressed with seamanlike strength, was a
definite settlement of the question. From the deck,
where I merely turned round and looked, I saw the
light of another summer day, the coast of Ireland
green and near and the sea of a more charming colour
than it had shown at all. When I came below again
Jasper had passed back ; he had gone to his cabin
and his mother had joined him there. He remained
there till we reached Liverpool—I never saw him.
His mother, after a little, at his request, left him alone.
All the world went above to look at the land and
chatter about our tragedy, but the poor lady spent the
day, dismally enough, in her room. It seemed to me,
the dreadful day, intolerably long ; I was thinking so
of vague, of inconceivable yet inevitable Porterfield,
and of my having to face him somehow on the morrow.
Now of course I knew why she had asked me if I
should recognise him ; she had delegated to me

mentally a certain pleasant office. I gave Mrs. Peck
and Mrs. Gotch a wide berth—I couldn't talk to them.
I could, or at least I did a little, to Mrs. Nettlepoint,
but with too many reserves for comfort on either side,
since I quite felt how little it would now make for ease
to mention Jasper to her. I was obliged to assume by
my silence that he had had nothing to do with what
had happened ; and of course I never really ascertained what he *had* had to do. The secret of what
passed between him and the strange girl who would
have sacrificed her marriage to him on so short an
acquaintance remains shut up in his breast. His
mother, I know, went to his door from time to time,
but he refused her admission. That evening, to be
human at a venture, I requested the steward to go in
and ask him if he should care to see me, and the
good man returned with an answer which he candidly trans-
mitted. " Not in the least ! "—Jasper apparently
was almost as scandalised as the Captain.

At Liverpool, at the dock, when we had touched,
twenty people came on board and I had already made
out Mr. Porterfield at a distance. He was looking up
at the side of the great vessel with disappointment
written—for my strained eyes—in his face ; disappointment at not seeing the woman he had so long
awaited lean over it and wave her handkerchief to
him. Every one was looking at him, every one but
she—his identity flew about in a moment—and I
wondered if it didn't strike him. He used to be gaunt
and angular, but had grown almost fat and stooped a
little. The interval between us diminished—he was
on the plank and then on the deck with the jostling
agents of the Customs ; too soon for my equanimity.
I met him instantly, however, to save him from exposure—laid my hand on him and drew him away,
though I was sure he had no impression of having
seen me before. It was not till afterwards that I

thought this rather characteristically dull of him. I drew him far away—I was conscious of Mrs. Peck and Mrs. Gotch, looking at us as we passed—into the empty stale smoking-room : he remained speechless, and that struck me as like him. I had to speak first, he couldn't even relieve me by saying " Is anything the matter ? " I broke ground by putting it, feebly, that she was ill. It was a dire moment.

FOUR MEETINGS

I saw her but four times, though I remember them
vividly ; she made her impression on me.   I thought
her very pretty and very interesting—a touching
specimen of a type with which I had had other and
perhaps less charming associations.   I'm sorry to hear
of her death, and yet when I think of it why *should* I
be ?   The last time I saw her she was certainly not— !
But it will be of interest to take our meetings in order.

I

The first was in the country, at a small tea-party, one
snowy night of some seventeen years ago.   My friend
Latouche, going to spend Christmas with his mother,
had insisted on my company, and the good lady had
given in our honour the entertainment of which I
speak.   To me it was really full of savour—it had all
the right marks :   I had never been in the depths of
New England at that season.   It had been snowing all
day and the drifts were knee-high.   I wondered how
the ladies had made their way to the house ; but I
inferred that just those general rigours rendered any
assembly offering the attraction of two gentlemen
from New York worth a desperate effort.

Mrs. Latouche in the course of the evening asked
me if I " didn't want to " show the photographs to
some of the young ladies.   The photographs were in
a couple of great portfolios, and had been brought

227

home by her son, who, like myself, was lately returned from Europe. I looked round and was struck
with the fact that most of the young ladies were provided with an object of interest more absorbing than
the most vivid sun-picture. But there was a person
alone near the mantel-shelf who looked round the
room with a small vague smile, a discreet, a disguised
yearning, which seemed somehow at odds with her
isolation. I looked at her a moment and then chose.
" I should like to show them to that young lady."

" Oh yes," said Mrs. Latouche, " she's just the
person. She doesn't care for flirting—I'll speak to
her." I replied that if she didn't care for flirting she
wasn't perhaps just the person ; but Mrs. Latouche
had already, with a few steps, appealed to her parti-
cipation. " She's delighted," my hostess came back
to report ; " and she's just the person—so quiet and
so bright." And she told me the young lady was
by name Miss Caroline Spencer—with which she
introduced me.

Miss Caroline Spencer was not quite a beauty, but
was none the less, in her small odd way, formed to
please. Close upon thirty, by every presumption, she
was made almost like a little girl and had the complexion of a child. She had also the prettiest head, on
which her hair was arranged as nearly as possible like
the hair of a Greek bust, though indeed it was to be
doubted if she had ever seen a Greek bust. She was
" artistic," I suspected, so far as the polar influences
of North Verona could allow for such yearnings or
could minister to them. Her eyes were perhaps just
too round and too inveterately surprised, but her lips
had a certain mild decision and her teeth, when she
showed them, were charming. About her neck she
wore what ladies call, I believe, a " ruche " fastened
with a very small pin of pink coral, and in her hand
she carried a fan made of plaited straw and adorned

with pink ribbon. She wore a scanty black silk dress. She spoke with slow soft neatness, even without smiles showing the prettiness of her teeth, and she seemed extremely pleased, in fact quite fluttered, at the prospect of my demonstrations. These went forward very smoothly after I had moved the portfolios out of their corner and placed a couple of chairs near a lamp. The photographs were usually things I knew—large views of Switzerland, Italy and Spain, landscapes, reproductions of famous buildings, pictures and statues. I said what I could for them, and my companion, looking at them as I held them up, sat perfectly still, her straw fan raised to her under-lip and gently, yet, as I could feel, almost excitedly, rubbing it. Occasionally, as I laid one of the pictures down, she said without confidence, which would have been too much : " Have you seen that place ? " I usually answered that I had seen it several times—I had been a great traveller, though I was somehow particularly admonished not to swagger—and then I felt her look at me askance for a moment with her pretty eyes. I had asked her at the outset whether she had been to Europe ; to this she had answered " No, no, no "—almost as much below her breath as if the image of such an event scarce, for solemnity, brooked phrasing. But after that, though she never took her eyes off the pictures, she said so little that I feared she was at last bored. Accordingly when we had finished one portfolio I offered, if she desired it, to desist. I rather guessed the exhibition really held her, but her reticence puzzled me and I wanted to make her speak. I turned round to judge better and then saw a faint flush in each of her cheeks. She kept waving her little fan to and fro. Instead of looking at me she fixed her eyes on the remainder of the collection, which leaned, in its receptacle, against the table.

" Won't you show me that ? " she quavered,

drawing the long breath of a person launched and afloat but conscious of rocking a little.

"With pleasure," I answered, "if you're really not tired."

"Oh I'm not tired a bit. I'm just fascinated." With which as I took up the other portfolio she laid her hand on it, rubbing it softly. "And have you been here too?"

On my opening the portfolio it appeared I had indeed been there. One of the first photographs was a large view of the Castle of Chillon by the Lake of Geneva. "Here," I said, "I've been many a time. Isn't it beautiful?" And I pointed to the perfect reflexion of the rugged rocks and pointed towers in the clear still water. She didn't say "Oh enchanting!" and push it away to see the next picture. She looked a while and then asked if it weren't where Bonnivard, about whom Byron wrote, had been confined. I assented, trying to quote Byron's verses, but not quite bringing it off.

She fanned herself a moment and then repeated the lines correctly, in a soft flat voice but with charming conviction. By the time she had finished, she was nevertheless blushing. I complimented her and assured her she was perfectly equipped for visiting Switzerland and Italy. She looked at me askance again, to see if I might be serious, and I added that if she wished to recognise Byron's descriptions she must go abroad speedily—Europe was getting sadly dis-Byronised. "How soon must I go?" she thereupon inquired.

"Oh I'll give you ten years."

"Well, I guess I can go in *that* time," she answered as if measuring her words.

"Then you'll enjoy it immensely," I said; "you'll find it of the highest interest." Just then I came upon a photograph of some nook in a foreign city which I had been very fond of and which recalled tender memories. I discoursed (as I suppose) with considerable spirit; my companion sat listening breathless.

"Have you been *very* long over there?" she asked some time after I had ceased.

"Well, it mounts up, put all the times together."

"And have you travelled everywhere?"

"I've travelled a good deal. I'm very fond of it and happily have been able."

Again she turned on me her slow shy scrutiny. "Do you know the foreign languages?"

"After a fashion."

"Is it hard to speak them?"

"I don't imagine you'd find it so," I gallantly answered.

"Oh I shouldn't want to speak—I should only want to listen." Then on a pause she added: "They say the French theatre's so beautiful."

"Ah the best in the world."

"Did you go there very often?"

"When I was first in Paris I went every night."

"Every night!" And she opened her clear eyes very wide. "That to me is"—and her expression hovered—"as if you tell me a fairy-tale." A few minutes later she put to me: "And which country do you prefer?"

"There's one I love beyond any. I think you'd do the same."

Her gaze rested as on a dim revelation and then she breathed "Italy?"

"Italy," I answered softly too; and for a moment we communed over it. She looked as pretty as if instead of showing her photographs I had been making love to her. To increase the resemblance she turned off blushing. It made a pause which she broke at last

by saying : " That's the place which—in particular
—I thought of going to."

" Oh that's the place—that's the place ! " I laughed.

She looked at two or three more views in silence.
" They say it's not very dear."

" As some other countries ? Well, one gets back
there one's money. That's not the least of the
charms."

" But it's *all* very expensive, isn't it ? "

" Europe, you mean ? "

" Going there and travelling. That has been the
trouble. I've very little money. I teach, you know,"
said Miss Caroline Spencer.

" Oh of course one must have money," I allowed ;
" but one can manage with a moderate amount judi-
ciously spent."

" I think I should manage. I've saved and saved
up, and I'm always adding a little to it. It's all for
that." She paused a moment, and then went on with
suppressed eagerness, as if telling me the story were a
rare, but possibly an impure satisfaction. " You see
it hasn't been only the money—it has been everything. Everything has acted against it. I've waited
and waited. It has been my castle in the air. I'm
almost afraid to talk about it. Two or three times it
has come a little nearer, and then I've talked about
it and it has melted away. I've talked about it too
much," she said hypocritically—for I saw such talk
was now a small tremulous ecstasy. " There's a lady
who's a great friend of mine—she doesn't want to
go, but I'm always at her about it. I think I must tire
her dreadfully. She told me just the other day she
didn't know what would become of me. She guessed
I'd go crazy if I didn't sail, and yet certainly I'd go
crazy if I did."

" Well," I laughed, " you haven't sailed up to now
—so I suppose you *are* crazy."

She took everything with the same seriousness. "Well, I guess I must be. It seems as if I couldn't think of anything else—and I don't require photographs to work me up! I'm always right *on* it. It kills any interest in things nearer home—things I ought to attend to. That's a kind of craziness."

"Well then the cure for it's just to go," I smiled—"I mean the cure for this kind. Of course you may have the other kind worse," I added—"the kind you get over there."

"Well, I've a faith that I'll go *some* time all right!" she quite elatedly cried. "I've a relative right there on the spot," she went on, "and I guess he'll know how to control me." I expressed the hope that he would, and I forget whether we turned over more photographs; but when I asked her if she had always lived just where I found her, "Oh no, sir," she quite eagerly replied; "I've spent twenty-two months and a half in Boston." I met it with the inevitable joke that in this case foreign lands might prove a disappointment to her, but I quite failed to alarm her. "I know more about them than you might think"—her earnestness resisted even that. "I mean by reading—for I've really read considerable. In fact I guess I've prepared my mind about as much as you *can*—in advance. I've not only read Byron—I've read histories and guide-books and articles and lots of things. I know I shall rave about everything."

"'Everything' is saying much, but I understand your case," I returned. "You've the great American disease, and you've got it 'bad'—the appetite, morbid and monstrous, for colour and form, for the picturesque and the romantic at any price. I don't know whether we come into the world with it—with the germs implanted and antecedent to experience; rather perhaps we catch it early, almost before developed consciousness—we *feel*, as we look about, that we're going (to save our souls, or at least our senses) to be thrown back on it hard. We're like travellers in the desert—deprived of water and subject to the terrible mirage, the torment of illusion, of the thirst-fever. They hear the plash of fountains, they see green gardens and orchards that are hundreds of miles away. So we with *our* thirst—except that with us it's *more* wonderful : we have before us the beautiful old things we've never seen at all, and when we do at last see them—if we're lucky !—we simply recognise them. What experience does is merely to confirm and consecrate our confident dream."

She listened with her rounded eyes. " The way you express it's too lovely, and I'm sure it will be just like that. I've dreamt of everything—I'll know it all ! "

" I'm afraid," I pretended for harmless comedy, " that you've wasted a great deal of time."

" Oh yes, that has been my great wickedness ! " The people about us had begun to scatter ; they were taking their leave. She got up and put out her hand to me, timidly, but as if quite shining and throbbing.

" I'm going back there—one *has* to," I said as I shook hands with her. " I shall look out for you."

Yes, she fairly glittered with her fever of excited faith. " Well, I'll tell you if I'm disappointed." And she left me, fluttering all expressively her little straw fan.

II

A FEW months after this I crossed the sea eastward again and some three years elapsed. I had been living in Paris and, toward the end of October, went from that city to the Havre, to meet a pair of relatives who had written me they were about to arrive there. On reaching the Havre I found the steamer already docked—I was two or three hours late. I repaired directly to the hotel, where my travellers were duly established. My sister had gone to bed, exhausted and disabled by her voyage ; she was the unsteadiest of sailors and her sufferings on this occasion had been extreme. She desired for the moment undisturbed rest and was able to see me but five minutes—long enough for us to agree to stop over, restoratively, till the morrow. My brother-in-law, anxious about his wife, was unwilling to leave her room ; but she insisted on my taking him a walk for aid to recovery of his spirits and his land-legs.

The early autumn day was warm and charming, and our stroll through the bright-coloured busy streets of the old French seaport beguiling enough. We walked along the sunny noisy quays and then turned into a wide pleasant street which lay half in sun and half in shade—a French provincial street that resembled an old water-colour drawing : tall grey steep-roofed red-gabled many-storied houses ; green shutters on windows and old scroll-work above them ; flower-

235

pots in balconies and white-capped women in door-
ways. We walked in the shade ; all this stretched
away on the sunny side of the vista and made a picture.
We looked at it as we passed along ; then suddenly
my companion stopped—pressing my arm and staring.
I followed his gaze and saw that we had paused just
before reaching a café where, under an awning,
several tables and chairs were disposed upon the pavement. The windows were open behind ; half a dozen
plants in tubs were ranged beside the door ; the pavement was besprinkled with clean bran. It was a dear
little quiet old-world café ; inside, in the comparative
dusk, I saw a stout handsome woman, who had pink
ribbons in her cap, perched up with a mirror behind
her back and smiling at some one placed out of
sight. This, to be exact, I noted afterwards ; what I
first observed was a lady seated alone, outside, at one
of the little marble-topped tables. My brother-in-law
had stopped to look at her. Something had been put
before her, but she only leaned back, motionless and
with her hands folded, looking down the street and
away from us. I saw her but in diminished profile ;
nevertheless I was sure I knew on the spot that we
must already have met.

"The little lady of the steamer ! " my companion
cried.

"Was she on your steamer ? " I asked with
interest.

"From morning till night. She was never sick. She
used to sit perpetually at the side of the vessel with her
hands crossed that way, looking at the eastward
horizon."

"And are you going to speak to her ? "

"I don't know her. I never made acquaintance
with her. I wasn't in form to make up to ladies. But
I used to watch her and—I don't know why—to be
interested in her. She's a dear little Yankee woman.

I've an idea she's a school-mistress taking a holiday
—for which her scholars have made up a purse."

She had now turned her face a little more into profile, looking at the steep grey house-fronts opposite.
On this I decided. " I shall speak to her myself."

" I wouldn't—she's very shy," said my brother-
in-law.

" My dear fellow, I know her. I once showed her
photographs at a tea-party." With which I went up
to her, making her, as she turned to look at me, leave
me in no doubt of her identity. Miss Caroline Spencer
had achieved her dream. But she was less quick to
recognise me and showed a slight bewilderment. I
pushed a chair to the table and sat down. " Well," I
said, " I hope you're not disappointed ! "

She stared, blushing a little—then gave a small
jump and placed me. " It was you who showed me
the photographs—at North Verona."

" Yes, it was I. This happens very charmingly,
for isn't it quite for me to give you a formal reception
here—the official welcome ? I talked to you so much
about Europe."

" You didn't say too much. I'm so intensely
happy ! " she declared.

Very happy indeed she looked. There was no sign
of her being older ; she was as gravely, decently, de-
murely pretty as before. If she had struck me then as
a thin-stemmed mild-hued flower of Puritanism it
may be imagined whether in her present situation this
clear bloom was less appealing. Beside her an old
gentleman was drinking absinthe ; behind her the
dame de comptoir in the pink ribbons called " Alcibiade, Alcibiade ! " to the long-aproned waiter. I explained to Miss Spencer that the gentleman with me
had lately been her shipmate, and my brother-in-law
came up and was introduced to her. But she looked
at him as if she had never so much as seen him, and I

remembered he had told me her eyes were always fixed on the eastward horizon. She had evidently not noticed him, and, still timidly smiling, made no attempt whatever to pretend the contrary. I stayed with her on the little terrace of the café while he went back to the hotel and to his wife. I remarked to my friend that this meeting of ours at the first hour of her landing partook, among all chances, of the miraculous, but that I was delighted to be there and receive her first impressions.

"Oh I can't tell you," she said—" I feel so much in a dream. I've been sitting here an hour and I don't want to move. Everything's so delicious and romantic. I don't know whether the coffee has gone to my head—it's *so* unlike the coffee of my dead past."

"Really," I made answer, "if you're so pleased with this poor prosaic Havre you'll have no admiration left for better things. Don't spend your appreciation all the first day—remember it's your intellectual letter of credit. Remember all the beautiful places and things that are waiting for you. Remember that lovely Italy we talked about."

"I'm not afraid of running short," she said gaily, still looking at the opposite houses. "I could sit here all day—just saying to myself that here I am at last. It's so dark and strange—so old and indifferent."

"By the way then," I asked, "how come you to be encamped in this odd place? Haven't you gone to one of the inns?" For I was half-amused, half-alarmed at the good conscience with which this delicately pretty woman had stationed herself in conspicuous isolation on the edge of the sidewalk.

"My cousin brought me here and—a little while ago—left me," she returned. "You know I told you I had a relation over here. He's still here—a real cousin. Well," she pursued with unclouded candour, "he met me at the steamer this morning."

It was absurd—and the case moreover none of my business ; but I felt somehow disconcerted. " It was hardly worth his while to meet you if he was to desert you so soon."

" Oh he has only left me for half an hour," said Caroline Spencer. " He has gone to get my money."

I continued to wonder. " Where *is* your money ? "

She appeared seldom to laugh, but she laughed for the joy of this. " It makes me feel very fine to tell you! It's in circular notes."

" And where are your circular notes ? "

" In my cousin's pocket."

This statement was uttered with such clearness of candour that—I can hardly say why—it gave me a sensible chill. I couldn't at all at the moment have justified my lapse from ease, for I knew nothing of Miss Spencer's cousin. Since he stood in that relation to her—dear respectable little person—the presumption was in his favour. But I found myself wincing at the thought that half an hour after her landing her scanty funds should have passed into his hands. " Is he to travel with you ? " I asked.

" Only as far as Paris. He's an art-student in Paris —I've always thought that so splendid. I wrote to him that I was coming, but I never expected him to come off to the ship. I supposed he'd only just meet me at the train in Paris. It's very kind of him. But he *is*," said Caroline Spencer, " very kind—and very bright."

I felt at once a strange eagerness to see this bright kind cousin who was an art-student. " He's gone to the banker's ? " I inquired.

" Yes, to the banker's. He took me to an hotel— such a queer quaint cunning little place, with a court in the middle and a gallery all round, and a lovely landlady in such a beautifully fluted cap and such a perfectly fitting dress ! After a while we came out to

walk to the banker's, for I hadn't any French money.
But I was very dizzy from the motion of the vessel and
I thought I had better sit down. He found this place
for me here—then he went off to the banker's himself. I'm to wait here till he comes back."

Her story was wholly lucid and my impression perfectly wanton, but it passed through my mind that
the gentleman would never come back. I settled myself in a chair beside my friend and determined to
await the event. She was lost in the vision and the
imagination of everything near us and about us—
she observed, she recognised and admired, with a
touching intensity. She noticed everything that was
brought before us by the movement of the street—
the peculiarities of costume, the shapes of vehicles,
the big Norman horses, the fat priests, the shaven
poodles. We talked of these things, and there was
something charming in her freshness of perception
and the way her book-nourished fancy sallied forth
for the revel.

"And when your cousin comes back what are you
going to do ? " I went on.

For this she had, a little oddly, to think. " We
don't quite know."

"When do you go to Paris ? If you go by the four
o'clock train I may have the pleasure of making the
journey with you."

"I don't think we shall do that." So far she was
prepared. "My cousin thinks I had better stay here
a few days."

"Oh ! " said I—and for five minutes had nothing
to add. I was wondering what our absentee was, in
vulgar parlance, "up to." I looked up and down the
street, but saw nothing that looked like a bright and
kind American art-student. At last I took the liberty
of observing that the Havre was hardly a place to
choose as one of the esthetic stations of a European

tour. It was a place of convenience, nothing more ; a place of transit, through which transit should be rapid. I recommended her to go to Paris by the afternoon train and meanwhile to amuse herself by driving to the ancient fortress at the mouth of the harbour— that remarkable circular structure which bore the name of Francis the First and figured a sort of small Castle of Saint Angelo. (I might really have foreknown that it was to be demolished.)

She listened with much interest—then for a moment looked grave. "My cousin told me that when he returned he should have something particular to say to me, and that we could do nothing or decide nothing till I should have heard it. But I'll make him tell me right off, and then we'll go to the ancient fortress. Francis the First, did you say ? Why, that's lovely. There's no hurry to get to Paris ; there's plenty of time."

She smiled with her softly severe little lips as she spoke those last words, yet, looking at her with a purpose, I made out in her eyes, I thought, a tiny gleam of apprehension. "Don't tell me," I said, "that this wretched man's going to give you bad news ! "

She coloured as if convicted of a hidden perversity, but she was soaring too high to drop. "Well, I guess it's a *little* bad, but I don't believe it's *very* bad. At any rate I must listen to it."

I usurped an unscrupulous authority. "Look here ; you didn't come to Europe to listen—you came to *see* ! " But now I was sure her cousin would come back ; since he had something disagreeable to say to her he'd infallibly turn up. We sat a while longer and I asked her about her plans of travel. She had them on her fingers' ends and told over the names as solemnly as a daughter of another faith might have told over the beads of a rosary : from Paris to Dijon and to Avignon, from Avignon to Marseilles and the Cornice road ; thence to Genoa, to Spezia, to Pisa, to Florence, to Rome. It apparently had never occurred to her that there could be the least incommodity in her travelling alone ; and since she was unprovided with a companion I of course civilly abstained from disturbing her sense of security.

At last her cousin came back. I saw him turn toward us out of a side-street, and from the moment my eyes rested on him I knew he could but be the bright, if not the kind, American art-student. He wore a slouch hat and a rusty black velvet jacket, such as I had often encountered in the Rue Bonaparte. His shirt-collar displayed a stretch of throat that at a distance wasn't strikingly statuesque. He was tall and lean, he had red hair and freckles. These items I had time to take in while he approached the café, staring at me with natural surprise from under his romantic brim. When he came up to us I immediately introduced myself as an old acquaintance of Miss Spencer's, a character she serenely permitted me to claim. He looked at me hard with a pair of small sharp eyes, then he gave me a solemn wave, in the " European " fashion, of his rather rusty sombrero.

" You weren't on the ship ? " he asked.

" No, I wasn't on the ship. I've been in Europe these several years."

He bowed once more, portentously, and motioned me to be seated again. I sat down, but only for the purpose of observing him an instant—I saw it was time I should return to my sister. Miss Spencer's European protector was, by my measure, a very queer quantity. Nature hadn't shaped him for a Raphaelesque or Byronic attire, and his velvet doublet and exhibited though not columnar throat weren't in harmony with his facial attributes. His hair was cropped close to his head ; his ears were large and ill-adjusted to the same. He had a lackadaisical carriage and a

sentimental droop which were peculiarly at variance
with his keen conscious strange-coloured eyes—of a
brown that was almost red. Perhaps I was prejudiced,
but I thought his eyes too shifty. He said nothing for
some time ; he leaned his hands on his stick and
looked up and down the street. Then at last, slowly
lifting the stick and pointing with it, " That's a very
nice bit," he dropped with a certain flatness. He had
his head to one side—he narrowed his ugly lids. I
followed the direction of his stick ; the object it indicated was a red cloth hung out of an old window.
" Nice bit of colour," he continued ; and without
moving his head transferred his half-closed gaze
to me. " Composes well. Fine old tone. Make a nice
thing." He spoke in a charmless vulgar voice.

" I see you've a great deal of eye," I replied. " Your
cousin tells me you're studying art." He looked at me
in the same way, without answering, and I went on
with deliberate urbanity : " I suppose you're at the
studio of one of those great men." Still on this he
continued to fix me, and then he named one of the
greatest of that day ; which led me to ask him if he
liked his master.

" Do you understand French ? " he returned.

" Some kinds."

He kept his little eyes on me ; with which he remarked : " Je suis fou de la peinture ! "

" Oh I understand that kind ! " I replied. Our companion laid her hand on his arm with a small pleased
and fluttered movement ; it was delightful to be among
people who were on such easy terms with foreign
tongues. I got up to take leave and asked her where,
in Paris, I might have the honour of waiting on her.
To what hotel would she go ?

She turned to her cousin inquiringly and he favoured me again with his little languid leer. " Do you
know the Hôtel des Princes ? "

" I know where it is."

" Well, that's the shop."

" I congratulate you," I said to Miss Spencer. " I believe it's the best inn in the world ; but, in case I should still have a moment to call on you here, where are you lodged ? "

" Oh it's such a pretty name," she returned gleefully. " A la Belle Normande."

" I guess I know my way round ! " her kinsman threw in ; and as I left them he gave me with his swaggering head-cover a great flourish that was like the wave of a banner over a conquered field.

III

My relative, as it proved, was not sufficiently restored
to leave the place by the afternoon train ; so that
as the autumn dusk began to fall I found myself at
liberty to call at the establishment named to me by my
friends. I must confess that I had spent much of the
interval in wondering what the disagreeable thing was
that the less attractive of these had been telling the
other. The *auberge* of the Belle Normande proved an
hostelry in a shady by-street, where it gave me satisfaction to think Miss Spencer must have encountered
local colour in abundance. There was a crooked little
court, where much of the hospitality of the house was
carried on ; there was a staircase climbing to bed-
rooms on the outer side of the wall ; there was a small
trickling fountain with a stucco statuette set in the
midst of it ; there was a little boy in a white cap and
apron cleaning copper vessels at a conspicuous kitchen
door ; there was a chattering landlady, neatly laced,
arranging apricots and grapes into an artistic pyramid
upon a pink plate. I looked about, and on a green
bench outside of an open door labelled Salle-à-Manger,
I distinguished Caroline Spencer. No sooner had
I looked at her than I was sure something had happened since the morning. Supported by the back of
her bench, with her hands clasped in her lap, she kept
her eyes on the other side of the court where the
landlady manipulated the apricots.

But I saw that, poor dear, she wasn't thinking of apricots or even of landladies. She was staring absently, thoughtfully; on a nearer view I could have certified she had been crying. I had seated myself beside her before she was aware; then, when she had done so, she simply turned round without surprise and showed me her sad face. Something very bad indeed had happened; she was completely changed, and I immediately charged her with it. "Your cousin has been giving you bad news. You've had a horrid time."

For a moment she said nothing, and I supposed her afraid to speak lest her tears should again rise. Then it came to me that even in the few hours since my leaving her she had shed them all—which made her now intensely, stoically composed. "My poor cousin has been having one," she replied at last. "He has had great worries. His news was bad." Then after a dismally conscious wait: "He was in dreadful want of money."

"In want of yours, you mean?"

"Of any he could get—honourably of course. Mine *is* all—well, that's available."

Ah, it was as if I had been sure from the first! "And he has taken it from you?"

Again she hung fire, but her face meanwhile was pleading. "I gave him what I had."

I recall the accent of those words as the most angelic human sound I had ever listened to—which is exactly why I jumped up almost with a sense of personal outrage. "Gracious goodness, madam, do you call that his getting it 'honourably'?"

I had gone too far—she coloured to her eyes. "We won't speak of it."

"We *must* speak of it," I declared as I dropped beside her again. "I'm your friend—upon my word I'm your protector; it seems to me you need one. What's the matter with this extraordinary person ? "

She was perfectly able to say. " He's just badly in debt."

" No doubt he is ! But what's the special propriety of your—in such tearing haste !—paying for that ? "

" Well, he has told me all his story. I *feel* for him so much."

" So do I, if you come to that ! But I hope," I roundly added, " he'll give you straight back your money."

As to this she was prompt. " Certainly he will— as soon as ever he can."

" And when the deuce will that be ? "

Her lucidity maintained itself. " When he has finished his great picture."

It took me full in the face. " My dear young lady, damn his great picture ! Where is this voracious man ? "

It was as if she must let me feel a moment that I did push her !—though indeed, as appeared, he was just where he'd naturally be. " He's having his dinner."

I turned about and looked through the open door into the salle-à-manger. There, sure enough, alone at the end of a long table, was the object of my friend's compassion—the bright, the kind young art-student. He was dining too attentively to notice me at first, but in the act of setting down a well-emptied wine-glass he caught sight of my air of observation. He paused in his repast and, with his head on one side and his meagre jaws slowly moving, fixedly returned my gaze. Then the landlady came brushing lightly by with her pyramid of apricots.

" And that nice little plate of fruit is for him ? " I wailed.

Miss Spencer glanced at it tenderly. " They seem to arrange everything so nicely ! " she simply sighed.

I felt helpless and irritated. " Come now, really," I said ; " do you think it right, do you think it decent, that that long strong fellow should collar your funds ? " She looked away from me—I was evidently giving her pain. The case was hopeless ; the long strong fellow had " interested " her.

" Pardon me if I speak of him so unceremoniously," I said. " But you're really too generous, and he hasn't, clearly, the rudiments of delicacy. He made his debts himself—he ought to pay them himself."

" He has been foolish," she obstinately said—" of course I know that. He has told me everything. We had a long talk this morning—the poor fellow threw himself on my charity. He has signed notes to a large amount."

" The more fool he ! "

" He's in real distress—and it's not only himself. It's his poor young wife."

" Ah he has a poor young wife ? "

" I didn't know—but he made a clean breast of it. He married two years since—secretly."

" Why secretly ? "

My informant took precautions as if she feared listeners. Then with low impressiveness : " She was a Countess ! "

" Are you very sure of that ? "

" She has written me the most beautiful letter."

" Asking you—whom she has never seen—for money ? "

" Asking me for confidence and sympathy "—Miss Spencer spoke now with spirit. " She has been cruelly treated by her family—in consequence of what she has done for him. My cousin has told me every particular, and she appeals to me in her own lovely way in the letter, which I've here in my pocket. It's such a wonderful old-world romance," said my prodigious friend. " She was a beautiful young widow — her

248

first husband was a Count, tremendously high-born, but really most wicked, with whom she hadn't been happy and whose death had left her ruined after he had deceived her in all sorts of ways. My poor cousin, meeting her in that situation and perhaps a little too recklessly pitying her and charmed with her, found her, don't you see ? "—Caroline's appeal on this head was amazing !—" but too ready to trust a better man after all she had been through. Only when her 'people,' as he says—and I do like the word !— understood she *would* have him, poor gifted young American art-student though he simply was, because she just adored him, her great-aunt, the old Marquise, from whom she had expectations of wealth which she could yet sacrifice for her love, utterly cast her off and wouldn't so much as speak to her, much less to *him*, in their dreadful haughtiness and pride. They *can* be haughty over here, it seems," she ineffably developed—" there's no mistake about that ! It's like something in some famous old book. The family, my cousin's wife's," she by this time almost complacently wound up, " are of the oldest Provençal noblesse."

I listened half-bewildered. The poor woman positively found it so interesting to be swindled by a flower of that stock—if stock or flower or solitary grain of truth was really concerned in the matter— as practically to have lost the sense of what the forfeiture of her hoard meant for her. " My dear young lady," I groaned, " you don't want to be stripped of every dollar for such a rigmarole ! "

She asserted, at this, her dignity—much as a small pink shorn lamb might have done. " It isn't a rigmarole, and I shan't be stripped. I shan't live any worse than I *have* lived, don't you see ? And I'll come back before long to stay with them. The Countess— he still gives her, he says, her title, as they do to noble widows, that is to 'dowagers,' don't you know ? in England—insists on a visit from me *some* time. So I guess for *that* I can start afresh—and meanwhile I'll have recovered my money."

It was all too heart-breaking. " You're going home then at once ? "

I felt the faint tremor of voice she heroically tried to stifle. " I've nothing left for a tour."

" You gave it *all* up ? "

" I've kept enough to take me back."

I uttered, I think, a positive howl, and at this juncture the hero of the situation, the happy proprietor of my little friend's sacred savings and of the infatuated *grande dame* just sketched for me, reappeared with the clear consciousness of a repast bravely earned and consistently enjoyed. He stood on the threshold an instant, extracting the stone from a plump apricot he had fondly retained ; then he put the apricot into his mouth and, while he let it gratefully dissolve there, stood looking at us with his long legs apart and his hands thrust into the pockets of his velvet coat. My companion got up, giving him a thin glance that I caught in its passage and which expressed at once resignation and fascination—the last dregs of her sacrifice and with it an anguish of upliftedness. Ugly vulgar pretentious dishonest as I thought him, and destitute of every grace of plausibility, he had yet appealed successfully to her eager and tender imagination. I was deeply disgusted, but I had no warrant to interfere, and at any rate felt that it would be vain. He waved his hand meanwhile with a breadth of appreciation. " Nice old court. Nice mellow old place. Nice crooked old staircase. Several pretty things."

Decidedly I couldn't stand it, and without responding I gave my hand to my friend. She looked at me an instant with her little white face and rounded eyes, and as she showed her pretty teeth I suppose she

meant to smile. " Don't be sorry for me," she sub-
limely pleaded ; " I'm very sure I shall see something
of this dear old Europe yet."

I refused, however, to take literal leave of her—I
should find a moment to come back next morning.
Her awful kinsman, who had put on his sombrero
again, flourished it off at me by way of a bow—on
which I hurried away.

On the morrow early I did return, and in the court
of the inn met the landlady, more loosely laced than in
the evening. On my asking for Miss Spencer, " Partie,
monsieur," the good woman said. " She went away
last night at ten o'clock, with her—her—not her
husband, eh ?—in fine her Monsieur. They went
down to the American ship." I turned off—I felt the
tears in my eyes. The poor girl had been some thirteen
hours in Europe.

I MYSELF, more fortunate, continued to sacrifice to opportunity as I myself met it. During this period— of some five years—I lost my friend Latouche, who died of a malarious fever during a tour in the Levant. One of the first things I did on my return to America was to go up to North Verona on a consolatory visit to his poor mother. I found her in deep affliction and sat with her the whole of the morning that followed my arrival—I had come in late at night—listening to her tearful descant and singing the praises of my friend. We talked of nothing else, and our conversation ended only with the arrival of a quick little woman who drove herself up to the door in a " carry-all " and whom I saw toss the reins to the horse's back with the briskness of a startled sleeper throwing off the bed-clothes. She jumped out of the carry-all and she jumped into the room. She proved to be the minister's wife and the great town-gossip, and she had evidently, in the latter capacity, a choice morsel to communicate. I was as sure of this as I was that poor Mrs. Latouche was not absolutely too bereaved to listen to her. It seemed to me discreet to retire, and I described myself as anxious for a walk before dinner.

" And by the way," I added, " if you'll tell me where my old friend Miss Spencer lives I think I'll call on her."

The minister's wife immediately responded. Miss Spencer lived in the fourth house beyond the Baptist church; the Baptist church was the one on the right, with that queer green thing over the door; they called it a portico, but it looked more like an old-fashioned bedstead swung in the air. "Yes, do look up poor Caroline," Mrs. Latouche further enjoined. "It will refresh her to see a strange face."

"I should think she had had enough of strange faces!" cried the minister's wife.

"To see, I mean, a charming visitor"—Mrs. Latouche amended her phrase.

"I should think she had had enough of charming visitors!" her companion returned. "But *you* don't mean to stay ten years," she added with significant eyes on me.

"Has she a visitor of that sort?" I asked in my ignorance.

"You'll make out the sort!" said the minister's wife. "She's easily seen; she generally sits in the front yard. Only take care what you say to her, and be very sure you're polite."

"Ah she's so sensitive?"

The minister's wife jumped up and dropped me a curtsey—a most sarcastic curtsey. "That's what she is, if you please. 'Madame la Comtesse'!"

And pronouncing these titular words with the most scathing accent, the little woman seemed fairly to laugh in the face of the lady they designated. I stood staring, wondering, remembering.

"Oh I shall be very polite!" I cried; and, grasping my hat and stick, I went on my way.

I found Miss Spencer's residence without difficulty. The Baptist church was easily identified, and the small dwelling near it, of a rusty white, with a large central chimney-stack and a Virginia creeper, seemed naturally and properly the abode of a withdrawn old maid with a taste for striking effects inexpensively obtained. As I approached I slackened my pace, for I had heard that some one was always sitting in the front yard, and I wished to reconnoitre. I looked cautiously over the low white fence that separated the small garden-space from the unpaved street, but I descried nothing in the shape of a Comtesse. A small straight path led up to the crooked door-step, on either side of which was a little grass-plot fringed with currant-bushes. In the middle of the grass, right and left, was a large quince-tree, full of antiquity and contortions, and beneath one of the quince-trees were placed a small table and a couple of light chairs. On the table lay a piece of unfinished embroidery and two or three books in bright-coloured paper covers. I went in at the gate and paused half-way along the path, scanning the place for some further token of its occupant, before whom—I could hardly have said why—I hesitated abruptly to present myself. Then I saw the poor little house to be of the shabbiest and felt a sudden doubt of my right to penetrate, since curiosity had been my motive and curiosity here failed of confidence. While I demurred a figure appeared in the open doorway and stood there looking at me. I immediately recognised Miss Spencer, but she faced me as if we had never met. Gently, but gravely and timidly, I advanced to the door-step, where I spoke with an attempt at friendly banter.

" I waited for you over there to come back, but you never came."

" Waited where, sir ? " she quavered, her innocent eyes rounding themselves as of old. She was much older ; she looked tired and wasted.

" Well," I said, " I waited at the old French port."

She stared harder, then recognised me, smiling, flushing, clasping her two hands together. " I remember you now—I remember that day." But she stood there, neither coming out nor asking me to come in. She was embarrassed.

I too felt a little awkward while I poked at the path with my stick. " I kept looking out for you year after year."

" You mean in Europe ? " she ruefully breathed.

" In Europe of course ! Here apparently you're easy enough to find."

She leaned her hand against the unpainted door-post and her head fell a little to one side. She looked at me thus without speaking, and I caught the expression visible in women's eyes when tears are rising. Suddenly she stepped out on the cracked slab of stone before her threshold and closed the door. Then her strained smile prevailed and I saw her teeth were as pretty as ever. But there had been tears too. " Have you been there ever since ? " she lowered her voice to ask.

" Until three weeks ago. And you—you never came back ? "

Still shining at me as she could, she put her hand behind her and reopened the door. " I'm not very polite," she said. " Won't you come in ? "

" I'm afraid I incommode you."

" Oh no ! "—she wouldn't hear of it now. And she pushed back the door with a sign that I should enter.

I followed her in. She led the way to a small room on the left of the narrow hall, which I supposed to be her parlour, though it was at the back of the house, and we passed the closed door of another apartment which apparently enjoyed a view of the quince-trees. This one looked out upon a small wood-shed and two clucking hens. But I thought it pretty until I saw its elegance to be of the most frugal kind ; after which, presently, I thought it prettier still, for I had never seen faded chintz and old mezzotint engravings, framed in varnished autumn leaves, disposed with so

255

touching a grace. Miss Spencer sat down on a very small section of the sofa, her hands tightly clasped in her lap. She looked ten years older, and I needn't now have felt called to insist on the facts of her person. But I still thought them interesting, and at any rate I was moved by them. She was peculiarly agitated. I tried to appear not to notice it ; but suddenly, in the most inconsequent fashion—it was an irresistible echo of our concentrated passage in the old French port—I said to her : " I do incommode you. Again you're in distress."

She raised her two hands to her face and for a moment kept it buried in them. Then taking them away, " It's because you remind me," she said.

" I remind you, you mean, of that miserable day at the Havre ? "

She wonderfully shook her head. " It wasn't miserable. It was delightful."

Ah was it ? my manner of receiving this must have commented. " I never was so shocked as when, on going back to your inn the next morning, I found you had wretchedly retreated."

She waited an instant, after which she said : " Please let us not speak of that."

" Did you come straight back here ? " I nevertheless went on.

" I was back here just thirty days after my first start."

" And here you've remained ever since ? "

" Every minute of the time."

I took it in ; I didn't know what to say, and what I presently said had almost the sound of mockery. " When then are you going to make that tour ? " It might be practically aggressive ; but there was something that irritated me in her depths of resignation, and I wished to extort from her some expression of impatience.

She attached her eyes a moment to a small sun-spot on the carpet ; then she got up and lowered the window-blind a little to obliterate it. I waited, watching her with interest—as if she had still some-thing more to give me. Well, presently, in answer to my last question, she gave it. " Never ! "

" I hope at least your cousin repaid you that money," I said.

At this again she looked away from me. " I don't care for it now."

" You don't care for your money ? "

" For ever going to Europe."

" Do you mean you wouldn't go if you could ? "

" I can't—I can't," said Caroline Spencer. " It's all over. Everything's different. I never think of it."

" The scoundrel never repaid you then ! " I cried.

" Please, please——! " she began.

But she had stopped—she was looking toward the door. There had been a rustle and a sound of steps in the hall.

I also looked toward the door, which was open and now admitted another person—a lady who paused just within the threshold. Behind her came a young man. The lady looked at me with a good deal of fixedness—long enough for me to rise to a vivid impression of herself. Then she turned to Caroline Spencer and, with a smile and a strong foreign accent, " *Pardon, ma chère !* I didn't know you had company," she said. " The gentleman came in so quietly." With which she again gave me the benefit of her attention. She was very strange, yet I was at once sure I had seen her before. Afterwards I rather put it that I had only seen ladies remarkably like her. But I had seen them very far away from North Verona, and it was the oddest of all things to meet one of them in that frame. To what quite other scene did the sight of her transport me ? To some dusky landing before

257

a shabby Parisian *quatrième*—to an open door reveal-
ing a greasy ante-chamber and to Madame leaning
over the banisters while she holds a faded wrapper
together and bawls down to the portress to bring up
her coffee. My friend's guest was a very large lady, of
middle age, with a plump dead-white face and hair
drawn back *à la chinoise*. She had a small penetrating
eye and what is called in French *le sourire agréable*.
She wore an old pink cashmere dressing-gown covered
with white embroideries, and, like the figure in my
momentary vision, she confined it in front with a
bare and rounded arm and a plump and deeply-
dimpled hand.

"It's only to spick about my café," she said to
her hostess with her *sourire agréable*. "I should like
it served in the garden under the leetle tree."

The young man behind her had now stepped into
the room, where he also stood revealed, though with
rather less of a challenge. He was a gentleman of few
inches but a vague importance, perhaps the leading
man of the world of North Verona. He had a small
pointed nose and a small pointed chin ; also, as I
observed, the most diminutive feet and a manner of
no point at all. He looked at me foolishly and with
his mouth open.

"You shall have your coffee," said Miss Spencer
as if an army of cooks had been engaged in the
preparation of it.

"*C'est bien !*" said her massive inmate. "Find
your bouk"—and this personage turned to the
gaping youth.

He gaped now at each quarter of the room. "My
grammar, d'ye mean ? "

The large lady, however, could but face her friend's
visitor while persistently engaged with a certain
laxity in the flow of her wrapper. "Find your bouk,"
she more absently repeated.

" My poetry, d'ye mean ? " said the young man, who also couldn't take his eyes off me.

" Never mind your bouk "—his companion reconsidered. " To-day we'll just talk. We'll make some conversation. But we mustn't interrupt Mademoiselle's. Come, come "—and she moved off a step. " Under the leetle tree," she added for the benefit of Mademoiselle. After which she gave me a thin salutation, jerked a measured " Monsieur ! " and swept away again with her swain following.

I looked at Miss Spencer, whose eyes never moved from the carpet, and I spoke, I fear, without grace. " Who in the world's that ? "

" The Comtesse—that *was* : my *cousine* as they call it in French."

" And who's the young man ? "

" The Countess's pupil, Mr. Mixter." This description of the tie uniting the two persons who had just quitted us must certainly have upset my gravity ; for I recall the marked increase of my friend's own as she continued to explain. " She gives lessons in French and music, the simpler sorts——"

" The simpler sorts of French ? " I fear I broke in.

But she was still impenetrable, and in fact had now an intonation that put me vulgarly in the wrong. " She has had the worst reverses—with no one to look to. She's prepared for any exertion—and she takes her misfortunes with gaiety."

" Ah well," I returned—no doubt a little ruefully, " that's all I myself am pretending to do. If she's determined to be a burden to nobody, nothing could be more right and proper."

My hostess looked vaguely, though I thought quite wearily enough, about : she met this proposition in no other way. " I must go and get the coffee," she simply said.

"Has the lady many pupils?" I none the less persisted.

"She has only Mr. Mixter. She gives him all her time." It might have set me off again, but something in my whole impression of my friend's sensibility urged me to keep strictly decent. "He pays very well," she at all events inscrutably went on. "He's not very bright—as a pupil; but he's very rich and he's very kind. He has a buggy—with a back, and he takes the Countess to drive."

"For good long spells I hope," I couldn't help interjecting—even at the cost of her so taking it that she had still to avoid my eyes. "Well, the country's beautiful for miles," I went on. And then as she was turning away: "You're going for the Countess's coffee?"

"If you'll excuse me a few moments."

"Is there no one else to do it?"

She seemed to wonder who there should be. "I keep no servants."

"Then can't I help?" After which, as she but looked at me, I bettered it. "Can't she wait on herself?"

Miss Spencer had a slow headshake—as if that too had been a strange idea. "She isn't used to *manual* labour."

The discrimination was a treat, but I cultivated decorum. "I see—and you *are*." But at the same time I couldn't abjure curiosity. "Before you go, at any rate, please tell me this: who *is* this wonderful lady?"

"I told you just who in France—that extraordinary day. She's the wife of my cousin, whom you saw there."

"The lady disowned by her family in consequence of her marriage?"

"Yes; they've never seen her again. They've completely broken with her."

" And where's her husband ? "

" My poor cousin's dead."

I pulled up, but only a moment. " And where's your money ? "

The poor thing flinched—I kept her on the rack. " I don't know," she woefully said.

I scarce know what it didn't prompt me to—but I went step by step. " On her husband's death this lady at once came to you ? "

It was as if she had had too often to describe it. " Yes, she arrived one day."

" How long ago ? "

" Two years and four months."

" And has been here ever since ? "

" Ever since."

I took it all in. " And how does she like it ? "

" Well, not *very* much," said Miss Spencer divinely.

That too I took in. " And how do *you*——? "

She laid her face in her two hands an instant as she had done ten minutes before. Then, quickly, she went to get the Countess's coffee.

Left alone in the little parlour I found myself divided between the perfection of my disgust and a contrary wish to see, to learn more. At the end of a few minutes the young man in attendance on the lady in question reappeared as for a fresh gape at me. He was inordinately grave—to be dressed in such particoloured flannels ; and he produced with no great confidence on his own side the message with which he had been charged. " She wants to know if you won't come right out."

" Who wants to know ? "

" The Countess. That French lady."

" She has asked you to bring me ? "

" Yes, sir," said the young man feebly—for I may claim to have surpassed him in stature and weight.

I went out with him, and we found his instructress

seated under one of the small quince-trees in front of
the house ; where she was engaged in drawing a fine
needle with a very fat hand through a piece of embroidery not remarkable for freshness. She pointed
graciously to the chair beside her and I sat down. Mr.
Mixter glanced about him and then accommodated
himself on the grass at her feet ; whence he gazed
upward more gapingly than ever and as if convinced
that between us something wonderful would now
occur.

" I'm sure you spick French," said the Countess,
whose eyes were singularly protuberant as she played
over me her agreeable smile.

" I do, madam—*tant bien que mal*," I replied, I
fear, more dryly.

" *Ah voilà !* " she cried as with delight. " I knew it
as soon as I looked at you. You've been in my poor
dear country."

" A considerable time."

" You love it then, *mon pays de France* ? "

" Oh it's an old affection." But I wasn't exuberant.

" And you know Paris well ? "

" Yes, *sans me vanter*, madam, I think I really do."
And with a certain conscious purpose I let my eyes
meet her own.

She presently, hereupon, moved her own and
glanced down at Mr. Mixter. " What are we talking
about ? " she demanded of her attentive pupil.

He pulled his knees up, plucked at the grass, stared,
blushed a little. " You're talking French," said Mr.
Mixter.

" *La belle découverte !* " mocked the Countess. " It's
going on ten months," she explained to me, " since
I took him in hand. Don't put yourself out not to
say he's *la bêtise même*," she added in fine style. " He
won't in the least understand you."

A moment's consideration of Mr. Mixter, awk-

wardly sporting at our feet, quite assured me that he
wouldn't. " I hope your other pupils do you more
honour," I then remarked to my entertainer.

" I have no others. They don't know what French
—or what anything else—is in this place ; they don't
want to know. You may therefore imagine the
pleasure it is to me to meet a person who speaks it
like yourself." I could but reply that my own
pleasure wasn't less, and she continued to draw the
stitches through her embroidery with an elegant curl
of her little finger. Every few moments she put her
eyes, near-sightedly, closer to her work—this as if for
elegance too. She inspired me with no more confidence than her late husband, if husband he was, had
done, years before, on the occasion with which this
one so detestably matched : she was coarse, common,
affected, dishonest—no more a Countess than I was
a Caliph. She had an assurance—based clearly on
experience ; but this couldn't have been the experience of " race." Whatever it was indeed it did now,
in a yearning fashion, flare out of her. " Talk to me
of Paris, *mon beau Paris* that I'd give my eyes to
see. The very name of it *me fait languir*. How long
since you were there ? "

" A couple of months ago."

" *Vous avez de la chance !* Tell me something about
it. What were they doing ? Oh for an hour of the
Boulevard ! "

" They were doing about what they're always doing
—amusing themselves a good deal."

" At the theatres, *hein* ? " sighed the Countess. " At
the cafés-concerts ? *sous ce beau ciel*—at the little
tables before the doors ? *Quelle existence !* You know
I'm a Parisienne, monsieur," she added, " to my
finger-tips."

" Miss Spencer was mistaken then," I ventured to
return, " in telling me you're a Provençale."

263

She stared a moment, then put her nose to her embroidery, which struck me as having acquired even while we sat a dingier and more desultory air. " Ah I'm a Provençale by birth, but a Parisienne by— inclination." After which she pursued : " And by the saddest events of my life—as well as by some of the happiest, hélas ! "

" In other words by a varied experience ! " I now at last smiled.

She questioned me over it with her hard little salient eyes. " Oh experience !—I could talk of that, no doubt, if I wished. *On en a de toutes les sortes*— and I never dreamed that mine, for example, would ever have *this* in store for me." And she indicated with her large bare elbow and with a jerk of her head all surrounding objects ; the little white house, the pair of quince-trees, the rickety paling, even the rapt Mr. Mixter.

I took them all bravely in. " Ah if you mean you're decidedly in exile—— ! "

" You may imagine what it is. These two years of my *épreuve—elles m'en ont données, des heures, des heures !* One gets used to things "—and she raised her shoulders to the highest shrug ever accomplished at North Verona ; " so that I sometimes think I've got used to this. But there are some things that are always beginning again. For example my coffee."

I so far again lent myself. " Do you always have coffee at this hour ? "

Her eyebrows went up as high as her shoulders had done. " At what hour would you propose to me to have it ? I must have my little cup after breakfast."

" Ah you breakfast at this hour ? "

" At mid-day—*comme cela se fait*. Here they breakfast at a quarter past seven. That ' quarter past ' is charming ! "

" But you were telling me about your coffee," I observed sympathetically.

" My *cousine* can't believe in it ; she can't understand it. *C'est une fille charmante,* but that little cup of black coffee with a drop of ' *fine,*' served at this hour—they exceed her comprehension. So I have to break the ice each day, and it takes the coffee the time you see to arrive. And when it does arrive, monsieur——! If I don't press it on *you*—though monsieur here sometimes joins me !—it's because you've drunk it on the Boulevard."

I resented extremely so critical a view of my poor friend's exertions, but I said nothing at all—the only way to be sure of my civility. I dropped my eyes on Mr. Mixter, who, sitting cross-legged and nursing his knees, watched my companion's foreign graces with an interest that familiarity had apparently done little to restrict. She became aware, naturally, of my mystified view of him and faced the question with all her boldness. " He adores me, you know," she murmured with her nose again in her tapestry— " he dreams of becoming *mon amoureux.* Yes, *il me fait une cour acharnée*—such as you see him. That's what we've come to. He has read some French novel —it took him six months. But ever since that he has thought himself a hero and me—such as I am, monsieur—*je ne sais quelle dévergondée !* "

Mr. Mixter may have inferred that he was to that extent the object of our reference ; but of the manner in which he was handled he must have had small suspicion—preoccupied as he was, as to my companion, with the ecstasy of contemplation. Our hostess moreover at this moment came out of the house, bearing a coffee-pot and three cups on a neat little tray. I took from her eyes, as she approached us, a brief but intense appeal—the mute expression, as I felt, conveyed in the hardest little look she had

yet addressed me, of her longing to know what, as a
man of the world in general and of the French world
in particular, I thought of these allied forces now so
encamped on the stricken field of her life. I could
only " act " however, as they said at North Verona,
quite impenetrably—only make no answering sign.
I couldn't intimate, much less could I frankly utter,
my inward sense of the Countess's probable past, with
its measure of her virtue, value and accomplishments,
and of the limits of the consideration to which she
could properly pretend. I couldn't give my friend a
hint of how I myself personally " saw " her interesting pensioner—whether as the runaway wife of a too-
jealous hairdresser or of a too-morose pastry-cook,
say ; whether as a very small bourgeoise, in fine,
who had vitiated her case beyond patching up, or
even as some character, of the nomadic sort, less
edifying still. I couldn't let in, by the jog of a
shutter, as it were, a hard informing ray and then,
washing my hands of the business, turn my back for
ever. I could on the contrary but save the situation,
my own at least, for the moment, by pulling myself
together with a master hand and appearing to ignore
everything but that the dreadful person between us
was a *grande dame.* This effort was possible indeed
but as a retreat in good order and with all the forms
of courtesy. If I couldn't speak, still less could I
stay, and I think I must, in spite of everything, have
turned black with disgust to see Caroline Spencer
stand there like a waiting-maid. I therefore won't
answer for the shade of success that may have attended my saying to the Countess, on my feet and as
to leave her : " You expect to remain some time in
these *parages* ? "

What passed between us, as from face to face,
while she looked up at me, *that* at least our companion
may have caught, that at least may have sown, for the

after-time, some seed of revelation. The Countess repeated her terrible shrug. " Who knows ? I don't see my way——! It isn't an existence, but when one's in misery——! *Chère belle*," she added as an appeal to Miss Spencer, " you've gone and forgotten the ' *fine* ' ! "

I detained that lady as, after considering a moment in silence the small array, she was about to turn off in quest of this article. I held out my hand in silence —I had to go. Her wan set little face, severely mild and with the question of a moment before now quite cold in it, spoke of extreme fatigue, but also of something else strange and conceived—whether a desperate patience still, or at last some other desperation, being more than I can say. What was clearest on the whole was that she was glad I was going. Mr. Mixter had risen to his feet and was pouring out the Countess's coffee. As I went back past the Baptist church I could feel how right my poor friend had been in her conviction at the other, the still intenser, the now historic crisis, that she should still see something of that dear old Europe.

267

NOTES

(The references are to page and line numbers. Details of works referred to can be found in 'Further reading'; dates, where given, indicate the edition used.)

PREFACE

xxxix.16 *ladies, who weren't in fact named* It has been argued that the original anecdote concerned a Mrs Newberry and her daughter Julia, wealthy Americans from Chicago, who had visited Vevey and Rome in their European wanderings. Julia had died suddenly in Rome in April 1876 and was buried in the Protestant Cemetery. (See Aziz, ed., *Tales*, 3, 15–16.)

xxxix.26 *the editor of a magazine ... at Philadelphia* John Foster Kirk, editor of *Lippincott's Magazine*.

xxxv.19 *pirated in Boston* In *Littell's Living Age*, 6 and 27 July 1878; and also in the *Home Journal* (New York) on 31 July, 7 and 14 August 1878. His failure to secure the American rights cost James the proceeds of the valuable periodical market in the United States.

xl.24 *the ultimately most prosperous child of my invention* There is a painful irony in this late claim that 'Daisy Miller' should have proved the most commercially successful of his works. In 1879 James told his friend W. D. Howells that he had made a mere two hundred dollars 'by the whole American career of *Daisy Miller*'.

xl.28 *Leslie Stephen* Editor of the *Cornhill Magazine* 1871–82; he had accepted 'Daisy Miller' 'with effusion'. James knew him personally, and kept up friendly contacts with his children, Toby Stephen, Vanessa Bell and Virginia Woolf, after their father's death in 1904.

xlii.24 *the original grossness of readers* 'Daisy Miller' had attracted a great deal of notice, both hostile and

268

appreciative, as a study of contemporary manners. W. D. Howells, editor of the *Atlantic Monthly* and a friend of James's, wrote that 'Harry James waked up all the women with his *Daisy Miller*, the intention of which they misconceived, and there has been a vast discussion in which nobody felt very deeply, and everybody talked very loudly. The thing went so far that society almost divided itself into Daisy Millerites and anti-Daisy Millerites. I am glad of it, for I hoped that in making James so thoroughly known, it would call attention in a wide degree to the beautiful work he has been doing for so long for very few readers.' See Gard, *Henry James: The Critical Heritage*, for a selection of reviews and reactions to the story. The *Cornhill* had carried other pieces on the greater freedom of, especially, young women in the New World. See, for example, the article 'On Some Peculiarities of Society in America', in Vol. 26, December 1872.

xliii.27 *The evolution of varieties moves fast* James traces here what he calls 'a whole passage of intellectual history' in the interval between the writing of 'Daisy Miller' and 'Pandora' and the much later 'Julia Bride' (1908), in terms which echo the earlier speech of the energetic lady in the gondola. The question concerns the extent to which the heroine of each story is to be taken as representative of a new type, or as 'pure poetry'.

xliv.13 *a brief but profusely peopled stay in New York* James had spent three weeks in New York in December 1881, after a five-year absence from America. He told Grace Norton that he had seen 'many persons—but no personages; have heard much talk—but no conversation.'

xliv.23 *the world "down-town"* Although a New Yorker born and (in the main) bred, James was conscious of how little he knew of the commercial world of Lower Manhattan. His autobiography records how alien to the James children was the notion of 'business'. Here the novelist meditates on what it meant to find himself 'unprepared and uneducated' on so essential an aspect of New York.

xlv.24 *the very moderate altitude of Twenty-Fifth Street* Street numbers in New York move from the Battery end of Manhattan, becoming higher as they go 'up' the island. James was staying in what was then well within the centre of the city, but in a district that was essentially residential—cut off from the active occupation of the male population of New York, the making of money.

xlviii.22 *piously persisted in* . . . James goes on to reflect on a story, 'Fordham Castle' (1904), included in Volume XVI of the New York Edition, as a case of his ingenuity in creating something 'larger' out of a 'scrap of an up-town subject'. He then returns to his theme of reviewing the group of stories which might seem to risk 'too unbroken an eternity of mere international young ladies'. See also the discussion of 'Julia Bride' at the end of the Preface to Volume XVII of the New York Edition.

lii.12 *the birthmark of Dialect* James's return to the United States in 1904 had quickened his interest—an interest both critical and imaginative—in the American language. He contributed a series of articles to *Harper's Bazar* from November 1906 to July 1907 (which have never been collected) on the manners and speech of American women. In 'The Question of Our Speech' (1905), he argued that 'Whereas the great idioms of Europe in general have grown up at home and in the family, the ancestral circle (with their migrations all comfortably historic), our transported maiden, our unrescued Andromeda . . . was to be disjoined from all associations, the other presences that had attended her, that had watched for her and with her, that had helped to form her manners and her voice, her taste and her genius.' Sensitivity to tone and idiom is especially marked in revisions to texts for the New York Edition. The heroines of these stories are, precisely, without the formative background of their European counterparts. If Mrs Walker pronounces with 'the voice of civilised society', the Miller family, touchingly, have no idea what they sound like; and Winterbourne is hardly prepared for Daisy to find *his* speech 'quaint'. The story plays on such uncertainties of response to tone and mode. Even a reader unfamiliar with James's American idioms may hear their effect through the precision of the writing.

DAISY MILLER

3.1 *Vevey* A small town on Lake Geneva in the Canton of Vaud, and a popular holiday resort. James had stayed there and visited the Castle of Chillon in 1873. The 'particularly comfortable' hotel is the Hôtel Monnet des Trois Couronnes.

3.23 *Newport and Saratoga* Newport, Rhode Island, was a very fashionable Atlantic resort; Saratoga, in up-state New York, was a health and holiday centre famous for its spa. James knew Newport well from childhood. He visited Saratoga in 1870 and found it 'characteristically American and democratic'.

4.2 *Ocean House . . . Congress Hall* Large hotels in, respectively, Newport and Saratoga.

4.9 *the Dent du Midi* A jagged, snow-covered peak across the lake from Vevey, in the Valais.

4.10 *the Castle of Chillon* The Castle stands on an isolated rock at the end of the lake, its massive walls and towers visible from a distance across the water. Byron's 'Prisoner of Chillon' (composed nearby in 1816) gives a moving though historically inaccurate account of Bonnivard as a victim of the Duke of Savoy's tyranny, confined alone for six years in the gloomy dungeons:

> Chillon! thy prison is a holy place,
>   And thy sad floor an altar,—for 'twas trod,
> Until his very steps have left a trace
>   Worn, as if thy cold pavement were a sod,
> By Bonnivard!—may none those marks efface!
>   For they appeal from tyranny to God.

5.1 *the little capital of Calvinism* Geneva was historically the heart of the Reformation. A refugee from Paris, Calvin became the chief spokesman for the new doctrines there, founding the Geneva Academy in 1559 as a school of Protestant theology. James also knew it as the city of Voltaire, Rousseau, Gibbon and Madame de Staël.

5.3 *the grey old "Academy"* Then part of the University of Geneva. William James had attended it in 1859–60. Henry, too young to join his brother, had spent the time at a school beside the prison and opposite the Cathedral of St Peter, in which Calvin used to preach. See *A Small Boy and Others*, pp. 162–6, and *Notes of a Son and Brother*, pp. 239–51.

12.5 *Schenectady* The town lies north-west of Albany in up-state New York. It was an important industrial centre with large locomotive works, and later became the headquarters of the General Electric Company. Henry James Sr. had attended Union College there in 1828, in conformity with his father's wishes.

12.28   *the cars*   i.e. the railway carriages.

19.7   *an obstreperous little boy*   T. S. Eliot admired Randolph Miller as one of James's 'distinct successes'. See also the comments on American children at Saratoga, *The American Scene*, p. 477.

20.4   *her stronghold in Forty-Second Street*   Mrs Costello lives in the part of New York known as Murray Hill, now bordered by many of the world's tallest buildings, but in the late nineteenth century an area of baroque brownstone mansions housing the city's social élite. See Edith Wharton's *Old New York* (1924).

24.6   *constatations*   Certified statements, findings.

24.28   *comme il faut*   Correct.

24.28   *she wore white puffs*   A hairstyle then fashionable in Paris. The ends of the hair were rolled in to form a rounded soft mass, usually arranged on the forehead.

36.1   *oubliettes*   Secret dungeons, whose occupants may be 'forgotten'.

36.7   *without other society than that of their guide*   A well-tipped guide has ensured the improbably secluded tour of the castle. James's own experience as a tourist at Chillon was very different: 'When I went, Bädecker in hand, to "do" the place, I found a huge concourse of visitors awaiting the reflux of an earlier wave. "Let us at least wait till there is no one else," I said to my companion. She smiled in compassion of my naïveté, *"There never is no one else,"* she answered. "We must treat it as a crush or leave it alone"' ('Swiss Notes', *Foreign Parts*, 1883).

36.26   *the story of the unhappy Bonnivard*   The historical François de Bonnivard lived from *c.*1493–1570. As Prior of St Victor, near Geneva, he supported the revolt of the Genevese against Charles III of Savoy, who kept him prisoner 1519–21 and again, at Chillon, 1530–6, when the Bernese finally stormed the castle.

39.13   *Cherbuliez's—'Paule Méré'*   Cherbuliez (1829–99) was a minor Swiss writer. *Paule Méré* first appeared in the *Revue des Deux Mondes* in 1864, where it enjoyed a vogue and was translated and widely read in America. James refers to it in his essay 'Swiss Notes' by way of defining the peculiar tone of Genevan society: 'An ingenious Swiss novelist has indeed written a tale expressly to prove that frank nature is wofully out of favor there, and his heroine dies of a broken heart because her spontaneity passes for impropriety. I don't know whether M. Cherbuliez's novel is as veracious as it is clever; but the susceptible stranger certainly feels that the Helvetic capital is a highly artificial compound.' Mrs Costello, it is ironically implied, misses the point of the parallel between the novel and the girl to whom she declines to be introduced. The novel's hero, Marcel Roger, has several qualities in common with Winterbourne: about thirty, he is wealthy, a self-styled 'spectateur désœuvré', and cosmopolitan in outlook. He shares with Winterbourne an ambivalent attitude to the heroine, who in each case courts criticism by her freedoms. The climax, similarly, comes as Roger sees the girl one night in an apparently compromising rendez-vous, and rejects her with finality.

46.5 *the Pincio* The handsome public garden laid out in the nineteenth century, linked to the park of the Villa Borghese. It offers an exceptional view across Rome, particularly at dusk when the golden light over the city is enhanced.

48.14 *if we don't die of the fever* Malaria, or 'Roman fever'; also known as *perniciosa* (75.27).

57.8 *the beautiful Villa Borghese* The largest public park in Rome, created for the Cardinal Scipione Borghese and containing his palace; now a museum.

59.23 *Elle s'affiche, la malheureuse* She's making a spectacle of herself, poor girl.

65.22 *having gone to Saint Peter's with his aunt* Writing of Rome in *Transatlantic Sketches*, James had said that 'Taken as a walk not less than as a church, St Peter's of course reigns alone. Even for the profane "constitutional" it serves where the Boulevards, where Piccadilly and Broadway, fall short, and if it didn't offer to our use the grandest area in the world it would still offer the most diverting.'

67.6 *cavaliere avvocato* Cavaliere is a title representing the most widely held (and therefore lowest) decoration bestowed by the Italian government. It usually denotes a minor official. The conjunction with *avvocato*—a lawyer—is strange: the implication seems to be that Giovanelli is someone of no special merit but with friends in the right places. In the autumn of 1877 James himself lodged with the family of the 'Cavaliere Avvocato Spinetti—a rather ragged and besmirched establishment' (*Letters*, ed. Edel, II 142).

67.21 *marchese* Marquis.

67.24 *qui se passe ses fantaisies* Who pleases herself, does what she likes.

68.16 *the Corso* The main street in the centre of Rome, lined with palaces dating from the Renaissance onwards. It is the traditional place for festivities such as the famous horse races (hence its name) and the carnival. See James's description in 'A Roman Holiday', in *Transatlantic Sketches*.

68.18 *the Doria palace* One of the great seventeenth-century Roman palaces. Writing elsewhere of Rome, James mentions particularly the Claudes in the Doria collection of paintings, admiring their familiarity with the landscape of the Campagna, just outside Rome.

68.36 *du meilleur monde* Of the best society.

70.25 *the Palace of the Caesars* The Palatine Hill, behind the Forum, was the site chosen by the Emperor Domitian for his Imperial Palace, since (according to legend) it was where Romulus and Remus had been discovered. The remains of the complex of buildings are very extensive.

73.18 *the Cælian Hill* One of the seven hills of Rome.

73.21 *the Arch of Constantine* One of the biggest of the Roman triumphal arches, built to commemorate Constantine's victory over Maxentius in AD 315. James describes its 'noble battered bas-reliefs, with the chain of tragic statues—fettered, drooping barbarians—round its summit', in 'A Roman Holiday'.

73.26 *the dusky circle of the Colosseum* The Colosseum is the name by which the vast Flavian Amphitheatre near the south-east end of the Forum has been known since the eighteenth century. The huge four-tiered oval, much of which still stands, has circle on circle of marble seats. The arena was the scene of gladiatorial contests, fights between men and beasts, races and other spectacles. According to tradition, persecuted Christians were thrown here to the beasts. The Cross erected in the centre of the arena in the eighteenth century to commemorate the martyrs was removed in 1874, but replaced in 1927. (James spent five months in Rome in 1873.)

74.1 *Byron's famous lines out of "Manfred"* The lines Winterbourne is speaking are from Manfred's soliloquy in Act III, scene iv. The imagery of the speech is markedly consonant with the episode in the story:

. . . the gladiators' bloody Circus stands,
A noble wreck in ruinous perfection,
While Caesar's chambers, and the Augustan halls,
Grovel on earth in indistinct decay.
And thou didst shine, thou rolling moon, upon
All this, and cast a wide and tender light,
Which softened down the hoar austerity
Of rugged desolation, and fill'd up,
As 'twere anew, the gaps of centuries;
Leaving that beautiful which still was so,
And making that which was not, till the place
Became religion, and the heart ran o'er
With silent worship of the great of old,—
The dead, but sceptred sovereigns, who still rule
Our spirits from their urns . . .

74.17 *he looks at us as one of the old lions or tigers may have looked at the Christian martyrs!* Compare *The Wings of the Dove*, where Merton Densher sees Milly Theale as 'a Christian maid, in the arena, mildly, caressingly martyred', not by the nosing of 'lions and tigers but of domestic animals let loose as for a joke'. William James, who visited the Colosseum with his brother in 1868, could not bear the place. He wrote to their father: 'when we entered under the mighty Coliseum [*sic*] wall and stood in its mysterious midst, with that cold sinister half-moon and hardly a star in the deep blue sky—it was all so strange, and, I must say, inhuman and horrible, that it felt like a nightmare. . . . Anti-Christian as I generally am, I actually derived a deep comfort from the big black cross that had been planted on that damned blood-soaked soil. I think if Harry had not been with me I should have fled howling from the place.' (Quoted in Matthiessen, *The James Family*, p. 291.) For a very different reaction, see Edith Wharton's story, 'Roman Fever' (1936), where the

outcome of another nocturnal rendez-vous in the Colosseum
is in marked contrast to Daisy Miller's fate.

79.24 *the little Protestant cemetery* The small open
cemetery for Protestant foreigners just outside the city walls,
next to Rome's one pyramid. It is the burial place of Keats
and Shelley. In an essay called 'The After-Season in Rome',
James described the charm of its neglected profusion of
stones and flowers and trees. He also mentions the monument
to a young English girl, Miss Bathurst, who drowned in the
Tiber in 1824. Its epitaph struck him irresistibly as 'a case for
tears on the spot': 'If thou art young and lovely, build not
thereon, for she who lieth beneath thy feet in death was the
loveliest flower ever cropt in its bloom.'

PANDORA

86.8 *as lately rearranged, the German Empire* The
rearrangement in question is Bismarck's creation of a North
German Confederation under Wilhelm I of Prussia after the
defeat of Austria in 1866.

87.27 *a Junker of Junkers* A young German noble,
particularly a member of the Prussian aristocracy. The term
implies the reactionary political views of a group set on
preserving its historical privileges.

87.33 *German emigrants* This was the main period of
emigration from northern Europe to the United States. The
photographer Alfred Steiglitz (1864–1946) is said to have
spent four days as he crossed the Atlantic on a German liner
watching the passengers in the steerage. The one, well-
known, picture he took, 'The Steerage', corresponds exactly
with James's description below.

97.2 *Pandora* The *Notebooks* say nothing of the
heroine's name or its possible significance. In Greek
mythology Pandora was the name of the first 'all-gifted'
woman, created by Zeus for the deliberate confusion of man,
to avenge the benefactions of Prometheus. She was sent as a
wife to Epimetheus, Prometheus's simple brother, with a box
(or jar) which Zeus forbade her to open. When she did open
it, it was to release all the evils of the world. Only Hope

remained in the box. There is, however, another meaning, not listed in the *Oxford English Dictionary* but very likely known to James. A 'Pandora' was the name give to the doll-sized figures used especially by Parisian fashion houses to model outfits for their customers. These dolls, complete to every accessory, were exported for display. I am indebted to Miss Goodfellow of the Bethnal Green Museum (which has several Pandoras) for the information. There is a temptingly apt irony, for a tale figuring Henry Adams, in the anticipation of the 'manikin' of *The Education of Henry Adams* (1918).

98.14 *Sainte-Beuve ... Renan ... Alfred de Musset* Respectively, a literary critic and man of letters; a philosophical and religious writer; and a Romantic poet and playwright.

98.28 *euchre* Like poker, a card game reputedly played on the old Mississippi steam-boats.

99.15 *Madison, Hamilton or Jefferson* Vogelstein has been reading a history of the United States and imagines both young Mr Day and the Randolph of 'Daisy Miller', his Tauchnitz novel, as possible (if improbable) future statesmen like these three great figures of the first decades of American Independence.

100.5 *a Daisy Miller en herbe* i.e. a budding Daisy Miller.

100.32 *the Chassepôt rifle, the socialistic spirit* The catalogue of 'modern' items catches the Teutonic character of the Count: the Chassepôt rifle, named after its French inventor, was first used in the Franco-Prussian war of 1870; the chief targets of Bismarck's internally repressive measures in Germany were the new and proliferating groups of Socialists and Marxists.

103.31 *Phidias and Pericles* Although no work of Phidias (thought of as the greatest sculptor of the ancient world) has survived, there is a tradition that he was responsible for the sculptures of the Parthenon and other buildings on the Acropolis. The birth of Pandora is depicted on the base of the great statue of Athena, suggesting her association with the cult of the goddess. Pericles (*c*.495–29 BC) stands as the Athenian statesman whose pre-eminence was due to an incorruptible character, a consistently intelligent foreign policy, and remarkable powers as an orator.

104.8   *Goethe's dictum*   The reference seems to be to a passage in *Wilhelm Meister's Years of Apprenticeship* (1796); in Carlyle's translation: 'Let no one think that he can conquer the first impressions of his youth' (Book II ch. 9).

104.9   *Utica*   The capital of Oneida County in up-state New York. Its name was drawn from a hat. It was in Utica that F. W. Woolworth opened his first five-cent merchandise store in 1879. Note the description of Mr Bellamy on p. 145.

105.2   *her parents are complete little burghers*   By 'burghers' the Count means something like tradesmen: he is equating 'social position' with evidence of 'cultivation'. But even allowing for what was 'contradictory' in America, Pandora Day defies the social placing of Mrs Dangerfield: 'A girl like that with such people—it *is* a new type.' The *Notebooks* are explicit: 'The point of the story would naturally be to show the contrast between the humble social background of the heroine, and the position which she has made—or is making for herself and, indirectly, for her family' (p. 56).

105.8   *an infinitely small majority*   The expected *minority* was altered to *majority* in revision, emphasising the conscious wit of Mrs Dangerfield, whose taste for the epigrammatic echoes that of Mrs Costello in 'Daisy Miller'.

112.13   *Mrs Bonnycastle's . . . receptions*   The *Notebooks* identify the Bonnycastles with Henry Adams and his wife, Marian (Clover), old friends of James's whom he visited freely during his stay in Washington in the winter of 1882. The Adamses' house in H Street has been called a haven of Boston hospitality in a sea of national politics; but James's experience bears out the social exclusiveness attributed to Mrs Bonnycastle in the story. He told Godkin (a mutual friend, and founder-editor of the *Nation*) that the Adamses disapproved of the company he was keeping in the capital, adding: 'though I notice that they are eagerly anxious to hear what I have seen and heard at places which they decline to frequent. After I had been to Mrs Robeson's they mobbed me for revelations; and after I had dined with Blaine, to meet the president, they fairly hung upon my lips' (quoted Edel, *Life*,

1977, I 648). Mrs Adams's sharpness earned her James's description of 'a perfect Voltaire in petticoats', though he also sincerely admired her as 'the incarnation of my native land'. 'Pandora' went some way to meeting William James's charge that as an American Henry should be studying life in Washington rather than London. James had replied (in 1878) that he 'would come to this in time', declaring: 'I know what I am about, and I have always my eyes on my native land' (*Letters*, ed. Edel, II 171).

114.4 *Her husband was not in politics, though politics were much in him* Henry Adams, descended from a line of Presidents and statesmen, had begun his career as private secretary to his father, who was the American ambassador to the Court of St James during the Civil War. He later became editor of the *North American Review*, and a historian of American politics. His first novel, *Democracy*, published anonymously in 1880, was a lively and satirical account of the Washington he knew. It appears that James was in the well-guarded secret of the authorship. Adams's wife, Marian Hooper, committed suicide on 6 December 1885.

115.11 *The White House had received a new tenant* James was in Washington shortly after the assassination of President Garfield, shot by a disappointed office-seeker in July 1881. On Garfield's death, his Vice-President, Chester A. Arthur (a man with a reputation for informality) succeeded to office until the next elections in 1885. Count Vogelstein's opportunity of seeing an electoral campaign clearly does not refer to this emergency transfer of power. It has been argued that the President in James's story is modelled on Rutherford Hayes, Garfield's predecessor, who held office 1877–81. (See Robert L. Gale, under 'Further reading'.) Hayes's administration was notable for his policy of Southern pacification and reform of the civil service. One of the more public victims of the reforms was Chester Arthur, then collector of the Port of New York and a friend of the powerful party boss, Roscoe Conkling. Political deals within the Republican party nevertheless secured Arthur's nomination to the vice-presidency at the 1880 convention. President within the year, Arthur surprised both political friends and enemies by the independence and integrity of his administration. Compare Henry Adams's treatment of the distribution of the spoils of office among *his* fictional President's personal friends in *Democracy* (1880).

116.6 *Members of the House*   i.e. the House of Representatives, or lower House of the American Congress.

116.26 *It was a society in which familiarity reigned*   James's impression of Washington was as 'the place in the world where money—or the absence of it, matters least'; as 'very queer and yet extremely pleasant: informal, familiar, heterogeneous, good-natured, essentially social and conversational, enormously big and yet extremely provincial, indefinably ridiculous and yet eminently agreeable' (*Letters*, ed. Edel, II 367).

117.29 *She's staying with Mrs Steuben*   Mrs Steuben proves a caricature of a Southern lady with literary pretensions. Yet her name ironically echoes that of the Baron Steuben, a Prussian officer who had served in the Seven Years War under Frederick the Great, and became Washington's inspector-general during the American War of Independence.

119.12 *Spielhagen*   (1829–1911) The son of a Prussian civil servant, and a prolific novelist. He was an aggressively committed realist and wrote polemically against Bismarck's Germany. The suggestion is that Bostonian earnestness outdoes even the Teutonic kind.

120.10 *a monstrous mystical infinite* Werden   The reference is to the abstract and metaphysical character of Hegel's philosophical writing generally; but the idea of *Werden*, a becoming, carries over to the description of Washington itself—a city planned to a vast scale on geometrical principles, monumental but unfinished.

125.25 *they've got a lady at the head over there*   i.e. Queen Victoria.

129.2 *Pennsylvania Avenue*   The White House is at one end of this.

129.14 *down the Potomac to Mount Vernon*   The Potomac flows from West Virginia, separating Maryland from Virginia, down to Washington and Chesapeake Bay. Mount Vernon, overlooking the river near Alexandria, was the original estate of George Washington. It had been made a national monument in 1860. James records his impressions of it as 'exquisite' in *The American Scene* (1907).

129.31 *She's the self-made girl!* 'I don't see why I shouldn't do the "self-made girl", whom I noted here last winter, in a way to make her a rival to D[aisy] M[iller]' (*Notebooks*, p. 56).

132.37 *the Capitol* The seat of the House of Congress and the Federal Courts, rebuilt with its present huge white dome after the British burnt down the original in 1814.

134.21 *cicerone* Guide.

135.4 *Arlington* The cemetery established as a national memorial after the Civil War, in 1864; originally part of George Washington's estate.

137.31 *gemüthlich* Comfortable, friendly.

138.6 *a Pomeranian count* Count Vogelstein came from the east German province of Pomerania, then part of Prussia.

138.24 *the pater patriae* i.e. George Washington, first President of the United States 1789–97.

THE PATAGONIA

151.1 *the perspective of Beacon Street* Beacon Street runs from the top of Beacon Hill down to the Back Bay, and was the most fashionable street in Boston.

151.3 *The club* The Somerset Club was the most exclusive in America at the time. It occupied a building with a double bow front at the top of Beacon Street, with a view over Boston Common.

151.10 *The heat was insufferable* Ezra Pound particularly admired the opening description of the hot summer night. The *Notebooks* recall the occasion on 22 August 1883 when James had himself sailed from Boston after a period of intense heat in the city. He had filled his days 'padding about in a state of undress in the Mount Vernon Street house and confining himself to lemonade and ice-cream' (Edel, *Life*, 1977, I 684).

151.14 *an old ship* The *Notebooks* entry recalls the last-minute substitution of an old Cunarder, the *Atlas*, for the faster-scheduled ship when James crossed the Atlantic in 1874.

151.24 *Mrs. Nettlepoint's house* occupies one of the

best positions on Beacon Street. Being 'on the water side' it commands the prized view across Back Bay—the point at which the wide mouth of the Charles River empties into Boston harbour.

152.4 *Mount Desert* An island off the Maine coast, developed as an exclusive resort in the nineteenth century. It had a standing similar to Newport, which James knew well.

155.19 *cordials* Refreshing drinks compounded from spirits with fruit and aromatic substances.

157.30 *the South End* The area of Boston south of Back Bay towards Roxbury; a new urban development which had been expected to become fashionable but had never done so.

158.8 *Mattapoisett* A town in south-eastern Massachusetts about sixty miles south of Boston.

162.20 *the École des Beaux Arts* The School of Fine Arts in Paris (also attended by Caroline Spencer's cousin in *Four Meetings*).

164.27 *the Horticultural Hall* Built in 1865 at the centre of Boston in the French Renaissance manner.

164.32 *tarletan* A thin muslin much in favour for ball-dresses.

169.33 *the* jeunesse des écoles i.e. the students.

175.6 *Elle ne sait pas se conduire* The narrator's reply in effect translates the phrase: 'As for her not knowing how to behave . . .'

190.25 *Ohne Hast, ohne Rast* A German proverb, meaning: Without haste, without pause.

191.33 *the Batignolles* Grace Mavis knows that the only part of Paris she and Mr Porterfield would be able to afford is the new mainly working-class quarter to the north of the *grands boulevards* of the city's mid-nineteenth century development. The comparison with Merrimac Avenue contrasts her realism with the narrator's more conventional responses.

216.26 *we'll tell tales when we get there* The *Notebooks* consider various versions that public knowledge of the scandal might take: it was an essential element of the original anecdote that the young woman felt threatened by her witnesses.

FOUR MEETINGS

227.1 *I saw her but four times* James inadvertently betrayed the connection between his tale and Turgenev's 'Three Meetings' when he referred to his own story in a letter as 'Three' (and not 'Four') 'Meetings'. See *Letters*, ed. Edel, II 219.

227.10 *Some seventeen years ago* The dramatic date of the story may be taken as roughly that of the present, making the narrator's first meeting with Caroline Spencer about 1860.

227.24 *The photographs were in a couple of great portfolios* Compare a similar winter's evening described in James's life of Hawthorne (1879). James's reflections bear eloquent testimony to his sense of the social restrictedness of the New England of the previous generation. See *Hawthorne*, pp. 69–70.

228.5 *sun-picture* A picture made by means of sunlight, a photograph.

228.30 *North Verona* The name seems to be fictional. In the first published version of the story, the town was called Grimwinter. James may have felt this too close to what he called Hawthorne's 'taste for conceits and analogies'; there is an ironic anticipation of the Italy Miss Spencer so particularly longed to see.

228.35 *a "ruche"* A frill or quilling of some light material, such as ribbon or lace, ornamenting part of a garment or head-dress.

230.11 *the Castle of Chillon* See note to 'Daisy Miller' (4.10). Miss Spencer not only knows her Byron better than the narrator, but has read 'histories and guide-books and articles and lots of things'. The narrator's account of Europe seems to owe much to Ruskin's *The Stones of Venice* (1851–3).

231.19 *They say the French theatre's so beautiful* Like the narrator, James was an avid playgoer and could claim to know the French theatre in particular. A record of his interests can be found in Wade (ed.), *The Scenic Art*.

233.18 *I've spent twenty-two and a half months in Boston* The revision to the twenty-three months of 1879 text emphasises that very literal 'veracity' of New England of which Mrs Luna complains in *The Bostonians*.

233.30 *You've the great American disease, and you've got it 'bad'* This speech, central to the story, is almost entirely new to the 1909 text. James described his own reaction to Europe as 'a lasting wound', a 'virus', and a 'poison' (see Edel, *Life*, 1977, I 287). The excess of sensibility in the American response to the old world is the subject of one of James's earliest stories, *A Passionate Pilgrim* (1871), whose hero, Clement Searle, declares: 'I was born with a soul for the picturesque. It condemns me, I confess; but in a measure, too, it absolves me.'

238.13 *Everything's so delicious and romantic* The 1879 text has 'picturesque', a word with wide and ambiguous currency in early James. 'Romantic' more candidly indicates the extent to which Caroline Spencer's image of Europe colours her perception of the actuality. In this scene the 'headiness' she attributes to her coffee anticipates the end where, waiting on the Countess, she serves 'the coffee of my dead past', laced more literally than here (see p. 265).

239.10 *circular notes* Letters of credit addressed by a banker to bankers in other countries in favour of a named person; the nineteenth-century equivalent to travellers' cheques.

239.36 *a beautifully fluted cap* A white head-dress with compressed pleats; part of the provincial dress of Normandy.

240.19 *her book-nourished fancy sallied forth for the revel* The note is on the extent to which Caroline Spencer's reading anticipates her experience. Compare the 'revel' of Roderick Hudson's first fortnight in Rome (The World's Classics, Oxford, 1980, p. 69).

242.12 *the Rue Bonaparte* The street in which the École des Beaux Arts is situated, on the Left Bank in Paris.

243.27 *Je suis fou de la peinture!* The revision of the simpler (though equally pretentious) 'J'adore la peinture!' of the 1879 text catches the vulgarity of this art student.

244.8 *la belle Normande* In revision James avoided the inelegantly literal rendering of the inn's name as 'The Fair Norman'. He had originally called it *la Belle Cuisinière*.

248.31 *She has been cruelly treated by her family* Caroline Spencer's version of the Countess's alleged marriage and history is virtually new to the revised text. It brings out both the intrinsic improbability of the story and Miss Spencer's readiness to credit its pathetic elements. For other accounts of the pride of the old French aristocracy see, for example, *The American* (1877) and 'Madame de Mauves' (1874).

252.14 *"carry-all"* American contraction for *carriole*; a light carriage for one horse, usually four-wheeled, and capable of holding several people.

258.1 *a shabby Parisian* quatrième The unfashionable fourth floor of a Parisian apartment house.

258.7 *à la chinoise* In a single knot.

258.8 *le sourire agréable* The 1909 text puts the phrase into French, stressing the element of consciousness which gains point in repetition.

262.14 *Tant bien que mal* Revised from the English of the 1879 text, 'After a fashion'.

262.23 *sans me vanter* Without boasting.

262.32 *La belle découverte!* What a find! (Ironically) How perceptive!

262.35 *la bêtise même* Stupidity itself.

264.12 *On en a de toutes les sortes* You can get all kinds of that.

264.22 *épreuve* Trial, ordeal.

264.35 *comme cela se fait* As is right, or as is done.

265.5 *'fine'* The revision changes 'cognac' for the colloquial abbreviation of Fine Champagne de Cognac.

265.22 *il me fait une cour acharnée* He's madly in love with me.

265.24 *some French novel* French novels were conventionally synonymous with romantic impropriety and the overt treatment of sexual relationships. Compare 'The Patagonia', 185.14.

265.27 *je ne sais quelle dévergondée* I don't know what kind of shameless, abandoned creature.

266.7 *I couldn't intimate . . . her terrible shrug* The passage is virtually new to the 1909 text.

266.34 *parages* Parts (colloquial); literally: latitudes, regions.

VARIANT READINGS

These lists include some of the more interesting changes to the early and final versions of the texts.

I. DAISY MILLER

	New York Edition (1909)	*First book edition (1879)*
5.2	even gone, on trial—trial of the grey old "Academy" on the steep and stony hillside—to college there	gone to College there
6.6	divesting vowel and consonants, pertinently enough, of any taint of softness	pronouncing the adjective in a peculiar manner
8.21	turned again to the little boy, whom she addressed quite as if they were alone together	turned to the little boy again
9.15	asked of all the echoes	loudly inquired
10.9	act unqualified by the faintest shadow of reserve	this glance was perfectly direct and unshrinking
10.10	It wasn't however what would have been called a "bold" front that she presented, for her expression was as decently limpid as the very cleanest water.	It was not, however, what would have been called an immodest glance, for the young girl's eyes were singularly honest and fresh.
11.15	So he artfully proceeded.	he said
11.23	"I should like very much to know *your* name", Winterbourne made free to reply.	"I should like very much to know your name," said Winterbourne.

286

	New York Edition (1909)	*First book edition (1879)*
15.1	an actual or a potential *arrière-pensée*	actual or potential *inconduite*
15.2	He felt he had lived at Geneva so long as to have got morally muddled; he had lost the right sense for the young American tone.	He felt that he had lived at Geneva so long that he had lost a good deal; he had become dishabituated to the American tone.
15.13	Yes, his instinct for such a question had ceased to serve him, and his reason could but mislead.	Winterbourne had lost his instinct in this matter, and his reason could not help him.
16.33	Winterbourne was thus emboldened to reply	said Winterbourne
17.3	He pretended to consider it.	Winterbourne hesitated a moment.
18.34	her natural elegance	the *tournure* of a princess
19.27	irreproachable in all such forms	attentive to one's aunt
20.18	just ignoring	not accepting
20.25	of the last crudity	very common
21.1	"An 'intimacy' with him?" Ah there it was! "There's no other name for such a relation. But the skinny little mother's just as bad!"	"An intimacy with the courier?" the young man demanded. "Oh, the mother is just as bad!"
21.33	uneducated	uncultivated
22.7	"Then she's just what I supposed." "And what do you suppose?" "Why that she's a horror."	"Dear me!" cried Mrs Costello. "What a dreadful girl!"
23.11	she did go even by the American allowance rather far	anything might be expected of her
23.13	it vexed, it even a little humiliated him, that he shouldn't by instinct appreciate her justly	he was vexed with himself that, by instinct, he should not appreciate her justly
24.6	The soft impartiality of her *constatations* as Winterbourne would	"Let us hope she will persuade him," observed

VARIANT READINGS

	New York Edition (1909)	First book edition (1879)
	have termed them, was a thing by itself— exquisite little fatalist as they seemed to make her. "Let us hope she'll persuade him," he encouragingly said.	Winterbourne.
27.19	"Common" she might be, as Mrs Costello had pronounced her; yet what provision was made by that epithet for her queer little native grace?	"Common" she was, as Mrs Costello had pronounced her; yet it was a wonder to Winterbourne that, with her commonness, she had a singularly delicate grace.
30.37	he hereupon eagerly pleaded; so instantly had he been struck with the romantic side of this chance to guide	said Winterbourne, ardently; for he had never yet enjoyed the sensation of guiding
32.36	"Oh no, with this gentleman!" cried Daisy's mamma for reassurance. "I *meant* alone with the gentleman." The courier looked for a moment at Winterbourne—the latter seemed to make out in his face a vague presumptuous intelligence as at the expense of their companions—	"Oh, no; with this gentleman!" answered Daisy's mamma. The courier looked for a moment at Winterbourne—the latter thought he was smiling—
33.17	all lighted with her odd perversity.	looking at him, smiling, and fanning herself.
34.2	dressed exactly in the way that consorted best, to his fancy, with their adventure.	dressed in the perfection of a soberly elegant travelling costume.
34.28	but she was clearly not at all in a nervous flutter— as she should have been	apparently not at all excited; she was not fluttered

288

	New York Edition (1909)	*First book edition (1879)*
	to match *his* tension	
34.20	so far delightfully irregular and incongruously intimate	so much of an escapade— an adventure—
37.30	that agent of his fate	there was a charmer
38.26	the girl at his side, her animation a little spent, was now quite distractingly passive.	the young girl was very quiet.
38.36	little abomination	young person
40.22	his little friend the child of nature of the Swiss lakeside	Daisy Miller
44.19	sweet appeal to his fond fancy, not to say to his finest curiosity.	sentimental impatience.
44.30	only to be riddled by your silver shafts	to encounter your reproaches
49.14	thing	man
50.4	he seemed to shine, in his coxcombical way, with the desire to please and the fact of his own intelligent joy	he had a brilliant smile, an intelligent smile
50.32	it was deeply disgusting to Daisy's other friend that something in her shouldn't have instinctively discriminated against such a type.	Winterbourne felt a superior indignation at his own lovely fellow-countrywoman's not knowing the difference between a spurious gentleman and a real one.
51.10	more of vulgarity than of anything else	of extreme cynicism
51.15	a wholly unspotted flower	a perfectly well-conducted young lady
53.37	irresponsibly	very agreeably
54.24	listen to the voice of civilised society	take Mrs. Walker's advice
55.22	*true*!	*earnest*!
60.30	"Of course you're incapable of a step," the girl assented. "I should think your legs *would* be	"Of course you don't dance; you're too stiff," said Miss Daisy. "I hope you enjoyed your drive

	New York Edition (1909)	*First book edition (1879)*
	stiff cooped in there so much of the time in that victoria."	with Mrs. Walker."
	"Well, they were very restless there three days ago," he amicably laughed; "all they really wanted was to dance attendance on you."	"No, I didn't enjoy it; I preferred walking with you."
	"Oh my other friend—my friend in need—stuck to me; he seems more at one with his limbs than you are—I'll say that for him."	"We paired off, that was much better," said Daisy.
61.20	"I'm afraid your habits are those of a ruthless flirt," said Winterbourne with studied severity.	"I am afraid your habits are those of a flirt," said Winterbourne gravely.
62.11	American flirting is a purely American silliness; it has—in its ineptitude of innocence—no place in *this* system.	Flirting is a purely American custom; it doesn't exist here.
63.11	Daisy at last turned on Winterbourne a more natural and calculable light	Daisy turned to Winterbourne, beginning to smile again
63.35	any rupture of any law or of any deviation from any custom	any violation of the usual social forms
64.5	a small white prettiness, a blighted grace	a pale, grave face
64.12	But this lady's face was also as a stone.	replied his hostess.
64.27	he really liked, after all, not making out what she was "up to"	the unexpected in her behaviour was the only thing to expect
64.31	and this easy flow had ever the same anomaly for her earlier friend that it was so free without availing itself of its freedom	there was always, in her conversation, the same odd mixture of audacity and puerility

	New York Edition (1909)	*First book edition (1879)*
65.8	It pleased him to believe that even were twenty other things different and Daisy should love him and he should know it and like it, he would still never be afraid of Daisy.	he had a pleasant sense that he should never be afraid of Daisy Miller.
67.2	The shiny—but, to do him justice, not greasy—little Roman.	The little Italian.
68.10	the measure of her course struck him as simply there to take.	he could not deny to himself that she was going very far indeed.
68.24	that little American who's so much more a work of nature than of art	that pretty American girl
68.31	"All alone?" the young man heard himself disingenuously ask.	"Who was her companion?" asked Winterbourne.
	"Alone with a little Italian who sports in his button-hole a stack of flowers.	"A little Italian with a bouquet in his buttonhole.
69.23	he recoiled before the attempt to educate at a single interview either her conscience or her wit.	he gave up as utterly irrelevant the attempt to place her on her guard.
70.2	He set her down as hopelessly childish and shallow, as such mere giddiness and ignorance incarnate as was powerless either to heed or to suffer.	He said to himself that she was too light and childish, too uncultivated and unreasoning, too provincial, to have reflected upon her ostracism or even to have perceived it.
72.12	you've no more 'give' than a ramrod	you were as stiff as an umbrella
73.8	He asked himself, and it was for a moment like testing a heart-beat	He was silent a moment
73.11	"But *if* you possibly do,"	"Well, then—I am not!"

	New York Edition (1909)	*First book edition (1879)*
	she still more perversely pursued—"well, I ain't!"	
74.19	These words were winged with their accent, so that they fluttered and settled about him in the darkness like vague white doves. It was Miss Daisy Miller who had released them for flight.	These were the words he heard, in the familiar accent of Miss Daisy Miller.
74.32	She was a young lady about the *shades* of whose perversity a foolish puzzled gentleman need no longer trouble his head or his heart.	She was a young lady whom a gentleman need no longer be at pains to respect.
75.30	Daisy, lovely in the sinister silver radiance, appraised him a moment, roughness and all. "Well, I guess all the evening." She answered with spirit and, he could see even then, with exaggeration. "I never saw anything so quaint."	Daisy, lovely in the flattering moonlight, looked at him a moment. Then—"All the evening," she answered gently. . . . "I never saw anything so pretty."
76.26	He tried to deny himself the small fine anguish of looking at her, but his eyes themselves refused to spare him	He kept looking at her
77.4	"It doesn't matter now what I believed the other day!" he replied with infinite point. It was a wonder how she didn't wince for it.	"It doesn't matter what I believed the other day," said Winterbourne, still laughing.
77.10	He felt her lighted eyes fairly penetrate the thick gloom of the vaulted passage—as if to	He felt the young girl's pretty eyes fixed upon him through the thick gloom of the archway;

	New York Edition (1909)	*First book edition (1879)*
	seek some access to him she hadn't yet compassed.	she was apparently going to answer.
80.1	"Also—naturally!—the most innocent."	"And she was the most innocent."
80.7	It came somehow so much too late that our friend could only glare at its having come at all.	Winterbourne felt sore and angry.
80.13	she did what she liked.	she wanted to go.
81.12	As he made no answer to this she after a little looked round at him— he hadn't been directly within sight; but the effect of that wasn't to make her repeat her question.	Winterbourne offered no answer to this question.

II. PANDORA

	New York Edition (1909)	*First book edition (1884)*
86.8	as lately rearranged, the German Empire places in the most striking light the highest of all the possibilities of the greatest of all the peoples.	at present the German Empire is the country in the world most highly evolved.
86.21	his sense of comedy, or of the humour of things, had never been specifically disengaged from his several other senses. He vaguely felt that something should be done about this, and in a general manner proposed to do it, for he was on his way to explore a society abounding in comic aspects.	he had not a high sense of humour. He had enough, however, to suspect his deficiency, and he was aware that he was about to visit a highly humourous people.

	New York Edition (1909)	*First book edition (1884)*
87.16	Mightn't it be proved, facts, figures and documents—or at least watch—in hand	It appeared to him that it might be proved
89.13	Differences, however, were notoriously half the charm of travel, and perhaps even most when they couldn't be expressed in figures, numbers, diagrams or the other useful symbols.	Differences, however, were half the charm of travel.
91.19	they were apt to advance, like this one, straight upon their victim.	they came straight towards one, like that.
95.8	"atrociously"	*exceedingly*
95.15	to the critical or only to the criticised half of the nation.	to the discriminating class.
99.4	must be choice specimens of that American humour admired and practised by a whole continent and yet to be rendered accessible to a trained diplomatist, clearly, but by some special and incalculable revelation.	were the most transcendental flights of American humour.
103.34	comparatively unformed ("comparatively!" he mutely gasped)	young
105.8	majority	minority
108.35	distributing chalk-marks as if they had been so many love-pats.	he distributed freely a dozen chalk-marks.
113.11	whimsically wilful	humourously inconsistent
113.17	fundamental fallacies and triumphant blunders.	necessary lapses.
113.30	American promiscuity, goodness knew, had been strange to him, but it was nothing to the	She perceived differences

	New York Edition (1909)	*First book edition (1884)*
	queerness of American criticism. This lady would discourse to him *à perte de vue* on differences	
115.3	let us be vulgar and have some fun	let us have some fun
121.16	ministered freely and without scruple, it was clear, to this effect of his comfortably unbending.	was making him laugh.
123.7	there was a high mature competence in the way the girl sounded the note of approval.	Pandora remarked, sympathetically.
129.37	sense of the ridiculous.	mirth
142.7	moonstruck.	transcendental.
144.11	a very fine man—I presume a College man	a very fine man
145.28	the laugh that seemed always to invite the whole of any company to partake in it	her friendly laugh
146.3	he seemed to look at the world over some counter-like expanse on which he invited it all warily and pleasantly to put down first its idea of the terms of a transaction.	a business-like eye.
147.5	but who, shrieking at the queer face he showed her, met it	but met it

III. THE PATAGONIA

	New York Edition (1909)	*First book edition (1889)*
160.4	There is notoriously nothing less desirable than an imposed aggravation of effort at	There is nothing more tiresome than complications at sea, but she accepted without a

	New York Edition (1909)	*First book edition (1889)*
	sea, but she accepted without betrayed dismay	protest
162.9	exemplary to positive irritation, and very poor, poor to positive oppression	exemplary and very poor
165.7	largely wiped her mouth.	declared.
166.18	rather marked embarrassment, or at least anxiety attended her.	there were some complications in her position.
170.7	I ventured a little to jeer.	I ventured to exclaim.
173.21	Miss Mavis, in her deliberate way, met my eyes.	Miss Mavis looked at me a moment.
174.24	It makes me, in any situation, just inordinately and submissively *see* things.	It puts it in my power, in any situation, to *see* things.
175.3	"There you are—you do feel she owes you something . . ."	"Well, she's very curious."
179.18	she 'squirmed' for her	she couldn't bear it
185.14	my French novel had set them in motion.	they were part of the French novel.
186.3	our common detachment	a marine existence
187.35	with high significance.	smiling at me.
188.8	you feel as if you had some rights in them—tit for tat!	you feel as if you were acquainted.
189.23	the terrible little woman	Mrs Peck
195.2	to 'take up with her'	to marry
199.31	I had taken really no such ferocious, or at least competent, note as Mrs Peck.	I evidently had not looked at them so continuously and hungrily as Mrs Peck.
199.36	rather perverse and even rather shameless	rather cynical and even a little immodest
200.19	Tucked away was the odious right expression and I deplored the fact so betrayed for the pitiful bad taste in it.	Concealed was the word, and I thought it a real pity; there was bad taste in it.

	New York Edition (1909)	*First book edition (1889)*
201.16	unless it had been a mere superstitious delicacy	unless of decorum
201.30	one had an extravagant sense of good omens and propitious airs.	one got a sort of exhilarated impression of fair conditions and an absence of hindrance.
212.8	her charge was a mere bore	she was a common creature
219.9	superficially it moved— and I admit with the last inconsequence—one's pity.	superficially it made her rather pitiable.
221.10	unwitnessed and unlighted tragic act.	mysterious tragic act.
223.29	He used to be gaunt and angular, but had grown almost fat and stooped a little.	He used to be lean, he had grown almost fat.
224.1	rather characteristically dull	a little stupid

IV. FOUR MEETINGS

	New York Edition (1909)	*First book edition (1879)*
228.7	a small vague smile, a discreet, a disguised yearning	a small, gentle smile
228.30	North Verona	Grimwinter
229.37	she quavered, drawing the long breath of a person launched and afloat but conscious of rocking a little.	she asked, with a little tremor in her voice. I could almost have believed she was agitated.
230.33	"Well, I guess I can go in *that* time," she answered as if measuring her words.	"I think I can go within ten years," she answered very soberly.
231.12	her shy slow scrutiny.	her sidelong glance.
231.26	as if you tell me a fairy-tale.	very wonderful.
232.36	you haven't sailed up to now—so I suppose you *are* crazy.	you have not gone yet, and nevertheless you are not crazy.
233.2	"It seems as if I couldn't think of anything else—	"I don't think of anything else. I am always

	New York Edition (1909)	*First book edition (1879)*
	and I don't require photographs to work me up! I'm always right *on* it. It kills any interest in things nearer home. . ."	thinking of it. It prevents me from thinking of things that are nearer home."
233.18	twenty-two and a half months in Boston.	twenty-three months in Boston.
233.30	"You've the great American disease, and you've got it 'bad'—the appetite, morbid and monstrous, for colour and form, for the picturesque and the romantic at any price."	"You have the native American passion—the passion for the picturesque."
234.11	What experience does is merely to confirm and consecrate our confident dream.	Experience comes and only shows us something we have dreamt of.
238.13	"Everything's so delicious and romantic. I don't know whether the coffee has gone to my head— it's *so* unlike the coffee of my dead past."	"Everything is so picturesque. I don't know whether the coffee has intoxicated me; it's so delicious."
238.28	encamped in this odd place?	sitting here?
238.34	cunning	delicious
240.10	She was lost in the vision and the imagination of everything near us and about us—she observed, she recognised and admired, with a touching intensity.	She was extremely observant; there was something touching in it.
241.24	She coloured as if convicted of a hidden perversity, but she was soaring too high to drop. "Well, I guess it's a *little* bad . . ."	"I suspect it is a little bad."
241.28	I usurped an unscrupulous authority.	I looked at her again an instant.
241.34	as solemnly as a daughter	with a kind of solemn

	New York Edition (1909)	*First book edition (1879)*
	of another faith might have told over the beads of a rosary:	distinctness:
244.9	"I guess I know my way round!" her kinsman threw in; and as I left them he gave me with his swaggering head-cover a great flourish that was like the wave of a banner over a conquered field.	As I left them her cousin gave me a great flourish with his picturesque hat.
246.18	after a dismally conscious wait:	after a brief hesitation:
250.24	the last dregs of her sacrifice and with it an anguish of upliftedness.	a sort of perverted exaltation.
251.1	she sublimely pleaded;	she said;
256.31	I took it in; I didn't know what to say, and what I presently said had almost the sound of mockery. "When then are you going to make that tour?"	"When are you going to Europe again?"
258.19	He was a gentleman of few inches but a vague importance, perhaps the leading man of the world of North Verona.	He was a pretty-faced little fellow, with an air of provincial foppishness—a tiny Adonis of Grimwinter.
258.27	as if an army of cooks had been engaged in the preparation of it.	who had a faint red spot in each of her cheeks.
258.35	while persistently engaged with a certain laxity in the flow of her wrapper.	gathering in her dressing gown with her white arm.
259.21	"She gives lessons in French and music, the simpler sorts . . ." "The simpler sorts of French?" I fear I broke in. But she was still impenetrable, and in	"She gives lessons in French; she has lost her fortune."

	New York Edition (1909)	*First book edition (1879)*
	fact had now an intonation that put me vulgarly in the wrong.	
260.13	Two years and four months.	Two years.
262.2	she was engaged in drawing a fine needle with a very fat hand through a piece of embroidery not remarkable for freshness.	She was drawing a needle through the piece of embroidery.
263.18	She had an assurance—based clearly on experience; but this couldn't have been the experience of 'race'. Whatever it was indeed it did now, in a yearning fashion, flare out of her. "Talk to me of Paris, *mon beau Paris*, that I'd give my eyes to see. The very name of it *me fait languir*."	"Talk to me of Paris," she went on.
265.5	'fine'	cognac
267.9	Her wan set little face, severely mild and with the question of a moment before now quite cold in it, spoke of extreme fatigue, but also of something else strange and conceived—whether a desperate patience still, or at last some other desperation, being more than I can say.	She looked very tired, but there was a strange hint of prospective patience in her severely mild little face.

300